LONDON SHIFTERS

ALSO BY PIPER J. DRAKE

Stand alone titles...

Siren's Calling

Red's Wolf

Finding His Mark

Gaming Grace

Evie's Gift

Keeping Cadence

True Heroes series

Book 1: Extreme Honor

Book 2: Ultimate Courage

Book 3: Absolute Trust

Book 4: Total Bravery

Book 5: Fierce Justice

Book 6: Forever Strong

LONDON SHIFTERS

TRILOGY

PIPER J. DRAKE

ACKNOWLEDGMENTS

Thank you to Donna Hillyer for taking me on a fresh editing pass of these books.

Writing a series is a heck of a project all on its own, re-releasing it is a whole new endeavor, with fresh challenges and lessons to learn. I would have been lost without Katee Robert, Asa Maria Bradley, and Gail Carriger. Thank you so much.

Thank you to Matthew for your patience and support.

Finally, thank you to my readers. I hope you enjoy these stories!

CONTENTS

BITE ME

BOOK 1

1

———

Seth struggled with the corpse as it twisted and groaned in his hold, trying to get a bite out of him. "Hurry up and get what we bloody well came here for before I kill the blighter."

The zombie wasn't near a match for him. In his phase-form, a supernatural meld of man and wolf, Seth towered over the struggling corpse. Killing it would've been easy. But they'd come out on this hunt for more than just the kill. He'd chosen phase-form so he had hands to hold the blighter for his pack mate but still had the protection his fur afforded him as the thing clawed and bit.

Course, if any normal human happened into the alley, they'd see the stuff of nightmares: two huge men with clawed hands and feet and the faces of wolves grappling with the living dead. Good thing most people kept to their homes these days.

"Steady on," Danny ground out, and he grasped the thing's skull with a clawed hand. "Got the muscle and skin samples, just trying to get a bit of what's left of his brain."

"Mush, that's all that's left in these, even the new ones." Seth hoisted the zombie off its feet.

"All right, that's got it. Good to kill the thing now."

With a snarl, Seth flung the monster across the alleyway and into a wall. It hit with a sickening crunch. He was on it before it could try to drag itself toward them again, crushing its skull and the remnants of its black-and-gray brain matter into, well, mush.

Victory.

He embraced the euphoria as it washed through his muscles, and if he'd not been standing in the streets of London, he'd have raised his muzzle to the night sky and howled his triumph.

Next to him, Danny shifted back from his phase-form to human. Painful, that, but Danny was still grinning through the finish of the change.

"See? Not so hard to get the samples I wanted. And that's one less zombie walking the streets."

Seth lifted his lip, baring his still elongated teeth at his smaller pack mate. "Would've been quicker to just kill the blighter."

"True." Danny cocked his head sideways, baring his neck and dropping his eyes to the ground in a submissive pose. "But killing them isn't enough. More keep coming, staying here in London, and we've not a clue why. At least if we could learn more about the stages, identify when the infection becomes irreversible ..."

"A human gets bitten, they die. Slowly, I grant you, and painfully, but they end up dead all the same." Seth snapped his teeth with an audible click. "Then the poor bastard gets back up and tries to eat anyone and anything alive around them. Worse, they can spread the virus before they die, after they die, *and* while they're stumbling their way around in the dark. Even bloody vampires don't create more of them-selves that easily. Nothing for it but to crush the zombies until they can't get up anymore."

"It's a virus—like ours, like the vampirism." Danny had a way of taking a point and chewing on it. But then, he was the pack's medic and a biologist by education. Research was just another kind of hunt for him. Answers to hypotheses were every bit as tempting as rabbits for the younger were-wolf. "It can be inoculated against at the very least, maybe reversed if caught early enough. We're the only ones who can safely obtain any samples."

And the vampires or the fae, but they'd agreed to stay in the shadows; preferred it, even. Better to let the werewolves stand in the glare of human scrutiny.

Frustration burned through Seth's veins, replacing the cleaner euphoria of the earlier fight. "Oi, I came out here to get your bloody samples, didn't I?"

Danny's shoulders slumped.

Seth reached out and nudged his pack mate's shoulder. "It was bad enough to see those scientists go out with those blinkered zombie hunters. Seeing one of them come back, dead and walking, was a damned shame. But don't feel guilty about it, Danny; you warned them."

"I could have gone with them."

"The humans didn't want us." And, as alpha, Seth wasn't going to let one of his own go into an infested park to be used as bait. A werewolf might be immune to the zombie virus, but he could still be eaten alive.

Dead was dead.

Danny sighed. "At least we've got these samples. With luck, I'll have enough findings to present to the council in a fortnight and maybe get a few other scientists in to coordi-nate a proper research group."

As if there were any other werewolf scientists. Danny was one of a kind and Seth held on to that with no small amount of pride. Academic, yes, but more than tough enough to hold a dominant place in the London pack as well.

Seth shook his head, resettling the fur across his neck and shoulders. "Those old wolves are going to be distracted keeping their own borders zombie-free. London is my territory, infestation or not. It's up to me to hold this territory. Any sign I can't and they're going to be at our throats."

"Zombies don't care what pack a wolf looks to. They'll eat us all given a chance."

True, that.

"But most of those alphas don't have to worry about more than one or two of the things wandering across the countryside. We're cursed, ever since the incident last year at one of the clinics. They've become a bleeding infestation across a good portion of London and the outlying towns." Seth bit off each word. "Humans are just easy prey. Even with our patrols, there're plenty of the hungry dead stumbling around the streets at night now."

He nudged the rotted remains of the zombie with his clawed toe, curling his lip in disgust. At least the decomposition sped up once a zombie was well and truly stopped. Another few hours and there'd be barely anything but dust and the smell of old death. Good thing too, or his wolves would have left rotted carrion in the alleys every time they encountered one. The humans would've needed biohazard teams just to clean up the mess.

"Some good has come of it." Danny shifted his weight from one foot to the other. Ever the optimist. "We're not in hiding anymore. The humans are right happy to have us patrolling London at night, keeping the zombies in check."

"Well, that's just brilliant, isn't it?" Seth didn't bother to hold back his snarl. "Can't help but wonder if they've all decided the enemy of my enemy is my friend, or whatever the old saying is. Got their barricaded checkpoints all set up along the M25 to help refugees, but you don't see them sending in real help, do you?" He shifted from his phase-form back to human semblance. Pausing, he rolled his head and his neck adjusted with a sharp pop. Better. "I've got the government and even the bloody Americans still wanting to have diplomatic talks with us after the zombie infestation is under control. It's all well and good for now, while they need us, but we'll have to walk carefully to see to our own once the humans feel safe again."

Danny nodded, gazing out toward the open street, looking like he wanted to run. Couldn't blame him, really. Pack politics were complicated, required too many compromises and not enough action to satisfy the wildness inside them.

And human politics? Seth liked human politicians only a little more than zombies—and the zombies were more honest for all that they were mindless. At least those monsters were driven by simple hunger, as opposed to convoluted power plays and greed.

"Come on, then; let's finish the patrol." He was too tired to keep the resignation from his voice. Snagging his long coat from where he'd dropped it earlier, he brushed away any dirt and shrugged into it, then shoved his feet into his sneakers. At least Danny had his samples and would be happily pottering around in his lab soon enough.

"More samples are always better." Danny fell into step at his shoulder, a bit behind him. "There's a chance the humans are hoping we and the zombies eliminate each other, won't deny that, but the other packs are following your lead and coming out into the open now too. The human military will find they're not just dealing with the London pack."

"The other packs haven't quite gone public yet. They're testing the waters. The vampires and fae, they may never come into the public eye." Watching to see what would happen to the London pack. Seth took a deep breath, taking in the scents of the city streets: his territory. He needed to keep his own safe. Then, maybe, he could look past to how the rest would fare as they followed his trail.

Aggravation tightened his chest and he growled, scanning the street beyond the alley for more prey. The fight had been good, clean. An outlet for the annoyance plaguing him under the scrutiny of the other European alphas and the distrust he had for the human governments. He'd not admit it to Danny, but the challenge of holding a zombie steady long enough to take the various samples had added a certain zest to the chore.

Any werewolf was more than strong enough to take out a single zombie.

As alpha, Seth wasn't just any werewolf.

"What we need to figure out is how this all started in the first place. There must be people conducting research, even if they aren't with the wolves. If you let me take in an infected human, maybe a study would—"

"Danny." Seth snapped off the end of his friend's name, more than a bit of power behind it.

The scientist lifted his hands, palms turned up to the sky. "Sorry. Can't help but think about all the possibilities. Zombies are another part of legend, aren't they? They'd have been around before now, like we've been all along. But none of us knew about them, saw or smelled any sign of them until a little over a year ago. And for them to pop up all over London, right in the heart of the city? And stay here? It's unnatural."

Humans would say the same about werewolves. "We wait too long for your precious research and they'll have multiplied too fast to keep under control. It'll become the bleeding apocalypse the mad ones go on about."

"At least they had proper guns stashed." Danny's lips twisted in a grim smile.

"You want to know how all this started. I care about when all this broke out of control and how to prevent it happening over again." Seth kicked at a stray bit of rubbish. There was too much frustration riding him today and a simple patrol wouldn't rid him of it all. He needed more action. "Some daft woman wandered into a clinic at the other end of town and infected half a dozen humans before anyone knew what happened. At least now we've got them all keen to look out for signs of the infected before they have a chance to go home and turn all their loved ones too."

"There has to be a trigger that started it all." Beginning to pace, Danny took himself on a diagonal line across the street and back again. "Something we've missed so far ... Maybe magic."

Seth snarled, the sound echoing off the buildings lining the small city street.

Danny hunched his shoulders and kept his eyes to the ground. "You've got a serious chip on your shoulder regarding anything besides killing the blighters. But we've *got* to find a solution to give those infected a chance. If this is magic induced, magic has to be part of the answer."

Rage burned through Seth again and the world blurred for a moment, then crystallized to a sharp clarity, an indication his eyes had shifted to wolf without his conscious action. Danny fell quiet.

"Head back to the pack house. I'll finish the patrol route." The words came out so guttural and rough, they were barely understandable.

"Seth ..."

"You've got your samples. Best get them preserved or stowed away however you need them. I'm going to work off some of this piss and wind I'm feeling." Seth rolled one shoulder and studied the almost empty city streets. "You're not wrong, but I'm not ready to talk on it."

He'd said the same words to Sarah ...

"It wasn't your fault, Seth." Danny's voice held too much sympathy.

"No? She's still dead. Dead trying to take a magical shortcut to the solution for all this madness." Seth brought himself up short. It'd do no good to go through it all again, rage at what couldn't be changed. No. He'd go out on patrol and make a tangible difference. "Go on, then. Off with you. And, Danny, check in with a text to my mobile when you get back to the house."

Danny could hold his own against any zombies he might encounter on the streets—a human couldn't. The only reason Danny had needed his help at all was because he wanted very specific samples taken while the blighted things were still animated.

He'd be fine. Safe.

"No one could've saved her. It's past time you forgive yourself."

Turning away, Seth blew his breath out slow and controlled. He fixed his gaze on the street ahead of him, searched the shadows for prey, for a way to make the world safer. "I haven't killed enough zombies yet."

No more words. Danny only nodded then headed off in

the direction of the pack house at an easy jog, his messenger bag slung across his chest.

Seth shoved his fists into the pockets of his coat and started walking. Alone.

Course, with the latest attacks, few humans walked the city streets after dusk. Zombies didn't seem to care whether it was day or night, but they appeared to have more energy to shamble and shuffle around after dark. Maybe their decomposed state made them slow in the daytime or maybe the undead had a reverse circadian rhythm from what they had when they'd been alive. Didn't matter to him. He'd leave the scientific explanations to Danny.

All he needed to know was how to kill them—faster and in greater numbers.

That infected victim should never have been allowed to move freely for so long, much less allowed to wander into a clinic full of helpless innocents. The clinic staff should have recognized something was horribly wrong, even if they didn't know exactly what. After all, it was bloody hard to try to save someone when they were trying to eat everyone else.

But no, everyone was too slow, too daft to recognize the threat. And then the cretins let the entire clinic go home—now infected—to their loved ones and either slaughter more innocents or make more zombies ... or both.

The bubonic plague had wiped out most of Europe in about two years at its peak. The zombie virus hadn't killed quite so many yet, but then the Black Death hadn't got up and stumbled after friends and loved ones, spreading the infection.

Even if they escaped, the survivors of zombie attacks sometimes didn't recover from the trauma of having a cherished person die and then try to eat them.

Since then, clinics had been shut down all over London

for fear of a repeat tragedy. For the most part the larger hospitals remained open—and many of those were guarded by newly armed human police, watching for any sign of the zombie infection.

Quarantine wasn't the answer. It only prolonged the torture for the person infected and the people trying to save them, watching them die a little more each day.

Better to end it clean and quick—for them and for the living.

And that's where Seth and his werewolves had stepped in.

The city officials had welcomed them—monsters to fight monsters. At least until would-be zombie hunters started filtering into the city, bringing firearms with them. A suddenly armed populace had brought on its own kind of apocalypse. Accidental shootings, stray fire hitting innocent bystanders, even self-inflicted injuries from misfires had the general populace scurrying into their homes, barring their doors against humans and monsters alike.

Seth growled, the sound rumbling up from deep in his chest. What few humans there were on the city streets were too far away to hear it, their heads wrapped in mufflers and shoulders hitched high to ward the cold from their necks. They scuffed along on the sidewalks, careful not to skid. No snow yet, but frost formed in the night.

He slipped on the slick surface, cursing the lack of traction in his sneakers. A few steps farther, he skidded again and his temper burned hotter. He'd wear boots, but they were more expensive to replace if he ripped them apart during a fast shape-shift. He hated watching his footing like a human, not that there were many out and about to see him fall on his arse.

It was still fairly early in the night—London used to be

alive with people heading from pub to pub or other entertainment. Just a few blocks away, Piccadilly would've been packed shoulder to shoulder with people. Not anymore. Now, only a few scattered souls hurried along on their way to a specific destination, no dallying.

A scream rang out through the night, the sound rising up through the cold air and echoing off the buildings. The humans on the street—all four of them—hurried on their way, oblivious to the sound too faint for their human range of hearing. If they could hear it, they would most likely head in the opposite direction.

After all, what could a human do against a zombie attack?

Dignity be damned. He headed in the direction of the scream, heedless of his slipping and sliding as he kept an eye on the darker alleys and side streets. As he drew closer, shots rang out. Curious. Someone was actually putting up a fight.

He crossed Bayswater Road and hit the grounds of Kensington Gardens at a run, pausing only to toss his coat into the shadows under a tree. Ignoring the official paths, he cut across the once carefully manicured, now despoiled grounds and began hunting. He caught the scent trail not too far into the park. A large group of zombies was on the move, maybe as many as half a dozen. Even without his enhanced senses, the smell of rotting flesh was easy to follow.

Another set of shots went off in rapid succession.

Another scream, the same woman he'd heard initially.

A child was crying ...

"Shit." What the hell was a child doing out in the middle of Kensington Gardens at night?

With zombies creeping across the night scene in

London, the few tourists still visiting the city went sight-seeing by day. More often, visitors were wannabe zombie hunters looking to claim bravery in the face of horror. Those tossers took their shots from a distance, behind the safety of a solid barricade or from boats on the river. Some never came past the blockades the military set up surrounding the outskirts of London.

Bloody cowards. Worse than useless, they were.

The wide expanses of lawn might give the people a small chance to run for it, but the area he tracked them to was surrounded by trees and edged on one side by the Long Water. Too many places for zombies to come shuffling out of the dark and not enough clear room to outrun them.

He circled the glade, taking in the details. No sense in drawing friendly fire before the shooter could identify him as help.

A family crouched at the foot of the Peter Pan statue, clutching the base in a terrified parody of the fairies gathered at the bronze statue's feet. The shooter leaned with her back to the base of the statue, taking down zombies two at a time—a pistol in each hand. She had a good eye and steady aim. Must've been using 9mms as every shot went into a zombie and didn't come back out on the other side.

Nice shooting.

Smart choice for a little bit like her. A larger caliber handgun might fire with too much force for her to be shooting one from each hand. Plus, larger caliber bullets would pass through zombies and potentially hit unlucky bystanders. The first cretins to come into London after the initial outbreak had made that mistake.

They'd come to kill zombies and instead hurt even more innocent people.

"Why don't you sod off?" The shooter let out a string of curses as she put bullets into another two zombies.

Seth raised his eyebrows. Such language. He chuckled.

And there were more than the group of six or seven he'd scented earlier. Other zombies were closing in on the small glade. Probably attracted by the other woman's screams and the scent of live meat.

No need to call in the pack. This, he could handle. More wolves and those humans could panic and go blinkered, run off screaming about werewolves attacking them alongside zombies. Damned delicate in the head, humans.

The last thing his pack needed was bad press threatening the tenuous partnership they'd built with the human authorities. Their energies needed to be focused on the real danger.

Better to clean this up alone.

If the shooter had full magazines loaded at the beginning, she was halfway to reloading. When she had to pause to do it—no matter how fast a human could handle a gun— those zombies would be on them all.

He'd seen enough. It was time to act.

2

———

Maisie admitted it'd been a bad night to go out for a walk. Hell, any night would have, but she'd been in such a snit over the landlord's greed she couldn't stay put.

Then, of course, she'd managed to find a batch of people even more stupid than she. And incapable of defending themselves. For the love of cretins, dumb and dumber, they'd only had one shotgun with them. One!

Any self-preserving person would stay far, far away.

And what did that say about her, then? Nothing she'd admit out loud.

The woman at her side needed to stop screaming. The noise would only attract more of the zombies ...

She had a half dozen shots left in each of her 9mms before she'd have to reload. With no one to cover her, it'd be an exercise in futility. Taking careful aim, she took a grim pleasure in making sure every shot was a perfect headshot. There was always a chance ...

And if not, she'd make herself one.

As the zombies had driven them farther into Kensington

Gardens, she'd chosen to make a stand at Peter Pan's statue rather than stumbling around in the dark with a man, woman and child. The man had gotten off two shots, never reloaded. Instead he clutched the shotgun like it'd magically save them all. She wasn't sure he even had any more ammunition. But she'd been counting and knew exactly how much she had left.

"Oi! Boom stick only fires if you point it and shoot."

"D-dead p-people. Walking! K-kill us. Rotting c-corpses ... t-trapped in hell ..." He trailed off in an incoherent babble.

Useless.

Six ... five ... four ... She took out the closest wave of undead and then had to split her focus between left and right as the next approached from opposing sides.

Three ... two ... She pulled her arms back in at her sides and then extended them straight forward.

Maybe this time she wouldn't be able to fight her way free after all.

A growl rolled across the glade as something new broke the cover of the trees, slamming into the group of zombies directly in front of her. The others broke stride, momentarily confused by the new predator in their midst.

"No, oh no!" the woman screeched right in Maisie's ear, reaching out and grabbing her left arm. "Help us!"

Great, fantastic ... hamper your savior by dragging down one of her shooting arms. Maisie opened her mouth to shout some sense into the woman when a zombie came around the side of the statue.

Maisie yanked down hard on her hindered arm and forced the woman to her knees. At the same time she brought her right arm around and fired off one shot, point-blank. The hole she put in the front of the zombie's head wasn't bigger than a quarter but it blew out the back in a messy way.

Ripping her left arm free of the hysterical woman, Maisie turned back to the main fight as she ejected the empty magazine and reloaded the one handgun.

No further sounds from the newcomer after that first growl. The only noise from the fight was the inarticulate hisses and groans from the attacking zombies. Her father had once told her the growling and snarling was all posturing but the silent wolf was the beast that'd kill you.

Apparently, Pops had been right.

The werewolf stood on two feet, his form caught between human and wolf with all the strengths of each. No zombie managed to get a grip on him, or fasten their hungry mouths in his flesh. He lashed out with deadly accuracy, muscled arms rippling under dark fur as he snapped necks and crushed skulls. The way he scattered the zombies, littered the glade with dismembered corpses, left her with few remaining targets.

Mostly, she made sure the ones that were down, stayed there.

Problem with zombies was the blighters had a knack for getting back to their feet again. Or dragging themselves after people.

Better to have loaded weapons ready than need them and curse Murphy's Law. She took careful aim and tagged a zombie entering the clearing before ejecting her other empty magazine and reloading.

Of course, more would keep arriving so long as they were attracted by the sound of easy prey—like the woman screeching in hysteria next to Maisie's ear.

"You need to stop screaming now." Maisie kept her voice low, calm.

Of course the woman didn't listen.

Maisie shoved one gun back in a holster at her shoulder, then with the freed hand grabbed a handful of the woman's shirt. Hauling her up, Maisie forced the other woman to face her. "Woman, he just saved us. If you're still carrying on all mad and the like, by the time he finishes off the rest of those zombies, he may rip your throat out just to keep you from attracting more. Do you get me?"

Hell, *she* wanted to do some damage to the other woman's vocal chords.

Shocked out of her hysterics mid-screech, the woman gulped. Eyes wide, she swallowed hard several times. Maisie could almost see her processing the words; it was like watching a hamster run in its bitty wheel to make the gears turn inside the woman's head.

"Gather up your family. Be ready to move. We don't know if he's going to stick around or not but we don't want to be here once he leaves." Maisie released her and glanced back toward the werewolf.

One final batch of zombies had come out of the trees. These seemed faster than the usual, and particularly blood-thirsty. They attacked with coordinated behavior—odd for the walking dead.

The werewolf was holding his own, but Maisie raised her guns anyway.

She picked off one, then another on the outside of the group as they threw themselves at the werewolf. He threw a third down to the ground just as three more jumped on him simultaneously. His hands—or claws or whatever—were full and the zombie on his back bit deep into his shoulder, at the base of his neck. The zombie could get to the werewolf's spine—a serious danger—and she didn't have a sure head-shot. She'd have to go a different route. Grabbing her last line of defense from its holster at her waist, she stowed her remaining 9mm.

Both hands on her .38 Super, Maisie took careful aim and fired.

A roar of mixed rage and pain. The bullet went through the werewolf's shoulder and carried the zombie off his back. Leaning hard to one side, cursing the pain in her leg, she fired a kill shot to the head before it got back to its feet.

As she did, the other two zombies fell in pieces on the ground. The werewolf reached down and crushed their skulls, finishing the kill so they couldn't drag themselves along the ground after their prey.

He straightened then, and stared at her with fierce golden eyes. Blackened zombie blood was liberally splattered across his fur and muzzle.

Maisie reminded herself that screaming would be a bad idea.

"You shot me."

They could talk in that form?

"I'm sorry." Maisie forced the words out, shoving terror to the back of her mind. Fear would only make him more dangerous. "Actually, I shot through you. I didn't know how close the zombie on your back was getting to your spine. Figured that'd be hard for even the likes of you to heal."

His growl stopped her heart, but the fur seemed to settle across his shoulders and what she could see of his back.

"More are coming. You all need to get out of the park." He pointed north along the path. "Go. I'll cover your retreat."

The woman gathered her man and child and scurried up the indicated walkway. Maisie leaned hard against the statue and wished for pixie dust.

Instead she tucked her .38 Super in its holster, hoisted

up the waistband of her britches and started to feel along the base of the statue.

"Are you daft, woman? Do as I say." The werewolf loomed closer.

"I plan to," she assured him as she groped with her free hand in the dark. Where had it fallen? They hadn't taken it with them. She would have seen.

"Now." He sounded even angrier, the words becoming harsher and more guttural.

There it was.

She nabbed the large stick she'd acquired earlier and dropped when they'd stopped here to make their defensive stand. She'd been lucky to come across it when she had hurt her ankle, twisting it in a fall and making it worse by trying to walk it off. But an injured ankle was better than being eaten alive. Now, she could use the stick as support and hobble her way out of the park. Her ankle didn't just throb, acute shooting pain let her know she was in for it if she didn't take proper care of it first thing when she got to safety.

He stared at her, suddenly so still he could have been another statue.

Even if she had the pixie dust, happy thoughts might be a touch hard to pull together past the severe onslaught of intimidation and fear she was attempting to quell.

"I'm going." Snapping at him might not be a good idea either, but at least her voice didn't shake.

"You're hurt. You can't run."

Temper spiked past her fear. "I wouldn't run from you even if I could."

She stabbed the tip of her makeshift cane into the ground and got started.

He moved with her, his otherworldly energy washing

across her side, raising the fine hairs on her arms. "I could carry you."

"You need your arms free to fight."

"There aren't any more infected in the near vicinity."

He would know.

"You told us more were coming." Wanker could've spared them some serious anxiety by being a bit more honest.

"At the rate you're moving, more will be in the area before you can get clear."

Ah well then, wasn't that a hard truth?

Before she could get past grinding her teeth, he bent down and swept her up in his arms, his grip gentle despite his obvious strength. "Hey!"

"This makes more sense." His words came clearer, less growly, quieter. "You can keep the stick if it make you feel better."

Carrying her did make more sense and clutching her stick securely in her hands did make her feel better. She didn't have to admit it though.

He walked with a steady stride, the rhythm calming her somehow. His fur was soft against her arm and the back of her hand, surprisingly so. Resisting the urge to bury her fingers in the pelt covering his chest took effort. Odd, but the longer he held her, the safer she felt.

Her injured leg continued to throb, though, and now that the danger was mostly past she had more trouble ignoring it. She'd put too much strain on it. She'd pay her dues in the morning with all sorts of aches and pains.

Resigned, she had no idea what to do with the awkward silence. "I'm Maisie."

"Seth."

Well, at least they knew each other on a first-name basis, then.

As they approached the outer edge of the park, he began to change without breaking stride. The arms around her reduced to muscular for a human, rather than huge and furry. She'd never been close to a werewolf when it shifted, much less cradled in one's arms.

"Isn't that supposed to hurt?"

"It does." His voice had lightened from the rough, guttural sound to a middle tenor. "But no reason to let it slow a body down."

"Aren't you cold?" She tried to sound casual about his bare upper body, but it was hard for a girl not to notice, pressed up against his chest as she was.

"Not so much when I've got fur. And right now, you're blocking most of the cold air." He paused. "I've a coat stashed at the edge of the park."

In human form, he was leaner and less bulky. The only "fur" he had sprinkled the front of his chest. She still wanted to run her hands over it. "A coat. No shirt?"

"Shirts don't last long when I'm out on patrol. They end up in shreds."

"You're wearing trousers just fine, though." And she needed to quit blurting out the first thing to come to mind.

The corner of his mouth turned up in a ghost of a smile. "I'm lean enough through the bottom that my change from human to phase-form doesn't rip up denims."

Maisie supposed it made sense that he'd managed to keep his pants through the change. Wolves and dogs like huskies or German Shepherds tended to be very trim through the hips. Seth's build held consistent from werewolf to human, simply taller and more muscular through the upper body in the former shape. Still, she wondered whether others had the same luck or if perhaps they lost their pants.

Best not to think about him losing his pants.

"Phase-form." She tasted the word. "That's what you call it then? When you're half wolf and standing up like a man? All tall and fierce-like?"

"It's one of the forms we can take, yes." His gaze roved over the area around them and she found herself searching the shadows too. "Some of us control it better than others."

She'd wondered about that. Werewolves appeared in top news stories on the TV and people whispered bits and pieces of remembered folk tales.

"Are the stories true, then? About you and the moon driving you mad?"

He missed a step and bobbled her in his arms. She thought she might have upset him, but then she realized he was chuckling. "The moon calls to the younger, less experienced pups, forces them into the change. But even they don't go mad. They learn to be well fed and find a good way to burn off their aggression. As they get older, more experienced, their control gets better. Go on then, what other stories have you heard?"

"Well, you don't eat the zombies, do you?" Her stomach churned at the thought. "Some people wonder if you're carrion eaters since there's no bodies to clean up."

"No." He sounded every bit as disgusted as she felt at the idea. "We don't eat rotting flesh."

"But you do eat things ... my kind of folk don't eat." Perhaps she shouldn't have asked, but she'd wondered. And well, he wasn't likely to eat her after saving her, was he?

The corner of his mouth twitched. Maybe that was as close to a smile as he got. "The things my kind eat aren't so different from what you'd prefer. Chicken, pork, steak when it's available, and occasionally some game meat. We just like it ... fresh."

"Ah, well, who doesn't like a good rabbit stew once in a while." Not so different, then, but she'd bet her idea of fresh and his were two different things.

Awkward silence ruled over the next few minutes as he walked the final distance out of Kensington Gardens and crossed over to the city streets.

Maisie fidgeted. "You can let me down now. There's not as much likelihood I'll run into stray corpses in this area. It's well patrolled."

"By my pack."

"And I thank you all for that, really. Ever consider setting up an emergency calling system? Like the Americans have when they call for Batman?" She'd meant it as a joke but his brows drew together in a dark expression. "Kidding. You can tell when someone is kidding, can't you?"

"Don't know you. Your heart rate is still up but I don't smell fear."

"Well, I'm not lying." Actually, she was more than appreciative of his rangy, well-toned torso now that he'd set her down and she could get a good look at the whole package. Lord help her. She'd been alone for too long.

He walked away.

"Oi." She waited for him to pause, not sure he would. "I *am* sorry about shooting you. If you come back to my clinic, I can clean that out so it heals proper."

Werewolves healed fast, she'd heard, and the evidence of it was right before her eyes. Bleeding had stopped and his flesh was closing over the wound. Still, it'd heal ugly if it wasn't thoroughly cleaned out. She hadn't been using hollow points, so he might even have a few fragments in his flesh. The bullet wound had to be more painful than he was letting on.

He stood motionless for a long moment, then bent and retrieved something from the shadows beneath a tree. She came close to retracting her offer and leaving, but then he returned, pulling on a coat as he did. "It'll set us even. Wait another moment."

Pulling a mobile from his back pocket, he tapped in a quick text message, his thumbs nimble on the tiny phone's keyboard. Hard for her to fathom after she'd seen those same hands rip dead bodies to pieces.

Finished, he looked up from the mobile, the light from the screen casting odd shadows across his face. Eerie. "The next patrol will check on that family. The wolves will pick up their trail here and follow them to be sure they all made it to a safe shelter."

Maisie cocked her head. Did he realize he looked like a figure from a bad horror movie? A handsome one, at least, but still. Best not to tell him, probably. She smiled up at him instead. "Ready?"

"Let's go."

3

<hr>

Seth stopped short as they turned onto the tiny side street. She'd said it was right there, but all he saw was an animal clinic.

Temper boiled up in his chest. He gritted his teeth and balled up his fists, every muscle in his throat tensing in the effort to hold back the growl threatening to roll loose.

"All right, then?" Maisie halted, turned toward him slowly. She studied him with clear gray eyes, her shoulders relaxed, passive. No scent of fear, even as he glared at her. Even his wolves were afraid when his anger washed over them, but not her. Focusing on the oddity helped him let the anger go.

"Really? Are you putting me on?"

She glanced to the simple, worn sign over the clinic. Her delicate brows drew together and she pressed her lips in a thin line. "Look, it's better than you trying to go home and wash it out under the kitchen faucet. I have all the tools I need here and the same cleaning supplies and disinfectants they'd use at a human clinic. Plus you won't have to go through the usual hoops they make humans go through for healthcare and other rubbish. Anyway, don't they try to have a police escort around before they treat you lot? You'd have to wait even longer."

He couldn't fault her logic there. He'd had more than enough of the ignorant comments blinkered people made. Even gone public, most wolves kept the fact to themselves. Like religion, the state of being a werewolf was for close, trusted friends only. A man would have to be daft or barmy to broadcast it to the general public.

Probably get himself shot for the trouble of all that honesty, as well.

"Oh, come on then; I can't stay on my feet all night." She hooked her pinky in his and tugged him along as easily as any stubborn child.

And he let her.

How long had it been since anyone, human or Were, had trusted him with so delicate a touch as hers? Most wouldn't give him their hand for fear he'd pulverize the fine bones. Or maybe they thought he'd rip their arm off. But here she was, limping along on her stick and dragging him behind her.

A pang of guilt hit him in the gut. He was a right bastard for making her stand there so long.

"You've been on your leg too much." He didn't have to pose it as a question. Her complexion had gone pale under already porcelain-white skin. Her gait had started out fairly strong considering she'd gone through an obvious retreat before he'd arrived on the battle scene. Now, her limp was more pronounced, as if she could fall with any step.

"You've carried me quite enough for one evening. I barely know you. What kind of lady do you think I am?" The humor in her voice came through clear, despite her fatigue.

He grinned. Petite, with soft brown hair streaked in caramel, she reminded him of a bit of custard tart.

"Well, then? I asked you a question."

With a hint of spice.

His grin widened as he decided he'd answer her with honesty and not politeness. "I was comparing you to food in my head."

A pause.

The woman stopped in her tracks. But she didn't turn back to look at him this time. No scent of fear rose from her, even now. Instead she simply started walking again.

After a moment, her stomach growled.

"No talk of food until after we get you cleaned and patched up."

When he chuckled, he wasn't surprised, even though he hadn't laughed for anyone in years. He also made a mental note to allow her to complete her task so she wouldn't get her knickers in a twist. Then he'd get a solid meal into her. But then, it could be fun to get her knickers twisted.

A memory of the earlier fight came back to him. Her standing at the base of the statue, small hands steady as she fired her gun. Fierce little minx too. He liked that.

"Oi, Brian!" Maisie called out as soon as they entered the clinic. "You still here?"

No answer. Ah well, no matter. She led her large companion across the waiting area and past the reception desk, heading down the hallway to the examination room.

"Someone else is supposed to be here?" Seth followed her readily enough as she continued to pull him in the direction she wanted.

Perhaps the lean werewolf was humoring her more than she'd realized ...

"What? Your superhuman senses haven't already told you about every person who's been here today and what we all ate for lunch?" She clucked to herself. "I'm sorry. I get a bit snippy when I've missed dinner."

He chuckled, a pleasant sound, loosening tension in her chest if not her twisting belly. "Not to worry." He paused. "There is someone in the building, listening to classical music with headphones. Maybe opera. The music is set very loud."

Brian *did* enjoy *La Boheme* after a particularly trying day and he *did* use headphones to encase himself in sound after hours. "How did you know he's wearing headphones?"

"The music would be louder and clearer if he played it from a sound system open to the room."

Ah. Well, the man did have remarkable hearing. "I'm amazed you didn't suffer when I fired my guns near you, then. My ears are still ringing."

"The shift healed my ear drums. Friendly fire happens fairly often around us." Sometimes not so friendly, she would have wagered. Seth shrugged when she turned to stare at him, alarmed. "Most times, we wear ear plugs if we know we'll be working alongside anyone bearing firearms. But tonight was a surprise."

"For both of us." Maisie dropped her gaze to the floor. As daft as that family was, she wished them safe—if they had a safe place to go to, that was. Especially with the chance Seth had given them.

Good of him, and his pack, to make certain as well.

She switched on the lights in the examination room and patted the metal bench against one wall. Seth sat without comment.

"Your friend is coming." His comment was delivered in a flat tone.

Must've heard Brian walking down the hallway. Saved her the trouble of going down the hall to pull her friend's headphones off his noggin.

"Maisie, what are you doing back? I tried to ring your mobile after you left." Brian called down the hallway as he approached. "Did you bring in another stray? I keep telling you we can't care for them for free …"

Brian stopped short as he caught sight of Seth.

Maisie tipped her head. "Not a stray. This one's got a home to go back to once I patch him up. And I owe him."

At least she assumed he had a home to go to. He'd mentioned pack mates and all.

The werewolf did appear a bit worn around the edges, but all things considered, still quite presentable if one didn't require a shirt. His jeans had come through the fight in good condition, with only a few rips and generous splashes of black goo. His upper torso was remarkably free of zombie blood or other fluids. Perhaps it had gone away with the magic of the shape-shift.

Then she realized her gaze had been fastened on Seth's chest for far longer than necessary. She forced her attention back to Brian. "I could explain but I'd imagine whatever is going through your head right now is likely to be more interesting." She didn't wait for Brian to tell her though. "I won't be using too many supplies. But it's sort of my fault he's been wounded and I'd like to do what I can to patch him up. Brian, meet Seth. Seth, Brian."

"How do you do?" Brian seemed more wary than genuinely concerned.

Seth only nodded.

Great. Not only were they both doing the manly thing,

but one of them could honestly win in a literal pissing contest if he chose. The thought brought an image to her head and a giggle burst from her lips.

"What's so funny?" Brian's wariness held a touch of exasperation.

He'd known her since childhood. Likely he could guess where her line of thought had taken her, or at the very least, imagine what nonsense she could come up with so late at night.

Aside from volume and distance, did a werewolf lift his leg to take a piss? Or just to mark territory? She really ought to learn more about werewolves.

A fresh fit of giggles welled up along with a wave of light-headed euphoria. Whoop. How long ago had she had a snack?

"Nothing's funny, really." She wasn't about to explain with Seth sitting right there. Besides, his powers, whatever they might be, were healing the wound she needed to clean out.

She busied herself with gathering her supplies. Placing them up on a small tray, she put them down next to Seth and put on her best bedside smile.

Up close, he smelled of night air and a faint musk—a bit like good pipe smoke but not quite as strong. Pleasant, really, and she wondered why she hadn't noticed it before when he'd been carrying her.

"This is going to sting a bit." How good was his control? He wasn't one of her animals, ones who couldn't know what she intended no matter how soothing she tried to be. They'd have snapped or tried to get away. She kept an eye on him as she started to clean the area around the bullet hole at both the entry and exit, paying extra attention to the way blood still seeped a bit from each. He grunted as she pressed the flesh around the exit point, trying to figure out if any fragments remained embedded. Shaking her head, she picked up a few more implements and a small curved bin and began flushing out the hole she'd put in the poor man.

Brian wasn't the heartless sort to simply stand there and watch. "Let me help, then. What happened?"

A low, intimidating growl emanated from Seth, and Brian stopped short halfway across the room. The promise of violence suddenly filled the air. All the color drained out of her friend's face and his eyes widened.

Maisie froze.

Under her hands, Seth hadn't moved but every muscle tensed and energy tingled along her fingertips.

Brian lifted his hands slowly in a show of no harm. "I was only coming to help her."

"You can stay right there." Seth lifted his chin to indicate the doorway. "Keep an eye on her and assure yourself she is safe but don't come any closer."

Brian wasn't a stupid man. He backed away as told. Full points, really, for not leaving altogether, but then he had quite a lot of courage too.

Still, the silence had become awkward and tense.

"I'd gone out for a bit of a walk to cool my head." Maisie decided the best thing to do would be to answer Brian's earlier question as she continued to flush out Seth's wound. Conversation would keep all of them from thinking too hard on what she was up to.

"A bit of a walk, Maisie? At night?" Frightened or no, Brian wasn't beyond making his exasperation clear to her.

"The landlord had his head up his ass and you can't deny it."

"I'm not, believe me. But at night? If I'd realized you'd be gone past sunset, I'd have made you promise to stay inside the clinic. You of all people should know better." Brian would bring up the biggest mistake of her life. Of course, he would.

One that cost her a family.

Everything she'd held close, lost in a single night, and she carried the weight of the memory in scars.

As she set down her tools and stepped away to dump out the used saline solution, Seth's stare burned into her. She wondered if he knew somehow …

But he couldn't.

Best to press on, then.

"In any case, my walk ended up a bit further than I'd planned." She ignored Seth's snort. "A family went running across the green at Kensington Gardens with a pack of zombies on their heels. Never seen anything like it."

"Really, Maisie."

"No, truly." She set her jaw and returned to Seth, prodding at his flesh again for fragments. "I mean, we've all heard of one or two zombies stumbling on a lone person in the alleys or a few wandering about in the parks. But this was a true group of the blighters, Brian, looking to feed."

"Zombies are always hungry." As if the little knowledge any average person might know about the undead was enough to explain it away. "Hunger is one of the few basic urges they still retain."

"Right, so how were these coordinating with one another? The behavior was off, I tell you." Maisie shook her head. "Like a pack of stray dogs. Sick ones, starving even."

"It's true." Seth grunted as she pressed a particular point. She looked harder and reached for a pair of forceps. He continued talking despite her work. "These did act in tandem and cooperative attacks. They were faster, fiercer too."

"So, when I fired a few shots to take down the lead zombie, the family bolted in the wrong direction. They went deeper into the park instead of coming up to the streets."

Odd, that. She hadn't stopped to wonder why, only cursed and followed after them. Once she'd gotten their attention, the zombies had almost caught up with them. She'd had to provide covering fire for them when the man proved to be no help at all even with a shotgun in his hands. He'd fired twice and then been unable to keep his hands steady enough to reload.

"No way you were on the edge of the park." Brian shook his head. "Admit it, you went back."

Perhaps having a childhood friend wasn't an advantage.

Seth shrugged. "I wasn't going to call you on it."

Maisie stared at him, hard. "Pardon?"

"Werewolves can smell a lie, hear it in the change of inflection in your tone and the rhythm of your heartbeat." Seth wasn't smiling, but his eyes were kind somehow. "It was a little white lie. I figured you had a reason for it."

She held her breath then let it out slow. "I suppose there's no point in denying it. Yes, I went back to the place where my family died. It's just inside the park and normally there'd be no danger at all."

During the day.

"Upset, angry ... I can see why you want to walk off your temper, even why you go there." Brian's voice had softened. "But you shouldn't have taken the risk at night."

"If I hadn't, that family would be dead, yeah?"

Brian opened his mouth to argue again but it was Seth who stopped him. "Lives were saved. She held the attack off for a good bit before I arrived. If they'd been normal zombies, she'd have gotten the family out and to safety all on her own."

"Yeah, well, I'm not the type to run off in a rush anyway." Maisie nipped out a bit of metal. Amazing her shot had retained enough velocity to carry the zombie off his back if the bullet had begun to fragment. Odd, that. The bullets were designed to flatten and do more damage to flesh on entry. A .38 Super could pierce armor, once upon a time. Werewolves must have tough hides ...

Luckily, it looked to be the only fragment. "Those dimwits popped out and honed in on the Peter Pan statue as if it might save them all somehow."

Just to be safe, she prodded the area around the bullet hole a bit more. Perhaps it had something to do with her suppressor. It was home-made. Maybe the fragment came from that and not the bullet ...

"They did head out of the park at the end there." Seth tilted his head toward her. His sudden close proximity surprised her and she fumbled a swab soaked in disinfectant. "I caught their trail leaving the park at the same place we crossed the street."

"I hope they have the sense not to try to double back." She paused. Why had they been in the park in the first place? "You don't think they were looting, do you? Seems even more daft than those cretins claiming they want to hunt zombies for trophies."

Seth grunted. "We've seen a few lone humans scavenging for trinkets and valuables. People like them wouldn't stand a chance competing with the tougher scavengers looting during the day when it's safer. Maybe the man got desperate and the rest of the family went with him to help. Maybe the woman pushed him into it. Dunno."

Maisie swallowed hard. She'd been near sick the first time she'd sifted through the bones and rags of the unlucky.

But the dead wouldn't need the firearms anymore and a person needed what defense they could find.

Desperate times.

She picked the swab back up and began to disinfect the area where she'd pulled the fragment out.

"I'm sure they've learned better now." Brian had a knack for sounding confident—able to bring a bit of peace, even when a body had no reason to believe him. "And they owe you their lives."

"I hope they take better care with them, then."

"Still, what you're describing ... Let's hope the zombies aren't evolving somehow," Brian mused. Likely he would mull over the possibility for quite a while.

She would too, in a "wake up in the middle of the night with cold sweats" sort of way.

"I wish there were more reliable information sources for the current findings on the virus, how widespread it's become, what progress there is to find a cure," Brian continued, more thinking out loud than to her or Seth. "Additional studies on why the lycanthropes, including the werewolves, are immune would be helpful too. Perhaps an antibody serum could be found."

Seth, for his part, had fallen silent.

Considering the tension still in the muscles under her fingertips, whatever he was thinking didn't consist of happy thoughts.

Well, her mind wasn't trending toward happy, so much as naughty. And that would not do, not at all.

Even as she admitted her thoughts, she realized Seth was watching her. Her cheeks grew warm and she addressed her attention to his front, trying not to spread her palms flat across his wonderfully broad chest. Running her hands over his tight abs and torso would get her into all sorts of trouble ...

Nope.

She needed to focus on the hole she'd put in the man.

"Still, Maisie. You've heard the morning broadcasts. They say the parks and gardens are the worst place to be." Returning to his lecture, Brian let the evolution of zombies rest. "And off you go, into Kensington Gardens and only your guns as company."

"Only." Seth made the statement without directing it at either her or Brian.

Brian apparently decided to answer for her though. "She has me, a friend, and there are other people who'd be there for her, if she'd let them."

"And have more lives to protect? No thank you. You know what one of them did tonight? Grabbed onto my arm in a panic and wouldn't let go. I only had one hand free for a gun."

"You need two to hold that favorite monstrosity of yours." Brian waved in the direction of her waist. "Much better to go alone and have your hands free. Makes a lot of sense."

Seth snorted.

Maisie shot him a quelling look. "A thirty eight Super is not a large gun."

"It is in your hands." Brian pressed on. "Especially with that makeshift silencer thing you put on it."

"It's a suppressor. And for your information, I carry nine millimeters too because I can shoot a nine millimeter just fine one-handed. You might look into learning to handle a gun yourself." She'd sleep better at night. For now, she settled for scowling at Seth's chest. Finding no more foreign bits, she returned to disinfecting the area. "I might have been foolish, yes, but not completely parted from my senses."

"It sounds like you were very lucky tonight." There was the note of worry Brian had been hiding up until now. "One need only look at you to realize how brave you are. You don't need to prove it over and over again."

Inexplicably, she blinked back tears. She hadn't meant to cause Brian worry. Truly. She'd gone out to cool her head. The sun had set before she'd come out of her thoughts and everything had happened so fast. There'd been no time to call for help. And even if she had, wouldn't she have put him in danger? Not something she'd risk.

Seth had arrived on the scene, strong and fierce. A stranger, and yet she suffered less guilt over his involvement in it all because he was like her. Moved to help in the midst of the circumstance. Seth had the power to survive and the immunity from the zombie virus to come away unchanged.

Relatively.

Most werewolves weren't born werewolves, as far as she knew. The articles in the daily papers gave little in the way of real information—mostly reassurances the werewolves were keeping the zombies under control.

She let out a small sigh.

"I'm sorry, Brian."

Maisie couldn't bear to turn and see his brows furrowed or the creases around his mouth. Once upon a time, the only lines on his face had been from laughter.

A large hand covered hers and she looked up into Seth's face, startled. His gaze was warm and sympathetic. There was an understanding there.

"I didn't say all this to get an apology from you, Maisie." Brian sighed in turn. "I only want you to be more careful.

I'm going to lose all my hair watching you go from one scrape to another."

Seth tightened his hand around hers and gave it a gentle squeeze. Her heart skipped but she felt steadier, and perhaps a touch distracted. In a good way.

She smiled, for both of them. "I'll try to hold back a bit, then, and simply give you a shot of gray instead of making you lose it all. You'll look distinguished."

"Oh, that's just grand." Despite the sarcastic tone, Brian chuckled.

Glancing back up, she found herself drawn to Seth's electric-blue eyes. Had they been so deep a blue before? She couldn't remember. But now, with Seth staring at her, she found herself very aware and suddenly shy.

"Now then, it seems to me you are all well in hand." Breaking the silence, Brian stepped backward, out the doorway. "I was going to offer to walk you home, Maisie, but I think perhaps your new friend can be trusted to accompany you. He did save your life, after all. I can't imagine he'd end it after going to the trouble."

Before she could think of a response, Seth answered. "I can see her home."

Truly, she must be tired if two men had beaten her to a comeback in less than a few minutes.

Her leg had gone past pain and into numb. Not a good sign. It wasn't that she didn't know her limits. She did. The fact was she simply pushed past them too often.

"Get some rest. No need to check the kennels. I've looked in on all our current beasties." Brian gave her a parting admonishment. "And for heaven's sake, get off your feet."

"Goodnight, Brain." She deliberately made use of his childhood nickname. Not brilliant, but definitely enough to push a button ... or three. Petty maybe, but the best she could do under the extenuating circumstances.

She'd finished patching up her new ... was he a friend? Perhaps not yet. Still, sending him off into the night might be a problem. And she didn't particularly want to. However, explaining where home was might pose a difficulty.

4

———

Seth studied Maisie's face as she cheerfully waved after Brian. Her friend headed out into the night armed with a cricket bat, ready to defend himself.

Unorthodox, that. At least innocent bystanders were less likely to be injured.

Anyway, Seth was more interested in why Maisie lied when she'd promised to go straight home.

The corners of her mouth trembled as she fought to maintain her smile. Her eyes darted to the left—no one was standing there.

She'd perked up once they'd come into the clinic, and he'd known better than to try to hold her off from treating him. She'd already demonstrated she put the good of others over her own well-being with a stubborn determination that bordered on mad.

But she was done now and the urge to get her off her feet and find something to feed her took over with surprising force. Since it was as likely common sense as instinct, he decided not to analyze it too closely.

"Sit down before you fall on your arse." Well now, that

hadn't come out in any sort of genteel manner, but he'd managed to keep the growl out of his voice. Mostly.

"Shove off," she shot back at him as she set about putting away the supplies used to patch him up.

Fine. He let the growl rise from his chest and roll through the room with a touch of power behind it. Most humans wouldn't have understood, only trembled in fear.

"You can cut that out too." No fear, only weariness and a bit of temper. Grumpy, in a cute way. "You're all patched up, so we're even now. You can go home if you'd like."

Oh no. Getting him to leave was not going to be as easy as all that. Her limp was more pronounced, and fine tremors shook her hands even as she tried to hide them. Besides, the color was quickly leaching out of her face.

Work in an animal clinic might be messy and all, but did her old clothes have to be threadbare as well? Surely she had sturdy clothing that'd provide her more warmth in the cold months.

"I'll buy you dinner on the way to your home." He could have made it more of an offer, but it came out mostly as an order.

She turned from the storage cabinets, then leaned against the counter. The wan smile she managed tugged at him. "Thank you, but really, you said this would make us even. I'd like to keep it that way."

"Freely offered." He was aware of debts—the pack took them seriously. She couldn't possibly know what an offer of a meal meant to a werewolf, not unless she'd dealt with any of the pack or with fae folk. He'd have heard about the former and hadn't noticed any sign of the latter about her. She wasn't fae-struck, as far as he could tell. Maybe just a coincidence then.

"There's not any particular place to get food along the way." Her gaze darted to the door and down to the floor.

Anger flashed. Was she afraid to go out into the night with him?

As quickly as he bristled, her gaze lifted to meet his. Sense washed away the heat of his temper in the face of her obvious awareness. Not afraid. Nervous then, but about what?

"Where is home?"

A blush spread across her cheeks.

Then her knees buckled.

He shot across the room and nipped her off her feet before she hit the floor.

"Oh, I ..."

Her eyes were unfocused for a moment and she had to blink several times before she pulled herself together.

"Food first, then you can explain what the fuss is while I take you home." The words were garbled with his growl but he knew she could understand him. She'd done it before, right after the fight.

The feel of her in his arms warmed every part of him, right down to his core. She weighed next to nothing. So fragile. He gathered her closer.

"It isn't anything to worry over." Her voice sounded even fainter.

He lifted his upper lip and snarled right in her face.

She stiffened. "Here now, no need to be mean about it. I'm tired is all."

There was that nice bit of temper. Relief washed through him and he relaxed his hold on her just a touch.

"Does anyone stop you doing this sort of thing? Ever? Really, you should let me down and go do ... wolfy things." Her voice had taken on an irritated edge.

Wouldn't be fun to let her go on too much more. Only one person ever argued with him and his medic wasn't there. Besides, Danny would've held the door open and gone with to have a pint of beer.

"There's a pub around the corner."

"There's a pub around every corner in this part of London." She grumbled, and then her belly rumbled louder.

Chuckling, he carried her down the hallway and out the door.

"Oi. I can walk."

"Your walking stick is back in the examination room." He kept his tone deliberately flat.

She glared at him.

He grinned and kept walking.

"We should have locked up."

Ah. He wasn't going back. "Should be all right this time of night." He'd text a patrol from his pack and have them watch the place for a few hours. "We'll go back and lock up after your stomach stops trying to eat you."

She wiggled—testing his hold on her, he'd bet. Little chit would hop right out of his arms and try to make a break for it if he gave her half a chance.

He grinned wider.

"What's all that about?"

"You're amusing."

She quit struggling and crossed her arms over her plump breasts. He couldn't help but notice her nipples had grown tight in the cold. Her shirt and bra were worn thin.

"Now what? You've stopped with the smiling and gone back to the brooding."

He glowered at her, even though he felt a smile teasing his lips. "I should have thought to get your coat."

"Don't have one."

Well, then ... "Why don't you have one? And don't tell me it's because you like the cold."

"Why do you wear one? The cold doesn't bother you as much, being a werewolf. You said as much earlier."

She blinked big gray eyes at him. He narrowed his own at her. She didn't drop her gaze. Stalemate.

Amusement, rather than rage, ran through his system. He gave her a little toss, grinning when she squeaked in surprise, and resettled her in his arms as he continued down the empty street. No dangers lurking in the shadows, only the rubbish and remains of what used to be a busy city.

"Do all werewolves like to mess with people?"

He cocked his head to the side, considered. "We all like a good game once in a while, about as much as a good fight."

It'd been a long time since he'd felt like playing ... anything.

"Do you fight a lot? I mean, aside from zombies. The news always has some new bit about you all 'taking out the zombie threat.'" The last bit was a fair imitation of one of the popular newscasters who stayed in London specifically to cover the infestation.

"My pack doesn't fight internally, if that's what you mean." He considered for a moment, then drew his eyebrows together. "Not all werewolves are honorable, mind you. I can only speak for my pack. My pack doesn't waste time with in-fighting because I lead them. If there's a challenge for a place in the hierarchy, it will be a dispute sanctioned by me."

And to disablement or death.

He always made the decision based on the circumstances. Humans might not understand, but he had to make some hard decisions for the good of the pack. Disputes couldn't be allowed to fester.

"So, you're the alpha." The words didn't bring him back to the conversation as much as her sudden stillness in his arms. He'd even stopped walking.

He gave her a brief nod and started toward the pub again. It really wasn't that far, but he'd been enjoying the walk so much he'd taken her around the block.

Funny. She hadn't protested.

"Have you always been the alpha?" A soft question, one with a pile more behind it he'd bet.

"I wasn't born a werewolf." Why tell her from the beginning? Maybe there'd be fewer questions if he gave her the whole of it. No one around but her to hear anyway. "Werewolves born to a pack are stronger, faster. The alpha is always the strongest, smartest, of the wolves. Stands to reason the alpha is usually born a werewolf as well."

"But you weren't." So calm. How did her calm settle him? She was like a warm blanket—soft, comforting.

"I'm old. It took me a long time to find a pack I could belong to." He paused. Remembering. "A long time to find an alpha I could put my faith in, one worth following."

"I don't suppose the former alpha retired to an estate out in Hampshire, did he?"

Ah, the old wolf would've enjoyed that. Plenty of hunting, lots of rich snobs to drive crazy.

"Werewolves don't often take themselves off to a grizzled retirement." No, they generally went insane, especially if left unbalanced by lack of a companion to ground them. Friend, mate, someone. "The anger, it grows inside us. Drives us mad, eventually."

He shouldn't tell her. They'd been careful to give their

best hero appearance to the public. They'd worked hard to hide the worst of themselves.

A small hand spread flat against his chest, over his heart. "You're not angry now."

The warmth of her palm seeped into his skin and deeper.

"No." He breathed deep, enjoyed the clean scent of her hair. Then he tossed her up in the air again and caught her close to his chest.

"Oi!" She pounded her fist into his chest. "I'm not a ball to be tossing around here."

He could've kept walking. Maybe after they'd both eaten, he'd take her for another walk.

The pub he'd chosen was one friendly to his pack. Convenient, really. He planned to include this portion of the pack's territory in his personal patrols in the future.

At the moment, though, he had a bundle of disgruntled lady to feed. She'd fussed to be let down at the front door and he had acquiesced, letting her limp her way to a booth. Her grip on his offered arm had to be as much temper as it was necessity.

She snarled almost as well as a werewolf.

"Haven't seen you in these parts in a while, Seth." The barmaid stopped by as soon as they sat down. "You know we normally require shirt and shoes for service.

He cocked his head to one side and gave her a nod of apology. "Sorry, Mel, hit a mess of trouble while I was out on a run. You're not too crowded tonight."

"No, and we're not too crowded any night lately. You can eat as you are." Mel gave an indifferent sniff. "At least you appreciate the quality of our food."

Not many had the quid to eat here, even the honest pub food. Of those who could, many were rich tourists here to hunt zombies. They came in armed with too much pride and lacking good taste.

Those with money had bought their way out of London before the quarantine had gone into effect and the military had established the checkpoints around the M25 beyond the city.

"I'll have my usual." He looked at Maisie, who was studying the one-page menu she must have nicked from the holder at the end of the table. "My ... friend might need a minute to decide."

Before Mel could step away, Maisie piped up. "Oh no, I'm ready. I'll have the haddock, please, and a side of mushy peas."

Seth raised his eyebrow. Maisie's sweet smile, which she hadn't yet given him, won an answering smile from Mel. The choice in supper probably won points too. *His* girl had a palate.

Of course she was his.

Content in the way Maisie seemed to have accepted his offer to buy her dinner, he slid a fresh glass of water across the table to her.

"Hydrate."

She stuck her tongue out at him.

He considered what he'd like to do with her sass, but got sidetracked by imagining what she might do with her tongue instead. He hardened at the thought and things didn't get any more comfortable when she wrapped both hands around her glass and brought it to her lips to drink.

Too distracted to make conversation, he was glad she wasn't one of those people who needed to fill silence with idle chatter. Instead, she seemed content to sip her water and look around the pub with those wide gray eyes.

And there were still things to see, even if few patrons

populated the pub. One or two brave souls sat at the bar and another quiet pair sat in a different corner booth. Conversation was hushed, as if everyone was too exhausted to be loud. This area had been hit harder by the infestation, as close as it was to Kensington Gardens and Hyde Park. Stray zombies shambled out of the parks and into the alleys at night. Some were even lured out by bait set out by mad hunters. Until the virus could be brought under control, this area would continue to struggle.

Jobs were gone. People eked out what existence they could supporting the new hunter tourism or trading each other for simple skills, like plumbing or handiwork.

Still, the pub had seen hard times before and it would weather the winter nights as well. Seth and his pack mates would see to it.

Once the zombies were gone and the quarantine lifted, London would bustle again.

"Here you are." Mel returned with two large platters. "On the pack account, Seth?"

"My personal tab, Mel. And buy yourself a drink for when you get off, will you?"

Mel smiled and gave him a nod, then left them to their meal.

As hungry as he was, Seth studied Maisie's plate first, to be sure it had been properly put together.

A salad of light greens had been arranged in a nice pile on her plate and a crisp breaded fillet of haddock laid on top. A perfectly poached egg sat perched on the haddock with a light drizzle of some sort of Béarnaise sauce over it all. In another small dish was her side of mushy peas.

Mel's cook did wonders with the shipments allowed in past the barricades as well as the little roof garden up on the top of the building.

Maisie laid a napkin in her lap and took up her fork, piercing the poached egg to let the rich golden yolk flow. Then she took a bite of the flaky haddock and a bit of salad. Her eyes rolled up and she gave an almost inaudible moan of pleasure.

Damn, but he might bust a zipper in his britches. The girl did enjoy her food. He desperately wanted to lick away the bit of sauce on her lip, but she wiped it away neatly with her napkin before digging in for another bite.

"Taste good?"

"Wonderful." She didn't even look up.

He didn't blame her. It smelled wonderful. So did his meal. He applied himself with a hearty appetite to the double portion of bangers and mash with his own side.

After a few moments, he noticed her watching him eat. "You have a question?"

She blinked, then tucked an errant curl behind her ear. "I'd have thought, you being what you are, you'd be eating a lot more ... protein."

"Bangers are protein."

She nodded. "True, but I wouldn't have thought you'd like bubble and squeak."

He looked down at his fried vegetables, mostly potato and cabbage with some peas and a bit of ham. Not many werewolves liked it; she had the right of it there. "Well, I used to have it all the time before I was changed. I guess I never lost the taste for it. You don't like it?"

She held up her hands. "I prefer mushy peas with dinner, myself. But a nice bubble and squeak is always pretty satisfying with breakfast."

How did she manage to get him to grin over and over again?

• • •

It wasn't until later, once he'd returned her back to the animal clinic, that he pushed her again. "I've answered your questions. You still haven't answered mine from before supper."

She blew out an exasperated huff, the puff of air lifting a wavy lock of caramel hair out of her face. She was probably grumpy again because he'd insisted on carrying her after they left the pub. He'd waited until after he'd gotten her to agree before lifting her, though.

"Because I don't want to tell you and don't want to lie to you," she said.

"But you'd lie to your friend." This female baffled him. She wasn't cowed by him and wouldn't lie to him, yet wouldn't trust him with the location of her den.

A part of him hurt.

It shouldn't. He barely knew her.

Somehow, it didn't matter that he'd only just met her. She was already his, if she'd have him in return. He intended to work on that.

"Well, and we've covered that particular talent of yours to smell a falsehood …" She began to squirm in his arms. "You don't have to hold me up like this."

"I asked first, and you did agree keeping weight off your injury would be the quickest way to heal." He tossed her up in the air, getting a satisfying squeak, catching her easily then cradling her in his arms again. That was beginning to be his favorite game. "More comfortable?"

"True. I did. But you really shouldn't make it a habit." But there was laughter in her voice beneath the admonishment.

He liked the feel of her—hoped she might be enjoying being held. He'd try not to indulge more though. The excuse of her injury would only last so long and then he should give her space and let her come to him. In the meantime, he'd take this moment and do his best not to get too distracted.

Especially since she still wiggled against him. "I didn't mean for you to toss me about like a stuffed doll. You could put me down now."

The examination room was most familiar, so he headed for it as she continued to grumble. At least her makeshift walking stick was in there. "Not likely to happen until I'm absolutely sure every room is clear, I'm afraid. My pack was keeping watch, but I always check to be sure nothing's amiss." The cinnamon-and-honey scent of her hair teased his nose. Made him want to taste her skin and see if it held the same spicy sweetness.

She beat at his chest with a small fist. He gave her his laziest smile.

She hit hard for a female.

"Fine then. It's not far." Her tone was exasperated but she looped her arm around his shoulders in a loose hold.

He grinned. "Then you be still while I carry you there."

Her response was both pithy and anatomically impossible. He laughed, and wondered whether she had the experience to know it wasn't possible.

"I'll need to bring my new walking stick in case I still need a bit of support to get back down here in the morning."

He raised an eyebrow. There was no way he could come up with an excuse to stay the night just so he could help her back down whatever stairs there might be. He did have responsibilities and while he wouldn't hesitate to stay with her if she invited him, he didn't want to push too hard too fast for her. It was clear to him that even though she was letting him carry her about, she was also still thinking for herself.

Point to her.

"I'll set you down here *if* you promise to stay while I get your stick and anything else you need. Otherwise, I'm taking you home and then I'll come back to get your things."

She narrowed her eyes, visibly assessing where she stood in their verbal sparring match. Well fed, the color had returned in her complexion. She'd already proved to be exceptionally nimble in thought. "Fine. I promise."

He placed her on the stretcher where he'd sat only an hour or two prior and caught up her walking stick in one hand. "What else do you need?"

Her lips twisted in a rueful grin as she acknowledged his foiling of her plan. "I've a purse behind the front reception desk."

The little woman had probably planned to scamper off on her walking stick. As if she would have gotten very far. He could run down any human, much less catch up to her, well fed or no.

Still, he was having fun playing.

Danny wouldn't hesitate to yank his tail over this if he'd seen it.

Violent, temper-driven Seth, pack alpha, playing games with a bitty human girl and enjoying every minute of it.

How long had it been since he'd been free of anger for any significant period of time? Yet with Maisie he'd smiled more in the space of a few hours then he had in a year or more.

Since he'd lost Sarah.

He retrieved the purse in short order, returning to find her perched right where he'd left her with wide, grey eyes and a supremely innocent look on her face.

"What are you up to? And why haven't you got a coat?"

"It really isn't all that far."

"It's cold outside." He growled at her.

She shrugged. "When I went out earlier in the day to cool my head, I didn't notice the cold."

"Harder to draw your gun?" He took a guess.

She shook her head. "I've been meaning to get one. When I do, I plan to put holes in the pockets for easier access and have an extra reinforced pocket in the front that acts as a spare holster."

Nice.

"Let's get you home. You can tell me how many guns you own on the way." He was genuinely curious. Where had she gotten them from, in a city where firearms were even more expensive with the rise of zombies?

The smile fled from her face and she fastened her gaze on the floor. She kicked her right foot out the way a kid would, sitting up on a high perch, then abruptly pulled it in and tucked it behind her left. "I *am* home."

He studied her. Yeah, the left ankle was swollen. However, it would probably heal once she had a chance to elevate it and rest. It'd just take a few days, because she was human.

Then her statement sank in.

Not a lie.

"You live here." It was a clinic. The windows to all the above floors were boarded up. They couldn't be livable.

She refused to meet his stare but lifted her chin in a sharp gesture. "Upstairs. The floors above the clinic are abandoned space. Landlord hasn't been able to rent out any of them as flats, in this building or the ones on either side, since last year. No one wants to live in them as they are and he's too cheap to renovate them to make them worth the rent. Says he'd make more in insurance at this point."

She bit off the last couple of words. Color rose up in her cheeks as she tensed with real anger. "If they're abandoned, the landlord doesn't have to supply heat or water to them."

He lifted his lip and bared his teeth. He didn't like the idea of her in the cold, curled up with no comfort.

"I wash up down here before Brian gets in for the day." She swept her arm out to indicate the whole of the clinic. "I'd sleep down here, but we lock it up and set alarms with motion sensors in every room but the kennels. I wouldn't be able to move around at night at all. And Brian would know if I didn't set the alarms at night. It's what keeps the clinic, the whole building, safe."

"Why doesn't your friend know you're squatting in abandoned flats?" He could remember the man's name, but couldn't say it. The attempt came out as a snarl.

Her friend should have known, should have seen through the farce. She deserved to be cared for much better than she'd been.

"Brian still has a family to care for, a mother and two younger siblings. Too many mouths to feed, and what we make at the clinic isn't enough for him to stretch to cover me too. Even though he'd try. I'm saving up. I'll have enough to afford a place of my own in time."

Still ...

"What happened to your family, Maisie? Where are your other friends?" A steady calm settled over him as he watched her. He was hunting now, hunting for the truth. It was important for him to know. He'd consider why later.

Her hands tightened on the edge of the stretcher and her shoulders hunched.

He waited. He didn't push her more and wouldn't ask

again if she refused. The question was out there and whether she answered at all would determine if he'd come back.

"Do you fight with your ... your pack mates? Is that what you call them?" she asked after a long moment.

"Yes."

"Do they forgive you?"

5
———

Maisie studied the man standing in the middle of the room. Still shirtless, he didn't seem to notice or care. He stood tall and confident, every fiber of him speaking of independence and strength.

Oh, he had a temper. She'd watched his rangy frame shake with it. It hadn't scared her. Maybe even was a bit of a turn on, if she'd admit it to herself. More than a bit.

Amazing he hadn't smelled it off her.

But then, she'd only just sponged him down in disinfectant an hour or so ago and had it all over her hands too. It would've been a miracle if he could smell anything besides the stuff.

"Most of the time, my pack mates will forgive." He rolled his shoulders and muscles rippled across his chest. "They might not forget, and they might find a way to get even, but most of the time we forgive each other."

She nodded. Her chest tightened. "Like a family."

"Yeah." His brows drew together in a scowl. Family seemed to be a difficult topic for him too.

Because of that, she trusted him enough to take the

plunge into her past.

"I'd had a fight with my brother." She stared down at her feet, right crossed behind the left. "It was stupid. They'd just started to broadcast the warnings about the zombie virus on the TV. Couldn't believe how much it would cost to get out of London before the quarantine kept everyone here. They'd make us all pay to go someplace safer? He wanted to stay here, wait it out, keep the family together. I thought he was bloody daft." She closed her eyes. "I'd stormed out of our flat, gone off to cool my head."

It was a habit.

Silence, though Seth had crossed the room to stand just in front of her, in arm's reach.

"My family, they came after me when they thought I'd been gone too long. Worried." She'd been too angry, too upset to think about where she'd gone, the danger she'd put them in that night. "I'd gone to the gardens. I could find the Peter Pan statue from anywhere in the park, you see. Even if it wasn't the original way the story's Peter should look, I still loved the statue. Every time I felt mischievous, devilish, I'd go there. It was as if I could put my hands on the cool bronze of it and let go of the devil in me, you know? Go back to the real world with a level head."

"It was your sanctuary." He didn't mock her. Maybe she imagined the understanding in his voice but at least he didn't make fun.

She nodded. "It was their voices, calling for me in the dark, that probably attracted the zombies. Two of the things came from opposite directions. If I'd answered my mum and brother sooner, maybe we would have had time to get out of the park. We weren't armed back then."

And she hadn't known how to shoot.

She'd fixed that.

"We didn't recognize them for what they were at first. Thought maybe they were beggars."

"You let them get too close."

Too much knowing there. He'd probably seen a lot of zombie attacks. The TV broadcasts said the werewolf pack was hunting down zombies, keeping them in check. Told the general public to stay indoors and not hinder their efforts. Based on Seth's comments, his pack truly was helping.

A relief, that.

But the werewolves hadn't been there the night her mum and brother died.

"I was the only one that made it out of the park, because my brother kept shoving me ahead of him and cursing at me to run. Mum had tried to hold them back and my brother went back to save her." She paused, swallowing past the horror building from the memories. "I didn't listen to him. Again. I followed him to help. One got a hold of me. I fell and the thing dragged me along the ground, gnawing on my shoe. I didn't see where Mum went, only saw my brother, diving at the thing, pulling it off of me. Then he told me if I didn't run, their lives would've been wasted."

She couldn't speak anymore. Shame burned through her.

"You ran." Seth reached out, brushed her hair away from her face. "It was good that you did, Maisie. Your brother and mother made their choices.."

"They wouldn't have been out there at all if it hadn't been for me." She choked on it. The irony was, she still went out into the night all the time. Maybe to look for their ghosts and say how sorry she was. Maybe to ask them if she could go with them. Still, she never let anyone follow her out there.

"They wanted you to live."

She laughed, but there was no joy in it. "I ran, as best I could. But I was bleeding and my right foot burned with the pain of it. By the time I made it here, I was delirious with fever."

"You'd been bitten." The growl had returned to Seth's voice.

Did he know his blue eyes turned golden when he got angry? When the wolf part of him took over? She looked back down at her feet.

"Brian found me in the foyer, dragged me into the treatment room." She tilted her head back, closing her eyes against the bright ceiling lights. They'd blinded her that night. "He had to cut away the dying flesh on my foot and ankle, get ahead of the decay and the virus. There wasn't time for anesthetic because the infection would spread through my bloodstream faster than the local anesthetic would. He managed it well, having put a tourniquet on below my knee to slow down blood flow just in case he'd have to amputate."

"Fast thinking." There was approval in Seth's voice, rather than pity.

Good. She couldn't have withstood pity. The tears would have fallen and then she'd end up a crying mess.

"Brian's always been a genius under pressure." She brought her head back to rights, opening her eyes to look Seth in the face. "So there, you have my story. After my mum and brother died, I couldn't afford our flat and Brian had already done so much, I didn't want him to worry. All our other friends had had the sense and the money to leave before the barricades started turning people back. Seemed perfect to squat in the apartments above the clinic until I'd saved enough to get a little place of my own. Save me the walk to and from work too."

Her attempt at a funny fell flat. Somehow, she couldn't even fake a small smile.

"You shouldn't be by yourself." Seth frowned.

As handsome as the man was, she liked him better when he smiled. Though it appeared he didn't smile often. His face seemed to find its way to a frown too easily. Surprise sparked in his eyes when a smile found its way across his lips. "I'm not alone, per say."

He snarled then.

Startled, she added quickly, "There's another squatter family or two up there in different apartments. One family has a pair of little kids. They don't come down here, but they make do up there and don't bring any harm to anyone."

As quickly as the fierce anger flared up, it faded away. She watched his eyes turn back from gold to brilliant blue, fascinated.

"What are you looking at?" He still sounded angry.

"What had you so riled up?" She tossed a question right back in return.

She hadn't expected him to step closer, so close she had to sit up straight and tilt her head back to maintain eye contact.

He stared at her for a long moment, then touched her hair. He took a single lock in one hand and held it up to his nose, taking a deep breath before letting it go. Her heart kicked into high gear.

Then he used the same hand to trace the line of her jaw. "I didn't like the idea of anyone, especially a single male, living near where you slept."

She parted her lips but wasn't sure how to answer that.

Seth solved the issue for her by crossing the little

remaining distance between them and closing his mouth over hers.

SHE TASTED sweet with a hint of spice—her lips incredibly soft under his.

Encouraged when Maisie didn't pull away, Seth raised his hand to cup the back of her head and deepened the kiss. He explored her mouth in gentle sweeps, happy when she returned with timid explorations of her own. Letting her up for air, he nipped at her lower lip then sucked at the fullest part. Teasing, he continued that way until she made a noise of frustration and caught his upper lip between her own teeth in a gentle bite.

He tightened his fingers around a handful of her hair and turned her head slightly for a better angle, ducking low to nuzzle her neck. She didn't struggle but her pulse fluttered at the delicate curve of her neck and her arousal scented the air. He kissed her pulse point and then her jaw before brushing his lips over hers. When she parted her lips for him, he took the invitation without hesitation and took her mouth in a deep kiss.

Her hands tugged at either side of his waist and he allowed her to pull him closer, snug between her legs. Releasing her hair, he let his own hands roam over her shoulders, over the curve of her back and down to her behind. Gripping her butt in both hands, he ground into her as he kissed her even harder, and was rewarded by an answering moan from her.

When he finally ended the kiss, they were both gasping and his arousal strained against the zipper of his jeans. She started pressing kisses across his chest, soft points of warmth drifting down his sternum until he had to step back to give her enough room to continue down to his abdomen. When her tongue flicked across the very tip of his dick, peaking at his waistband, he groaned. Helping her as her slender fingers struggled with the button, he undid his pants and the rock-hard length of him stood free.

She giggled, looking up through cinnamon-colored eyelashes at him. "You go commando?"

A question at a time like this? And he was supposed to answer with words?

"Easier when I need to do a complete shift to wolf." His voice came out husky. She didn't seem to mind.

No. Her attention centered on his very hard, very obvious arousal. As she nuzzled him, he gathered her hair in one hand, trying with every ounce of will he had not to fist her hair and shove her head into his groin.

He wouldn't rush her.

But damn he wanted her mouth on his cock.

And then moist heat closed around him and he couldn't help but tighten his hold. If she was reading his mind, she couldn't have known better what he wanted and how. She took him into her mouth and worked her tongue, keeping her teeth clear of his sensitive flesh. Her fingertips drifted over the line of his hip, tracing the V down to his balls. She sucked gently on his cock as she tickled the skin on the underside of his scrotum. Everything inside him tightened in response.

She was hungry, his Maisie. Now he needed to slow things down so he could please her in return. Her clever mouth coaxed another groan out of him as his balls tightened.

It'd been a long time since he'd last been with a woman.

"Easy, there." He tried to keep his tone gentle, but his

voice came out low and rough.

She looked up, cheeks flushed and lips moist.

"You'll have me too fast." He bent low to kiss her again. "I'm about sharing, luv."

"Sharing?" Her breath came in little huffs.

What kind of men had she been with in the past?

No. He didn't want to think of that.

Still, the thought washed through his desire and cleared his head. Looking around at the cold room, the steel treatment counters and sterilization equipment, he stilled her hands by pressing them against his waist.

"This is not the place to keep going where we were headed." She deserved better.

"Wha—"

He took her mouth again and then put every ounce of persuasion he had behind his next words. "When I have you for the first time, Maisie, I want you comfortable in my bed, because I promise you won't have any energy afterward for anything but a long nap."

Her eyes narrowed. "I don't know whether to be miffed or pleased."

Seth didn't blame her. He'd be paying for his virtue later as well. "Hopefully you'll choose the latter." He paused, then gave her a grin. "I can promise I'll more than make it up to you."

She bit her lip, gaze falling to his groin as he tucked himself back into his pants.

Damn, he got harder under the weight of her stare.

Finally, she ran a shaking hand through her wavy hair. "Well, bollocks. Start the night killing zombies, tote me around the London streets, take me to dinner and wind me up. You do know how to show a girl one hell of a first date."

He laughed.

6

"I want a blood sample."

Seth narrowed his eyes. "Why?"

"Whatever it is you're on, I figure it'd be useful to help the newer wolves with their rage control." Danny paused. "Or I could sell it as a recreation drug. I'd make a fortune."

Seth tossed a towel at the pack medic and stood up from the weight bench where he'd been pressing more weight than any three human body builders could have handled. "Get on, then."

"Seriously, mate, I left you out on a solo patrol cause you had to burn off some temper, and you come back all sunshine and posies." Danny handed Seth a water bottle. "One of the pups freaked out, thought he might have seen an actual smile on your face. Maybe."

"I smile."

"Only fresh from killing zombies, covered in gore and high on adrenaline. You've got a reputation for being a bit mad, you know. Seeing you smile like a normal man, in the middle of the day? Nah. That's enough to creep me out too."

Seth growled. Danny had known him for years, well enough to know there'd been a time when he'd smiled like a normal.

Danny held up his hands. "All right, fair enough, but I am curious. What happened last night to trigger such a big change? I won't say how long it's been, but it's good to see."

True enough.

Mollified, Seth turned his attention to removing the heavy weight plates from the bar and returning them to the rack. "There might have been some zombie killing involved."

"Not the main reason, I gather." Danny was a smart man and didn't push the joke further.

"I might have found a lady."

"Did you save her from the zombies?"

Wouldn't that have been classic?

If she'd have been an ordinary damsel in distress, he'd not have stuck around after saving her. Nah. And if he'd have called Maisie a damsel in anything, she'd have stabbed him with her walking stick. Or used it to crack him over the head.

Seth chuckled. "Well, now, she was in the process of saving someone else from zombies, but I decided to step in when those cretins' screaming attracted more."

"Sounds like an interesting woman." There was a cautious note in Danny's voice.

Rightly so. Seth hadn't mentioned details and the last time a lady had entered his life, her betrayal had almost been the death of him. It was ironic the way he and Danny had been talking about Sarah only a short time before Seth came upon Maisie, but a day rarely went by when Seth wasn't reminded of Sarah. He made it a point to remind himself about her, so he'd not allow anyone close to make the mistake of relying on magic again.

Maisie relied only on herself ... and her guns. Clean, practical.

"She's a plucky girl, not like any I've met before."

He'd said it as much to reassure Danny that Maisie wouldn't be a repeat in history as to give him a hint of her character.

Danny never let caution stop his curiosity. The medic might be spending too much time with the leopard pride. The big cat shape-shifters had moved into London proper in the last year, after hiding out in the countryside for a couple decades scaring the bejeezus out of farmers around Devon and Cornwall. While the werewolves were glad to have their help in controlling the growing zombie infestation, only Danny and the leopard pride healer could visit either group without triggering territorial aggression so far.

"And how's she different?"

"She shot me." Seth grinned at the memory.

"She what?" The anger in Danny's voice turned the last word into a growl.

Seth raised a hand to forestall Danny's temper.

"The zombies last night, a few of them had a completely different behavioral pattern." Seth's mood sobered. "Fierce simultaneous attacks. Two came at me, one from either side while another jumped on my back. She shot through my shoulder. Blew it to the ground then administered a kill shot to its head. Woman knows how to handle a gun and she knows how to put a zombie down permanently."

A moment of silence fell in the gym. Then Danny seemed to gather his wits. "Seems she's a practical sort."

"That she is."

The pride he experienced in saying so tangled with another emotion. One he'd never thought he'd feel again.

Next time he took her out for a meal, he'd get the story out of her as to how she learned to shoot and how she'd gotten a hold of firearms with so little money at hand.

He figured he knew, but he wanted to hear it from her. Then he could set about arguing with her not to do it anymore. Setting his will against hers ought to perk up both their days.

Danny apparently hadn't left yet. "So, I'm assuming she's still alive after putting a hole in you. Didn't hear you fussing around in my supplies. You go to the emergency room?"

Seth didn't miss the disgruntlement under Danny's words. As much of a clown as he was, the medic was fiercely protective of his pack brothers. "Nah. You know I hate hospitals. Woman works in a clinic. Patched me up as an apology for shooting me in the first place."

"A clinic? Not many around the area, not with the hospital so close by."

"True enough and you know it. She works at an animal clinic."

Danny snickered.

He might take a minute to pound his friend into the floor after all.

The medic turned his head to bare his neck and held up his hands. "Now, Seth, you can see the humor in it with your newfound good mood, can't you?"

"Not so much as to let you go on about it."

Keeping his gaze on the floor, Danny backed up a step or two. "I'll leave it alone then, for the time being."

Seth growled.

"Aw, you can't expect me not to tuck this away for a rainy

day, can you? It's a choice bit of fun to poke you with when you get ahead of yourself."

Folding his arms across his chest, Seth scowled. "I give you a lot of slack, Danny. But one of these days, it's going to run out."

"Point taken. And I suppose it does rain bloody often in London." Danny scratched his head. "This clinic was out near last night's patrol route though, yeah?"

Seth nodded.

"If you're going to be visiting her more often anyway, and I'm guessing you are, it wouldn't hurt to see if the clinic could become a field triage location for the pack. We're going to be needing a few locations for those."

"I don't know about a few ..." It wasn't a bad idea. But he hadn't kept his pack safe in the middle of a major city by trusting every bloke out there. Werewolves were best taken care of by their own.

"Start with this one, then," Danny urged. "Humans who work with animals on a daily basis do better at working with shape-shifters. They're more likely to understand the body language. Werewolves and were-cats are touchy enough to deal with hale and whole. Any of our wounded will need medical attention from people who aren't going to be stupid and incite our prey drives."

A point, there. Another reason Seth hated normal emergency rooms was the stink of fear from the nurses and doctors. Whether they were afraid he'd hurt them, attack them, or they thought they'd "catch" the werewolf disease by wiping away his blood, they all tiptoed around, ready to bolt if he moved a muscle. It took all of his considerable will not to run them down when they behaved so much like skittish deer. Either he or Danny always had to be present if any pack member with less control had to be cared for in a human hospital.

"I'll think about it. There's two of them working at the clinic and they'd both work well with werewolves." Even Brian had responded amazingly well considering the circumstances. "But I want to get a better feel for their current routine before we send it arse over elbow. You and the rest of the pack wait for me to make the introductions. Understood? For now, we keep the clinic under our protection."

His claim on Maisie needed to be clear. Once she accepted his suit, then he'd worry about the rest.

"You gonna let me take a look at the hole she put in you?" Danny nodded with a pointed look at Seth's chest. "It'll have healed by now, but I'd like to be sure it healed clean."

Seth sat on the weight bench with his back to Danny. The position gave Danny access to the healed wound and represented a show of trust Seth wouldn't have given to other pack members. It was about as close to a peace offering as Seth would give for his temper regarding Maisie.

"Healed clean. I don't smell any infection or leftover lead." Danny gave his assessment with a hint of grudging respect. "She did a good job of it."

"Aye, she did."

Danny moved back into Seth's field of vision, a grin on his face. "You going to let her put more holes in you or just get yourself randomly injured here so you can go get her to patch you up?"

Seth bared his teeth.

"Well, you've made it clear you're going to go see her again. What excuse are you going to have ready?"

"I don't need an excuse." Seth paused, then shook his

head. Did he? "One night, Danny, one night and I can't get her out of my head. Every part of me wants to head back over to her place, catch her up and bring her back here. I want her in my den, where I can keep her safe, mark her with my scent."

"Whoa there." The medic's brows were raised in surprise. "Never thought I'd see you bitten this way."

Neither had he. The wolf in him could identify a mate—the mate for him—far sooner than the man in him. He'd thought the woman for him had died years ago, yet the last twenty-four hours had turned him upside down.

"While I'd dearly enjoy pressing you for more details on this very special lady friend, we've got an interesting report in from one of the patrols." Jerking his head in the direction of the door, Danny gave him an apologetic grimace. "Pretty certain you'll be interested in light of the observation you just made."

"Why did you wait so long to tell me?"

"Not used to you all warm and fuzzy, wanted to be sure to get a feel for what was on your mind before setting this issue in your lap."

Seth considered the situation. These new developments with the zombies might require in-depth investigation. Normally he let his seconds handle reports, but if Danny had brought this one to his attention ...

He began pulling the weights off the bar and placed them back on the racks. "Let me finish setting these to rights and I'll meet you in the wreck room."

Danny nodded and gave him a moment of peace. The wreck room was actually more of a sort of TV and entertainment room at pack headquarters. Informal. Most of the junior pack members spent time relaxing, watching shows on the vid or playing cards. The bonds of the pack were built as much on quality social time as in combat.

If the report had come during the day, it was probably from one of the junior pack members and the pup would give a clearer report in a setting more familiar and less of a strain for him.

Finished setting the plates back on their rack, Seth used his towel to give the bench a quick wipe down. Then he headed out of the gym and down the hall.

As he'd thought, the patrol waiting was composed of three young Weres. One had been with them for more than a decade, the other two were more junior, having only made the change in the past five years. The younger pups fidgeted despite the casual environment.

Seth nodded to each of them, then Danny, who waited off to one side. He chose a big armchair and sat, keeping his body language relaxed. The others sat as well, staying even with the level of his head in a gesture of respect.

"Something unusual in today's report?" Calm voice, soothing.

The two pups kept their eyes glued to the floor but their shoulders relaxed. The older werewolf kept his eyes on Seth's shoulder, still not making eye contact but not staring at Seth's throat the way some of the others did, hungry to advance in the pack hierarchy. He did the talking.

"We were out on a standard patrol route, sir. And the humans were all stirred up about an apartment complex. Lots of bodies—in pieces, all rotted or tainted." Sentence structure broke down as he reacted to the memory associated with the report. Werewolves remembered everything in a cascade of sights, scents, sounds, touch and taste. Humans might experience some particularly strong memories that way, but not always. The wolf might be older than his two pack mates, but he still had a long way to go before he had the control the senior wolves had.

"Go on." Seth didn't need to prompt for details. The wolf would have trouble not giving every detail. The trick was only sharing the key points.

"The dead, all humans. Zombie stink everywhere. Trails all around the building, like they came from every direction. The humans in the building had no escape route."

Danny gave Seth a worried look.

Zombies usually hunted in the open, preying on the stray humans wandering out in the night. One might find its way into a building, but only if the doors were wide open or if it were directly following live meat.

"Any survivors?" Not his favorite question. The way the situation sounded, they might have to go put survivors out of their misery. The hospital wouldn't do what needed to be done—not until it was too late. By then more innocent people would be infected.

And wouldn't that be fodder for the news-hounds?

The reporting wolf shook his head. The action seemed to clear his head some. "There were ambulances, sir, but no survivors loaded up or taken back to the hospice. Mostly police on the scene, investigating, and standard gawkers."

Seth cocked his head. Something off, there. "Rubber necking, but no one upset? Crying?"

A pause. One of the very junior pups answered. "No, sir. No crying. All the humans smelled of fear, but no one grieving. None of the gathered crowd were friends or family."

Smart pup.

Friends and family would have been summoned to the scene if the news hit the TV. Still, even if it hadn't aired yet, someone in the crowd should have known the residents, suffered for the loss.

"Have the three of you gotten sleep? Fed?"

"Fed before the patrol, sir," the original reporting wolf assured him.

Good. It was standard procedure to send out well-fed patrols, but never hurt to confirm. Wouldn't do for a younger wolf to lose control and start feeding on a dead body. None of them would be tempted by one of the rotting zombies, but a fresh human kill before it made the transition? It could happen and the humans would turn on the shape-shifters in a fear-driven monster hunt. Too easy to lump all the supernatural under the "things that need to be destroyed" category.

"Rest up, feed again, then I want you to go back and scout the scene a second time. I want to know if any friends or family show up."

Something. There was something odd about that building and the change in the zombie attack pattern.

Nods all around.

Seth stood, allowing the rest of them to stand and leave the room. It didn't surprise him when Danny remained.

"You're hunting." And Danny wasn't talking about fat bunnies in Hyde Park.

Seth shook his head once. "I've got a gut feeling; still no real trail to follow yet. Something's not right about the changes we're seeing in the zombies. You see anything different in those samples we got for you?"

"Tests can take more than a single night." Danny grimaced, sitting on the arm of a sofa. "Based on my initial findings though, the virus is still active in the tissue samples we've seen and looks to be the same with the limited equipment I've got. It hasn't mutated. Whatever the source is for this new behavior, it doesn't seem to be the virus itself. I'll ask the boys to bring in samples on the next patrols just to be sure."

Seth made a mental note to track down some of the new ones—the faster corpses.

"It's not the virus and it's not the hosts, because the humans aren't evolving or some of them would be developing an immunity to the virus." Seth had done his time in university not once, but several times over the decades he'd been a werewolf. "There's some external factor, something we're missing."

Magic.

Rage simmered, but Seth couldn't ignore it any longer, couldn't let his hate blind him to the potential threat.

"And why?" Danny was right there with him in worrying.

"It's not likely to be the were-cats, but keep alert next time you go see them." Territorial aggression or not, they'd all been upfront with each other thus far. No. If there was a bid for power, it was some of the other supernaturals. Vampires, for example, loved cities as hunting grounds, and the chaos of the epidemic gave them freedom to prey on humans amid the confusion. And there were fae who fed on those emotions. "If one of the other groups fishes for information, I want to be sure they know we're aware of an issue, but I want all cards on the table. We *all* share what we know and I want to be there if there's anything to be said."

A nod from Danny was all he needed. The medic would be careful.

"Let's see what this next patrol turns up." He walked past Danny, dropping a hand on his friend's shoulder. "And keep an ear to the ground for any other occurrences like this one."

"I'll check in with our contacts. Our patrol stumbled on

this by accident. Could be one of the others saw something similar."

Seth curled his lip. "I hope not. If a pattern does come up, let me know."

"This smells like magic, Seth. There's no natural cause, not from the virus. If one of the other groups confirms it, we're going to have to be prepared to deal with it."

Danny wouldn't flush the game out in front of the junior pack members. He knew what it did to Seth.

Anger churned in his belly, a familiar burn. He'd lived in a state of almost constant temper since he'd lost Sarah—dead because the witch couldn't resist the call of power. She'd brought the consequences to their doorstep, their home, when he hadn't been there to protect her.

Damn magic users and their hunger, their need for more and more power. Nothing but evil.

"Sarah didn't share the spell with others." Seth choked on the name of his deceased lover.

"No. What she did was find a way to control zombies. If she could, so could others. She was good, but she wasn't singular." Head down, shoulders hunched, Danny was obviously prepared in case Seth lashed out. The medic had big balls to put the truth out there for discussion.

He was indispensable to the pack, and to Seth, because of it.

"The price won't change for a different magic user. Spells, power, always require a price." Seth wanted to spit in disgust, get the bitter taste out of his mouth.

Sure, Sarah had figured out how to control zombies, but she hadn't considered the cost. When her endurance had run out, her spell had backlashed. The "controlled" zombies had been drawn to her and attacked her where she rested—in *his* home. He'd lost everything he'd held dear in one night, unable to get there in time. All because his lover couldn't resist the temptation to solve things with magic and had gone back on her promise not to.

She'd broken her word to him and he hadn't been able to save her.

"Magic can be harnessed for good things." Danny meant well, but Seth didn't want to hear it.

"Yeah. The tossers who try to use it go mad with the power, or else they're too daft to control it properly to begin with." Seth struggled to untangle the roiling emotions in his belly. He needed to get out, run, find some clean violence. "The magic might be a cure for the zombie virus, but only sometimes and only in the hands of a user in his right mind. It's never a consistent thing. And at what price? All power requires a price, Danny. You've seen it. The magic that makes us what we are takes its price from us every day. The magic this would take, it'd cause chaos."

Sarah had said the same thing as Danny. She'd wanted to help clear the city of the zombies, use the zombies under her power to contain the epidemic without risking infection to humans. Good intentions, bad decisions and a broken promise had left him mourning her.

No.

He would put his faith in himself and the pack, and destroy the walking dead.

"Where are you going?"

Seth snarled, his anger a living thing inside of him. "Out on patrol to burn some of this off until we have more information."

7

———

S eth halted on the landing of the pack's headquarters —a terraced house built in the 1780s and identical to its neighbors in every regard save for the reinforced, sound-proofed cellars meant to keep newly changed were-wolves safely confined. He imagined he looked like any other man, about to go off on an errand.

A man dressed in naught but a trench coat and denims. He'd left off a shirt again.

Broad daylight as it was, would Maisie mind?

Was he going to see her?

He'd thought to ring her up, not look in on her so soon. Was it too soon? It bloody well would be if he'd no reason to be bothering her in the middle of her day. She was likely busy. He'd no way of knowing.

Stand around much longer and Danny was going to pop his head out to ask what all was going on.

Cursing, Seth yanked his mobile out of his pocket and dialed a number.

It took half a dozen rings before a tart voice answered. "Clinic."

The tension melted away at the sound of her voice.

"Maisie."

"And who's ringing me up, then?" Suspicion and spunk —that was his girl being cautious. Good.

"It's Seth." Well, what else was he going to say? He didn't really know why he'd called other than to hear her voice. "Wanted to see that you'd had a good night's rest."

Awkward. She was going to think he was mad.

"Oh." Actually, pleasure seemed to infuse the one word, or maybe he was just hopeful. "I ... um ... I did. Thank you. And you?"

"Well, yeah, I guess." Damn, man, find your balls. "I had a bit on my mind and it might've made sleep a little frustrating."

She laughed. "I might remind you, you're the one who put a stop to it." A pause. "Though I appreciate why you said you did."

"And did you give some thought to it too?" The idea of her in his bed heated his blood in a completely different way.

"I might have." There was an answering heat in her tone, more encouraging than her light words.

He wanted to see her, enjoy the color that must be rising up in her cheeks. Her scent would be turning musky about now and drive him out of his right mind.

Ah hell, he was doing a good job of it all on his own.

"I'd like to take you out for dinner again." He'd like to lay a plump bunny at her feet and know she'd accepted him as a provider, but he'd settle for taking her to a nice restaurant. He'd convince her to accept him over time.

"You don't have to." Maisie sounded distressed and his chest tightened. "I mean, it'd be nice to see you, either way.

No need to buy me dinner. You'd be welcome to stop in at the clinic."

He grinned. He might stop by sooner than she thought.

Could be she wasn't used to anyone spending money on her, his girl.

She'd have to get used to it.

He planned to spoil her silly. But telling her so might put her off, so he settled for a baby step. "I'm a big bad wolf, Maisie, and I eat a lot. If you wouldn't mind watching me shovel a mountain of food into my gullet, your company would make a mealtime more pleasant. I enjoyed talking to you over dinner last night."

"Oh. Well then, I enjoyed your company too." She sounded flustered and pleased.

Warmth spread through his chest.

"I ... uh ... I have to go, Seth. We've got a patient in the waiting room."

Seth jolted out of his thoughts. "Oh. Course. I'll be talking to you later, then." Maybe dropping by the clinic, as in now, would be too soon.

He seemed to be worrying a lot about what was "too soon."

He ended the call and cursed himself for acting like a puppy. It hadn't been so long. How did men manage to court a lady with stupid mobiles limiting them to only sound? Conversation wasn't so awkward in person and he could get a better feel for her moods and reactions, watch her expressions change across her face, her body language.

He'd go see her after all. Besides, she seemed to like him near her right fine.

Since he planned to take her out to dinner, he needed a different reason to stop by. Flowers? Nah. Surely he could think of something more personal, something she'd really want. Maybe something would come to mind while he was out on patrol. If all else failed, he could always get her extra ammunition. Ammunition for that .38 Super of hers wasn't easy to come by.

Best get her full metal jacket rounds. If she ever decided to shoot him again, he'd rather her not have the cheaper hollow points.

He shook his head. When had any man ever grinned over the prospect of being shot?

The grin didn't leave his face as he started off down the road. He set a path at random, foregoing the normal patrol routes as they were already covered by his wolves. He preferred to be the wild card for those times when chaos could cock-up even the best-laid schedules.

The sun was high, and most of the fog had burned away this late in the morning. More people walked the streets, rushing from place to place on their errands. They might dawdle a little to have a word with a friend here and there, but there was an edge to every exchange.

"Another building. Horrible, it was," a woman said to one of the ration distributors.

He didn't turn his head toward the speaker but he slowed his pace to catch more of the conversation. "The zombie hunters are going in with the police. They say they want to try to track the zombies back to where they came from, maybe find a nest of them. Clean 'em out like rats."

Not a bad idea, that. If the police mustered a decent force to go in and clean out the parks in a coordinated effort, Seth would be willing to support the effort. But he wouldn't offer his wolves up to be fodder or bait. He'd wait to see whether the police approached him with a decent plan.

He headed up Savile Row, past shops boasting the latest in survival and hunting gear where once they were the finest tailors in London. What businesses remained open had evolved to cater to the clientele with the money to spend.

A pair of constables, apparently on patrol as well, paused near him. They never went out alone anymore—smart move. These two slowed to eye him up and down for a long moment before the older of the two gave him a nod.

In a good mood, Seth nodded in return. He paused to see if they'd say something to him. Dealings between police and werewolves were tentative thus far. He didn't remember meeting these two, but a man walking about in a trench coat and no shirt probably tipped them off to him being a were-wolf. Or, one of them might be observant enough to see the difference in the way he moved.

A shop door swung open and first one then another man stepped out laden with new gear.

"I'm telling you, Sam, we're going to get us some fan-fucking-tastic trophies. My contact guarantees us plenty of targets. We can shoot all we want. This isn't like hunting moose." American, by their accents. Amazing how they could use the same words and still make a bloody mess of the language. "They don't make you submit an application and wait on the results of some lottery to see if you'll be awarded a permit."

"Can't wait to get out there." The other American's voice was a veritable boom on the quiet street. "Show these Brits how to get things *done*. No worries about any apocalypse once we start taking them down."

The older constable shifted his weight, catching Seth's eye. The corner of the human's mouth twitched. Seth raised an eyebrow in return.

He'd be a bad, bad man for finding amusement. He should try to give these hunters a fighting chance, some idea of why zombies were different from hunting natural prey.

"These locals, they didn't carry decent weapons before the zombies started appearing. I hear they haven't even settled on a standard issue rifle for their cops yet." Tourist hunter number one hefted a fancy rifle. "I bet they never used a Henry Big Boy. Mine's custom."

Was that ivory inlay on the stock of that rifle? Pretty ... pretty for a big man's weapon.

Tourist hunter number two hefted a sack of garlic heads, holding it far away from his pristine camouflage. Not a speck of dirt on those, anywhere. He must have ordered them custom fit and decided to wear them right out of the store when he'd come to pick them up. "And I've got plenty of garlic to throw the monsters off my scent."

Garlic? Were they hunting zombies or vampires?

Far as Seth knew, the local vampires had no particular aversion to it.

The sharp scent of salted beef cut through the garlic. Seth glanced to his side to see the younger of the two constables holding out an open sack.

"Beef jerky? My mum made it." Both were chewing away at the snack. "Figure your kind would like it better than tobacco."

Seth accepted a piece. Nice of the man to offer.

The three stood in companionable silence, taking in the continuing tourist entertainment.

"I hear the Brits are getting so desperate, they've got werewolves hunting them zombies down for 'em. Before you know it, they're going to be out there on horses in those nifty hunting jackets." Tourist one guffawed. "Can you see it? One of 'em sounding off on their horn with a pack of werewolves running out in front chasing down zombies. It's all about the sport, I'm tellin' ya."

To hell with warning these men. Burning in hell wasn't

so bad. Seth chewed on his beef jerky and kept his advice to himself. He'd caught enough of their scent to remember them. It'd be interesting to see if he came across the trails of these two again.

"Best to let those types go on their way." The older constable spat on the sidewalk once the two hunters left. "All shiny and new, they were. Out to prove something."

"Try to give them a word of warning and they won't listen in any case." The other constable scratched his head. "At least they tend to go into the parks, away from normal people. Won't have to worry much about them shooting innocent people when they get all worked up waiting for a zombie to stumble by."

True enough. They would worry about having all their "trophies" to themselves. Little did they know, their precious trophies would be naught but ashes by the time they arrived back in the States.

"As long as they don't make trouble for us, they're welcome to take their shots at the blighters." Seth tried for an amiable tone. He couldn't bring himself to smile, even in the name of camaraderie.

Funny how a smile had come to his face so readily the night before.

"Well, and we all appreciate what you and yours do to help keep the public safe." The older constable coughed. "Takes some getting used to, won't lie to you there, but we're learning new tricks. If you get my meaning."

"We all are." Seth gave them another nod as they headed off on the rest of their patrol.

He made a mental note of Constables Middleton and Turpin. Danny would find them amenable to contact in the future.

His mood held out for the next hour or so. Cloud cover

came and went as the day moved into afternoon. Shadows raced across the streets, alternately revealing then hiding the way London had deteriorated. As he walked, he kicked at fallen mortar and stones from the various buildings falling into disrepair.

Not enough residents left in the city to maintain them.

Most had moved into apartment complexes clustered closer to the police stations. Any homes near the various parks had been long since abandoned, with only the odd small businesses remaining—aside from the businesses directly capitalizing on the new tourist hunting excursions.

A low moan snapped Seth out of his musings.

There, in a tiny alley. The movement raised the fine hairs on the back of his neck. He approached slowly. Careful.

The zombie hadn't caught his scent yet. It was scrabbling against the far wall of the alley. The corpse stood on two feet, fairly solid for a rotting thing. As it scraped its hands over the rough stone of the building, bits of flesh came away and streaked the mortar in rot. The tips of bone had been exposed on its fingertips and added a sickening sound with the friction of bone on stone.

It could get out. No encumbrances were visible around its legs. Hell, he'd seen a few of them drag themselves against a snare until a leg came loose. They didn't care much about leaving a body part behind if they were determined to go after fresh meat.

There was none, though. No one on this smaller street besides him. So what was this zombie after? It kept at the wall, trying to get through. Seth studied the building. Windows boarded up, falling apart, not even a small business in the ground floor to make any noise that'd attract the thing. It wasn't far from Maisie and the clinic. Most of the buildings in this area were abandoned or close to it.

And still, Seth had a gut feeling the blighter was trying to get *into* the building. It had moved to the very end of the alley, a dead end. It began half climbing a stack of crates as it continued to do its best to pass through a solid wall.

A hiss echoed through the alley.

The zombie froze, made a slow turn. Something live was in those crates. As the corpse crouched over, it uttered another low moan.

A thin yowl issued from a crate. A tiny paw shot through the cracks and swiped the zombie across its jaw, taking away a chunk of flesh.

Really?

He moved without thought. In a flash, he had the zombie by the throat. It took a simple twist to snap its neck and then he crushed its skull.

Another hiss.

He glared at the crate. There. A patch of dirty orange. In moments, Seth had an itty bitty bundle of tabby kitten in his grip. It literally fit in the palm of his hand.

"Poor bastard."

Golden eyes glared at him with a defiance the tiny body couldn't back up.

"Where's your mum, then? You don't stand a chance on your own."

No sign of any other cats in the alley, not by sight or scent. However the little bloke had gotten there, it was obvious he was on his own.

He should leave the cat.

It huddled in the palm of his hand, waiting. Seth leaned in close then jerked his head back as the kitten took a swipe at his nose.

He chuckled. This one had fight to him.

"You're supposed to be frightened." The kitten seemed unimpressed. Still, most dogs and cats were scared to spitting of werewolves. They gave Seth a wide berth, cowering and running for cover long before he approached touching distance. This one, not so much.

Well, he'd wondered what reason he'd have to visit Maisie at the clinic.

8

"There now, settle down, won't you?" Maisie gave the Yorkshire terrier a final scratch behind the ear before closing the door to its kennel. Sweet boy needed a nap after running about so much earlier. "You've had a long walk and hours of playtime with the others; don't you think it's time to rest and let me have a cup of tea?"

The Yorkie had been about to take her advice too, then suddenly he was up on his hind legs lunging at the door to his kennel, barking for all he was worth. The others erupted in a chorus of growls and yaps until the entire room was in chaos.

"If I get you that cup of tea, do you have a few minutes to spare?" Seth's voice sent a shiver down Maisie's spine.

She took a deep breath before she turned to face him, and hoped her cheeks weren't too flushed. "Well, see what you've done now."

He dropped his chin a bit, mouth twisted in what he must've thought was an expression of contrition but really, anyone could tell he was grinning. There was a distinct lack of a verbal apology. Really, the man was incorrigible.

And incredibly sexy.

"Enough." She'd had to raise her voice to be heard, but the barking and growling decreased immediately. A few brave ones gave a final bark or snarl before she pinned each of them with a glare.

"You seem to have quite a lot of business." He didn't move and his voice remained low, deliciously dark. A few warning growls, but the peanut gallery remained relatively quiet.

"People've always liked to travel with their pets when they could." She checked the doors to all of their kennels, pausing to give each of them a reassuring skritch to the nose as she passed. "Customs doesn't seem to be holding most of the supposed zombie hunters to the normal quarantine times. Gives them the ability to bring in their hunting dogs, I suppose. But really, we get a decent number of these pets to board while their owners see their fill of zombie-infested London."

She eyed Seth. She'd seen him in action. Energy fairly vibrated in the air around him, and yet he'd somehow managed to tuck it all away as he stood there, perfectly still. She wondered if it only lasted while he remained standing there. And why did he have his hand clutched to his shoulder like that?

"What happened? Have you gotten yourself hurt again, then?"

He lifted an eyebrow.

"Well? Has someone shot you besides me in the last twenty-four hours?"

He flashed teeth in a real smile. "I might have had a run-in with a stray zombie."

"What zombie isn't a stray, shambling about aimlessly until it stumbles across live meat?" She wanted to spit the bitter taste from her mouth, but it'd set a bad example for the boys and next thing she knew, they'd be drooling everywhere.

"I've been wondering that myself." Could the man be more cryptic?

Seth turned and lowered his hand to the small utility table in the center of the room at the same time. She had to step around him to see.

There stood the tiniest orange tabby kitten, standing on wide braced paws and looking very annoyed.

"He fits in your hand!" She hushed herself and leaned in for a closer look.

The kitten immediately puffed into an orange ball of temper.

"There now, easy. We're only trying to help." She cooed and made soft nonsense sounds, to let him see she meant him no harm. As his fur settled, she extended a single finger.

It took another long minute before the lad met her halfway to sniff her fingertip.

"All right then, now we're friends, let me look you over in the other room." Before the boys set to barking their furry heads off again and scared the bejeezus out of the kitten.

She gathered him to her chest and tried not to wince when needle-sharp claws immediately anchored into the front of her shirt. Poor thing didn't trust her not to drop him.

Couldn't blame him. Easier to survive in this world relying on no one.

Seth followed her into the examination room. "Found him in an alley, fighting a zombie."

"You must be joking."

"He reminded me of someone, so I brought him here."

Oh, wasn't that charming. She gave the werewolf a scowl for his trouble.

"He can't be more than a few weeks old." It took a bit of wriggling to detach him from her shirt. He'd better not rip it—she only had a few good enough to wear down to the clinic. "He's in good shape, though, if he's got this much fight to him."

She set him down on the table and checked him over with gentle hands.

"Cats've been doing well in the city this past year, better than dogs," Seth said.

"You think so?" She'd not seen many dogs at all. "I thought most of the dogs might have run off."

Seth shook his head. "Most people keep their dogs in their houses with them or tied up to a kennel. Usually dogs can't run away from a zombie if one of the blighters gets into a home or yard."

Her breath caught. Poor things. She focused on breathing away the pang of sadness and she spent an extra moment caressing the soft fur around the tabby's face.

"Some of the dogs probably did run off," Seth added. His voice had taken on an odd sound. Trying to ease the harsh reality a bit for her?

No need.

She straightened and reached for the thermometer and a few swabs. "I'll take a few readings, then some samples to test him for worms and mites. Then, he's in desperate need of a thorough bath. We've got shampoo for kittens and a powder to dust him for fleas."

Seth's face twisted in a funny expression. A giggle tickled her belly as she wondered if a werewolf ever had to be dipped for fleas.

"Don't enjoy baths?" She tried for innocent. She sounded more like she was choking on something.

"I like baths." His gaze pinned her, sent shivers across her skin. "When there's someone to wash my back."

"You do have a broad back." Suddenly words were tripping over her tongue. "Could see how you'd need a bit of help reaching a few places."

Silence fell across the room, wrapped her in an odd tension. She bustled the kitten through his tests and much-needed bath despite yowls and squirming on his part. Seth even lent a hand to keep the orange spitfire in the sink.

Every time their shoulders brushed or their sides bumped, excitement tingled across Maisie's skin. She remembered the touch of his hands ... Wanted more.

And oddly, seeing how gentle he was with the kitten caused a twinge in her heart. She'd seen him crush zombie skulls, rip body parts off the monsters. And here he was, helping care for a stray kitten. So much control over all that strength.

Finally, the kitten was bathed, dusted and settled into a kennel in the room they kept for cats. When she placed a dish of wet food in front of him, he dove face first into it, smooshing the food with his paws as he greedily sucked up the much-needed sustenance.

Seth chuckled.

"He's a bit young to be neat about it." Maisie felt a need to defend their little charge.

Seth raised his hands in acquiescence. "I can leave him with you, then?"

"Of course."

Then Brian's latest lecture whispered at the back of her mind and she grimaced.

"A problem?"

"It's just that all of our business is boarding the pets of the tourists lately. It's enough to keep us afloat, but not by much. We don't have the means to care for strays really, and there are a lot of them out there." She shook her head. "I'll find a way around it."

"Put his care on a tab and I'll take care of it."

She blinked. "We're not a pub."

"I don't plan to eat him." Seth reached across the space between them and tapped her nose with his fingertip. "But I did make sure he didn't become a zombie snack, so I figure I ought to see to his care through until he can look after himself."

"And what use do you have for a cat?"

"No idea." Seth grinned. "We've got a few rats plaguing the cellar and I hear cats are good for those."

"So are Yorkies, and they'd seem a better choice for a werewolf."

"Tch. You saw how those little ... things reacted to me when I first got here."

He had a point. Anything so frightened of him and his would be useless in their home. It'd also be a bit cruel. Not a good fit for any of the parties involved.

"This kitten is the first I've encountered that's willing to make friends with a werewolf. Least I can do is see if he wants a home with one once he's big enough to mean I won't be stepping on him."

She'd no idea what to say to that. Warmth spread through her chest all the same. The kitten would have a home after all.

Before she realized what she'd done, she was in his arms and kissing him.

"Maisie?" a voice came from the hallway. "Maisie, luv, are you back here? Brian said to come on back."

Oh, for heaven's ... No time to gather her wits. They were scattered all over the room.

She stepped away from Seth and cleared her throat. "Here, Mrs. Wells."

Seth kept a hand on the small of her back as the older woman entered the room. When Mrs. Wells caught sight of Seth, the woman dropped her gaze to the ground almost immediately.

Did she know what Seth was? Or did she just do it without thinking?

"You've been such a help, these past few weeks, dear. I wanted to bring you something but it's been so late when you've been coming back, I didn't want to wake the children to give these to you."

Maisie glanced past Mrs. Wells to the corridor, hoping Brian wasn't within earshot.

"Oh, you shouldn't have, really."

Mrs. Wells pressed something soft into her hands. Knitted ... gloves? Maybe leg warmers, for very thin legs.

"They're arm warmers, dear. You can slide them on, all the way up to your shoulder, or leave them slouched around your forearms and wrists. I left them with just the thumb hole to keep them in place so your fingers would be free to do your work around the clinic."

Handy, and good to keep her fingers clear to squeeze a trigger. Cozy too.

"Found a few balls of yarn while the weather was warmer," Mrs. Wells continued. "Enough to make scarves for the children and something to keep you warm as well. You do such a good job of watching over us."

Well, Mrs. Wells had her hands full with the children.

"Mr. Wells still out?"

"He should be home soon." The strain in Mrs. Wells's voice prevented Maisie from asking further.

Mr. Wells had been gone two days. With the hard cold leaving frost on the pavement, it wasn't likely Mr. Wells had been spending the nights away from shelter. Still, he'd been going out every day looking for work. Maisie didn't want to believe he'd abandoned his small family …

Maisie did a mental count. She might be able to "accidentally" purchase enough supper for all of them tomorrow. Besides, she could go light for a few days after the solid meal Seth had bought her.

As if he'd sensed her thoughts had turned to him, the lanky werewolf stirred at her side.

"I'm sorry, my mind is wandering. Mrs. Wells, this is Seth."

"How do you do?" Mrs. Wells gave Seth a glassy-eyed glance, more polite than truly seeing him.

Maisie guessed Mrs. Wells didn't even notice the way her gaze slid over and away from the big werewolf.

"Nice to meet you," Seth answered, playing nice.

Maisie got the impression from his awkward tone that he didn't do it often.

"Didn't you see Maisie home last night?" Mrs. Wells apparently missed very little, even if she wouldn't look Seth in the eye.

Shit.

Mrs. Wells gave Maisie an apologetic smile but directed her words to Seth. "Hard not to hear the fuss when you were stomping about checking the boards to the windows and going on about entry points."

"It's a good thing to sleep where a person can see all the entrances to a room." Seth didn't seem unsettled by the commentary.

"It's a good thing to see someone taking care of Maisie for once." Mrs. Wells clucked and reached out to brush a loose hair away from Maisie's face. It took effort for Maisie not to fidget.

"No need." Maisie had worked hard to make sure no one would need to look after her again. No one should put themselves before her, or die for her.

"Now, Maisie." Mrs. Wells shook a finger under Maisie's nose. "You're far too young to be going on through life alone, no matter how you think you can take care of yourself."

"I'm more concerned about getting through the next month, let alone life beyond that." A change of subject was becoming an imperative. "The landlord stopped by today. That's why Brian is up at the front desk shuffling through papers. The bastard says he has to raise the rent again and wants to send in his bullies to clear out any squatters in the building so he can renovate and sell the flats to trophy hunters. Otherwise, it's back to the 'collecting on insurance' threat."

Mrs. Wells's hands flew to her mouth and her eyes widened in alarm.

Maisie reached out to her immediately, took the older woman's chill hands into her own. "Brian stood up to him. Showed the bastard the lease to the clinic. We've got at least two more years before the landlord can raise the rent."

Brian had pointed out that as a resident in good standing, he had every right to deny those bullies access to the premises. Maisie wasn't certain how true it was, but the landlord had backed down.

She glanced over at Seth, then took a good look at him. "Now you go on upstairs, Mrs. Wells. No need to worry. Brian has things well in hand." She needed to get Mrs. Wells out of the room. "Thank you for the arm warmers."

A moment after Mrs. Wells left for the stairs leading to the flats, Maisie cautiously turned to Seth.

Every muscle tensed, his hands clenched into fists, Seth seemed even taller. He filled the room with his anger, his eyes gone from blue to golden.

"Brian has things well in hand." Maisie kept her voice calm and soothing.

Seth studied her, his gaze so intense she could hardly breathe. After a long moment, he spoke in a deep voice gone wolf. "You have my mobile. You'll call if that man comes back."

He'd not made a request.

She could argue with him on principal, but she was a practical sort. Even if Brian had things sorted for now, it didn't hurt to have allies they could trust. She'd known Seth only a short time, but she felt she could trust him.

Another moment, this one almost awkward again. "Dinner … might not be as good an idea tonight."

Her heart dropped down to her stomach. She dredged up a smile. "All right."

Of course he would've changed his mind, she thought. He'd have lost interest in her eventually in any case.

"I've got a text from the pack. I've got to head back for a meeting and I don't know how long it will take. I don't want to set a time to pick you up then have to cancel later."

Her heart popped back up into her throat.

"Could I ring you up tonight? After the meeting? And then set a time to pick you up for dinner tomorrow?"

Settle. Calm. Use words, not squees. "Course. And you'll come in and check on your little friend as well, yeah?"

He smiled for her. Her heart did a skip and a jump.

Could a person die of a heart attack from all the cardiovascular acrobatics?

Seth meant to pull himself together on the way back to the pack's headquarters. It'd taken a whole two blocks to wipe the stupid grin off his face. He could still smell Maisie's scent on his hands, taste her on his lips.

Danny would've had too much fun slagging him, so Seth had stopped in at a shop. By the time he'd stepped back out —a new coat for Maisie in hand—it was dark. The shopkeeper was eager to close up and hurry home. Seth pondered the coat as he headed back. It was warm and she obviously needed it.

Would she accept a gift from him so soon?

His mobile rang in his pocket. He ignored it. It rang again. Only Danny would have called back. And only if it were urgent.

"You are going to want to get here as soon as possible."

"I'm just down the street. Give me the highlights."

"At least two other apartment buildings were hit last night. All abandoned. None of them should have had people in them." The worry in Danny's voice was nothing compared to the anxiety that struck Seth.

"Squatters."

Maisie.

Danny rushed on, words terse. "Those buildings were owned by the same man. He's got half a dozen more and it's just past nightfall. He has to have something to do with it. You can bet there will be more deaths tonight ... I sent the list of addresses to the entire pack."

Seth cursed. "I'm headed back to Maisie's clinic. I want you and one patrol to follow me as backup as soon as you can pack your kit. Send two patrols to each of the other buildings. Our most senior team goes after this man. I want him for questioning before dawn."

"You got it."

Seth turned on his heel and ran through the darkening evening, the coat dropped and forgotten on the curb.

9

"All right there, Maisie?" Mrs. Wells called as Maisie limped down the hallway. She and her two children kept residence in the small apartment on the same floor as the flat Maisie had chosen for her own.

"Fine." Though it took effort to keep her voice upbeat. It'd been a long day at the clinic after Seth had left.

At the thought of the lanky werewolf, heat touched her cheeks. She leaned hard on her walking stick. She probably should have found more time to elevate her injured ankle through the day, but it felt so much better to be doing things. Her ankle would heal eventually, perhaps not as quickly as it could. As soon as she lay down for the night, she would prop up the ankle with pillows for a real rest. A part of her wanted to demonstrate to the werewolf that his worry was unnecessary.

Another part of her took a careful look around just in case luck would prove him right to be worried.

The apartments might be abandoned and fallen into disrepair, but the water still worked for the businesses on the lower levels. Fire wasn't likely and definitely not the first danger she'd worry about.

Still, she stood there with a nonsensical grin plastered across her face as she remembered—his concern had made her happy.

It wasn't as if there weren't people in the world who cared about her. Not a single one of those people would have forgiven her for shooting them, though. Hell, he seemed amused by it more than anything.

Maisie shook her head and made her way to her corner, setting her back to the wall and letting herself slide slowly down. Tired didn't cover it. His visit earlier had been a pleasant surprise though. She'd left the kitten sleeping soundly with a rounded belly full of food. After that, every time a man walked past the door of the clinic her heart had leapt. She didn't want to admit how much she was hoping Seth would have a reason to come back.

He'd said he would.

But then, Mr. Wells had said he'd come back too.

A loud bang startled her out of her roller coaster thoughts.

It had come from downstairs, outside. What in the hell could have made such a noise for them to hear it all the way upstairs.

Her first thought was that Wells might have returned, in trouble, banging on the door of the clinic to get inside and out of the night.

"Luv? Is that you?" Apparently Mrs. Wells thought the same.

Maisie struggled to her feet, keeping her walking stick with her as she made for the door. There was no answer, only another loud crash, like the sound of something large hitting the front door. Hesitating, Maisie grabbed the shotgun she left by the door to her apartment.

"Don't go down there." She stopped Mrs. Wells as the other woman stepped out of her apartment.

Being a reasonable woman, and possessing of a fair dose of sensible fear, Mrs. Wells waited for Maisie to limp down the hallway. With a nod, Maisie stepped past her into her apartment and went to the window overlooking the front street. She peered out through the cracks, straining to see into the shadows.

Was something moving?

Mrs. Wells probably hadn't looked out this window because it didn't give a direct view of the front of the clinic. A person would have to lean out the window to see the clinic entrance, as it was directly below them. Nevertheless, Maisie wanted to get an idea of what was out there on the street and across in the alley shadows.

There. Darker shadows shuffled back and forth outside the light of the few unbroken streetlamps. Another bang sounded down below and she saw someone, something, fall into view.

"Bloody hell." Maisie turned and gestured for Mrs. Wells to come back into the apartment. "It's not the mister. Quickly gather up the children. We need to get them to my apartment. Now."

Mrs. Wells began to peer out the window. "What—?"

Maisie grabbed the other woman by the arm and stared at her hard. "You do *not* want to look out there. You want to see to the children and I'll do what I can to get you all out of the building. But you can bet we won't be going out the front door."

A crash cut off whatever Mrs. Wells had been about to say.

"No more time. Quick now, before it's too late."

Maisie hurried out of the apartment and to the stairwell.

Nothing handy there, nothing she could throw down to slow their progress. Once they found their way through the clinic and up the stairs, the zombies would be on them. The best she could do was take a few of them out to slow the others as they climbed. She desperately hoped none of them were the new sort she'd seen the night before.

"Maisie."

Stupid git of a woman. Maisie bit back a curse. The first zombie appeared at the bottom of the curved stairwell and she couldn't afford to turn to the woman and provide any explanations.

"Heaven help us," Mrs. Wells whispered, backing away. Well, then, no words needed.

Maisie lifted her shotgun, leaned over the railing and took aim. Her first shot took the one she could see in the head. It toppled and from what she could hear, the ones that followed struggled to get past it on the landing.

Good.

For the next four shots, at least, she could litter the stairs with bodies. Maybe even have time to reload ...

She doubted it.

What were they doing coming into the building anyway? They'd never seemed to do anything but fall on the unfortunates crossing their paths out in the open. What would possess them to come looking for prey and inside places like theirs? There were other buildings, truly abandoned, that would've been easier to access. Why break in through the locked clinic?

Hoping there weren't many wouldn't do her any good. The best she could manage was to draw them all into the building, or at least around to the entry point they'd already made. Then she might have enough time to break past the boards over her window and send the family down the fire escape while she kept the zombies busy upstairs. If she had their attention, Mrs. Wells could slip down the street with her children and find a safer place.

Not much, but it was the best plan she could come up with on short notice.

Damn, she wished she'd had the presence of mind to ask Seth for his mobile number. A werewolf on speed dial might have been handy. Not that it would do her any good—she'd have to make it down to the clinic to use a phone in any case.

Of course, her line of thought bordered on the ridiculous.

Watching zombies make their way up the zigzag flight of stairs could do that to a girl.

She fired her last shot and hurried to her flat.

Mrs. Wells waited for her, helping her shut the door and run the shotgun through two rungs Maisie had installed across the back of the door and the wall as a makeshift way to bar it.

"The window. We need to clear away the boards and get you all on the fire escape." Maisie kept her voice to an urgent whisper. The zombies shouldn't be able to understand her, but shouting her plan seemed a daft thing to do all the same.

The nails holding the boards to the windows from the outside were loose and Maisie had the presence of mind to peek through the gaps to make sure no zombies waited outside before shoving the boards off. Careful to make as little noise as possible, she brought the boards in through the window and gestured to Mrs. Wells.

"Go. Get the children down and make a run for it."

"But—"

An overwhelming urge burned through her to shake the woman. The children would take too much time to climb down. "All of us won't make it down the fire escape before they come back out the building. Go now and I'll keep them occupied as long as I can. Send help if you find it."

Maisie didn't waste time taking the boards back to the entrance to swap them with the shotgun. It took longer than it should have to reload, but her hands were shaking. She had enough ammunition to reload it the one time and get off a few shots before she had to switch to her handguns.

Mrs. Wells might have stayed if it'd been only her, but she was a mother. She had her children out on the fire escape as the zombies reached the door.

Maisie backed away as they clawed and threw their weight against it. Propping herself in the windowsill, she spared one last look at Mrs. Wells.

"Coast is clear up and down the street. Run for it."

Mrs. Wells gave her a nod, her lips pressed in a grim line.

Wood split with a sickening crack and Maisie focused her attention on the dead coming through the door ... for her.

One shot, and the first fell in the doorway. It slowed them a fraction of a minute and she shot another. The others stumbled over the fallen. Her third shot came up lucky, the force of it blowing the zombie back into the ones behind it.

And then Mrs. Wells screamed.

Maisie shouldn't have looked, but she did anyway. She just might be able to pick one or two off from her vantage point. When she turned in the windowsill, it wasn't to see zombies on the street below. No. It was Mrs. Wells clutching her children to her legs, pointing upward.

"Run!" Maisie screamed at her.

At the same time, a grim sort of realization settled over her. She wouldn't be seeing Seth again, or Brian.

When the zombie leapt down, landing on the fire escape outside her window, she was ready with a handgun and fed it a bullet at point-blank range.

"Maisie!"

She thought she heard her name.

Seth's voice boomed from the street, distorted the same way she'd heard it when they'd first met. He was partially shifted.

Brilliant. Maybe she *would* see him again.

She lifted her shotgun one more time and fired the last round. Then she propped it next to her and pulled out her second handgun. Too many zombies poured into the room, despite the corpses to which she'd already given a final death.

Something grabbed her by the back of her shirt, yanking her arse over elbow out the window.

Pointing both guns upward, she blew a hole through the attacking zombie's face and managed a body shot to another zombie higher up on the fire escape.

Before she could even think of struggling up to a sitting position, something heavy hit the fire escape, shaking the damaged zombie loose to fall to the street. Thanks to her unique point of view, she saw the blighters jumping from the roof. She aimed one gun at the roof and one at the window, but before she got her next shot off a snarl erupted at her shoulder.

Seth surged past her, knocking a zombie out of the air.

Adjusting the angle of her arm before she shot him

again, she took out another zombie in the window. A shaky laugh bubbled up out of her throat—the tiny balcony momentarily clear of ravenous dead people.

"Are you mad, woman?" Seth snarled, turning to crouch over her.

"Likely." She paused. "Was starting to think you wouldn't be coming back for a second date." To be honest, she didn't think she'd survive the next five minutes.

Whatever he'd intended to say got cut short as a fresh batch of zombies hit the fire escape from the roof, one or two even succeeded making the jump. As he turned to deal with them, a cold hand gripped her ankle and yanked.

Cursing, she shot but didn't catch the thing before it sank teeth into her. Pain ripped through her good leg and her hand shook as she aimed more carefully. Her shot blew off the thing's head, but as it fell away she could see a few teeth buried in her flesh.

"Seth!" He'd been too busy tossing zombies to see. He needed to leave her and get out. "Seth, you bloody mutt! Listen, or I'll shoot you again!"

"What?" Seth shouted the word as he turned, ripping another zombie from the window and right over the edge of the fire escape. She hoped they were all landing headfirst.

"I'm done for. I've been bitten. Get out while you can and I'll cover you. There's a family, Mrs. Wells and her children. Help them!"

He bared his teeth, long canines in his partially shifted form. His jaw and cheekbones had lifted and pulled forward, making his growl even more effective.

"I won't leave you here."

Seth barely noticed the scratches as a zombie clawed at his back. Maisie cursed and emptied whatever she had left in her handguns into the mass of arms and heads straining to get out the window. Before she could use her last bullet to carry out her threat, he scooped her up in his arms and leapt off the balcony.

Only one story, and he had no trouble keeping his feet as he hit the pavement. He bent his knees to take the shock and kept her carefully pressed against him.

More werewolves were on the scene as Danny arrived with backup.

"Danny!" The name came out as more of a sharp bark than a word, but the pack medic instantly responded, sprinting to him. The others came at a run to flank them.

Walking fast to get clear of the building, he ignored Maisie's muffled protests.

"Any others in the building?" Danny asked.

Seth shook his head. "One family escaped, woman and a couple children. Send a pair of wolves to get them to safety. You need to see to Maisie, *now*. She's been bitten."

Danny's face stilled. "Put her here, Seth, on the corner. Let me see."

A brief, fierce battle warred inside his chest as he put a leash on the urge to protect his woman. Danny gave him space to decide and shouted orders to the other werewolves in the meantime. When Seth opened his arms, setting his precious Maisie down, her face had already gone pale, her skin clammy.

She shook her head. "Too long. There's not enough time."

The rot was taking over her leg. Blood vessels darkened under her grayed skin and the torn flesh around the bite had already turned a sickly green-black.

"We didn't put a tourniquet on it this time." Maisie's voice came in a whisper and her eyelids fluttered.

"She's got a high fever, Seth. Is she serious? This isn't the first time?" Danny had his kit open, using forceps to remove the grisly teeth and trying to clean the infected skin. "It's spreading faster than I ever saw it before. Her heart's racing, accelerating the infection's progress through her circulatory system."

Seth's mind raced, searching for a solution. "Her friend, Brian, he cut away the dying meat the first time."

"And he used a tourniquet to slow the blood flow?" Danny spit out several curses of his own. "Bloody brilliant." He moved to do the same. Even as he got the tourniquet on he shook his head. "It won't work, Seth. It's spread too fast."

Something. Something about what Brian had said. Werewolves were immune. The vectors of infection weren't compatible.

Maisie had lost consciousness, her head lolling against his shoulder. He cradled her in his arms, turning her face away as he stared at her slender neck.

"Forgive me." He whispered the words and then bared his teeth.

"Seth! What? No!" Danny shouted in horror.

Seth sank his teeth into her neck and shoulder, biting down through skin and muscle until the delicate artery burst. Immediately he withdrew, licking at her neck.

"Are you mad?" Danny shoved his face out of the way, pressed a folded pad of bandaging against her neck and applied pressure.

If Danny hadn't been a healer, Seth might have removed Danny's arm from his body for touching his girl.

"I needed to infect her faster."

Danny stared at him with wide eyes, comprehension

gleaming. He slashed her slacks at her thigh. "Bite her one more time, here above the tourniquet, at the femoral. Quick, now, before the infection makes it the rest of the way up her leg."

Growling, Seth bit her again, his teeth cutting deep past her muscle. Her blood still ran clean in his mouth. Relief flowed through him.

"Enough. You've mauled her bad, Seth. More than we do for the voluntary candidates." Danny wiped the back of his hand across his brow, leaving behind a smear of Maisie's blood. "We've got to get her back to the den and get some fluids into her. If she's going to survive, we need to help all we can."

Gathering her up in his arms, Seth stood.

"But if she doesn't Change, if the zombie infection takes over first …"

"I'll kill her myself." He could at least do that for her.

Maisie hadn't ever believed the bollocks about following the light.

Course when she started to come to, blinded by a bloody bright one, she wondered if she might have to amend her belief system.

Then the memories came crashing back and she bolted upright.

Or rather, she tried.

"Easy there." A familiar voice, comforting tenor. "I'm right here. Don't do yourself any harm."

Heavy leather straps held her at the wrists and upper arms. Her legs too. "Seth?"

Her throat ached and she croaked more than called his name. Fear drove her to struggle against the bindings.

"Pupils are dilating fine. Blood is testing negative for the zombie virus. She's in the clear." The unfamiliar voice reminded her of Brian. When the speaker finished his assessment, the awful light disappeared. "Come calm her before she hurts herself."

"Easy, there, Maisie. I'm here." Seth's voice.

A familiar touch on the side of her face. Relieved, she lay still for a moment.

"Where?"

Seth sounded as if he were just beside her. "Safe. You're in my home. We set up a hospital bed for you in my room. We're taking care of you."

Blinking hard, she tested her bonds again. As happy as she was to hear his voice, she was about to spit curses about the bindings. What was going on?

His silhouette came into focus as she scowled up at him. Was he *grinning*? Bastard.

"Such a face." A chuckle. "Hold still, just for another minute." Seth's words ran over her, sending a delicious shiver down her spine.

How did he make a simple request sound so intimate?

A slight tug at the straps over her right arm and they came free. In moments, all of the cuffs were removed and Seth had slipped an arm around her shoulders to help her sit up.

She stared at her legs. Someone had removed her trousers. Her right leg was still as she remembered, badly scarred. She was incredibly happy to still have it. But her left …

Experimentally, she wiggled her toes. Whole set of five. No scars or muscle missing. Her left foot wasn't misshapen or damaged at all. Yet she remembered the zombie sinking its teeth into her left leg, leaving teeth behind. Not a bite mark anywhere. Well, except on the inside of her thigh, and it seemed larger than a human—or zombie—bite.

What?

"All right there, Maisie?" Seth's concern brought her back to the present.

"Am I dead?"

"No."

"Should I be?"

Silence. A grimace.

More memories flashed through her head and she stared hard at her left leg, specifically at the spot mauled by a zombie that should have had teeth still buried in the flesh.

"I'm ... hungry." The admission frightened her.

"That's expected." The stranger spoke up again. "You'll have more of an appetite now, and a higher metabolism. It's important for you to get proper nutrition in the early days around your Change."

Fear stabbed her heart.

"Well, I'll give you two some privacy. We've got a different sort of visitor to attend to. Call me if you need anything." Despite the short words, the man's voice had been gentle. Understanding.

She barely registered the sound of a door opening and closing, wasn't ready to think yet.

"Who?"

Seth's voice came to her, gentle, but anger simmered beneath the surface tone. "Your landlord. He's got a lot to answer for. We'll be keeping him here for questioning before we turn him over to human authorities."

"Oh." She wanted to care. She should. All she could do was stare at her good leg. Still good.

How had she changed? Why was Seth allowing her to live? If she was alive ... She couldn't believe he'd allow her to become a danger to anyone else.

"Maisie."

Panic took hold. How was this her? Her legs didn't look right. Zombies didn't have whole limbs. They rotted and fell apart.

"Maisie! Look at me!"

The force of the command snapped her head around and she couldn't help but look into Seth's blue eyes. For some reason, she was annoyed about it.

His lips spread in a slow, cocky grin. "That's my girl."

"What's happened, Seth? If I look in a mirror, will I still be me?" Taking another look at her uninjured leg convinced her he'd swapped her with somebody else.

A chuckle rumbled up from his chest as he reached over to a nearby counter and handed her a round mirror. "You're still you—" the chuckle ended "—and you're different as well."

When she looked into the mirror, she saw her own face. With trembling fingertips, she touched the scar at the place where her neck and shoulder met. Other than the new scars, she seemed to be better than she'd ever been. She felt stronger, steadier. One at a time, her senses fed her a flood of information and then, her mind caught up with what it all meant.

How was it one became a werewolf again?

"It was the only way I could think to save you," Seth told her in a gentle voice. "Your friend, Brian, gave me the idea with what he said the night we met, about shape-shifters being immune. The zombie virus was spreading too fast to save you the same way he did the first time. You'd already fainted with fever. I couldn't ask you."

A bite, or clawing, infected a human with the lycanthropy virus.

"You bit me."

He slipped a hand under her jaw, holding her chin between his thumb and forefinger. "I'm not sorry."

It'd take a lot to process, and she wasn't all sure she was ready to admit she wasn't human anymore. But one thing stood out in her mind. "I wasn't ready to die."

"No. You're a fighter." He nuzzled her temple.

So close, he smelled of a hundred different things. Blood and rotted things, streets and pavement, but also of soap and aftershave, grass and his own earthy musk.

"Why?"

He pulled away just enough to gaze directly into her eyes. "I wasn't ready to let you go."

The kiss he pressed to her lips started gentle, but quickly stole her breath away.

"I wanted to take my time courting you, give you time to decide." He murmured his explanation against her lips, his hands gently stroking either side of her face. "But there you were, dying in my arms."

His hands tightened and he kissed her again, and she responded with everything in her. She wanted to reassure him, both of them, that she was still alive.

And wanted him.

When he pulled away a second time, he pressed his forehead to hers, his hands trembling. "The only choice I have left to give you is whether you want to stay with me or not. You don't have to if you don't want to. The pack will provide for any need, and I'll leave, give you your space."

No weakness in evidence in any aspect of this man, none at all. Yet somehow, he'd bared his throat and his heart to her simply by giving her a choice.

"Brian. He's safe?"

"My wolves cleaned up the zombies in the building. We stopped Brian going in until it was all clear." Seth choked out a laugh. "You'd locked up the dogs and cats so tight, the zombies couldn't get into those rooms. All of them are safe."

"What happened to Mrs. Wells? Her children?" Struggling to gather her thoughts, she latched onto a neutral topic first.

"Hale and whole. They'd run rabbit down the street when my men found them. We've put them up in a decent shelter until we can find the mother a job." Seth's voice sounded strained. "You don't have to answer now, Maisie. But if you tell me to go, I will."

Even imagining him gone, never seeing him again, caused Maisie's chest to tighten until she thought she might not breathe. She placed one hand over his chest, feeling the strength of his heart beating underneath, and closed her eyes.

She leaned into his hand buried in her hair and turned her cheek to his palm, savoring the warmth of his touch.

For a moment, alone in that abandoned apartment building, she'd thought she'd go down fighting with no one at her side. No one to help her protect friends and dear ones. But he'd come to her.

He'd fought a virus to give her a chance to make a choice.

"Love me, Seth. No stopping this time."

He stared at her for a long moment, not breathing, his heart a staccato beat under her hand. Then he covered her mouth with his in the most possessive kiss he'd given her yet. His tongue explored in long, lazy sweeps until he withdrew to nip at first her lower lip and then her upper lip. Every nip was followed by a gentle suction as he tasted her mouth and whispered endearments against her lips.

His hands caressed her gently as he continued to kiss her, framing her face and then wandering down her neck. He cupped one of her breasts in his hand and she gasped as he brushed her nipple to a hard point with his thumb.

For a moment, he withdrew his hand and she almost protested, but claws flashed. Her shirt lay to either side of her, neatly shredded to expose her.

"What?" Startled, she instinctively moved to cover herself, but he stopped her with a gentle yet firm grip on one wrist.

"No stopping?" His voice had dropped an octave, husky with desire.

Hesitating, she didn't pull her wrist free and he loosened his hold. When she didn't protest, he extended a single clawed finger to the center of her cleavage. As she watched, he sliced the tiny bit of fabric holding the front of her bra together. The pleased sound he uttered as he viewed her naked breasts made her blush. Still, she didn't try to hide from his regard.

Setting her free, he stood and undid his denims. No briefs, again, and his arousal stood out as he dropped his pants to the floor. Stepping out of them, he climbed directly onto the bed until he was crouching over her.

She shivered with excitement and anticipation in equal measure. He didn't cover her immediately.

"You said no stopping, but you didn't say how fast." He grinned as he stared up the length of her body.

Cheeky bastard.

SETH LOVED the way her cheeks, and other interesting bits, blushed deep red when he got her riled up. Oh, and he planned to make up for it, no doubt there. He waited only another couple of moments to enjoy how beautiful and alive she was, lying in his bed.

Dipping his head, he dropped a light kiss on her big toe and then another on the graceful arch of her foot, making his way up her ankle and calf to her knee. Taking his time about repeating the gestures with her other, scarred leg.

"I—" She gasped and he looked up to see her fingers fiddling with the edge of the pillows. "It's been a long time since anyone has actually touched me there."

He smiled and caressed her unscarred left foot, the one she probably expected to be as damaged as her old injury. "The zombie infection took over most of this leg this time, Danny said. When the lycanthropy virus, the factor that turns us to werewolves, took over faster, it healed your bitten leg from the inside out. He said something about genetic map and stem cells and things. Either way, the only scars we have as werewolves are any we had as humans before the Change and the original bites that made us. Usually."

He kissed her foot again, then ran his claws lightly along the underside. She twitched, ticklish, and he laughed.

She cursed at him and he laughed harder.

But he didn't lose focus, oh no. His Maisie still had her panties on and he intended to remedy that shortly.

He ran his hands over her legs in soothing circles, enjoying the way her skin heated under his touch, placing a kiss here and there, on her knee, on the inside of one thigh, in the crease of her hip.

By the time he hovered over her panties, he was half drunk on her scent. When he blew gently over the thin cloth, a hint of wetness spread across the fabric.

Almost ready for him, and he planned to be sure she wanted him every bit as much as he wanted her.

Lifting the side of her panties, he started to slice the fabric with a single claw, careful not to damage her creamy skin.

"What am I going to do for clothes?" The words came out a little breathless.

He tossed away her panties, admiring her naked body under his. "Oh, you won't need them for the time being."

Covering her with his own body, he pressed his hips snug to hers, the length of his erection hard between them. She placed her hands on his shoulders, the hesitation in her touch reminding him he'd wanted to go slow, give her time to get used to him.

So he took his time. He kissed her breathless and nibbled at her neck until she giggled. He ran his hands over her body, along her sides. Her breasts were a perfect fit for the palms of his hands and he enjoyed kneading them, teasing her nipples between thumb and forefinger, and then suckling them until she moaned.

Once she writhed under him, gasping and pulling him against her, he slid his knee between her legs. She pressed kisses over his shoulder and drifted them across his collarbone, whispering against his skin, "Please."

He couldn't, wouldn't deny her anything in his power to give.

"Please, Seth. I've got to have you, now."

And now, he wasn't as likely to hurt her, not when she was a werewolf too.

Bracing himself on one arm, he used his other hand to guide himself between her legs. As he pressed the tip of his cock to her entrance, he found her hot and slick and ready. Gritting his teeth for control, he nudged inside her, just the tip, teasing her tight entrance until she angled her hips upward. He gave in then, sliding into her, stretching her as her inner muscles clenched around him.

She called out as he entered her. Gathering her against him, he kissed her temple. Turning her head, she found his lips and kissed him hungrily even as her hands settled on his waist, tugging and encouraging him.

He'd planned to be gentle, slow, but she wrapped her legs around his hips. His Maisie wanted more.

He gave it to her.

He ground his hips into her until he was buried to the hilt, then pulled out and slid back inside her again and again. Picking up the rhythm, she lifted her hips to meet him until they both were holding on to each other for the ride of their lives.

"Seth!"

She bucked against him as her inner muscles spasmed, and his balls tightened. As she screamed his name, he followed her over the edge into orgasm.

MAISIE MUST HAVE DOZED off in the aftermath. She woke tucked against Seth's side, covered by a light blanket.

As she looked around her, really seeing the room for the first time, he stirred.

"Awake, are you?" He tugged a lock of her hair.

"This is your flat?" She found it spartan and neat, but not cold. It lacked none of the necessities and what furniture he had was of high quality, like the bed. There was a feeling of simple living to it.

"Yours too, if you like." He propped himself up on one elbow, kissing her bare shoulder.

A home, a man who cared for her—hadn't she dreamed of it?

"We'll get you a proper collection of clothes too." He touched the tip of his finger to her nose. "And a name for that damned kitten, once he's ready to move in too."

She gave him a thorough kiss for that. Enough of a kiss to wake other parts of him.

They played for a bit, learning each other.

Abruptly, he stopped, braced on his elbows and looking her over. "So, you've decided, then?"

"This has happened fast. So fast." She watched his eyes go blank, his warmth withdraw. He was bracing himself. "I'm not holding back, Seth, or toying with you. But I want us to build this one day at a time. Can we do that?"

His answer came slow. "I'll not promise you I won't be difficult, or downright overbearing." He took a slow breath. "But I'll do my best."

"Then, I'll stay with you." She bit her lip, suddenly embarrassed by the happiness in his eyes matching the joy blooming inside her chest.

It'd take some getting used to, being happy.

She wrinkled her nose. "This doesn't get you off the hook, you know."

"For what?" He drew his brows together.

She liked the way he looked grumpy.

"You bit me."

"I said it before." He kissed the scar on her neck. "I'm not sorry."

SING FOR THE DEAD

BOOK 2

1

S orcha ran.

Taking the Serpentine bridge helped speed her along, man-made though the bridge was. Crossing running water posed no deterrent for her. Others of fae blood might have paused in the hunt, but the zombies shambling through the bare trees in these parks were not her quarry.

No. Pursuit was not her purpose. Rescue was.

The feeling of wrongness, the taint of spoiled magic, worsened as she crossed from Hyde Park into the Kensington Gardens. Perhaps the lake separating the two parks kept some of it from spreading. What humans called the Long Water remained relatively clean of the pall of death exuding from the land. The trees in Kensington Gardens were bare skeletons this deep into winter in London—sleeping, but restless, tugging at her heart. Would the trees be too sickened to bring forth new life after their roots had bathed in blood? Parks like these provided sanctuary for the lesser fae and Fair Folk living in cities such as London. Without them, the fae who'd made the city their home, had braved cold iron, would fade. And for every city lost, the Under Hill shrank as well. Even if mortals ruled the world, the fae needed to maintain a presence in order to keep the balance of things or their own world would fade from existence.

She'd been sent to investigate why the fae of London were disappearing, and she'd found death walking.

Stupid humans, coming in after dark, to hunt and be overwhelmed, to loot and be taken by surprise. Perhaps such short lives made for stunted memories. Though the zombies found prey too often in these gardens, the humans kept coming. She didn't Sing for those, the ones who'd done humanity a favor by taking themselves out of the gene pool. No. Her Songs aided the passing of worthier souls.

A tortured cry rang out in the night, sending ripples through the magic saturating the land, tainted as it was.

She ran harder. Perhaps she could be savior this time, and not simply witness to death.

The zombies were gathering, called not only by the sounds of struggle, but also by the disturbance. Like sharks drawn to an injured fish in water, it was as if the zombies could sense easy prey. Unnatural as they were, she had no doubt zombies were animated at least in part by magic of some kind.

The parks used to be the reservoirs of old magic in the city. Now they were death traps.

As she broke through the trees, a brownie stood atop a mound in the children's playground, a curved dome with tunnels for children to crawl through in play. Good that he'd chosen higher ground, bad that he'd allowed himself to be surrounded away from any trees or route of escape. Maybe the mound had reminded him of a hollowed hill, the way the tunnels led beneath it. Gentle in nature, brownies like him tended places and buildings, their magic sympathetic to home and hearth. They weren't bred to fighting, weren't trained as soldiers the way she'd been. While he could turn boggart and create minor havoc, he wasn't meant for true violence and was no match for the dead trying to eat him.

But she was.

Red haze encroached on her vision. Sorcha reached for her swords, drawing them free without slowing her pace, embracing the sweet song of savagery rising in her blood.

With an effort, she held back the rising tide and the red haze, binding it tightly with her will. There was an innocent on the field and she couldn't afford to lose control, but she could harness a few drops of it to lend her strength.

Running past the mound, she'd sliced through two zombies before they realized another being was amongst them. Turning, she whipped her blades around and beheaded two more. The others moved toward her, distracted from their prey. Or perhaps they were excited by the scent of her living flesh.

She grinned. Excitement danced along her nerves. The red crept closer on her vision.

Not yet. After she'd saved the innocent, maybe she would give herself over, but not yet.

She planted a front kick into one zombie's chest. The smell of rot clogged her nose and black blood streaked the sand. She spun, lunging forward and impaling another. Then she pulled back with a yank and brought her sword around in an arc to remove its head from its body. Always remove the head, slice through the skull or crush it. Otherwise, the blighted things would rise up and continue trying to feed.

The brownie cried out again, the horrible agony of the scream dousing the heady burn of combat from her mind like a bucket of ice water. Sorcha spotted a zombie sprawled across the mound, rotting hands wrapped around the brownie's leg. Another sank its teeth in his shoulder.

"Bloody hell."

She might not be in time. She fought harder, spilled more black blood and fouled brain matter onto the sand of the playground.

In a moment, she was up on the mound. One of the two zombies lifted its head—dead eyes fastening on her as it bared its teeth. The blood of the brownie stained its lips and chin red. The thing launched itself at her. Fast—too fast. She barely raised her swords in time to remove its head. But the force of its charge drove her off the mound. The others hadn't had this … ferocity.

The second zombie charged her as soon as her back hit the hard-packed sand. It wrapped both hands around one of her swords, trapping the blade between them and bearing down with all its weight. Releasing her other sword, she groped for her combat knife. The shorter knife came free of her chest harness sheath just as the zombie snapped its teeth less than an inch from her face. Fetid breath choked her and black blood splattered cold across her face as she drove her knife into the side of its head. She rolled until the zombie lay on the ground and she could struggle to her feet.

On the mound, the brownie moaned.

No. No. Please, let me have come in time.

"Hush." She hastily retrieved her knife and wiped her swords. Sheathing all of them, she freed her hands too late, too late. "Shhh. I am here. I will help, but you mustn't cry out anymore. It will only call more to us."

His mouth worked, but no words came. Fae blood pumped from his neck in time with his heart beat. She clamped a hand over the wound, applying pressure and what minor touch of healing magic she had. A cold fist of despair tightened in her chest. She could slow the bleeding, but hadn't the true power to save him. Her talent lay in the dying, not the living.

Tears sprang to her eyes. Her stomach lurched.

He was full fae—of the wee folk. And he'd valiantly kept the small playground taint-free until tonight. Every corner showed his care, from the upkeep of the huge wooden pirate ship to the clean white of the canvas pavillions nearby. The sensory trails were clear of ice and snow, leaf litter, and, most importantly, no hint of tainted magic lingered.

His breath caught, and he struggled in her grasp.

"Peace. No. 'Tis not the end. We will find help."

Where, she did not know, but she sent out a silent plea to the magic around them. *Please, help him where I can not.*

But his struggles would draw more of the undead. She needed him calm. She could carry him, but they'd be vulnerable to more attacks with her hands full. And where would she take him? There were no strong fae nearby.

No, the Court of Light had sent *her,* a half blood, into London instead.

Bitterness flowed across her tongue but she clenched her jaw. No time for selfish distractions.

At a loss, a part of her magic reached out to the brownie, sensed his hold on life weaken, felt his fear shiver through her veins. She parted her lips and Sang the fear away.

If death was coming for him, at least that much was in her power to do.

SOMETHING HAD STIRRED up the zombies. Kayden's nightly patrol took him along the borders of Kensington Gardens, checking the scents for signs of idiots headed into the park to loot the remains of other idiots.

It wasn't just the stupidity of humans, nay; they were opportunists, and it spoke to their survival through the centuries. The walking dead in London, they brought out the darker side of human nature and somehow, the zombies' numbers were increasing. Shape-shifters were finding themselves outnumbered.

Shape-shifters weren't common anywhere, and as a were-leopard, Kayden was rare amongst the uncommon. Unlike the werewolves, were-leopards didn't usually gather in packs or prides. Normally, the largest gathering was a small family unit and then, only long enough to raise young. Leopards were solitary as adults. And though he'd come to London and allied himself with the London wolf pack, he still ran his patrols solo.

Tonight, he'd managed to head off several bold street urchins and one so-called hunter before they'd made it too far into the park. It should have made him feel better, afforded him some relief from the ever-present guilt he carried.

It didn't.

Kayden disarmed the man, more a scavenger than any hunter, and escorted him to one of Seth's patrols. The werewolves wouldn't tolerate those kinds of humans anymore, the ones who tempted starving kids into heading into the park as zombie bait. Lambs sacrificed to make it easier to steal from the dead.

What the hell was wrong with people?

The walking corpses all over the place suddenly seemed less horrific.

The winds changed direction, carrying with them information in sound and scent. A low sound tweaked his ears, below the range of human hearing. Odd. It wasn't unpleasant, but it unsettled him. If he'd been in his animal form, he'd have tried to shake the feel from his coat.

Mournful, aye, a song to tug at the soul.

Who was daft enough to sing in a park full of monsters?

He shed his jacket and shirt, stowing them in the branches of a tree alongside one of the paths. His pants followed, then the rest of his clothing. Crouching down to make the change easier, he shifted to leopard form. Joints popped and muscles stretched.

No matter how quick or slow, the change still hurt.

He panted as he let the last bits of the shift settle into place. Ready to hunt, he padded through the shadows, following the song through the otherwise-silent trees.

It was as if the entire park had paused to listen.

He didn't have far to search. The Princess Diana Children's Playground was just within the bounds of the Kensington Gardens. He'd not been inside over the course of the winter—his hunts limited to forays amongst the denser stands of trees and the wide-open lawns where hunters chose to pick off zombies.

And yet, there was something ... not right about the playground.

It was pristine.

All other part of the gardens had fallen into disrepair or gone wild with neglect. But the playground was swept clear of leaf litter and twigs. The walks were clean of ice and snow. Granted, this part of the isles saw little enough of either, but these pathways showed no sign of the cracks and holes the other walks had from being under a thin layer of ice all winter. The swings were in good working order, the hinges oiled and the chains free of rust. The great ship in the middle of the park was cleaner than it had probably been when children crawled all over it. Before the zombie infestation had changed the city of London.

The playground was as perfect and welcoming as the day it'd been built.

Well, except for the pile of zombie parts littered around the wee mound to one end. He'd be guessing the woman was responsible. The swords strapped across her back gave him the first clue.

She hadn't noticed him yet—cradling a tiny body in her arms and singing as she was. A child? Even in cat form his chest tightened. No. Maybe? Hard to tell.

He padded closer.

The sound of steel sliding free of a scabbard should have been alarming. Stranger still, the woman hadn't stopped singing as she drew her blade. An odd calm hung over the entire playground, wrapped it in a soothing blanket and hushed away all fear.

Magic. And not of the human kind either. Human magic had a different scent to it. Aye, and a different feel to it as well. The power a human summoned for casting was drawn of sacrifice. No, this magic had a different flavor to it. It'd come of nature and the essence of living things. Harder to quantify, but then, the fae were uncanny in many ways.

The woman watched him, ghost-pale under the faint light cast by the crescent moon. A ponytail held back most of her long, shining hair but a few long locks fell loose to frame her face. The color of moonlight, such a pale shade of blonde as he'd never seen before. Probably soft as silk, as well. Why did he want to touch it? Rub his scent into her hair? He didn't halt his approach, only slowed so she had plenty of time to assess the danger. He'd bet it was her singing keeping more zombies from coming. Without such magic in the air, half the zombies in the city would have followed the rich scent of blood.

She'd done a fine accounting of herself, if he tallied the body count correctly. Body parts lay all around her, decomposing as he watched. It had been a pack of the undead she'd fought off. They'd not stood a chance against her, though it might have been too late for her friend.

A wheeze and the small chest rose once.

Perhaps not too late after all.

This woman had a chance to save her small companion, and he'd be damned if he didn't help her do it. Kayden shifted back to human form. It left him vulnerable if she chose to attack, naked and weaponless as he was, but he was fair certain she wouldn't. Mayhap it was folly on his part, but he didn't think she'd leave her fallen comrade. Nae. She'd wait for an opponent to make the first move, finish him before he began. The precious minutes it took to change to human form were worth it, if he could help her save the life in her arms. And for that, he needed speech.

His extremities were still finishing the change when he forced his vocal chords to shape human words. "Do ye need help, lass?"

The singing stopped. She blinked, her posture relaxing a fraction.

But her grip tightened around the pommel of her sword.

Blast. No time for niceties.

"I am Kayden." He left out his full name. Giving your name to a fae was unwise. A true name had power over the bearer. Dangerous, especially in the hands of any fae old enough to know how to use it, some witches too. As young as she appeared, she could be centuries older than any of the shape-shifters in London. Old enough to have the knowledge of how, and to have grown in power enough, to bind him into doing her will with it. "I can lead you some-place where they can close his wounds, give him a chance of surviving. It's not far."

She said nothing, her beautiful face a frozen mask. Instead she pulled the wee man closer to her. Ah, the Fair Folk were proud creatures. He tried to remember what little his grandam had taught him before she'd passed. Human and superstitious, his grandam, she'd held to the old ways of leaving out a bit of milk and bread, some honey, for fairies. She'd told him stories of the wee fairies to make him chuckle and scarier tales of the larger fae, the ones who could feed on children. Fragmented and vague, human stories of the fae folk generally all had the same moral: avoid them whenever possible.

He'd have to work on remembering whatever else he could later. One thing was certain, it was important to know what kind of fae a man was dealing with if he had to. There were many kinds and each had their own peculiarities.

Kayden held out his hands, fingers spread, and stood tall. "I've no intention of hurting you, lass. As you can very well see, I'm unarmed."

Her gaze flickered over him in a swift assessment and there he stood, naked as a babe.

"The dual-natured need no weapons, be they fae or mortal shape-shifters." Ah, so she did speak, and with a hint of his own Scottish brogue. Not surprising, though his second guess would have been Irish. "And men do enough harm with their bare hands."

She had a point there. "You'll have trust me, then." The old stories said a fae never broke his word, nor did he take another being's word lightly. Still, Kayden ought to be clear about what he was saying. "I give you my word I mean you no harm. I only want to help you save the wee man there."

He waited a heartbeat, two.

What was she? Dressed in dark browns and black, with her two swords and more knives in a shoulder harness. Her skin was the pale color of the insides of seashells, white with undertones of faint pink. Her eyes were round and almost too large for her face. She had the look of the Fair Folk, that was certain. Her appearance matched more than a few of the descriptions in his grandam's stories of various fae women and no human had features so delicate.

Beautiful. Not only for her physical features, but also the air of lethal potential around her. She was a warrior, this one. Aye, and skilled, judging from the decomposing remains turning to dust around her. Women skilled in the art of combat were wonders in bed. His blood heated at the direction his thoughts wandered and he stifled it before things became more physically obvious. Pants would've been handy.

She sheathed her sword, finally, and gathered the wee man to her. As she stood, she lifted her chin. "Where are we going?"

"Follow me." Another precious minute to shift once more. Since she was carrying the injured, he'd have to cover them both and he didn't fancy defending them all unarmed and his cods bare to the breeze. The night air was still chill.

He halted his shift part way between man and beast. Fur kept him warm and claws tipped his fingers. His head was a meld of leopard and man, but he stood and strode forward on two feet. This phase-form was a compromise. Protect and still communicate.

"This way." His voice came out deeper, almost strangled as his vocal chords strained for speech.

No fear from her, not in her scent and not in her steady heartbeat. She followed him, close but far enough behind to allow him space to fight if something should happen. She knew something of shifters, obviously.

He set a fast pace, one that would have been challenging for a human man, much less woman. Yet she had no trouble covering the ground, burdened as she was.

Speed, strength, stamina—all good qualities for fighting … and for other things. Exhilarated by their mission to save her companion, he tucked his more heated thoughts away. He allowed himself a grin though, because he always could appreciate a lovely woman even in the worst of circumstances. And this one, this lady, was worth appreciation.

The streets were nearly deserted. The moon had risen to its zenith in the dark sky and most clinics would have been closed.

Not this clinic, though. It had been open late nights since midwinter.

The human, Brian, had begun living out of his clinic rather than his flat once the werewolves had bought the building.

As they approached, the lass called out to him. "What is this place?"

"It's become a sort of triage location for the local shape-shifters." The sign still said veterinary clinic. "I'm guessing your friend would have too many questions to answer in a human emergency room. This place is safer for him and the doctor here has a steadier hand around the supernaturals."

"Is he dual-natured?"

Coming from her, the phrase held a sophisticated lilt. Fancy that. *Dual-natured.* Shape-shifters didn't often call themselves such but the label fit. Fae changed form as well—some of them. They changed or they used glamour to hide their true appearance. He'd encountered one or two of the lesser fae in his travels around Europe. He'd not ever run into the likes of this fae and his grandam's stories were all he had to guess at what she was. Ah well, where his memories fell short in the past, he'd relied on his wit to fill in the blanks and he'd do it again.

"Not a shape-shifter, no. Human." And a good man, a gentle man. Kayden hoped he wasn't bringing ill luck to Brian.

They'd cross that bridge when they came to it. A life hung in jeopardy. Kayden exchanged nods with a werewolf in human form, standing guard across the street. Then he pulled the door to the clinic open.

"Please enter." He'd been there several times before to get a wound cleaned out after a fight. He guessed he had the right to invite a fae in and the fae were looser about their interpretations of an invitation in any case. Vampires had much more stringent requirements.

She raised an eyebrow in eloquent surprise as she stepped past him into the warmth of the clinic.

"Oi! Brian! Emergency!" Kayden gestured for her to continue through the waiting area and into an empty examination room.

She wasted no time easing her burden onto the hospital bed. Blood covered her entire front and she kept pressure on the side of the little man's neck. He'd gone paler under his brown skin and his eyes barely fluttered in response to being laid down.

Quick footsteps came from upstairs. Brian ran in a few moments later, his sandy-brown hair standing on end in several different directions. They'd waken him right out of sleep.

Light sleeper for a human.

"What have we got?" Brian rolled up his sleeves, then

began washing his hands in the room's sink, all business and no wasting time.

"Well, I don't exactly know." Kayden looked to his new ... friend?

"My ... companion is a brownie." The woman made the statement in a quiet voice, wary.

Brian halted. "I've never treated one of the fae."

Her shoulders stiffened. "But will you?"

Brian waved off the challenge. "Of course, I'll try. Let me see his injuries."

The woman turned to allow Brian to approach and inspect the wounds. The human was thorough, only touching the brownie as necessary, and with gentle hands. "I'll need you to let off the pressure so I can see the extent of the wound on his neck."

When she did, his brows drew together as he studied the damage.

"You're doing something to slow the bleeding?"

She frowned, but gave him a slow nod. "I haven't the power to stop it completely, only slow it."

Brian moved swiftly around the room, gathering a tray with supplies. When he returned, he paused, hands hovering over his instruments. "Fae are sensitive to iron and some iron alloys, aren't they? My needles might burn him. They're made of surgical steel, but I have liquid sutures. I can close his wounds with those."

"You hesitate." The threat darkened the woman's voice. She was damned suspicious.

Kayden tensed, ready to defend Brian if necessary. He'd brought the woman in an effort to help, but he wouldn't allow her to harm an ally.

Brian only nodded to the woman, possibly oblivious to the danger. "Liquid sutures create a barrier, which could make things worse if his wounds are contaminated. This is a zombie attack. Can fae be infected by the zombie virus? I don't see the tissue death I normally observe with these kinds of wounds."

She relaxed a fraction, giving the doctor space to work. "The fae cannot become zombies. Our magic can keep him free of contamination if you can close the wounds and stop the bleeding."

Kayden let out a breath he hadn't realized he'd been holding. The wee man had a chance. None of them had been certain until that moment. It was obvious in the fae woman's posture, in the relief pouring off Brian.

He stepped out of the room to give them privacy, staying near in case the fae woman had another swing in mood. He'd have been willing to bet his trousers the woman was unpredictable.

Speaking of trousers ...

He reached under the front desk and pulled out the extra clothes kept in a bin for the shape-shifters. The pullover and sweatpants weren't his preferred clothing, but he could head back to where he'd stashed his clothes later. They were up a tree high enough to be out of reach of any looters. "Normally it's me bringing in the strays."

The gentle voice didn't surprise him, though the tart bite to the words made him smile. He'd heard Maisie come in through the side entrance. "You spend a lot of time in the flats above this clinic, though you don't live up there anymore."

Maisie brandished a paintbrush. "Not too many contractors left in the city. Of those that are, none are interested in renovating apartments flooded by zombies just a few weeks ago. Afraid the blighted things will come back."

A possibility. Which was why the clinic had a patrol of

werewolves watching over it at every hour of the day and night. Especially since the alpha's mate spent so much time on the premises.

"From what I heard of that attack, you held your own. Now? You'd be able to rip any zombie limb from limb." He gave her a hug, sweeping her up, then setting her carefully back on her feet with enough time for her to get her balance.

He'd been amazed to meet a werewolf so newly Changed. Shape-shifters tended to keep the newest members hidden until they'd had a chance to learn control. Maisie had quite the will, though, and her control was the best he'd encountered. When he'd first met her, he'd been overcome with the urge to protect and shelter one of the newly Changed. Maisie had wasted no time informing him she was well able to care for herself, thank you very much.

Seth was a lucky man to have such a mate.

"Hah. You're only this cuddly when Seth isn't here."

"I'd hug you even if he was here." Kayden grinned down at her. Such a tiny package of spunk, she was. "But then we'd have a tussle and you'd smack us both for being male."

She huffed. "The man knows I've chosen him. No need to get on with the growling nonsense. It's as if he thinks every male in the city is going to try to steal me away."

"You're one of a kind." Kayden reached out and tapped her nose with a finger, yanking his hand back as she took a swipe at it. "I've not heard of many women resorting to shooting a man to save his life."

She rolled her eyes. "Danny never will get tired of telling that story, will he?"

"Not likely."

She wrinkled her nose. "Enough with old stories. What

have you brought to our doorstep? I wanted to get a good look before Seth got here and got all protective on me."

What indeed?

"New friends, I think." Not enemies, at least. The brownie was no threat for certain and he'd only had a short time to assess the fae woman's character but he was a good judge.

He'd better be. He always forgot how fast Maisie could be.

He only had enough time to dash down the hallway after her and slip into the treatment room as she came to a halt.

"Hello." Maisie cocked her head as she studied the fae woman.

The sound of drawn steel rang through the room.

"Now that's a bad idea in a treatment room." Maisie had a .38 Super handgun out.. "A better idea would be for you to put that away, and I'll put this away and we'll talk as if we weren't dangerous people."

Females. Was it any wonder males would rather throw themselves into the face of danger than deal with two strong women in a tiny room?

"The dual-natured carry weapons now?" The fae woman's words were brittle with distrust, but there was hesitation too. She edged to the end of the hospital bed, clear of her brownie companion and Brian but not closer to Maisie.

Maisie's hands remained steady, the gun never wavering. Everything about her body language projected wary readiness but her scent was spiced with a hint of anger. "I've only recently made the Change. Old habits are hard to give up, especially the prudent ones. Besides, I can put a bullet in you faster than you can slice me."

"I thought this was a place of healing." The woman

didn't look at Kayden, but her tone made it clear she felt betrayed.

Kayden narrowed his eyes. Despite holding her swords at the ready, the woman was loose and her muscles appeared limber. She might not be able to cut Maisie first but she probably could dodge the bullet and close the distance.

He moved between them to prevent further escalation, only to be knocked back a few steps by a blur of dark-furred testosterone.

Bollocks.

Kayden's leopard rose to the edge of his control as he spun to face Seth.

"Who are you?" The questioned rolled free with a loud growl from Seth's phase-form, directed toward the fae woman.

Kayden stood tall, keeping his fae behind him as he faced the werewolf. Hard to keep an eye on Maisie where she leaned to one side behind Seth, trying to maintain a clear shot. "Let's everyone calm down."

Easy to say. Harder to set the example. He wouldn't back down until Seth did. Instead he kept his voice steady and didn't shift. Shifting would take too long in any case.

"I've been remiss in my introductions." Kayden held his hands up, palms out. Seth glared at him. At least the other shape-shifter wasn't attacking. Kayden half turned to face them all. He kept his gaze on Seth, but aimed his words at the fae woman. "This is Seth, alpha of the London pack, and his mate, Maisie."

Safe enough to offer their given names. Nowadays, names could be shed as easily as clothing. This fae would need to know at least one, and more likely three, of the full given and surnames any of them had gone by for a significant portion of their lifetimes to bind any of them in a true naming. Funny the way names and numbers held such power over a person.

A sigh broke the momentary silence.

"This *is* a place of healing. It's also a place of survival." Maisie echoed the fae woman's earlier accusation. She did have a fine way of clearing things up. "And we *are* here to help. The only violence offered is in equal measure to what you give."

Silence. Again.

"Not many mortals have a gift for the truth." After another hesitation, the woman sheathed her sword. "I am … anxious."

And wasn't that the closest to an apology he'd ever heard of a fae offering?

"From the looks of it, you have every right to be." Maisie had stowed her handgun as well. Suddenly, she was just a wisp of a woman again.

It was a wonder Seth's muzzle hadn't gone grey dealing with such a mercurial mate.

And how in hell was Brian still working away through all of this without a single flinch?

"Your friend is in good hands. Brian has saved many lives, mine included." Maisie's voice had softened. "Why don't we all step out into the hallway before we drive poor Brian to distraction?"

"Please do." Brian didn't even look up. "I've got a bit more work ahead of me before my patient is in the clear and the two of you are enough to drive a daft man sane."

Her slender shoulders relaxed, but the fae woman's face remained a cold mask. "You may call me Sorcha."

2

Kayden followed Sorcha up the stairs to the flats above the clinic. He fought the temptation to follow a wee close on her heels, because he was a predator and he also wanted to be inside her personal space, if she'd let him. But what he wanted didn't matter as compared to her feeling safe in his presence and he thought they'd both be a lot happier if she invited him closer herself. So he kept a respectful distance and tried a different way to engage her.

"We'll just have a look around while Seth stays down-stairs and gathers himself. Maisie'll have him calmed in a minute." Kayden needed a moment too. He'd meant to head off the alpha before things escalated into an all-out fight, but he hadn't anticipated the fierce protectiveness that'd pushed him to the edge of his own control. Two dominants going head to head wouldn't have ended well, whether they were allies or not. Now, following Sorcha, ushering her to some-place with only her and him, his leopard began to calm. Clear of distraction, he wanted to know more about the fae woman. The urge to learn her scent, feel her skin under his hands, pushed at him.

"Why is this place important?" She took her time on the stairs, peering into the darkness above, every line of her shoulders and back taut with wariness.

The predator part of him approved of her caution.

"This building was attacked by zombies fairly recently." Kayden watched her for a reaction. She didn't look back at him or tense further. There was only a sense of stillness, as if she listened and waited. "The former landlord found a way to lure zombies to buildings. His way of getting rid of squatters and difficult tenants to make way for more lucrative clients—like foreigners here to hunt the zombies."

She nodded, her head tilting to one side and then the other as she searched through the darkness above them. "Zombies are driven by hunger. They are mindless and slow. How would they be lured?"

Kayden liked her train of thought. He'd gnawed at the same questions when he'd first come back to the city. "Not by blood. None of the shape-shifters scented any sort of bait trail and there were plenty of things along the way to distract the corpses from their course. Still, they came right up here."

"Past the animals in their kennels downstairs."

He raised an eyebrow though she wasn't looking at him. "Observant, aren't ye, lass?"

"It's an animal clinic. I could hear the barks and calls from the kennels, though they do have good sound buffering in those back rooms." Her words were dry, but he fancied he heard a hint of humor, there and then gone. "Even if instinct had silenced the kenneled dogs, at least some of the zombies should have wandered into the lower clinic area following the scent of living flesh."

She didn't say more, only climbed up the steps, humming to herself.

Fair Folk were an odd lot. The stories he knew from childhood made them out to be either shy or downright reclusive. The former were harmless, the latter ... perhaps not so much. White-haired, fiery-eyed Sorcha hadn't been the least bit timid when he'd come upon her. Left him wondering just what sort of fae she might be.

Not a faery. The tiny winged folk might be fae, but they were only one kind amongst many. He smiled, imagining Sorcha might take offense at being mistaken for a wee bit of a thing with butterfly wings. His grandam's stories described beings of any number of shapes and sizes with powers ranging across any element of the natural world.

The fae lass remained oblivious to his musing as she reached the landing on the second floor.

"No flats on this level." He offered what information he knew from previous visits. "The space is taken up as offices for the clinic, walled off from this staircase."

Silence. She studied him, her face as still as carved marble. Then her lids fell to half-mast, only partially hiding the gleam of amber in her pupils as her magic came to life.

Beneath the stringent odor of cleaners and fresh paint, the air freshened as if someone had opened up a window nearby. Only there were no windows in the stairwell. Fae magic.

He waited a step or two down off the landing. Figured it best to give her space to do her work. After a moment, her eyes flashed open. "Nothing on this level."

"And what is it you're looking for?" He kept his tone relaxed, but he'd stop her from causing mischief if necessary. Seth and Maisie, aye, and Brian too, were still down below.

"Something out of place." When he didn't respond, she waved her hand in the air as if searching for words. "I am looking for a missing puzzle piece, but I do not know what shape it is. I need to know more about what is happening in this city."

Fair enough. He'd wanted to know more when he'd come back to find London overrun with hungry corpses too. "I believe Maisie's old flat was one more level up."

"And that is where we are going?" A tiny wrinkle marred the pale skin of her forehead. Not sure when she'd choose to use her power again, Kayden gave her a bit more of a lead as she continued across the next flight of stairs.

"It's as good a place as any for a talk." He grinned as she narrowed her eyes even as she moved away from him. Wary, but not running.

Whatever image she was trying to project, it wasn't working. Maybe a human would see her as calm, cool, all business. But no, her scent filled the air with a spicy edge, sharp and fierce. She searched every shadow, nook and cranny, as tensed as a cat ready to pounce. If there was anything to find, she'd be on it faster than he could blink.

Interesting, interesting woman.

A hallway extended from the landing of the third floor. The renovations had ended with the stairwell, apparently, because a good portion of the walls and floors were in ruin. Dirt lay in piles all along their path to the first doorway, remnants of dead zombies.

"This is ankle-deep." Sorcha scuffed her foot until the floorboards were revealed.

"Aye, and I'm certain everyone in this building is glad they turn to compost after you take out their brain. Otherwise, this would have been hell to clean up." He wrinkled his nose. He didn't fancy breathing in the dirt, harmless or not.

"Most I've seen take a few hours to disintegrate at least. It's not instantaneous like staked vampires. There must have been dozens of zombies crowded into this hallway. Why were they here?"

The suspicion in her voice was impossible to miss.

"Well, that's part of why it'd be good to have a talk considering you've proved handy with those blades of yours. As you might have noticed, we've got a bit of a zombie problem in the city."

Sorcha stared hard at the man. He gave her a slow, lazy grin. Fighting not to let the corners of her own mouth turn up in response, she crouched down and took up a pinch of the stuff. "It's not powder or ashes either. It's a bit more like fine silt. If it is returned to the land, I wonder if it would help soil or hurt it."

A question for another day. Perhaps the brownie, with an affinity for hearth and home, could tell her. While the parks remained overrun and tainted, she'd not seen or sensed any of the smaller faery folk who had an affinity for plants and growing things.

"Maisie's flat is at the end of the hallway. I'm told a lot of the burning and damage here was her doing."

Sorcha turned her face up to him and raised an eyebrow.

"It's my understanding she did a lot of damage." He grinned. "And she was human when she did it, too."

"Werewolf or human, I imagine there is more to her than most would give her credit for on first meeting."

Sorcha rose and brushed her hand off on her pants leg. "It is good she has survived."

Kayden opened his mouth to comment, but Sorcha halted, fingers raised to her lips. Something was there that shouldn't be. A flicker of magic, calling out. She stepped across the hall and placed her hand flat on the wall, then began walking farther toward the end.

Yes, summoning. Not of her, no. But it resonated inside her chest; like calling to like. Why? She did not know yet. But she would find out.

Coming to a stop just inside Maisie's door, Sorcha drew the knife from her shoulder harness and used the edge to scrape at the wall. "Well placed. This spot is likely hidden in shadows at any time of day."

The wall crumbled to reveal a small hole, barely large enough for a man to squeeze his hand inside. Sorcha reached in, her slender arm fitting and allowing her to search inside the wall.

"Ah." She breathed out the word. When she withdrew her arm, she held a bit of cloth sewn together at the edges to make a crude pillow.

"And what is that?" He peered at the dusty thing.

Sorcha handed it over and began brushing the plaster dust from her arm and hand. "A faery charm, I think you'd call it. What it actually is doesn't matter so much as the power placed in the object. This was the lure, placed to call the walking dead to the building. Once they got here, they must have targeted the nearest living beings."

"A fae made this?" Kayden sniffed it and sneezed.

She didn't blame him. It smelled of old sweat, must and mildew. Based on the rough stitches and ragged edges, maybe the landlord himself had sewn the thing together. "The fae behind this is strong. It is a difficult thing to summon so many of any being with just a charm. The stronger fae do not trouble themselves with the making of bits of hearth craft like this. No, the human servant would have fashioned the lures first and the fae would have poured a drop of power into each of them."

Kayden tossed it up and caught it again. "This is something we'll be wanting to share with Seth, then."

"Why?" She wanted to snatch it out of his hand.

His gaze locked on hers and, despite his easygoing nature, the force of his will slammed into her own. "This is an important puzzle piece to what's going on here. The London pack should be informed." His voice softened. "It is your find, and you'll have it back. My word on it. But we are allies here in a common goal, I think."

Perhaps. At the very least, she did owe him a debt for his aid earlier in the evening. "I will cooperate for the time being. However, my main interest is in the fae behind that charm and not the human servant, this landlord."

"You can use the charm to track this mystery fae?" Only a question because of his tone. Still, it demanded an answer.

Her temper sparked.

"Yes." A hunt would begin. Not the Wild Hunt nor anything like the glory of legend when the fae rode out across the skies in relentless pursuit of their quarry. But a solo mission all her own gave her almost as much satisfaction. She hungered for the kill at the end of the trail.

Kayden studied her, still in the way only another predator could stand. "Just what kind of fae folk are you?"

Sorcha hesitated in giving him the answer. But the answer to his question was the part of herself she should be proud of, the part she cherished. "I am half Bean Sidhe. Humans nowadays call us banshees."

Eyebrows lifted. "I'd not have thought it. The old stories

paint the Bean Sidhe as harmless—bringers of bad tidings, but not the cause of death. You did a fair bit of fighting earlier tonight, and mind you, I've not seen many take out so many zombies on their own. I've been wondering if you have any guns squirreled away somewhere."

"I prefer to deal my damage more directly." Oh, and she wished she could call the words back the moment she'd snapped them out. How could she be so careless as to let the admission slip? She shouldn't be so ready to share how much she enjoyed what she did.

And that was her shame, wasn't it? Violence sang through her blood—the mortal part of her heritage surging to the fore at the mere memory of the earlier fight. More. She needed more.

Kayden watched her, still and yet poised on the balls of his feet. "The Bean Sidhe are peaceful fae."

At any moment, he'd be moving and she'd be countering the motion. She craved the action, the potential.

"Yes." She gritted her teeth, struggling to focus on choosing her words with care. "We watch over the old families, Sing for those who will be lost. The Sight sometimes comes to us, so we might know their fate. It is not within our power to change it, only give warning. Sometimes, we Sing the pain away so the dying find peace sooner. It is our gift."

A step closer, another, until he was close enough to heat the air whispering across her skin. "And does your Sight show you many more deaths here, in London? Do you feel like Singing?"

"There are so many." Her whisper came out harsh, bitter. London had become a killing zone and the deaths crowded her vision until she had to stare into his eyes to find an anchor. "And the Song won't come for those who walk after death."

"Why?"

"Their peace was stolen from them, taken beyond my power to Sing them to their rest. Zombies have no soul." Beyond the horror of what they were was the sadness of what they'd lost. Her mother would have shed tears for them.

His eyes shone golden; what did he see when he stared at her?

"You don't want to bring peace though. Not now." He drew in a long breath through his nose, let it out his mouth. "Anger, rage, your scent is hot with need."

Her heart thumped hard, things tightened low in her abdomen. "Yes."

His hand rose, hovered for a moment a millimeter from her cheek, then lowered to her shoulder. He barely brushed her shoulder yet her skin burned where he'd touched her.

"When I found you earlier tonight, a dozen zombies littered that park." He bent close, his words tickling her ear. "No peaceful fae sliced them to pieces."

No. Red crept along the edge of her vision—the color of her madness.

"I need to go." It came out harsh, guttural.

Kayden stilled, his hand hovering at her elbow. "Where?"

Where she wouldn't be a danger to those around her. "Back to the gardens."

"There's no peace there." He watched her, his gaze burning into her.

She wanted to grab his shirt, rip it to shreds. Her fingers curled into talons in response. "There is something else I need."

"I'll go with you."

"No." Oh, but he was strong. She hadn't seen him fight

yet, but she knew. Shape-shifters were a magnificent breed, physically hardier than the fae who could take animal form. Kayden's energy beat against her skin until she could scarcely stand the heat of it, and the idea of pitting her strength against his?

Yes, oh yes.

"What do you want?" His voice had deepened; the timbre of it sent shivers down her spine.

Was there a word for it? How would he think of it? This man with a soul equal parts man and cat, a predator in every aspect of his being?

"Hunt." She breathed the word. "I ... I need to hunt."

She needed to kill.

He hooked a finger under her chin, gently but inexorably lifting it until she met his gaze. "What are you?"

"Aberration." The word echoed through her memories. Despite the need riding her, the cool wetness of a tear traced its way down the side of her hot cheek.

"No."

She couldn't see his expression, he was so close. Instead, she closed her eyes, tried to make him understand. "My mother was Bean Sidhe and my father ... was mortal, but not only a human. Father was a berserker, a nightmare on the battlefield. When he stepped onto the fields and the rage took him, he became an unstoppable soldier, an indiscriminate killer. And I am truly my father's daughter. I have his blood madness. I am cursed."

Lips pressed against hers, hot, demanding. His tongue swept inside her mouth when she gasped. Desire washed through her and she returned his kiss, hungry.

He pulled away suddenly and she snarled.

The bastard smiled. "You are beautiful."

3

———

Beautiful? No. Impossible.

"*Mew.*"

Sorcha spun toward the source of the noise. A slender orange tabby cat stood in the doorway staring up at her. Thoughts tumbled through her mind as she tried to make sense of what had just happened and the absurd little animal in front of her.

She failed.

"You just let that cat wander around like she owns the place, Seth?" Kayden called out from behind her.

"Seemed like letting the cat take point might be a good idea." A tall, lanky man appeared in the doorway dressed in denims and an overcoat with no shirt to cover his sculpted chest and abs. He crossed his arms over his chest and leaned one shoulder into the door frame.

Power and charisma emanated from the man. This was the alpha werewolf. He'd shifted to human form.

"Dunno. Maisie might have something to say to you if anything were to happen to her friend here." Kayden continued to sound relaxed, but he stood close to Sorcha's back and an odd tension in his posture bothered her.

"Maisie might have something to say to you." Seth lifted his chin toward the cat, who'd advanced into the room and lay stretched out on its side with languid disregard for the display of testosterone Sorcha was beginning to realize was going on. "Tiny beast is hers and he knows this is his territory."

"I thought true cats didn't like canines, especially not werewolves." Kayden rested a hand on her waist, the heat of it seeping through the fabric of both her vest and tunic and steadying her. The cat in question looked past Sorcha, presumably at Kayden and flicked the tip of its tail.

Seth chuckled. "Most cats run from zombies too."

For all their casual talk, both males spoke with edges to their words. Was it possible to relax with so much aggression filling a room? Again, the cat being the exception to the rule.

"Maisie figured it best if she remained downstairs." Seth shrugged. "I'm more levelheaded when I'm not focused on protecting her."

Ah, it made sense to her. A mated pair would be fiercely protective of each other, and she and Maisie had been on the brink of violence.

Sorcha was still off-balance despite Kayden's hand.

Kayden shifted his hand from her waist to her shoulder. "I'd like to sponsor her as a new ally to the pack, if you will accept her."

"Can the pack trust her?" Seth stood tall and his words rang with formality.

"I do." Kayden stood equally as tall, but his eyes remained cast downward.

Sorcha bit the inside of her cheek. She wanted to ask

what they were going on about, but the weight of a decision hung in the air.

The energy building between the two men pushed all of her instincts to choose some course of action—fight or flee. Sorcha tensed and she flexed her hands, wanting nothing more than to reach for her swords.

Something needed to happen, anything.

The cat rose, stretched and picked its way across the floor toward her. Her gaze was drawn to it, even as her common sense screamed to keep an eye on the dangerous males. Oblivious, the tabby sniffed at her boot toe, then her ankle.

"Mew." Such a tiny sound.

The cat turned and sat on her foot.

What in … ?

"Welcome." Seth stepped forward, hand outstretched.

Sorcha yanked her gaze from the cat and looked straight into the werewolf's eyes. Power slammed into her mind and a dominating will pressed upon hers. Her own rose up to meet it and she struggled to hold her magic back.

She'd been the one to challenge by meeting the alpha's gaze.

Swallowing hard, she gave him a firm handshake in the human way. She had to lean; otherwise she'd dislodge the cat.

"Our friend Kayden here finds the most interesting people." Seth gave her a smile and released her hand.

"And what do allies of the pack do?" She wanted to know more, before she formally aligned herself with the shape-shifters. They could be of help as scouts or direct intelligence regarding the hidden places in the city, perhaps, but the fae had little need of the dual-natured to handle fae matters.

Seth tilted his head to the side, considering her. "In some cases, run patrols like Kayden or coordinate search and rescue efforts. We need all the help we can get out there, keeping the numbers of zombies down. The pack is outnumbered, and we can't kill the lot of them in one night."

Oh, but wouldn't it have been wonderful for the solution to have been so simple?

"My purpose is not to keep the corpses under control." Seth's mouth tightened at her choice of words. Kayden's gaze burned into her as well. "The fae only intervene because fae influence is involved."

"So, you're not here to find a cure or wipe out the problem; you're just cleaning up the evidence of faery fun?" Seth crossed his arms.

The cat sitting on her foot began to play with the laces of her boot.

"Yes." Truth, for the most part, and to put an end to the one causing it. What did she care if he wanted to put it that way? Allies did not have to be friendly to one another. "I am a soldier for the Court of Light—the Seelie Sidhe—sent to investigate why the lesser fae living in the city of London are dying and to stop it if I can. My lords in the Court have no concern for the mortals in the city, only the fae."

Silence fell. Only the sound of the cat tugging at her laces broke the heavy atmosphere. Sorcha might have shivered as well, but her annoyance was slowly burning to a true anger. She would not jump through hoops for the pleasure of one of the dual-natured simply to gain their cooperation.

"Help is help." Kayden shrugged.

Seth snarled.

"What?" Kayden shot back. "The lass found evidence of fae magic. If it can be eliminated, it's one less thing to worry ourselves over. As much as I enjoy going out there every night and killing the blighted things, there are other approaches to the problem."

Enough was enough. Sorcha deliberately took her gaze off the irritating men and bent to reclaim her laces. After she retied them, she scooped the cat up and cradled him in her arms. "I have my purpose here. I will proceed whether I have your help or not." She paused. "It would be preferable to work with you as opposed to avoiding you."

The cat purred in her arms, the sound impossibly loud to her ears.

"Get on with you." Seth sighed. "No point in arguing over the how of it all. That you're helping is enough. I suppose you'll want to talk with our prisoner then?"

"Prisoner?" Sorcha looked to Kayden.

It was Seth who continued, "My wolves took the landlord who did this into custody for questioning." His brows came together in a dark scowl. "No matter what we've tried so far, he hasn't revealed any information. He just opens his mouth and nothing comes out."

"He's gone mute?" Disbelief colored Kayden's voice.

Seth shook his head. "He can cry and beg for mercy, curse us and blubber."

"When he tries to give you the answer you seek, the words are stolen before he can speak them." Sorcha's mind raced. Only magic could have bound the man's words, a safeguard against betrayal. It was a *geas*, a binding of his will. The fae responsible for laying the *geas* on him would have left other safeguards on the human servant. "He's been bound not to speak of what he knows. To let him see me, talk to me, might warn the responsible fae of my arrival."

"What do you need, then?" Seth's brows drew together and his expression grew more severe.

"Fae magic is powerful, but it has its limits." That much

should have been common sense, perhaps, but best to begin at the beginning rather than backtrack to explain. "Usually magic intended to hide something can only do so from one set of senses or another. I was unable to find any trace of this fae's meddling in the Kensington Gardens though magic floods the area. Yet zombies seem to be summoned from there to buildings like this one."

Kayden nodded. "Based on the investigation we've done since the attack on this building, we've confirmed most of the batches of undead have come from the nearest parks. Kensington Gardens and Hyde Park are the largest in this part of the city."

Sorcha motioned to the charm Kayden still held. "Hard to tell yet if this summons specifically marked undead or if it simply calls to the closest in a given area. What I do know is that it was hidden from your senses of smell though it probably reeks of the man you hold in custody and the fae who gave it to him. If I or another fae hadn't come up here, it wouldn't have been found. This fae has invested an immense amount of effort to hide his comings and goings in the city from others of our kind and to keep all of you ignorant of his intervention." She reached out to touch Kayden's wrist. "However, he can't hide from both of us at the same time."

"You want a partner." Seth sounded as if he might continue but stopped when Kayden placed a hand on her waist again.

"Let's hunt him together, then." Kayden's words came in a whisper, intimate and to the exclusion of the alpha.

Both men glared at each other. This time Kayden did not drop his gaze.

"Were-cat, I granted you status as an ally." Seth's teeth flashed in the dim light of the room.

"And leopards are normally loners. I don't play well with your pack no matter how good the intentions are on both sides." Kayden spread his hands at his sides. "How many of your wolves have tried to challenge me? They can't help it, not when I'm too dominant to have a clear place in your hierarchy. This is the perfect solution. With me as her partner, I won't be constantly crossing paths with your patrols. Win, win."

Sorcha studied Kayden. More had gone unsaid, but at least now she understood why Kayden and Seth came together with such tension. There were many aspects of personality and behavior involved in the complex concept consolidated into the simplified term: dominance. Even among the dual-natured fae, the dominance in the animal aspect played a major part in status and standing.

"I'm not challenging your claim, cat, but I need to be kept up to date on the progress of this investigation. My wolves report in regularly." Seth fished a mobile out of his pocket and waved it.

Claim? Sorcha sucked in a breath but Kayden bumped her shoulder and she bit back her question.

A wry grin spread across Kayden's face. "Aye, and I'm not the best at reporting at all, am I? All right then, I'll do my best to at least text updates."

"That'll meet minimum requirement." Seth slid the mobile back into the front of his denims. "Ring us up using your mobile sometimes. A text is too easy to fake."

"I'd best be heading back to headquarters before Maisie decides to call and see if I've eaten the two of you." Seth took a step toward Sorcha, hands outstretched.

A rumbling growl rose up in the room. Startled, Sorcha stared at Kayden.

"The tabby. Just retrieving the tabby, or Maisie'll have

my hide." As reasonable as Seth's words were, his voice had dropped deeper as well, the words rougher.

Sorcha handed over the purring cat before the two men abandoned civility and settled whatever the remaining issue was with violence. A part of her wailed inside her mind, urging her to hold onto the cat and push the men to bloodshed.

No, no, no.

They were allies, both dedicated to protecting those weaker than themselves in this city. She would not manipulate them for her pleasure. But oh, for warm blood to spill ... Not that of the walking dead but that of the living.

Silence intruded on her thoughts. The cat had stopped purring. Both men were watching her. Her bloodlust had nearly taken over and they must have been able to see it in her eyes, or catch it in her scent.

"I need to get back to the gardens." Back to where she had room to move, things she could kill.

Seth gave her a slow nod. "I have patrols on the perimeters. They haven't been briefed yet about your new status as an ally. It'd be better for you to wait until tomorrow."

As if she needed him to vouch for her in order to walk where she desired.

Kayden took a step toward her and suddenly the rest of the room phased out of her attention. Taller than her and more heavily muscled than Seth. But he moved quickly. Faster than her? She wanted to find out.

"Staying in might not be a bad idea. Wouldn't want to get in a tussle, being allies and all." Kayden's voice was low, mild. It took a few moments for his words to sink in.

No. It wouldn't be good to clash with new allies. Not when she craved a battlefield so badly and not when the blood of living people excited her so much more than the dead. After all, the dead didn't provide much of a challenge besides their sheer drive and numbers.

The living fought with skill … and a desire to stay alive.

"Sorcha, my lady. You'll stay with me, won't you?"

She swallowed hard, latched onto Kayden's voice as an anchor. The teasing in his tone sparked at her temper, distracted her from the sort of fight she normally hungered for. No words came to her to respond, though. All she could manage was a nod.

"We'll meet in the morning, then." Seth's voice came from farther away. He'd stepped back to the door, small cat tucked in the crook of one arm.

Kayden touched two fingers to his forehead in a cocky salute. "We'll be seeing you tomorrow."

"It was … interesting to meet you, Sorcha." No anger in Seth's voice. And she couldn't bring herself to respond. Embarrassment warred with the pounding of her heart as she struggled to control the urge to scream, the need to pick a fight. As he left, he turned and touched two fingers to his temple in some sort of salute. He never gave either her or Kayden his back.

After a moment, Kayden tugged at her ponytail. "Well then, we can have a bit of a sparring match here where Brian can patch us up after or we can go back to my flat. I'd much prefer there."

Did he want the advantage of his home territory? "Why should I go there?"

"Because you're fussing for either a fight or a good tumble. There's nothing but dirt and rubble here but I've got a nice big bed at home and one hell of a hard-on."

4

—————

Kayden met her stare with an easy smile until she sighed, some of the tension leaving her body. He'd not meant it, really. Well and maybe he did, a wee bit, but he'd barely known the woman a scant few hours and she'd already gone toe-to-toe with the biggest, baddest supernaturals in the city. Kayden wasn't about to take her to bed without a thorough weapons check.

Luckily, the alpha of the London pack was a man with patience and a sense of humor. They could both sense the bloodlust upon her, so much like a young shape-shifter out of control. Anger and aggression clung to her like a perfume and her struggle to keep herself under control had been obvious. Shape-shifters were good with body language and he was particularly fascinated with hers.

He tipped his head toward the door, then led the way out of the room and out of the building.

"Where are we going?" She trailed him by a few steps.

He'd have preferred she walk side by side with him. He could hope she enjoyed his rear view as much as he was certain he would enjoy hers. Perhaps the way to build trust between them first was for him to give her a measure of it now. So he walked ahead, leaving his vulnerable back open to her.

He glanced over his shoulder. "We're headed toward my flat, just as we told Seth. Going to make a bit of a stop along the way."

The wind whipped a few platinum strands around her cheeks. She reached up to tuck them back behind one slightly pointed ear. "Why are we stopping?"

"As much as I'd love to help you take the edge off your temper, lass, I've got a liking for my own hide. And since you're still itching for a goodly portion of violence, I figured I'd be a quality friend and show you where you can find it. "

Her delicately arched brows drew together. "Not one for following orders, are you?"

"Not to the letter, no. Might be more accurate to say I'm not always the best team player. I tend to go a bit rogue now and then." He gave her a wide grin before continuing on down the street. They had just another block or two to go.

"I suppose I made a fool of myself in front of the alpha." The words had been spoken quietly, but his sensitive ears caught them before the wind could steal them away.

"Nah. Don't fret yourself. Seth only took himself out of reach before the temptation to have a scrap with you got too strong." Not the only temptation where she was concerned, but Seth was immune to that most likely. Mated as he was, Seth's bond with Maisie was solid and a pretty fae wouldn't turn his head.

An unmated male like himself though ... Oh aye, she was a monumental distraction.

Best to redirect her before her bloodlust rose up again or they very well might engage in a struggle of some sort.

When he reached his goal, he stood at the top of the steps and waited for her to join him.

"This isn't your home." She'd made the statement as if she hoped it wouldn't be and his grin widened. She probably didn't fancy sleeping in the London Underground.

"Nay. This is my favor to you, to help take the edge off that wee problem of yours before we try to settle for the night." He started down the steps and dropped his voice to a low whisper. Normally, only another shape-shifter would have been able to hear him but the old stories indicated fae had heightened senses as well. "Seth's pack doesn't patrol here. No chance of an accidental run-in with one of his."

"But there *is* hunting to be had." Excitement lent a sexy lilt to her return whisper and she reached for the grip of one of her short swords.

"Aye. Even the Underground has electricity here and there where the wiring is still intact." He waved to the few flickering lights in the dimly lit stairwell. Most were broken, but there was enough light for a supernatural to see by. "There's few enough humans left in London, let alone brave enough to risk the Tube if they can help it. Too many accidents when an infected got on the train and spread the blight to everyone else trapped in the car with them. The werewolves don't have enough numbers to waste time keeping the trains running."

"So they focus on making the city above livable." The way she'd said it made it clear she was no stranger to difficult decisions.

Kayden nodded. Since she didn't seem to have problems following his lead in the darkness, he assumed she could see him just fine. "Once they get the infestation above sorted, or at least under control, the plan is to clear out the tunnels below systematically, but until then, the dead walk the tunnels in larger numbers than the rats."

"Is that what they feed on down here?" She paused, reaching out to touch a sign with a tiny fingertip. She traced the red circle and then the blue line through it, even the lettering: Notting Hill Gate.

"The cold will drive more than rats down here in the wintertime." The old anger simmered and his chest tightened. He gritted his teeth against the bitterness flooding his mouth. "With a few drops of electricity and water pipes that aren't frozen, there're some poor souls cold enough and desperate enough to risk living in the subsurface level."

She watched him, and he was fascinated by the way her eyes shone in the darkness. They didn't reflect the ambient light the way his did. Her irises glowed faintly with magic, as if a bit of moonlight lit them from within. "Are we here to avenge a death or to make it safer for the living?"

"A little of both." He shifted to his phase-form then. The familiar pain burned along his extremities and his bones rearranged until he stood a bit taller, his chest expanded further to take in more air and his jaw extended to accommodate his fangs. He flexed stronger hands, fingertips ending in claws. He forced words through his changed vocal chords, pitching them loud enough for humans to hear. "Come, fae, hunt with me."

The invitation, and the warning, echoed down the corridors, followed by the ringing sound of steel pulled free of sheathes. He'd have to ask later whether her half-berserker ancestry protected her from the effects of cold iron. The folktales claimed it as a protection from the fae. She hadn't touched the wrought-iron railing on the way down, but she carried steel blades, not silver. The contradiction presented a mystery for later. For now, the walking dead drew near.

He stalked through the corridors, headed for the subsurface Circle and District lines first. There was more room to maneuver on those.

The platforms were beautiful in the last of the night. Huge brick walls rose up to support an arching roof of alternating glass and wood panels. Some of the glass had broken and the rest had been covered in dust and soot from the weather. Here and there, moonlight flooded through broken panels pooling on the platform below. The shadows hid from the human eye what he and Sorcha could see.

Bones.

Shattered skeletons lay scattered across the floor, piled higher in each of the archways set into the far wall.

"Why so many here?" Sorcha's voice was pitched to echo through the room and down the train tunnels. The sound would attract their prey.

Why, indeed.

Kayden studied the shadows, searching for memories, and shrugged. "With more light from the glass windows overhead this was the first place the homeless came. Easy to see around them, easy to huddle in the archways and hide from the cold. They could still get daylight here."

A scrapping sound, a shuffling step and then another. Kayden moved to an open space, appreciating the distance Sorcha gave him as she chose her own spot. Not too far, but enough for her to have a clear field of battle.

She made a frustrated sound. "Would be faster if I opened up a vein."

"Don't." Why? She wanted to attract more, destroy more. He'd even spilled a drop or two as bait in the past. He had no idea why the image of her ivory skin marred could bother him so much. He reached for a sensible reason. "Some of the new ones, the faster ones, will be unpredictable. Fight them first if they come and gauge how many you want to take at a time."

With two of them, hot and breathing, they'd attract every zombie in the nearby corridors. It'd be more than enough for the both of them to get their fill of killing.

The trick was to be sure they could get out again without being overwhelmed. There could always be too much of what they were asking for.

"Kayden."

He glanced at her, then stared. Her eyes had gone blood red, still softly glowing. "Yes?"

"It's very important that you stay clear, out of my line of sight. I will not know you for a friend when the bloodlust takes me." A pause. "And ... thank you." There were tears behind those words. And ecstasy. The odd mix of emotions tore at his chest.

And then she was running, charging to meet the pack of shambling prey as it emerged from the train tunnel.

"Careful of the tracks! The electricity goes on and off with them!" No time to check and see if she heeded the warning. He had incoming zombies from the central ticketing area.

Pickings must have been slim for the zombies in the last month. These were slow, but they were more voracious, if it was possible. He ripped into the first, literally tearing its head from shoulders. Rotting flesh gave way under his claws and the scent of death clogged his nostrils. Emerging from hallways and corridors, they came in an almost steady stream. Hungry.

Don't ever look into their faces.

It didn't matter who they used to be.

Bitter anger rose up inside him, fueling his need to destroy them all and he gave himself over to his leopard aspect. His animal instinct pitted against the zombies' mindless hunger. Fight, kill and live.

One after another fell to his claw-tipped fingers as he slashed back and forth. His guilt and rage ripped free with every corpse he put to rest. He leaped free of the mob as it threatened to surround him, landed in another open spot and began to rend and tear anew. No matter how many he took apart, he couldn't sate the need to kill more. Two of the monsters managed to lay their hands on him, forced him to use tooth and claw to fight his way free. He coughed at the disgusting taste of rotting flesh in his mouth.

He glanced in Sorcha's direction to see how the lass faired.

"Bloody hell."

He needn't have worried about the fae woman.

Enough of the shambling dead had come through the tunnels to press her back, but only far enough for her to take the high ground on the station platform. Bodies littered the tracks and ground around her, some twitching and others limp with the finality of death. Still she wielded her short swords in fatal arcs, the moonlight catching the blades in flashes of silver as she parted limbs from torsos and heads from shoulders.

Someone had trained the lass to kill, and they'd had an eye for beauty when they'd done it.

Sorcha made combat a killing dance. She kept to her own center and dealt damage in all directions, rarely leaving her back open to attack as she constantly pivoted and moved. Her peripheral awareness must have been exceptional. He'd never seen such carnage and considered it ... elegant. Aye, Sorcha gave each of those poor wankers a final rest with elegance and a cold sort of mercy.

He made his way toward her in between his own

batches of action, careful to stay out of her range but close enough to come to her aid if need be. The zombies were arriving at a slow trickle now, a few each moment, rather than the steady stream he and Sorcha had attracted initially. The rage he'd come to burn off was fading to a bearable smolder. Killing zombies brought him no joy, no satisfaction.

They charged him. He tore them apart. Over and over again, the cycle.

This was a hunt, but no meat and no feeding at the end. His inner cat derived scant satisfaction. Such battles resulted in scarce triumph. When every corpse lay still, there was only a weary surcease.

He was empty.

Changing from his phase-form to his human, he retained only his clawed hands. And the guilt whispering through the back of his mind fell silent. For now.

He paused as the fae woman took down her last opponent. No match, really—a single straggling zombie against a cold killing beauty like her. And when she stood victorious, she was so *alive*.

"What are you looking at?" She could growl as well as any female shape-shifter. And if her eyes had remained red, he'd have kept his distance, remained cautious.

But they were clear and dark, pools of calm after the fighting had drained the rage from her. Her chest rose and fell as she regained her breath. A fine sheen of sweat shone on the creamy skin that peeked from between her shrug and the snug tank top she wore.

He stepped closer, noted her hands tightened on her swords, but she didn't raise them. Nor did she give ground.

Oh, he liked that.

He caught her gaze in his, delighted in the stubborn

challenge he saw there mixed with confusion. "Are you afraid?"

She lifted her chin. "Of course not. Look around us, cat, we stand amidst—"

He kissed her. Tasted her words of victory. Her lips were the sweeter for them. When she gasped in surprise, he settled his mouth over hers and teased her tongue until she tangled with him, returning his kiss. She was the one to grab at his belt and pull him closer. He took hold of her upper arms, crushed her to his chest.

Heat rushed through him, desire. He wanted. It'd been a long time and he didn't just want; he *needed* this woman. And to all accounts, she hungered for him at least as much.

She arched against him and he released one of her arms to slide his own across the small of her back.

Teeth sunk into his forearm.

"Argh!" He flung the creature away, yanking Sorcha behind him as he did, and it hit the far wall. Too small, too light. It hadn't been an adult human before it'd succumbed to the zombie virus. No. What picked itself up and shambled toward them, arms outstretched, was a child.

"Aw, lad, I looked for you. All of you." Devastation spilled ice into Kayden's veins.

The thing moaned—its lips stained red with his blood.

"Kayden," Sorcha snapped. "What are you doing?"

"I owe him this." Kayden couldn't take his gaze from the approaching zombie child. "He and his friends. Each of them. I owe them a pound of flesh."

"He's already had that from you ... and maybe more." She strode forward.

"He deserves a clean death." Too wrapped up in chains of guilt to stop her, Kayden stared at the approaching child. In his mind's eye, Kayden saw a nonstop grin and heard unfettered laughter. But it was a memory, not what the boy had become, only what should have been.

The metallic tang of fresh blood filled the air. Kayden blinked and snarled, ripped his gaze off the child to see Sorcha, not a foot away it, tempting him with her own freshly cut forearm.

"Get away from him, lass!"

"It." She stepped back once, took another, luring the zombie child away from him. "How is this one different? What power does it have over you?"

Another zombie came shuffling, and another. These were bigger and Kayden lost a precious moment to look at them.

"Damn!"

Apparently, so had Sorcha. She yanked her arm away from the zombie child and it fell to its knees as she backed away.

"You let it get a bite out of you?" He couldn't believe it. The woman hadn't had a scratch on her after dispatching dozens of the blighters.

She sheathed one sword and gripped the bitten arm. "Oh aye, now you say that, after you've been bitten yourself then gone daft. Never, ever kiss me on a field of battle again! Too much distraction for the both of us."

Kayden's retort died unspoken as the child raised its head. New light shone in its eyes and it opened its mouth in a wide grin and hissed at them both. It was up on its feet faster than any live child could move and charged Sorcha. She brought her blade across the tiny body at an angle, parting it at the shoulder and cutting deep into its chest cavity. As it was forced to its knees, it reached for her. She yanked her sword free and stumbled away.

Kayden saw her face twist, knew the move she would

have taken and didn't. Normally a bladesman would have set his boot to the victim and pushed them off the blade. His chested twisted with a sick sort of gratitude that Sorcha hadn't done it to the child, zombie or not.

He rushed to the fallen child, pausing to glance in the direction of the oncoming danger, then up at Sorcha. She gave him a jerky nod and turned to deal with the newly arrived undead.

Grasping the child by the scruff as he would a kitten, he lifted its face to his. The eyes were covered in the thin, cloudy film of a corpse. Amazing they were intact, to be honest. Eyeballs softened after death—less fluid pressure— and the longer a zombie managed to walk around the more likely softer bits were to burst or putrefy. Maybe the spark of intelligence Kayden saw earlier was only imagination.

The zombie child jerked in his grasp, lunging for him. Stronger, faster, definitely more intelligent. It'd tried to fool him with a moment of passive waiting, Kayden was sure of it. He'd used the tactic himself in the past.

The boy had been bright as a button, he had.

"What's become of you, laddie?" The worst thing imaginable. And Kayden had seen too many horrors to have to imagine worse. Oh, the child had been the best of his group, the brightest, their leader. And Kayden had failed them all. The proof lay in his hands, seeing the boy as a mindless zombie ... Ralph, his name had been.

Thin lips, dripping crimson with Sorcha's blood and his, pulled back from yellowed teeth. "Why ... did ... you ... leave ... us?"

Shocked, Kayden let loose his hold. It shot up toward his neck, grabbed handfuls of his collar. It gave a gurgling cry of triumph, cut short by the sound of steel slicing through the air.

Its head toppled backward, rolled and came to a stop at Sorcha's feet.

"IF YOU'RE the one who's gone mad, why are you checking over me?" Despite her logic, Sorcha sat passive as the big cat in human form studied the bite on her arm. The last kill had obviously disturbed him—more than the fact that it'd been a child. And she'd learned a long time ago not to further upset an already stirred-up predator.

"Something different about the effect of biting you as compared to me," Kayden muttered, his brows drawn together in a deep scowl.

The sky began to lighten from what she could see through the broken glass panes above them.

"Do they always give way to the dawn?" Patience came easier after the hours of killing she'd done. It had been a long time since she'd been able to kill without remorse, her talent for bringing death as a gift to end suffering as opposed to a curse. For the first time in decades, she felt something akin to restful.

Perhaps exhausted was a better description. Still, she had Kayden to thank for it.

"It's not as if they can't stand the light, like vampires." He took her chin between his thumb and forefinger and exerted gentle pressure to turn her head so he could study her scalp line. "More, they slow down during the day, become less active."

Perhaps he had a need to see to her care. None of the dual-natured fae she'd interacted with had exhibited this much concern though. Obviously the mortal shape-shifters were a different breed. It would not surprise her if immortality made fae set a lower value on the lives of others.

"So the zombies didn't retreat."

Apparently satisfied, Kayden straightened and offered his hand. "No. We just ran out of walking corpses to kill."

That would explain how the bloodlust had finally loosened its hold on her. The berserker in her would have kept going as long as there had been enemies to slice apart.

"But there *are* more." She took his proffered hand in a firm grasp and let him help her to her feet. He kept her hand, though, and tugged her across the street and down another.

"There are always more." As he spoke, she wiggled her fingers, wanting both hands free in case of trouble. He looked at her hand in his, brows drawn together, and released her slowly. "There's a steady supply of daft hunters and tourists coming in, some scientists bent on studying the monsters. The pack can't keep them all safe. And the homeless, the ones who couldn't prove they had a place to go if they got out of the city; they're stuck here."

Her steps stuttered to a stop, her mind latching onto what he'd said. There was something there. Something important.

"I owe you an explanation for what happened back there with the wee zombie. I know it. But can we let the topic rest until I can get us both settled and safe?" He glanced downward, then took her hand in his again. "Time to get cleaned up and maybe sleep a bit."

Whatever her intuition had caught in the moment flickered out of being as he pulled her back into a walk. A peculiar tightening in her chest brought her attention to her hand in his. Large hands, strong, and roughly calloused.

And yet, his hold wasn't unpleasant. Rather, she was strangely hypersensitive to his touch. Odd.

"Yes. It can wait." Curiosity wasn't one of her drivers in any case. If it upset him this badly, she could wait until he chose to share—or not—as he needed. The long-lived could afford the time to be patient.

Silence fell between them, awkward perhaps, and yet it gave her time to ponder her change in mood. A strange man, Kayden, vibrant and alive where the fae she'd grown up with were pale ghosts of living beings. She'd found him cocky, arrogant, at first. This latest version of him puzzled her.

"Shape-shifters live long lives, do they not?" She'd thought so, but in her experience, only mortals' finite lives burned with such brilliance.

Kayden didn't look back, instead shrugging his shoulders. "Seth is older."

"You are not young for your kind either." Where did he get his energy from, then? If not the fear of death or the blessing of youth, why did he *live* so fiercely?

"No." Kayden chuckled. "Are you hoping for me to be younger or older? I've seen a lot in my time. Some of it can age a man beyond his years, but then again, that sort of time can also give a man an appreciation for the time he has on this earth."

She shook her head, struggled to make sense of it. "You are unlike any being I've ever known."

"Ah well, then." He tugged her round by the hand to lead her up a set of steps onto the landing of a townhouse. "Isn't that the truth? And I'd be willing to bet you'll never meet the likes of me ever again. Best get to know me while you have the chance."

He winked at her.

Whatever the encounter with the zombie child had done to him, he was recovering quickly. Before she could think of any sort of response, he opened the door and ushered her inside. "The lift works, but I tend to prefer the stairs."

As did she. She set her foot to the first step and began climbing. "Lifts are too close, fail too often."

Attacks were too easy when one was trapped in a tiny box of metal, some made of cold iron.

"For one of the Fair Folk, you seem to handle the ... machinery of modern housing without much of a fuss."

She kept on up the stairs, but she appreciated his attempt at circumspection. Good to be around another warrior, one who respected the reluctance to discuss potential weaknesses. "My mortal blood affords me some resistance. A metal box is still a metal box, though."

Even some humans harbored issues with such closed spaces.

"Aye, it is." Kayden chuckled, the sound sending delicate shivers up her spine.

She missed a step.

"Careful now." Strong hands came around her, one cupping her elbow and the other at her waist providing a steadying support. "Only a few more flights. My flat is on the sixth floor. Are ye coming down off the combat high, then?"

"I'm all right." In truth, it was worse. Her limbs shook with fatigue and her coordination obviously had gotten away from her. There'd been battles in the past where she'd fallen in her own tracks once the bloodlust had drained from her. Too afraid to approach, her own allies had left her where she lay. In moments, she'd fall into oblivion. Helpless.

Not yet.

"Shall I carry you?" Beneath the teasing lilt, she heard an undercurrent of worry in Kayden's voice.

Shaking her head, she gritted her teeth and pressed onward. She wouldn't be humiliated by a few flights of stairs. "No need."

"I've not got many supplies, but there's a pot of soup on the stove. We'll have a bowl each to warm us up, and then I'll see you tucked into bed."

"A blanket would suffice." The words tumbled out faster than she'd meant. Would he think her afraid?

"Ah, lass, my mother'd turn in her grave if she found she'd raised a boy who couldn't take proper care of a lady." Kayden clucked and pressed her forward onto the landing of the top level. "I've slept plenty a night on the floor and can do it again. I'll not get a wink of sleep if you refuse the comfort of my bed and we'll both end up on the floor for no reason but pride. Better you let me see to your comfort and we'll both get some rest. It's the way of it for good men raised proper, more so for shape-shifters. The more dominant we are, the more it fusses us when we cannae care for the friends we've made."

He opened the door to his flat and entered first. She did not particularly mind what some might have considered a breach of courtesy, especially when he took in a deep breath of air as if searching for scents. Too many of her old comrades had died in the imagined safety of their own homes.

Appearing satisfied, Kayden indicated the interior with a sweep of his arm. "Come in, my new ally, and be welcome."

Not a traditional welcome, to be sure, but closer in sincerity than any she'd heard in a long time. Not many kept to the older ways, be they human or fae and she had no knowledge of interactions between the latter and shape-shifters.

Humans were the connection between all the supernaturals, the one race to interact with them all through the centuries even as the supernaturals had hidden from the world. And from humans, had come the zombies. "It is always humans," she murmured, more to herself than to him, and she entered his home.

$$5$$

It was large, for a single studio in London. Or perhaps it seemed larger than most, simply because it lacked anything much to fill it. A pair of mattresses had been stacked at the far end, covered in clean-looking sheets with plenty of blankets folded neatly at one end. A lone duffel bag lay in one corner, easily retrieved if the need to leave arose. A camp set of pots sat on the tiny stove unit in the kitchen area. He'd not lived here long, from the looks of it, nor was he planning to settle in either.

Of course, she had no room to criticize, as she had nothing but the clothes she wore and the weapons she carried. Her purpose in London was one of reconnaissance and eliminating any potential threat to the fae if she found it. At this point, she wasn't sure if the zombies would be considered a true threat to either of the Courts, in any case, despite the evidence of their ability to feed on fae flesh. The more powerful fae were strong enough to avoid being cornered by the walking dead. Of greater concern was the mystery fae behind the creation of the magical lure.

Kayden stepped to the stove and began pulling things

from the cupboard. "It's a bit new, this place. The previous owners were able to evacuate and there are no other tenants in the building. I managed to lay claim to it before some of the more enterprising landlords thought to rent these out to visiting hunters."

"You own the entire townhouse, then?" Surprised, but perhaps she shouldn't have been. A longer-lived mortal like a shape-shifter could amass a decent amount of wealth by human standards if he were so inclined.

"Rent. I'd no desire to own. Everything is temporary when you move through the human world 'on the down-low' as the Americans say."

A laugh escaped her. More of an amused huff. "And have you been to America?"

"Aye. Interesting continent. I prefer Europe, though, especially Scotland and the countryside around London." He took a pitcher with some sort of filter affixed to the top and poured water into a pot. Shape-shifters had hardier constitutions than normal humans and she, as fae, needn't worry about consuming tainted water either as her small spark of healing could take care of any damage it might do to her. Not that he would know it, but perhaps he filtered the water for the taste. She smiled, watching him. A mortal with refined taste; something about the concept—and every nuance of him—fascinated her. As a shape-shifter, other fae might look upon Kayden as a savage, a beast. And here he was chopping a few onions to flavor a soup.

"The countryside has always been beautiful." She preferred the sweeping fells of northern England, though the rolling green hills farther south had once been every bit as beautiful by moonlight. Only in the more recent centuries had she learned to tolerate the press of iron and concrete of the major cities. "Why are you here, then? Why the center of London?"

His hands paused, his grip on the kitchen knife tightening for a moment before he went on cutting dried strips of meat. "I passed through a year ago." Another long moment grew heavy with silence. "When I heard of the zombie infestation, I came back to have a look around and decided to give Seth's pack what aid I could. It's always a good idea to have a few well-placed men who owe you a favor. An alpha of any breed is a good connection amongst shape-shifters."

A truth, but not the whole of it. He was a cat, after all, and when did any of them give a straight answer? She spared a faint smile for her momentary whimsy. Perhaps wine would drink itself and she would find the way down to the answer she sought.

Again, her gift for the future sparked, but no vision came. No knowledge of an impending death washed over her. Only a hint of surety—she needed to dig deeper and continue on her line of investigation. She'd have let the thread of conversation end there if her gut hadn't insisted she needed to know more about why he was here. Perhaps she'd learn more from a slightly different approach.

"The station tonight, I know why you took me down there, and for that, I am grateful." Rubbing her upper arms, she turned in a slow circle, taking in the sparse furnishing, the lack of keepsakes of any kind. Mortals with good memories tended to keep both somehow. But this man, this man had nothing that wasn't newly acquired. Everything had the look and smell of having been freshly unwrapped from some package. Facing him again, she tilted her head as she studied him. "Why do you go hunting down there?"

He shrugged. "Much the same as you, lass. Patrolling

isn't always enough to take the edge off the need to hunt. I see a lot of stupid humans waste their lives heading into the parks every night. They make the mistake of thinking mindless zombies would provide interesting sport, a whole new kind of trophy hunting though a walking corpse goes to dirt. You can't stuff one of those and hang it on a wall somewhere. Those hunters, they get cocky, brandishing some bit of clothing or some trinket they've looted and then they get themselves cornered or surrounded. Dumb and daft, they end up eaten, and worse, they add to the infestation. It makes me angry to see all of this every day and best to take my anger out where it will at least do us all some good."

Some part of Sorcha warmed to the idea. How many beings would simply vent their wrath without a care for the harm or the good it would do others? "Why did tonight surprise you?"

His jaw tightened.

A bit of intuition, another spark of foresight darted through her consciousness. The child, the child. It had everything to do with the child. But how had that zombie been different to the others in any other way but what it used to be?

Kayden had stopped stirring the soup. Ever so carefully, he set down the spoon and switched off the heat. "I knew him."

He picked up the pot and poured a bit of soup into two camp mugs. Taking one in each hand, he offered her one. Careful of the hot sides, she took hers gingerly and followed him to one side of the room.

"The boy was one of those street urchins you'd see running about the city." Kayden braced his back against the wall and allowed himself to slide down until he sat on the floor. "Doesn't matter what decade, there's always bound to be some. Orphans, mostly, or runaways. If they're lucky, they band together in packs of their own to survive life on the streets, pickpocketing and nicking a few things here and there for their survival."

She joined him, sitting within arm's reach by his side. "But he was human?"

Kayden nodded. "Aye. And he was a bright lad. He could tell I wasn't strictly normal, though he didn't say as much. He knew enough to let a man keep his own secrets. He was holed up with his pack in some of the old tunnels in Notting Hill Gate, closed off and not in use. They'd all learned not to trust adults, young as they were, but I'd been camping in another tunnel nearby. After a couple of days I guess they decided since I hadn't tried to harm them, I must be safe enough to talk to. Besides, they wanted to know how I'd avoided being caught by the station guards. Even street-smart kids are still curious."

"Was it so easy to avoid detection?" For a shape-shifter, it probably had been. Normal human guards would easily overlook a shadow in some abandoned tunnel. Even a large predator like that could lie in the shadows and hide from eyes that didn't expect to find it.

"If a mess of children could successfully hide from the station guards every night, of course I'd have no problems doing the same in order to have a quiet piece of sheltered territory to sleep in for a few days." Kayden snorted. "I suppose they might have been looking for a bit of something to believe in, and a supernatural is a brilliant discovery to a wee one."

He hadn't avoided her original question, but he was working his own way to giving her his answer. Smiling, she took a sip of soup. Surprisingly rich flavor burst across her tongue, savory and warming. How had he managed to turn a few onions and jerky into such a satisfying comfort?

"You like it, then?" He'd been watching her. "I made this for the kids too. It's mostly in the seasoning for the jerky. Any greens you can find are a bonus, added nutrition and flavor. I carry the jerky when I travel in case I'm not in a place where I can run down fresh meat, but you can make it stretch by turning it into a soup. I left them an entire package of this jerky when I moved on."

He fell silent. She continued to sip, waited.

"They didn't want me to leave. Said there were rumors of people falling ill. Random people gone mad on the trains. Too cold for them to find another hidey-hole up on the streets so they had to stay in the Underground." Kayden set his mug down on the floor with exaggerated care and then crossed his arms over his knees. "But I didn't want them becoming too attached to me. Liked them all well enough, but big cats like me are loners by nature. We drift, we move on. And that's what I did. I left them."

And how much chance did a group of children have in a city with an epidemic running rampant? Oh, she didn't fault him. Impossible for him to have known how bad it all would get. But she was beginning to understand the weight he must carry with the memories.

"I didn't know," he whispered. "The zombie virus was only a rumor at the time. I was already out of the city by the time they set up the quarantine. And when I came back, I lost time arguing with the human officials. Had to contact Seth's pack to have a reason to be here, to look for them. And by the time I could, the children were gone. Their scents were scattered, too lost in the chaos for me to track any of them. But I keep going down there, hoping to find out what happened to them. And tonight, I saw Ralph."

Safe enough to assume Kayden's reaction had more to do with the guilt and the shock than any supernatural power the zombie might have had over him, then. Relief swept through her. The chance of zombies developing powers was unlikely but the effect would have been devastating. After a moment she set down her own mug and reached out to give him a tentative pat on the arm. Awkward, but she wasn't used to giving consolation to someone who wasn't dying. And yet, she wanted to. Her heart ached for him, even as the emotion surprised her.

He covered her hand with his, then curled his fingers around it. "I didn't take it well when I caught the scent of your blood, lass. If we're to fight together, you mustn't do that again."

"I ..." His gaze caught hers, held her with unsettling intensity. She fell silent—no desire to argue with him but unwilling to give him a false promise either.

"You're a fierce warrior, of that I have no doubt." He lifted her fingertips to his lips. "But it undid something inside me to see you bleeding."

The heat of his lips pressed against her fingertips sent thrills up her arm. Her breath caught and her pulse quickened. Her nipples tightened beneath her tank top. How did he trigger such hunger in her? How was she still thrumming with energy after slacking the blood madness?

What was he waking inside her?

Intuition poked at her. But it wasn't answering her questions so she mentally shoved it aside.

He released her hand and reached for her, his gaze never leaving hers as he cupped her cheek. She parted her lips, tried to think of something to say, but words scampered across her mind in every direction. Then his thumb brushed over her bottom lip and a wildness sparked inside her, an urge to break whatever hold he had on her without backing away. Oh no, backing away was the last thing she wanted to do.

Instead, she set her teeth into his thumb.

THE SNARL ESCAPED Kayden's throat before he could control it. Little minx. Defiance lit her eyes as she released his thumb and then pressed a light kiss on it. His control broke. He slid his hand behind her head, grasped her nape and pulled her close for a deep kiss.

She was liquid heat in his arms, her tongue dancing with his. He shifted his hands to get a good hold on her and pulled her across his lap. But she didn't just lie there. No, she lunged up out of his grasp and straddled him. Her hands plunged into his hair as she first nipped at the corner of his mouth and then claimed it as hers, drinking him in and kissing him as if their lives depended on it.

Never still, her body pressed against him. Her hips ground into his. He let his hands roam over every inch of her, reveling in the fantastic strength of the taut muscle under her sleek surface. No fragile flower, his fae, his faery woman. Tearing free of their kiss for a moment, he buried his face into the sweet depths of her cleavage as he pressed his hands into her back, encouraging her to arch for him.

He tugged at the thin fabric stretched across her shoulders. "Take it off before I tear it off."

She leaned back, just a bit, and stared at him, deciding. Then she set her hands to the hem and peeled the garment off. He slid his hands underneath her tank top, followed it upward as she removed the tank as well.

So soft, so smooth.

Her bra was at odds with the stark plainness of her outerwear. Sheer lace held the most perfect breasts he'd ever seen, cupped in almost invisible support. He palmed one breast in each hand and squeezed, grinned when she gasped and took hold of his upper arms. She didn't try to pull his hands away. But she did need the support. Her head fell back and she let out a soft mew as he massaged, molded, her breasts in his grip. She gasped again as he switched to teasing her taut nipples between thumb and forefinger, and the sound almost brought him to his own peak as his cock strained to get past the loose fabric of his borrowed sweatpants.

He wanted her the way he needed food, water. He needed to bury himself inside her heat and *live,* the way too many people took for granted and no one in London ever forgot to. Why now, why with her, he didn't plan to think on. Instinct drove him. His beast waited just beneath the surface.

"It's been a long time, my lady." The words tumbled out as he struggled to pull his control together. Important to let her know what she was getting into. "I've not got the patience to go slow this first time with you."

"Then come inside me." She leaned in, paused to meet his gaze in one long moment and then pressed her lips to his. Her response whispered against his mouth. "Patience ... is not one of my virtues either."

This time he let the growl roll free from his throat as he set his hands on either side of her hips and deadlifted her, tossing her the short distance to the bed. He was on his feet with shifter speed and shredded the gods-be-damned sweatpants. She'd kicked off her boots the moment she landed and he helped her free of her pants, tossing them somewhere behind him. Fabric tore and his leopard surged to the fore in approval, aroused past control by the sight of his shirt in pieces in her hands.

He pressed her backward on the bed in a tangle of ravaging kisses and sharp nips. She opened her legs for him and wrapped them around his hips. He dragged his mouth across her neck, her collarbone, as she arched her body against his, and then he shifted his hips until the head of his cock nudged at her hot, wet entrance.

Nails pricked the skin across his shoulders as she clutched at him, encouraged him.

"When I'm inside you, don't claw me until you're coming."

Her eyes flew wide at his order and her nails dug deeper into his skin. He grinned, loving the temper in her stormy eyes and pressed himself inside her. The heat of her surrounded the tip of his cock and her entrance contracted as she cried out. He almost lost it, right then. Dragging in deep breaths of air he reached for control.

Just a bit longer. He wanted to savor this incredible woman longer.

He worked himself inside her, stretching her inch by inch, growling through the blinding pleasure of the snug fit, the muscles of her vagina hugging the length of him. Her thighs squeezed at his waist, incredibly strong. He answered by rolling his hips, pressing the tip of his cock against more sensitive places inside her. The change in friction, in pressure, sent pleasure shooting down the length of his cock until his balls tightened.

Sorcha shuddered beneath him, sucked in a breath of her own. "More."

He pulled out an inch and was rewarded by her snarl. In answer, he plunged deep inside her, burying himself to the hilt in her heat. She threw back her head, arched her back until her breasts pressed against his chest. He withdrew and thrust into her again; her hips rose to meet him. He gritted his teeth.

He was going to bring her with him, damn it.

Again and again, he thrust into her—his growl rumbling through his chest at the building pleasure. He gave her everything he had, pushing every muscle in his body to the limit with the need to fill her. She convulsed with a cry, her inner muscles clenching around his cock with the force of her orgasm, and her nails dragged across his back.

Everything crested all at once and his release exploded through him, tearing an inarticulate yell from his throat.

He collapsed over her, shuddering in the aftermath, twitching as her muscles spasmed around his cock still buried inside her. Her heartbeat hard against his own chest, he held her until both their pulses calmed, running a hand along the soft skin of her side and pressing a kiss to her temple.

So very alive. Fierce and beautiful. Had he ever met anyone as magnificent? Certainty settled deep in his bones —a knowing he'd never experienced before but couldn't ever fail to recognize.

"Stay with me," he whispered into her hair.

She nodded, her face tucked into the hollow of his neck and shoulder. "I will stay the night."

He rose and retrieved a soft cloth, dampened it to clean her up and himself. Then he brought her a cup of water and tucked her into his bed, snug against his side. Sunlight streamed in the window, warming them both as he dozed with her head pillowed against his shoulder. Content.

When would she realize he hadn't asked her for the one night? He chuckled to himself and then sleep took him.

6

———

The sounds of glass on glass chimed and Sorcha's eyes flew open. Sitting up, she took in her surroundings with one hand holding the duvet to her chest and another finding the hilt of her dagger underneath her pillow. Despite their brief coupling—or perhaps of mutual accord—both she and Kayden had made sure they had weapons close to hand before they'd fallen to sleep.

"Easy there. Just getting a few things together to break our fast." Kayden stood in the kitchen area of the studio, putting several small plates on a tray. "No need to draw steel on a man who's bringing you your tea."

Odd, but she missed the weight of him at her back. She'd not indulged in such a deep sleep in a very long time. Unconsciousness, yes, but it wasn't the same kind of rest.

Kayden continued his task, accompanied by the clinking of plates and silverware. "It's probably not the finery the Fair Folk enjoy Under Hill, but I do appreciate a few of the niceties modern civilization has created."

"Under Hill has many fine things for the powerful and

the pure-blooded. Wonders of magic, fine treasures only those with all the time in the world to master their skill can create." She snorted. "All the glamour and gilded riches are cold hospitality when one is only a half-breed."

A moment of silence and Kayden's gaze weighed heavily on her.

She shook off the old memories and gave him a smile, a true smile from the night he'd given her. "I've found the warmth of home and hearth with honest people a much better experience."

His gaze never wavered, and he never blinked, but he took hold of the tray and headed toward her.

"These were sitting in a bakery window display when I went out to get more supplies. Store owner let me borrow them since I work with Seth's pack." Sitting on the edge of the bed, Kayden settled a tray between them. He lifted the simple white china teapot and poured steaming tea into matching cups. A faintly floral scent wafted up to her nose —light and yet it had a musky spiciness to it as well.

A far cry from the camp mugs he'd used to feed her the night before.

"You don't prefer a traditional English tea?" Not that she minded. There were many good teas in the world. She sniffed again in appreciation and her stomach rumbled.

"Well, normally I enjoy an easily obtainable cup of Earl Grey or Lady Grey." Kayden handed her a cup then brought his own to his lips. "But since it's gone well past morning, this one matched my mood better. I can brew you up a cup of one of those instead."

"No need." She sipped, careful not to burn her tongue. "I like Darjeeling."

He might have smiled behind his teacup, but he made no immediate comment. Instead he took his time about drinking his tea and then set it down. "The bread's a day old, but it ought to taste all right toasted. Wasn't sure what sort of breakfast you'd be wanting."

He'd obviously put some effort into it though. A couple of bangers and tomatoes cut in halves had been grilled and plated aside a generous helping of baked beans and a fried egg. Rather than speak to reassure him, she picked up a fork and began to eat. He watched her for the first few bites, then a peculiar tension across his shoulders eased and he began eating too.

Strange, the calm inside her. For as long as she could remember, her days and nights had been filled with an ever-present turmoil. When the pressure of it boiled over, the bloodlust took her. But now? There was only a comfortable ease.

"You slept deep, hardly stirred when I rose. And I slept late into the afternoon." Kayden dipped his toast in the rich, golden yolk of his egg. "I would've thought you'd have come awake when I left, maybe at the sound or smell of me cooking."

Sorcha chewed her mouthful of toasted bread and swallowed. "It's the consequence of the battle rage, the berserker part of me. It lends me strength beyond what I should have, greater stamina, but the price is a sleep so close to death that I've been left for dead on the battlefield in the past."

And she'd woken wishing she hadn't, once she'd seen the bodies strewn all around her.

His brows were drawn together, the corners of his mouth turned downward. "I'm hoping you find a safe place to hide away when your sleep takes you, but I'm guessing you've not bothered in the past."

Was that disapproval in his voice?

She shrugged. Little value to be had in hiding the way of

things. "There's usually nothing for miles left alive to hurt me."

"Still, it'd be easier on you to have friends, or family maybe, to watch over you. Kill all of your opponents and the world will always create new enemies for you."

No denying his words rang so very true. They were dancing around a set of questions, touching, poking, fishing for answers but not willing to lance a potential wound. She scooped up beans on her fork and ate as she considered how to respond.

Family? Friends?

Such an assumption to believe every being had those. And yet, she noticed he hadn't jumped to the conclusion so much as, well, fished. How very feline of him. "My father died in a great war when I was still an infant."

Still, she'd been born with a fae's wisdom. She'd cried inconsolably for the loss of him and her mother had never tried to stop her. Her mother had keened for her father as well.

Sorcha drew a steadying breath then continued, "He never knew he'd passed on his curse to me. My mother foresaw his death and could not convince him not to go into that battle. Babe though I was, I still remember her Song to soothe his soul into the next world, very different than any she'd ever Sung before."

The humans told legends of banshees screeching or howling, foretelling a man's death. Only part of those stories were true, and with time those stories had warped and evolved as any mythology would. A Bean Sidhe's song had a purpose other than foretelling, and the sound of it could ease the passing of the dying or drive the wounded into death. Half-blood she might be, what magic flowed through her took the tone of her heart. Had she been a century older, she'd have brought the opposing army to its knees in agony for the pain her father's death brought to her mother ... and her.

"I remember, but my gift didn't come to me until much later. I was too young, too weak, to ease her pain as she passed." Her mother died pining for her father—of a broken heart. Tragic, romantic and everything the human fairy tales might find classic. Sorcha could think of no torture worse than those days. Kayden didn't reach for her, didn't babble out awkward words of condolence or regret. A good thing, that, as all of it was long gone and none of it his fault.

"Leopards are solitary creatures." His words were spoken in a low tone, a strain to hear even with her fae ears. "I was born a leopard shape-shifter and left the den early to fend for myself. I never knew to miss family. But friends, I do miss friends."

"And when you are long-lived, friends not only come and go, they pass away." How many had she Sung for? Whether for immortal brethren ended before their time or for mortals she'd come to know, it had never been easy. Though to be honest, she'd cried for the mortals more so.

Kayden only nodded. "Aye. But solitary doesn't mean hermit. I seek out companionship, find brotherhood with other shape-shifters. Seth and his pack are an honorable lot. It's good to stand shoulder to shoulder with men like him."

"Perhaps I'll learn more of him." She'd been more at ease with Maisie. At least she hadn't tried to challenge the female werewolf to a fight that might have left them both bleeding or worse. "He's named me ally, for this ... mission ... at least."

Human military would call it a mission. Perhaps there was a better word for it, but she couldn't think of one. Assassination was what it would come to, though. And wasn't the outcome what truly mattered in the end?

"But would you trust your allies to watch over you when you're forced to rest, the way you did last night?" His gaze caught and held hers.

The answer: it wasn't simple. She had a sense that what he wanted as an answer wasn't simple either.

"I was here last night." When at a loss for what to say, she always gave a bit of truth to hold off the inevitable. If she had a more direct answer for him, she wasn't sure she wanted to think on what it might mean. Better to move on.

Apparently, Kayden thought so too. He surveyed her empty plate. "A good fight always leaves me plenty hungry. I was guessing you burn through your own share of energy. Have room for a sweet to finish off this meal?"

A weakness, and she rarely gave in to it. But when Kayden stepped away and returned with warmed scones, her mouth watered anew. Hard to believe a bakery would sell such large scones. They were still soft as she broke them in half and spread clotted cream, then berry preserves on them. "Bakeries still manage business?"

"Zombies don't break into shops at night unless there's some sort of prey inside. The bakers don't begin until after sunrise, late for them but they've managed. And they shut down before sunset. They've a respectable clientele in the way of visitors and hunters. Amazing how many people will stop their entire day to sit down and have a nice cream tea before going back to ogling the horror walking in the parks."

It wasn't the bitterness of his words that bothered her. The higher fae mocked humankind at every opportunity and the behavior of the humans in the face of this zombie outbreak had left the mortals open for every kind of criticism. Kayden's sentiments only echoed what she'd already heard in the Court of Light. No. It was something else.

"Unless there is prey inside." She chewed on the words, mulled them over. "How would the zombies have been attracted to any of the shops? How often have those break-ins occurred?"

Kayden swirled his tea in his cup, apparently doing a mental count. "Not many, but more than I'd have expected. As far as the wolf pack has told me, only one or two incidents have occurred where someone being chased took refuge inside a shop and led the zombies to the building. The rest couldn't be explained by normal investigation."

"So there are more lures in the city." Of course. Whatever fae was behind this, a single landlord wouldn't be the only pawn to set them out. "It wouldn't be effective to search them all out. They've already served their purpose after the attack, and I can't be sure I can detect them in time to prevent one."

"Can they be reactivated?"

Not the proper term for renewing the magic imbued in those bits of cloth and binding. Still, she could answer his question well enough. "Only if the fae who gave them power touched them again. And they would have to come back into his hands. It couldn't be done at a distance."

"His." The shape-shifter was sharp.

"Magic like this carries a personal signature. I have not met this particular fae before, but I can tell he is male and very, very old."

Given enough time and a greater sample of his power, she might be able to tell more about the nature of his magic. But the small charms wouldn't give her enough. It would have had to have been a great work of magic.

Kayden blew out a breath. "Can you use it to track him, the way we follow scent?"

"No." She paused. "Not unless he'd been wielding his magic as he moved through the streets of the city. Not many have the power to do so, and those who do are wiser."

A nod. "But you could tell if he was using his magic nearby."

"I'd have to be close, but yes. I could home in on the source."

"Looks like we'll be doing a fair bit of walking this evening, faery, in order to see if we can find more clues as to this bastard's whereabouts."

Or if they were lucky, they would find the fae. Not likely, but luck was another gift the fae were known to have on occasion. And when had he decided she was one of the little folk? She considered, her flash of irritation quickly dissipating. The man was baiting her, teasing without any real intent to harm. She'd been too alone too long to remember that sort of easy camaraderie.

It took her a moment to realize no further question had come her way. She raised her eyes and found herself caught in his gaze. Her pulse quickened, her nipples grew sensitive, and she gripped the duvet tight against her chest. A different kind of hunger began to pool low in her belly.

A ringing tone cut through the silence. Kayden's gaze never left her as he reached to the side of the bed and retrieved his mobile. "Yeah."

"Seth here." The alpha's voice came across loud and clear to Sorcha's fae senses. "Is Sorcha with you?"

Kayden raised an eyebrow at her. In response, she touched a fingertip to the side of her ear and nodded.

"Aye, Seth. We're both here and we can both hear you." Kayden dropped the mobile on the bed between them.

"Good." The news didn't seem to faze Seth. How much did they know about the fae? More than most humans, but neither had demonstrated an alarming amount of knowledge. As she pondered, she listened with partial attention to Seth continue. "A patrol crossed paths with one of those groups of faster zombies. Haven't run into them in a while but this batch definitely moved faster, used coordinated attacks. They hared off into the bigger park and my wolves are trailing them."

"You want us to join the chase?" Kayden stood, every line of his body tense with eagerness. His anticipation of a hunt didn't replace the sensuality he'd had pouring from him only a moment before, only added to it.

"We've got it covered." Seth cleared his throat before he continued. "The patrol is young, it'd be best to let them continue. I was hoping you could backtrack and follow the trail to see where these things came from. You've got better experience and there's a chance you'll encounter more."

Better control? Sorcha mulled over the possibility. Her encounter with the alpha of the London pack had proved Seth, at least, had better control than she did. A group of younger werewolves might not. Kayden, on the other hand, was ready to go back out into the dusk and kill more zombies.

A slow smile stretched her lips and she began looking for her clothing. Fighting first, and maybe a good tumble afterward. The perfect night to her mind.

7

"Interesting."

"We're back at Kensington Gardens." Sorcha had her short swords out as she studied the outdoor car park.

With the darkening sky, zombies would be more active.

"Right at the end of Perk's Field, no less." Kayden made his way along the edge of the paved area, coming to a stop at a tree. It was the largest of a small copse separating the car park from the broad expanse of overgrown lawn that was called Perk's Field. Many hunters chose the stand of trees as a vantage point when hunting the random corpses wandering across the wide-open area.

"And the pack of zombies headed straight into the gardens?" Sorcha kicked the tire of an abandoned car.

"Not quite." Kayden circled the tree, studying the ground. "Dirt's scuffed to hell here and the turf is torn up all around the tree. The zombies milled around this one, scraped and scratched at the tree trunk."

Rot and decay filled his nostrils. He looked up into the branches. There—a few small branches were broken.

He made a controlled shift and claws extended from his fingertips. Making an easy leap, he grabbed the lowest branch and hauled himself up. And there was the scent he was looking for. "A boy was in this tree. A human one."

Sorcha came to stand beneath the tree. "Any sign of him?"

Poor kid could have fallen, but there were no torn clothes or sign of remains. The zombies weren't clean eaters. Shreds of fabric or gnawed bones would at least be left behind. Kayden jumped clear of the branch and landed easily next to Sorcha. "Looking for it, but the zombies' scent cover his. I'm going to range out a bit and see what else I find."

When they'd entered, he'd been focused on the marker Seth's pack had left. And then he'd been on the zombies' trail. Now, he was casting around for other fresh scents from the boy or from others recently passed through the area.

"Kayden." He turned to see Sorcha standing a few yards from the tree, deeper in the gardens. She crouched and retrieved something. "Another charm."

Aye, they were onto something then. And his instinct told him it wasn't the zombies they needed to track. He circled the tree in ever-widening circles until he found the boy's scent, finally—sharp and unmuddled by the decay of walking dead. "We've got a trail."

Sorcha caught up with him, eyes on the ground, watching for signs as he used his nose to follow the scents.

"A small boy," she commented.

He didn't break his stride, didn't look up from the trail in case he missed something. "The footprints?"

"Aye." She paused. "Smaller than mine, even. And there's more of them."

Talented tracker, though tracking by sight more than

scent. The leopard aspect of him approved. She was a good hunting partner, this one, one to keep if he could.

Several other boys had joined their clue as he hit Bayswater Road and crossed. He picked up five distinct scent signatures, all dirty and unwashed, but human. They had headed together down the street, not long ago. The trail was hot.

In minutes, Kayden and Sorcha stood in front of an old church. They crept up the steps and heard voices raised.

Kayden glanced at Sorcha, nodding as she tested the door, then opened it slow and soundless. They slipped in and kept to the shadows inside the entryway.

Their quarry was on the dais gathered around an adult, equally dirty and balding. The man had one of the boys by the front of his shirt.

"Ye done a botch job of it, now!" The grimy man shook the boy. "Didn't I tell you the next time I wouldn't just box yer ears. I'm sendin' ya down below to Himself personally. Ya understand me?"

"N-nah. Don't." The boy's teeth clicked. Whether from terror or from the force of the man shaking him, Kayden wasn't sure. but he didn't care. Anger built inside him, a rising wave of heat.

"Keep hold of it, I told ye. Don't lose it!" The man punctuated each sentence with a hard shake. "Ye were supposed to carry it all the way to the playground. There's summit Himself wants there."

The playground. Diana's children's playground was the closest to the area where they'd found the lure. Kayden shot a look at Sorcha. She was crouched low, ready to dart down the aisle.

"I give ye a safe place, keep ye outta the cold, and this is wot you do?" The man continued his tirade. "I ought to send the lot ye down below wit no protection. See if Himself will listen to yer excuses."

"They were fast." Another boy broke in. This one had spiky dark hair and dark skin. "Too fast. We couldna stay fer enough ahead o' them. Barely had time to toss Goggles up the tree 'fore they were on us."

"Ye had enough time to run fer it, didn't ye?" The old man clenched his free hand and backhanded the dark boy.

Kayden's temper snapped.

He charged with a roar. The entire room darkened in his vision, only the man remained in focus. The man dropped his captive, and the boys dodged to one side. Kayden didn't care. His target was the old bastard.

How could he? How dare he send children into harm's way?

The man didn't even run. The acrid scent of urine burned Kayden's nostrils and the man's scream filled his ears. He reached for the man with clawed hands and lifted him clear off the ground.

"Please! Please!" the man screeched. "Don't!"

"Monster!" Kayden roared into his face.

"Kayden! The children!" Sorcha's voice cut through his rage.

The children, the children. He hadn't been there for them. They'd stood no chance.

And monsters like this pitiful human had probably left them to die, used them as bait.

The man struggled and Kayden tightened his hold, bones breaking under his grip. The man screamed.

"Not in front of them. Do you hear me, Kayden? Not in front of the children." This time her words were a cold strike against his anger. She was right. They'd seen enough horror.

Kayden stared into the man's terrified gaze and snarled,

letting the full force of his dominance loose. The man uttered a whimper, his eyes rolled up into the back of his skull and he went limp.

"I-is he dead?" a young voice echoed in the startled quiet of the church.

Kayden panted, reaching for control and penning up his rage. "No. Coward passed out."

He tossed the man aside in disgust, not caring how hurt the bastard was. When he turned toward the speaker, he found the five boys crouched in the side aisle under a stained-glass window, partially boarded up. Sorcha had blocked their escape route and stood by them.

Their fear hung sour in the air, mingling with the terror of their keeper.

What could he say?

They probably feared him more than the old bastard.

"Shite, Ollie, ye were right about them Weres. They don't waste time pissing around when something sets 'em off."

THE RESILIENCE of human children amazed Sorcha.

The boys had transitioned from being afraid of Kayden to a hesitant sort of expectation, taking note of his every move. The puzzled look on Kayden's face probably helped convince them he meant them no harm.

She'd told them as much when she'd stopped them from running. Kayden's response to her had given them something to hope for.

Kayden recovered his balance quickly though, and she tucked the memory of his flummoxed expression away for another time. It'd bring her a smile.

"Oi, you lot." Kayden addressed the pack of boys. "What're you called?"

The boys eyed the big man warily and Sorcha didn't blame them. Kayden's voice still sounded sharp with temper despite his calmer appearance.

"I'm Ollie." The skinniest one stepped forward, his skin dark even under the grime of street living. He jerked his head to indicate the others. "Them's Dan, Dan, and Dan and Dougie."

Not related, at least as far as she could see under the dirt and rags. The five of them had different builds, different shapes to their faces.

"How'd you all know which Dan you're talking to?" Kayden leaned against the wall, crossing his arms. The press of his intimidation lessened with his casual pose.

Ollie gave him a lopsided grin. "He's Peas, he's Goggles and he's Doc."

Each of the "Dans" gave a small wave based on his nickname. No longer poised to bolt, the boys relaxed into slouches. Their gazes drawn in by the charisma of Kayden.

Did Seth have the same effect on his wolves?

"Why Peas?" Kayden asked, nodding to the smallest of them.

It was the boy named Dougie who spoke up. "'Cause when we go huntin' fer leftovers behind the pubs, he always goes fer the mushy peas."

Doc shook his head.

"What's wrong with that?" Sorcha asked.

"Ye never know if what looks like mushy peas *is* mushy peas till it's too late."

She wouldn't know. Judging from the nods of agreement and the twitch at the corner of Kayden's mouth, Doc had a point.

Dougie was studying her. "Yer not quite right."

Ollie took a swipe at Dougie, catching him across the back of the head. "Oi, what're you, daft? Ye don't talk to ladies that way."

"I didn't mean it in a bad way." Dougie rubbed the spot, thick brown hair falling across his eyes. "I'm sayin' she's not properly like a lady."

Goggles raised his hand, but Dougie blocked him before the other boy could take a swing. Letting out a huff, Goggles threw up his hands. "Ye don't say that to a lady either."

The boys leaped at each other, scuffling until they were a mob on the floor. Ollie and Dougie had some decent grappling skills. The others added in and they were a pile of long arms and legs.

"Enough." They froze under Kayden's command, then relaxed as he chuckled.

"Dougie's right, you know." She didn't speak to any of them in particular. "I'm not a proper lady."

"You're a grand fighter. Can tell by all your weapons. You hold 'em like ye know how to use 'em." Dougie piped up before Kayden could say something. "And you've got this glow about you. Silver-like."

"Don't say it." Ollie's quiet command had Dougie shutting his mouth on whatever else the boy might've added. "The Fair Folk, they dinnae like it when you tell what they are."

She raised an eyebrow at Kayden. Dougie might have some fae in his bloodline. Not Sidhe, not with his broader shoulders and thicker bone structure. But maybe he had a touch of Red Cap or one of the other warrior fae. Ollie, with his dark eyes and skin, might as well but she rather thought he came to conclusions after adding bits of information together. "And how do you know we don't like being revealed as fae?" Aside from the brownie she'd saved, she'd not found other fae as yet. The fae were good at hiding.

Guilty looks and more than a spark of fear in their eyes.

Kayden crossed his arms over his chest. "We overheard a bit before we came in. You lot might as well spill what you know."

"Gaffer ... the old prick there." Ollie jerked his head toward the dais. "He took us in. Gave us a safe place an' a meal a day in exchange fer errands. Made us give our word on it, right up there."

Smart. She wandered over to the dais as the boys continued to speak to Kayden.

"At first 'twas just a few runs cross town, fetching bits o' cloth an' things we could find. Then he started sendin' us out ta sneak inta ol' uilding's with courtyards, places with some green to 'em that the zombies couldn't get into 'cause they were inside high walls. Looking for ..."

Sorcha looked up as Ollie trailed off. The boys had their heads down, peeking at her from under thatches of unruly hair.

"He sent you looking for fae folk, like her." Kayden drew their attention back to him.

She stepped onto the dais and ran her hand over chairs, then along the podium, before she found it.

"Aye, Gaffer had us find smaller ones. Said Himself had a use fer 'em. Sometimes we just had to tell him where they were. Other times, he gave us one of those bundles and they'd follow us."

She believed it. A lure could be set to call fae as easily as it could be set to call zombies. It was in the will of the creator when the magic was imbued in the charm. The one left in the podium wasn't a lure, but it explained why the boys were bound to their agreement. The magic forced them to keep their word. The old man must have had them swear on it at the podium, where the magic would bind them.

"Where did you lead them?" Kayden kept his voice calm, but she could hear the anger beneath the surface. Good. She was angry too. Not at the boys, but at the fae.

"Down below." Ollie's words quieted to a hush. "Himself lives in the dark there, in the Tube. He's got zombies there, guardin' the way. We took all different station entrances, but the closest to him is Notting Hill Gate. When we led the others inta the black, we always had a special bundle in our pockets to keep the zombies away."

Lures and repellents and bindings. Whoever the fae responsible for this was, he had a way with charms she'd not seen in her many centuries. He must be more than just old, to have perfected his skill. He had to be very good at hiding from the greater powers of the Courts of Light and Dark.

Kayden sighed. "If you had a way to keep the zombies off you, why did they almost have you tonight?"

"Gaffer always took them bundles back. Said we could only have 'em if we were going down below. 'Twas up to us to be fast when he sent us into the big parks."

"There'll be no more of that." The boys breathed audible sighs of relief at Kayden's statement.

"Agreed." She held up the tiny charm that bound them to their word. "Your Gaffer broke his word. This place was no longer safe the minute he hit any of you."

And it probably had happened many times, but the power was in their belief and not in the vow he'd extracted from them.

She tossed the charm on the ground at their feet. "The bargain is nulled. You don't have to do as he says anymore."

Besides, Kayden was likely to kill the old man once he'd seen the children safe. If he didn't, she would.

Bright smiles broke out on their faces. They were free. A warmth spread through her chest and she turned away, embarrassed. Never had her fellow soldiers looked at her with gratitude. Always before they'd feared her, distrusted. Ill luck, bad omen. For centuries none had welcomed her much less given her such sincere smiles.

Kayden cleared his throat. "There's an animal shelter a few streets over. You know it?"

"Aye." Ollie nodded. "The one the werewolves guard."

Observant boy. Though, Sorcha guessed the shape-shifters hadn't been making an effort to hide their presence so much as not be obvious.

"You lot head straight over to the shelter at first light. And no faffing around either." Kayden straightened. "You tell them I sent you and you're to wait for me there. We'll be seeing to it you have a safer place and some honest work."

"Really?" Peas had shadows in his expression, despite the hope in his eyes.

"No more baiting zombies. I'll not have you anywhere near the parks." A low growl rumbled up from Kayden's chest. "I'll see to it you've got something better to keep you busy. It's not going to be easy, mind, but you're a lot less likely to end up dead or worse."

"That's good enough fer me." Ollie hopped up and brushed off his trousers.

"More than good enough." Dougie got to his feet, paused, then looked directly at Sorcha. "Yer going down into the dark, aren't you?"

"Aye."

They were all staring at her again.

"Don't worry, I'll be with her to watch her back."

Kayden's promise seeped into her heart. "We've been down and back again before; we'll be doing it again."

Five pairs of eyes grew round with surprise.

"Off with you then, get up to wherever it is you sleep for the night." Kayden waved his hand toward the back of the big church. "Make sure you're holed up good and safe, then get to the animal shelter in the morning. Understood?"

He was rewarded with a chorus of "ayes" and the boys scrambled past the pews and up to the second level of the church.

"In and out of my own hunting grounds and I didn't notice. What are the chances?" Kayden stood inside of Notting Hill Gate tube station. Again. They'd come all the way inside and to the top of the escalators leading downward to the second level.

"You had no reason to take note of the scents and the boys used other Tube entrances as well." Sorcha stood a step behind and to one side, swords drawn to guard their rear.

"Still something happening in my territory." He stared down the stairwell splitting the two escalators. Neither the upward nor the downward heading escalator was running, but the stairs were the steadier footing in case they found themselves face-to-face with zombies. Going down there had never occurred to him, not when there were plenty to fight on the subsurface level. Besides, the Circle Line had been closer to where the kids had been.

The child zombie's face flashed across his memory, followed by the smiles on the boys' faces from earlier in the evening. He'd texted Seth, requesting a wolf patrol to keep an eye outside the church through the night. Hopefully, the boys would do as they were told come dawn. They were safe and he would make them even safer.

It was like a game trail, the scent trails coming up out of the tube station. He'd not noticed it before because he'd always assumed zombies wandered and found their way above from the tunnels. But what if zombies traveled in both directions, coming and going, more than anyone had realized? And what was the one place sane people wouldn't go searching?

All those times he'd come, killed, vented his guilt and rage. Something hid below and laughed.

Why would the fae want others of his kind? What use did he have for them?

The image of the child returned, the corpse's mouth covered in blood. Sorcha's blood.

"Last night, you created one of the new ones." Too many things were falling together too fast. He needed to talk it through.

"Pardon? I did what?" How many men died moments after she'd used such a quiet tone of voice, the icy cold deceiving in its calmness?

"Remember the boy, the dead boy? Did you see what he did after he bit you?"

"I was occupied." The frost hadn't left her voice and the bite to her words told him he'd better explain himself more quickly.

"The moment he had a taste of your blood, he changed. Hell, he spoke. And if you hadn't ended him, he'd have had me too." Aye, Kayden would admit it. He'd left himself open. How many normals had died when they faced the corpses of their friends, their family? He'd not imagined he'd have been a victim himself until it happened and if not for Sorcha ... "Lass, the fae you're looking for is likely—nae, I'm sure of it ... he is the reason for the new breed of zombies plaguing us."

Surprise flashed across her face lightning fast, and then her features hardened as she set her jaw and gave him a sharp nod. "What you say rings true, and I should have made the connection earlier when Ollie and his friends told us of their errands."

"Well, I'll take some accountability for distracting you." He gave her a brief grin before focusing his attention on the darkness. "Since I'm fair certain our quarry is hiding himself down below, the question is how far?"

"How many levels beneath the surface?"

"There's four."

"Call in the wolf pack." The command cut sharper than her blades and if she hadn't already been to him what she was, they might have had a problem. As it was, he simply raised an eyebrow. His fae woman was truly sexy when she took the lead. And she *was* his. "We'll go to the very bottom level and search, work our way up. If our prey is flushed out of hiding, he'll flee into the jaws of our allies."

"The bastard could bolt down the tunnels."

"He could." She tipped her head to one side. "But he's not as likely to. Whatever else, he is fae and in enough of a panic, he will take the shortest route out and into the open air. It gives us the best chance to make use of our glamour to mislead any chase and find a new place to hide."

"I'm not going to doubt your word, faery, but I do need to know the why of it. The better I understand our prey, the more help I can be in bringing him down." Kayden checked his mobile, thankful the thing still had a bare bit of signal. Any farther into the tube station and he'd lose reception. He tapped out a quick message—a call to arms. "What if this fae feels the Underground is his very own Under Hill."

"This is nothing like Under Hill."

He glanced up from his mobile and studied her blank expression. No anger, no happiness either. A master of the unearthly unreadable expression, his Sorcha. But he'd seen her free of conscious thought, caught in the throes of passion. He knew the relaxed softness of her sleeping face. And the longing hiding at the corners of her mouth, in the hunch of her shoulders? Homesick, she was.

"Will you be going back there?" He'd have to work hard to give her a reason to stay. She'd not yet understood his full intent, and he wanted to see her mission fulfilled before he convinced her.

When her gaze met his, the sadness in her eyes nearly swallowed him whole. "No. Not for a long time to come. There are many in the world like this one, and with the zombies spreading, it is my purpose to eliminate any who might harness the walking dead to threaten the Court of Light."

"And the Court of Dark?" He knew only that there were the two. Most of the lone fae he'd heard of living outside the Courts were bits and pieces of folk tales and lore, old superstitions.

"What I do benefits the Court of Dark, just the same. But I do not serve them and they have soldiers of their own." She hesitated and then continued when he hadn't thought she would. "It is more truthful to say there is no place for me Under Hill. I've become too useful a weapon in the mortal world, more … comfortable with my purpose than my brethren."

"Well, let's eliminate this bastard. And then you and I, lass, we'll have a longer talk of what you plan to do next."

She nodded and stepped down the first step of the staircase, then halted.

"What is it?" His mobile pinged and he glanced at the message, setting the device to silent as he did.

She didn't turn to face him, but instead leaned back until her shoulder blades pressed against his chest. "I always hunt alone. Those who know of me would assume as much. And the fae ..." A pause. "They think little of shape-shifters. Less, if possible, when you are in animal form. It would be easy to overlook you."

He placed his hands on her shoulders and gave them a squeeze. "Good for us to plan for every advantage we can."

He stepped back and stripped down. She looked over her shoulder and he gave her a wink. "Are ye sure ye dinnae say that just to see me in the nude again?"

"Get on with ye. I'll not wait too long." She took a few steps farther.

Embarrassed, his fae? He'd enjoy doing that to her more often.

It only took him a few moments to change. Shaking off the last tingling pain of the shift, he left his clothes piled where they were and padded down the steps after her. Butting her hip, he leaned his head into her hand when she reached down. He enjoyed her caress, glad she had no issue touching him in this form.

"Let's go." She kept her voice to a murmur.

He let her take the lead, staying back in the shadows. They made it all the way to the landing of the second level before the first of the zombies shambled into their path.

No way to dispatch them in silence. Their hungry groans and hisses echoed through the tunnels. Anyone would know something had riled up the walking dead. Instead, Kayden made an effort to keep his presence a surprise. He fought silent—no growls or snarls, no roars.

The fae might hear them coming, but hopefully, he would only be expecting Sorcha.

Efficient and quick, Sorcha did away with most of the zombies as she walked toward the next set of stairs and escalators. Kayden only cleaned up the few stragglers to keep the way behind her open. Her two swords cut through decaying flesh and bone as easily as air and her stamina held with no signs of flagging.

"He is close." Her whisper floated back to him, the sound a caress.

They descended to the third level. She'd sent a zombie tumbling down the stairs into a pile of them with a front kick. It took Kayden and Sorcha both a few minutes to make their way through. Kayden was careful to stay clear of her blades. Her spicy scent changed as they fought their way forward, heated with anger and lust. Her berserker heritage was wakening.

Once they stood alone on the third-level platform, she paused, her muscles trembling. "Stay back if the blood madness takes me. Don't let me kill you."

Aye, he'd stay back, but he wouldn't leave her. He hadn't forgotten the desolation in her eyes when she'd told him she'd woken alone on the battlefield.

He'd never abandon her.

As they took the last set of stairs, the darkness below moved. Groans floated up the stairwell from the absolute black. She paused, waiting for a few to climb the stairs to meet them. Blades swept through the air and body parts fell at her feet. A few more steps, another couple of zombies eliminated.

Kayden lingered farther back, hugging the wall along the escalator instead of the center stairs. They weren't coming in more numbers than she could handle and he worried about their return path. He turned to check, make sure they didn't have more flanking them.

The squeal of metal wheels pierced the dark. Sorcha cried out in surprise.

Kayden spun and darted down the escalator steps. When he saw her, caught up in a huge net, swinging above a mass of zombies, it took everything he had not to dive into them to get to her. His muscles trembled and his leopard aspect clawed the inside of his mind.

No, no. She'd not be happy with him if he got himself killed before she won her way free. He needed to watch, wait for their quarry. Hope she stayed alive.

His heart pounded in the cage of his chest.

She had to live.

"I set out to catch dinner, and, lo, I catch a prize!"

Sorcha blinked her eyes against the pain in her skull. She'd taken a hard hit to the head. Considering how much rubbish pressed against her on all sides, it was no wonder.

"And what do we have here?" Her captor peered up at her, suspended as she was in some sort of ... cargo net? Big eyes—round and bulging—studied her from a wizened old face. "A fae, yes, feel lucky my snare caught you. And don't try to struggle against my magic. I assure you, the *geas* will only turn your power back on itself, and your will is mine."

Panic shot through her, her breath harsh. What sort of *geas* had he managed to lay on her? She wouldn't know the true extent until she tried to do something ... and failed.

She made a few cautious movements. Whatever netting held her, it held strong, suspending her above a sea of zombies. Their inarticulate groans floated up as their upraised hands reached for her. How long had she been unconscious? Not long or Kayden would have moved to free her.

"You are quite fortunate I had my servants set this so high, my dear."

Her captor wandered through the mass of undead, the corpses giving way before him and giving him wide berth. Power radiated from him, an effortless miasma and if she could have, she'd have taken herself far away from him too. Wherever Kayden hid, she hoped he was safe and biding his time. The wrong moment and her companion would be zombie bait. On the other hand, he hadn't been the one to set foot in a trap.

Stupid. How could she have been so careless?

"Ah mortals and their technology. It is a shame so few of them have the spark of intelligence to create such things." Her captor moved to the base of the stairs and tapped a tiny nub tucked in a crevice. "Isn't it a wonder a tiny infrared device sensitive to temperature could be so useful? One of my servants provided these. I was so pleased I let him live. So much easier to have a means of snaring unwary intruders without the cold corpses setting it off as they stumble everywhere. I forbade him speak of it, of course. I couldn't have him betraying me."

Never had she feared so much in the heat of battle, where every moment was an action or reaction, kill or be killed. Trapped as she was, helplessness crushed her. Sorcha fought to shove her panic far down. Discipline from years of training lent her focus and she gathered her thoughts in a methodical progression, banishing fear as she did so.

Alone. Of course this fae had to be alone. Immortal or not, too long without interaction and even the long-lived spoke simply to hear themselves. Otherwise, they went mad.

She studied this one, his stooped form and ragged clothes. He didn't bother to use glamour to hide his blemished hide or his overlarge skull. As he shuffled around her, muttering, she wondered if he hadn't already gone mad anyway.

"Why set a trap?" Would he respond, engage in conversation? Possibly not, if he considered her on a level with the mortals he used as servants. Still, he had to have given them orders.

"Sustenance, of course, for my pets." It wouldn't have been unheard of for a fae to feed on humans. In fact, she'd encountered many. "And they make for interesting test subjects."

"Testing?"

He chuckled as he used a stick to poke at something high up on the wall. "Of course, testing. One doesn't develop a strategy without testing the effectiveness of the weapons he has at hand."

She fell to the ground, unable to catch herself or break her fall, tangled up in netting and random debris. A roar echoed around her and suddenly Kayden was there, standing over her in his leopard form.

"Careful, careful." The fae held up a long finger. "If your pet kills me, there will be nothing to hold back all of these."

Beyond him, a sea of zombies rocked back and forth.

Shit.

Had she ever seen so many? She'd faced regiments smaller than the host of undead filling the train platform. There were too many for her and Kayden to fight, even if she had her swords.

"And if I keep my pet under control, what will you do, old one?" Wrapping her arms around Kayden's shoulders, she prayed he would remain in animal form for the time being.

Stay, stay. If you take human form, he will try to Name you. Stay.

No way to warn Kayden. Her silent pleading was useless and she could only hope he had enough knowledge of the Fair Folk to keep to the form the fae wouldn't bother to bind.

She needed time.

Luckily, Kayden had stilled under her touch, a low growl the only sign of his continued anger.

"Ah. It's been so long since I had the company of another fae. Especially one like you. If the high lords of Light sent one of their blades to investigate, I am becoming a threat. The news delights me. So much so, I might show you my great work." The fae clapped his hands, the motion giving him a childish demeanor before his eyes narrowed. "Whether you can truly appreciate it or not, you will still be of use. It was no small effort to gather this many humans."

"What have you done?" Horror washed through her as she took in the sheer number of them again.

"Have you seen them? Scuttling about, beneath the ground, less able to see to their survival than rats. The homeless and wretched, the tired and poor, the lost. I gave them a purpose." The delight in his voice held a brittle edge. "A better purpose than my banishment here, to this forsaken city of mortal wrought iron. I've made the filthy humans more than what they would have been."

Like Kayden's young friends, the orphans who'd hid and gone missing? Her heart ached. They'd done a good thing to save Ollie and his friends tonight. Otherwise, the boys would have suffered the same fate. The bloodlust began to pulse in her veins, burning away at her control. And she welcomed it—anger and joy mingling as she began to embrace it.

"Ah, ah. We cannot have your mongrel blood ruining

this fortuitous meeting." Magic—not hers—tightened in a clawed grip around her. The pain of it cleared the red haze in her mind and locked away the bloodlust, leaving her shivering. Never before had any fae managed a binding great enough to hold her blood madness in check. The *geas* was more than powerful. She trembled again. Who was he?

He laughed, a cold and ugly sound, harsh against a backdrop of moans from the undead. "Come. See."

She wrestled her swords free of the net and random bits of bent metal, glad to have found them and not have been skewered when she fell. She followed the fae, Kayden a breath behind her, as the zombies closed in around them.

The fae came to a stop on the edge of the platform, the tunnels stretching out to either side. He threw his hand up into the air and a tiny bit of ... something ... lit the darkness. Apparently, charms were the primary focus of his power. Some might have decided it to be a limitation. Obviously, he used it to good effect.

"Do you see, my dear? They gather." The old fae swept a hand toward the mass of zombies standing just beyond the far platform.

"We are trapped here." Her swords were a small comfort in her grip. Never before had she seen such a solid mass of the walking dead, hungry and reaching for them, held back by an invisible force of fae magic.

"I am too old to be trapped anywhere." Pricked by her statement, the fae straightened and lifted his chin. "I made gifts for my human servants. Some of the gifts drew the monsters to them, yet the charm I keep holds them at bay. A safety precaution, for now and for future endeavors. Charms, my dear, are a simple tool, effective. It was easy to use them to call appropriate human servants to me, to bind them to my will. I've found humans to be incredibly greedy, easy to trick into a bargain. Then, it was simple. Place these bits of power into the hands of my servants and have them act out my will. Humans, alive or dead, do as I wish."

Perhaps to prove his point, the fae walked forward a few steps and the press of zombies gave way to him. Much farther and he'd leave her and Kayden to be overwhelmed. Instead, he turned to her with his hand outstretched.

"Come, beautiful Sorcha, child of the Morrigan. Did you think I did not know what they call you? Walk with me."

She gritted her teeth. More clues were needed before she had the naming of him in return. And without his true Name, he had both her and Kayden at a great disadvantage. Pride and obstinance were her weapons now as she struggled against the *geas*. "I will not leave my companion behind."

Thin lips lifted in a contemptuous sneer. "By all means, bring along your pet mortal. But put away your weapons. You'll have no need of them as we walk. Better advised to scruff your big cat and keep him from charging off into my soldiers. Come, shall we begin our tour?"

A growl rose from Kayden, but he remained at her side. She slid each of her swords home in their scabbards across her back, then reached down to bury one hand in the fur across his shoulders. Not to hold him. No. She had faith in his ability to pick his battles. But to draw comfort? Yes. The press of his shoulder against her thigh gave her reassurance. If this did not play out well, they might not win their way free to the light of day. At the very least, she had a trustworthy ally at her back.

And yet, he'd become so much more. When, how, she didn't know, only that he had.

"I will not invite you again."

Sorcha's attention snapped back to their opponent.

Annoyance tinged his voice and her mind raced as she considered why he'd not simply commanded her using the power of the *geas*.

She placed her fingertips in the fae's hand and he began to lead her, as if stepping onto a dance floor. She tugged Kayden—the big cat remained close enough to brush her thigh with his shoulder.

Beyond the circle of light cast by the old fae's charm, over a dozen of the faster, stronger zombies snapped and hissed. The same horde Seth's pack had been chasing? No. There hadn't been time for those to return and they would have brought the wolves with them. These must be a different grouping. And around them, packed shoulder to shoulder, were hundreds of the mindless corpses. She and Kayden couldn't eliminate so many, gathered in so close an area. They'd be overwhelmed, no hope of keeping a space clear enough to take the things on.

"A tour of my new army is in order, I think." They began walking farther along the platform until they could see the whole of it and the tunnels beyond.

Her heart sank. The entire platform was filled, wall to wall, with shuffling zombies. Where had they all come from? She and Kayden had only fought their way through a few dozen on the way in. To get out, they could literally run atop the shoulders of the mass filling the platform to get to the escalators now. If only the dead wouldn't pull them down.

"How is this an army?" She fought to keep her tone flat, bored. "Soldiers, the most basic infantry, follow orders. These simply wander aimlessly until they happen across a food source."

"I have seen many wars fought, my lovely berserker, and freedom of thought in infantry is overrated. Their only value is in numbers large enough to overwhelm the opposing force, and in that, I am quite confident." The fae continued forward, and though the hungry dead gave way before him, the fae-fed atrocities followed close at their heels. "It is only the few elite soldiers that need any semblance of cognizance, and then only to make decisive strikes on my enemies. Even in them, the ability to think for themselves is overvalued and potentially dangerous. I prefer to harness these—simple and easy to lead the herd in the direction I desire."

"They might be better hunters than the rest, but they are not soldiers." Sorcha studied them closer. A spark of cognizance, recognition, in those ravenous gazes and maybe a touch of hate, but those eyes were still covered over in the milky-white film of death. Whatever fragment of self that fae blood had tied back into the rotting corpses, it wasn't enough.

Shriveled fingers tightened around hers, and she halted. They stood there, her arm fully outstretched between them. The old fae grinned, his thin lips stretched across gleaming pointed teeth. "Not yet, no. You see, lovely Sorcha. These were fed on what fae blood I could find here in the city of London. And what is here? A few brownies, the odd troll and random others. I didn't know there was one such as you inside city limits until you foiled my scouting party's mission to retrieve the brownie from the Kensington Gardens. None of them was worth keeping to prolong the control. None of them had the strength you do, or the power of your heritage."

She laughed. "You want to give these the bloodlust? It's been tried before, old one, and every warlord who tried to use a berserker's blood failed. It is singular to the berserker and the only way to make more is to breed them."

And she sent silent thanks to any power listening that zombies couldn't be bred. Propagation was solely a miracle of the living.

"Oh no. It's not a question of your berserker taint, halfling." His words twisted her gut. They shouldn't have.

Kayden snarled at her side. Her fingers curled in the warmth of his fur.

Tainted. Halfling. She'd heard the labels in the past, enough for them to have become sufficient for her naming. A true naming could be completed with more than given names or surnames. It could have a power over a person if something inside them recognized the label too.

That had been before she'd gained the confidence to find her own identity. And before she'd met Kayden. She was changed now, and more than what she'd been. As she acknowledged it, a bit of the *geas*'s power over her loosened its hold. Not enough for the fae to notice, if she could keep him talking, distracted.

Amazing, what a bit of self-awareness could do in the face of magic. Like Ollie and his friends, knowledge could set her free.

"If not berserkers, then how is halfling blood better than full-blooded fae?" The brownie. He'd been one of many, the only to survive this old one's madness. Her anger simmered hotter beneath her skin, the berserker inside her impatient. The power of *geas* tightened around her painfully, but she was beginning to not care.

Wait.

Kayden's presence washed over her with a true predator's calm. She hadn't heard the word in her mind so much as understood it as it resonated through her chest. He didn't quench the fury, only helped her hold it in check.

Was this the way he controlled the beast aspect of himself?

"The magic in fae blood acts as a boost, yes." Their host had lost himself in the pleasure of his own clever plans. He gestured to the pack of faster, fiercer undead. "As glorious as they are, they do not follow orders. Sufficient, but we can do better. With you, the effect will be different, give me greater control."

"The spells wouldn't work better with the dilution." Her powers were limited, weaker than a normal fae of the Court of Light.

"It is not about the purity of the blood, for once. It is about the nature of the magic and the resonance."

Realization washed through her and with it, Kayden's presence receded. "Death."

The old fae's grin widened impossibly farther, until his face half split with the slash of white, pointed teeth. "The humans call it necromancy. And for once, I am fond of the term. We'll call it that, shall we? Necromancy—power over the dead. And what fae blood would work best to forge the bond but that from a fae whose magic resonates with the coming of Death? Your blood, my dear, will give me officers to lead my army, elite soldiers who will actually carry out my commands."

No. No. No!

"The power of the Bean Sidhe is peaceful. Its purpose is to help the soul find rest." Horror shot like ice through her veins at the thought that her mother's blood would be used for anything else. Her mother's blood was Sorcha's only redemption. Turn it, use it for such atrocity, would make every part of her existence a curse.

Abomination.

Forget the zombies. If she allowed him to use her this way, *she* would be the nightmare.

"With such an army, we can leave this husk of a city and retake all of the Isles. As the Fir Bolg were driven from the western coast, so shall the Tuatha Dé Danann." Oh, and his madness continued in a long litany as he named each of the Sidhe mounds. Some of those had closed to the human world already, lost. He had been hiding, bound by iron and stone, for a very long time.

"The humans have quarantined the city. They will raise arms against your precious horde." Perhaps she'd injected too much confidence. His grin only faded a fraction, but the reaction was there.

She needed to buy more time. Ah! But they should have found a diplomat for this nonsense. She was better at destroying things.

"The humans are too short-lived, too shortsighted. They never do anything with the kind of thorough eye for detail the longer-lived races have. They've not the patience."

Well, and neither did she.

Wait.

Again came the sense of Kayden, pressing upon her with an insistent pressure and a sensation of claws pricking against the outer edge of her Self. If shape-shifters could communicate this way amongst themselves, it was a wonder they hadn't become the dominant supernatural race across the lands above. It would've been a distinct advantage. The dry assessment gave her a moment's relief. And perhaps she'd imagined the sound of Kayden's chuckle.

"The trick is to ensure the zombies do not feed indiscriminately." By this time, the old fae was muttering to himself. Humans might have mistaken him for an absent-minded professor, the way he blinked his overly large eyes in an owlish way as he patted his robes in search of something. "To simply cut off pieces of you would drive them into a feeding frenzy and, besides, you'd bleed out. No, the humans have a clever apparatus for this ... perfect."

"As wonderful a solution as this ... trinket might be, I must decline." She kept her tone formal and tried to withdraw her hand. Shriveled fingers snapped tight on hers, suddenly strong. She found herself held fast in his grip. She tugged, tugged again. Each time, his fingers squeezed tighter around hers until a joint popped. She'd have to rip her hand free from her fingers to pull her arm back. Strong old fae.

"There is no choice for you. How naive of you to think you ever had one. I told you before, your will is mine." He continued to pat down his robes with his free hand, absently keeping hold of her. She continued to pull—let her arm fall lax, then tug again. Let him think her struggle was limited to the physical contact.

Now.

Sorcha used her free hand to draw her sword in a single, smooth motion, bringing it down on the arm of her captor. A howl rose up, echoing through the halls of the train station and a wave of grey poured down the far escalators as the werewolves dove into the assembled zombies.

The zombies turned, their attention drawn by warm flesh and hot blood. Her attacker only cackled, a high-pitched laugh. She backed away a few steps, flinging off the disembodied hand still holding her. The old fae stared at her, still grinning, as his lost arm reformed in gleaming silver.

She had his true Name.

"Dian Cecht." She called out, mustering the full strength of what magic she had. The *geas* trapping her will, forcing her to listen to his daft schemes, shattered around her. "Can you not master your son's magic yet? He had the power to truly restore a living body and he gave the King of the Tuatha Dé Danann back an arm of joint and sinew, flesh and blood. Yet here, you cannot reclaim your own arm. A shame you killed your own boy when his potential outshone what you could do."

"Little half-blood bitch!"

She narrowed her eyes. "Truly, bitch is the only epithet you can add to make it worse?"

"I still have the charm. All I need do is step away and leave you and your pet to the mob. You will die, a lone waste of a fae when you could have served a greater cause."

"I am not alone." Sorcha's chest swelled with the London wolf pack's howling and the fire of Kayden's anger. "And my companion is no pet. I have your Name now, and so you cannot have his."

With her words, Kayden shifted. He rose up on his hind legs, a roar set loose from his chest as his shoulders broadened and his forelegs reshaped into arms, his fingertips ending in claws. His head remained mostly leopard. In his phase-form, he towered over her. The fastest change she'd ever seen him make.

It was the blood-fed zombies who reached them first. They attacked all at once, tried to mob them. But Kayden was too strong and her swords too sharp. One moment, they were a flurry of rotting limbs and gnashing teeth, stinking of putrification. The next, they were body parts strewn on the ground. Sorcha didn't dare stop slashing. The zombies had pressed close. Even with much of their attention turned by the wolves, the closest of the corpses were tearing at her and Kayden.

Kayden reached past her then, tossing the zombies out of her way, sweeping clear her path to the fae. She did not waste the opening. Darting across the intervening space, she used her blades to slice past grasping hands. But the fae was fast and he dodged directly into his horde. She and Kayden had to hack and slash, clearing the path the way explorers would through a jungle. Their allies had formed a wedge and were making their way to meet them. It wouldn't be long and the fae would have nowhere to go.

... but the tunnels.

Kayden was there, on the fae's back as he leaped off the platform, bearing him down to the tracks below. Sorcha's heart jumped into her throat. The tracks!

No flash of electricity, no convulsing bodies. These tracks, at least for the moment, had no electricity in them. Only then, as she realized Kayden was not about to die, did she notice he was waiting for her. He practically sat on the fae, using his forearms to swipe and crush the zombies approaching. The wolf pack flowed around them both, clearing a space and surrounding the fae to block off all routes of escape.

Kayden's triumph didn't last for long. The fae surged up, knocking Kayden off as if he weighed no more than Ollie. Dian Cecht leaped back onto the platform, but she was there to meet him. She brought her sword up in an arc, and he twisted midair to avoid it. She'd anticipated the move, her second blade rising in a smooth motion, slicing through his wrist.

At the same time, she parted her lips and let loose all of her power in a scream.

KAYDEN CLAPPED his hands over his ears and every wolf but Seth dropped to their bellies on the ground. The zombies toppled over. Sorcha's screech echoed through the tunnels, amplified and shattering the air over and over again. Pain and agony, bitter loneliness, tore through all of them, but the strongest note in her song was the anger. She was Bean Sidhe—not every Song they sang was gentle.

Her eyes shone blood red. Angry and half-blood she might be, but the berserker part of her must revel in her anger. The merging of the two sides of her ancestry gave her a different kind of power.

The old fae began screaming, the sound of it a horrific counterpoint to her song. Blood trickled from his ears and nose. It poured from his stub of a wrist. His lost hand lay at her feet, the charm to keep the zombies away still held in the fingertips.

She stopped, all at once. Kayden breathed, his ears ringing from the damage. The wolves struggled to their feet, shaking their heads and snarling as the zombies began moving again. He jumped to the platform and pinned the wounded fae down before he could reach for Sorcha.

"Dian Cecht." She stepped closer, her voice cold, each word cutting Kayden's damaged hearing. "You meant harm to the Court of Light." She stood over the pinned fae and lifted her swords. Magic coalesced around her and flowed along her arms to her swords until cold flames danced along the edges. "You are sentenced to Death."

"I am immortal! I will live forever!"

"Just because you are long-lived does not mean you cannot die." She raised her swords to either side. "I have Seen it. My will be done."

Her blades came down in an arc of light and death. The old fae's head rolled across the platform and fell over the edge onto the tracks.

"Kayden." Sorcha stood, flames still dancing along her blades. Every muscle trembled and her eyes burned red.

"Go. We are here. Do what you were made to do." His words were coarse, forced through the vocal chords of his phase-form.

"Back, keep them all back." Despair and desperation made her words tight, high-pitched.

Kayden sought out Seth, their gazes locking. "Get your wolves away from her. *Now.*"

He could only hope the alpha could hear him after the damage of Sorcha's song.

The wolves drew back, up the stairs and escalators and into the tunnels, tearing apart zombies as they went. And they left Sorcha in a sea of the hungry dead.

He stayed to one side, but he didn't leave her. Kayden leaped down on the tracks and fought to keep his own space clear as his love cut through zombie after zombie on the platform. Anything that stepped in her way fell in pieces at her feet. A silver aura grew around her, tinged in ruby-red. And black blood spilled across the ground. Dozens upon dozens of corpses fell until they were piling around her. Still, she kept her footing, moving around her own center in a deadly progression.

It went on and on, the carnage, until there were no more zombies to kill. She stood in the center of the platform. Her breath came ragged and her eyes burned so bright, he couldn't see the pupils. Black blood from the zombies she'd killed sizzled on her blade. She turned in a slow circle, searching, until her gaze fell on him.

He wouldn't run from her. He held his ground, pouring love and warmth in her direction. The connection they'd snapped into place earlier remained. He could reach her.

The light faded from her blades, then her body. The red

dimmed in her eyes. For a moment, she stared at him with dark pools of calm. Then her eyes rolled up.

He shot forward onto the platform, caught her as she collapsed.

"I've got you, love." He brushed platinum hair from her gore-stained face. "I'm with you."

9

"There had better be dragons in the sky or a swarm of locusts or something." Kayden's voice came disgruntled and sleepy as he answered his mobile.

Disgruntled could be a good thing. She'd never thought it before. Of course, there had been many things she'd never considered possible before she'd come to London.

For one thing, how was she calm about waking in such a disoriented state and not trying to make everything around her dead?

"Zombies still wandering around London and you want more fun of the apocalyptic kind?" Seth's response over the mobile was dry, yet the alpha still sounded amused.

"Tell me you have a reason to be calling aside from being an arse." Kayden rubbed his hand over her hip, his touch reassuring.

"You send a pack of kids to Maisie and Brian's clinic at the crack of dawn and you're asking me this?"

Sorcha released her grip on her dagger, leaving it under the mattress, and turned to rub her cheek against Kayden's chest. Of all the times she'd woken from the berserker state, the few hours they'd shared before falling into true sleep and this morning had to be the most peaceful. He dropped a kiss on her forehead. His free arm held her close. For the moment, she was content to savor the comfort of his embrace.

Kayden gave the alpha a slightly less grumpy follow-up. "Aye, I meant to tell you about them. I figured they could help with the renovations and run errands for Maisie in return for staying in the flats above the clinic."

"Maisie might like the help. And we were all a bit distracted last night." It was good Seth was willing to be so amiable about it. "We can work out the details later. I've got something else to discuss with you."

"I think we get at least a day off for destroying about ninety percent of the horde of walking dead last night. And a diabolic mastermind."

"No rest for the heroic."

"A shame." He released her and sat up. When she would have risen with him, he pressed her down into the pillows and tucked the sheet around her.

Content to let the night last a few moments longer, she watched him walk naked across the studio. His tight behind was no hardship to look upon in the twilight before dawn. When he half turned to give her a knowing grin, heat rose up in her cheeks. He was also sporting an erection of fairly epic proportions. Her nipples tightened and her breath caught before she realized Seth was still talking on the other end of the mobile line.

"Your Sorcha was right in warning us." The amusement had faded from Seth's voice, the words clipped and all business now. When had she warned them of anything? The time after killing Dian Cecht was a blur. Her only clear memory had been coming out of the bloodlust and into Kayden's arms. He'd brought her back to his flat and she'd been so hungry to feel alive, to feel him inside her. And he'd been happy to oblige. "We contacted the human military patrolling the quarantine perimeter along the M25. At least two of the Underground's lines extended underneath the perimeter and the blockages at those stations were insufficient. Zombies got out of the city last night."

Sorcha bolted upright and began to dress in a hurry. Where the hell had her bra gotten to?

"Which lines?" Kayden scooped up discarded pieces of clothing and threw them to her, then grabbed his own pants.

"Central and the Metropolitan Line." Seth cursed. "I don't have the resources to send any of my wolves outside of London at this point and the human governments are taking too long talking us to death over whether they'll allow the London pack free access to come and go across the quarantine."

"Convenient the way that's worded." Kayden chuckled.

Well, alliances dissolved as easily as they were forged. She'd never intended to stay in London in any case. The Sidhe lords would have more missions for her and she needed to make her reports. Whatever agreements or politics went on between the humans and the London pack did not bind her.

Seth continued, "I was figuring your Sorcha would be itching to go after them, especially since several seem to be traveling in a group and headed in a specific direction. South."

Kayden drew his brows together, though the smile playing on his lips never faded. She'd miss his smile.

"Thought you said your wolves weren't allowed across the perimeter."

"Allowed." Seth growled. "What matters from a practicality standpoint is I can't spare the resources to go after the blighters before they spread the virus across the English countryside. We both know the human military won't be able to track them all down. I had a couple of patrols do some preliminary scouting when we got the contact from the quarantine lines. They'll have placed scent markers where they left off. You think her sense of smell is good enough to find them?"

It'd have to be. Her chest tightened unbearably as she shrugged into her shoulder harness, then checked each of her weapons. No time for farewells, and probably better if they weren't said. She didn't even try to walk past Kayden to get to the door.

The window was just as easily accessible. And truth be told, the easier escape.

Having to say goodbye would have ripped her heart out of her chest.

She dropped down the fire escape to the street below and began running toward the city's edge.

"No worries, Seth. We'll head out now and get past the quarantine with the humans none the wiser. They can't be angered over what they don't know about, now can they?" Kayden didn't mind finishing his conversation. He would give Sorcha a moment to herself, but just what did his faery woman think she was doing?

"It'd be appreciated if you'd check in." Good thing Seth hadn't worded it as an order. Alpha, he may be, but he wasn't Kayden's. Since finding Sorcha, Kayden hadn't been one to answer to any other male, ally or no.

"Will do." Kayden didn't bother with a shirt or shoes. He ended the call and climbed out onto the fire escape. Sorcha was gaining a further head start and his faery was faster than a normal woman on a streak of madness.

And she must be mad to think he'd let her go off on her own now that he'd found her. Especially without her having told him when she'd come back to him.

He hit the pavement in two hops and drew in a deep breath, catching her scent. The hunt was on and at the end would be his prize. He'd spent too many centuries alone to live another day without her. His mate.

He caught her at the entrance to Notting Hill Gate, the silver crown of her head disappearing as she descended the steps.

"Oi!" He put on an extra burst of speed and vaulted the wrought-iron railing to land in front of her. "Where do you think you're going?"

Halting, one sword drawn, she stared at him. her dark eyes wide in surprise. "There's no time to lose."

Ah, she was beautiful flustered. Apart only for the short time it'd taken to catch up to her and now his pulse quickened at the sight of her. From the hot rose spreading across her cheeks, she was aware of their bond too. Good.

He straightened and crossed his arms across his chest, grinning when her eyes narrowed. "Aye, and so I'm wondering why you'd be taking it into your head to go underground when it'll take you longer to fight your way through the remaining monstrosities down below to catch up to the blighters you're trying to hunt."

"I ..." Her free hand balled into a fist. Oh, and he did like to rile her up too. "It's the best way I know to follow either of the Underground lines out past the quarantine. I could go above but I'd not be sure I'd exit at the same place the zombies did."

"I could be sure."

Her sweet lips turned down into a sad frown. "I hadn't wanted to trouble you with showing me the way."

His cat stilled. Something was off. "Strange thing to call it. Trouble?"

"You've got your responsibilities here." She switched her weight from one foot to the other, and despite all her grace, she looked like a fawn only just finding its way to standing. Her lips pressed into a line. "In either case, I find farewells difficult. I don't know why you followed me."

And so you'll leave me, then?

Her eyes narrowed. "Get out of my head. What sort of shape-shifter talent is this?"

He spread his hands out to his sides. "Not a common one. Truth be told, you started it."

Her mouth fell open. "I ... what?"

"I heard you down there, telling me to stay, warning me to keep safe from his finding my name." It'd caught him by surprise, the sense of her inside his head, his heart. But then, it shouldn't have. He intended to keep her, so he'd let her in. "This is not a thing shape-shifters do, unless Seth and Maisie have been keeping secrets."

"Seth ... and Maisie ..." Sorcha caught her lower lip between her teeth. "Mated."

"Why would there have been a farewell, lass?" He approached her, making sure he was within arm's reach in case she planned to bolt. He wouldn't let her go unless she didn't want to be with him.

"I've got to leave."

"Aye, and I'll be coming with you."

If you'll have me.

He didn't say the last out loud, wouldn't doubt the connection they shared. 'Twas more than a mere connection, their bond, but she had to acknowledge it. Accept it.

"You can't." Confusion clouded her gaze and her brows drew together in consternation. "You wouldn't."

"And why wouldn't I want to come with you?"

"I'm cursed!"

He stepped closer to her. "Ah, and if you remember, I told you what I thought the first time you made that particular revelation. Why do you hate yourself so much?"

"You don't understand! I was born to gentle fae, meant to bring peace to those whose time drew near. Instead?" She laughed, a harsh croak. "I revel in the violence of a battlefield. I savor the kiss of iron and test mine against any foe I come across."

His resolve only strengthened. It was past time for someone to cherish her the way she deserved.

"There's many a man hoping for peace to come of their moment on the fields of battle, lass. 'Tis often the reason they fight in the first place." He reached for her. "And cold metal isn't what comes to my mind when I think of you and kisses."

She flinched but didn't pull free when his hand closed around her upper arm. He kept watch on her sword-wielding arm all the same, but her eyes were free of the red glow of bloodlust. "You see, lass, I'd be willing to bet every teacup left in London that violence isn't what comes to your mind when you think of me either."

Her breath left her in half a sob, half a huff of laughter. "You. You are incorrigible. Irrepressible. You defy your own descriptions of yourself."

He paused, tipped his head sideways. "How so?"

Her eyebrow lifted. "You say you're a loner. You talk of big cats and a solitary nature. I've not seen you seek out your solitude in the entire time I've known you."

Fair enough. "And isn't that just the point of all this, then? Everything I was changed the moment I saw you in the moonlight, the ground around you littered with your fallen enemies."

"Saw me?" Her mouth fell open. She tried to say more, failed and then snapped her mouth shut with a click of her teeth. Color spread across her pale cheeks. "You must be fae-struck. I can't think of any other reason you'd speak such sweet words and set your mind to this insanity. I could kill you by accident, caught in the bloodlust. Everything I am looks for opponents as strong as you to fight and destroy."

"Aw, now, I've not once let you land an actual blow in any of the times I've tangled with you." He grinned and tugged her closer. "There's no other way you'd strike me, faery. Your glamour doesn't work on a man who knows you as well as I do."

"Not true." There was no conviction in her whisper.

"We won't find out any time soon. Will we? Because you've not used your glamour on me once." He didn't have to see the truth in her eyes for confirmation. He'd had enough of faeries and their glamour in the last couple of nights to know it when he encountered it. And she'd been honest from the very first about the magic only being able to fool one set of senses at a time. No. He knew because she'd been herself with him from the very first. It hadn't occurred to her to appear as anyone else. "Think. Why? You know it."

"And if you know, why are you asking?" So vulnerable. Fear cracked her voice.

"I love you." He caressed her cheek. "And because I do, I need to hear you say it, faery. Say it for me."

She leaned into his palm, her lids falling over her eyes until her long lashes cast shadows across her cheeks. "How did so much happen in the light of a few nights? I've lived centuries and never believed I could fall so fast."

And she wasn't speaking of the night before, soaked in gore and reveling in killing. No. She'd been there before, a different battlefield. Kayden's confidence swelled. Their first night together, though, that was when everything changed.

"One of these days we'll compare our centuries and see which of us is the elder." His own voice came out gruff. Now, when she was so close to saying the words he wanted to hear, everything in his chest tightened. It mattered more than he ever could have imagined it would.

"I love you, Kayden." She sucked in a deep breath of air and lifted her gaze to his. The full force of her being crashed into his. "I've loved you since the moment you kissed me on a battlefield and now, more than anything, I want you to kiss me again."

SURVIVE TO DAWN

BOOK 3

1

———————

Danny decided to give the humans two more minutes to argue their cause with Seth before he stepped in to save them from themselves. His alpha had a firm leash on his temper, but it was notoriously short. This particular group of scientists was clearly trying the limits of Seth's patience.

"The cage is integral to our purposes, you see." The older human kept his eyes down, his posture relaxed, and used no sudden hand gestures to punctuate his argument. No movements to trigger a defensive and potentially violent response. "We need tissue samples."

"Plenty have been taken, but if you're in need of more, our teams can hold the zombies." Seth ground out his assurance.

True. Seth himself had held one or two of the mindless dead while Danny had taken the samples. As shape-shifters, they were immune to the zombie virus that could turn the human scientists into the very blighters they were trying to study.

"But if your people hold the zombies, they'll kill them right away." A woman stepped forward, right up to the quarantine line, too fast in her urgency. Danny's attention, as well as his alpha's, fastened instantly on her. The British soldiers on the outside would've been too slow to stop her from crossing into London even though they were standing just a meter or two from her. She dropped her deep brown eyes a second late, but at least she'd remembered. Looking a werewolf in the eye was a challenge, aggressive behavior, especially when entering their territory. Werewolves, like all predatory shifters, tended to deal with such acts immediately and definitively. Primal instincts were an integral part of who they were. Anyone attempting to cross the quarantine line was supposed to receive a werewolf primer now, as the London pack had absolute authority within the city. Based on this team's behavior and the relaxed attitude of the military guards, it might be time to look into reinforcing those. Luckily for the woman, Danny and his alpha had more control than most and could allow her the leeway.

Seth let loose a low growl. The color drained from her tanned face, but she held her ground even as a couple of the other scientists retreated a few steps. Several of the soldiers tightened their grips on their weapons.

Jumpy around the big bad wolves, eh?

They might be on constant guard on the quarantine line, but they didn't have direct dealings with Seth often. Danny fought to keep a properly stern expression. Based on his alpha's relaxed posture and the lack of anger in his scent, Seth was amused. But then, the both of them appreciated a woman with a spine. And this one was a right beauty to boot.

Medium height, a touch on the leaner side, with the natural bronzing of someone who spent a lot of time outdoors someplace sunny. Her dark hair was pulled back in a serviceable ponytail, but a few escaped strands framed her heart-shaped face. Very pretty. Currently, her lips were pressed together in a thin line of stubborn determination and that did even more to hold his attention.

"We need samples from the same specimen over time. Your people can't eliminate the ones we catch right away. There'd be nothing left to test after the accelerated decomposition leaves us with just ... potting soil."

"Actually, what's left after a zombie is well and truly dead is a bit drier than the stuff they use for plants." Danny scratched his chin, enjoying the woman's surprise when he spoke up. Very focused, this lass. She forgot to lower her gaze. Since it didn't prick his temper, he gave her a wink. "But then, nobody I know has been mad enough to try setting up a garden from the stuff. Might be worth a go, see if it's actually good for something."

She blinked. At the sight of her baffled expression, Danny could hold back no longer. He grinned at her.

Her gaze darted back and forth between him and Seth, but lingered on him. "Th-the hypothesis we're testing revolves around the effect of our experiment over time, like I said. Samples from different individuals would skew the results, introduce unnecessary bias to the findings." Dusky rose stained her cheeks.

Good, the interest was mutual. "As much as I personally do enjoy the very lovely sound of science passing your lips, lass, it doesn't change a hard and fast rule. If you had sent your study protocol on ahead to Brian, he'd have told you the same."

Danny would've been interested to read it, regardless. Their experiment sounded structured more to test a potential treatment. The usual kill-the-zombies-instantaneously solutions the science-types had been trying to develop generally meant a one-time, lethal dose.

"The protocol and the related investigational drug product are proprietary." She pressed her lips back together, just for an instant. "It wasn't available for dissemination to anyone without top-level security clearance. Plus, we require a signed nondisclosure agreement."

The way she shaped words, took a breath as she was about to let loose a long sentence in one go ... he liked it, wanted to coax her into a more in-depth conversation. The bigger the vocabulary, the better, as far as he was concerned.

Oy yes, talk science to me. It's a bit of a thing for me.

Besides, she wasn't only cerebral. She was clever. She'd given him a touch more of what he wanted to know while telling him she couldn't. The pleading look she was giving him now convinced him not to ask more at the moment, but he wouldn't mind a chance to get her alone and have a little chat. He liked several aspects of that idea.

Seth shook his head. "Too many zombies in the city as it is. We can't afford to keep however many you decide to capture for study and risk having them loose again, especially when you don't know what will happen once you do ... whatever it is you plan to do to them. I won't have cages in the city. Too many cretins have used them for the wrong things."

Others, trophy hunters, had left bait in their cages. Live bait. Danny's vision swam with red at the memory. Volunteers would have been bad enough, but no. They'd taken street urchins, orphans too young to know what they'd been nipped out of the alleys for, too hungry to question until they couldn't escape. If their pack ally, Kayden, hadn't rescued Ollie and the boys, they'd have eventually been set up for the same.

The atrocities people were capable of committing on each other never ceased to horrify Danny. It hadn't been only Seth to go on a rampage that night. Danny had let go of everything human as he'd let his rage loose on not only the zombies lured to the site, but on the bastards who'd devised the traps too. They'd been able to rescue a few of the children, but not all. And the trophy hunters? The wolves had ripped them apart and left them in the park. A better death than they deserved. Cleaner.

Since then, no cages in London.

Of course, there were a few other taboos too, but only one came to mind that would anger Seth more.

It was best for them all if they avoided the topic.

The woman had collected herself and returned to championing her cause. "While we were able to demonstrate a significant effect on the tissue samples sent to us, in this phase we'll look to demonstrate the effectiveness on an actual, animated specimen. We need the cage to hold a zombie so we can monitor the effect of the vaccine injected over time. Samples need to come from the same zombie at each of our planned time points to provide comparative data. It's key to the next step in our research."

Danny perked up. Good to know the tissue samples he'd been sending all over the world were being put to some use. If there was a cure, it needed to be found. Things were far past the containment point and something decisive needed to be done soon.

Seth sighed. "We have rules for reasons, miss ..."

"Deanna, everyone just calls me Deanna." Her eyes opened wide with hope.

Ah no, the big-eyed puppy look wouldn't work on Seth. 'Course, if she decided to turn that look on Danny, no telling what would happen.

"Deanna, then, even if you and your team have good intentions, letting the cages into London is a mistake. They could be stolen. Other things could happen to your team." Seth's voice took on a grim tone. Too many groups of humans went into the parks either to try their hands at the latest "dangerous game" hunting or to study the walking dead. Most of them ended up eaten or as zombies themselves. "Based on our friend Brian's recommendation, we're willing to offer pack escort into the city and for the duration of your studies. But, as alpha, I'm not going to break my own rules. The cages stay outside city limits."

She opened her mouth to argue, but one of her other scientists called out, "You can't just step all over us and tell us what equipment we can or can't bring. We have the United States government's backing on this research trip."

Seth stood straighter, the muscles across his back tensing. Governments and politics were a sore spot. Parliament's lack of action had allowed the zombie outbreak to take over and lay London to waste. Officials had been frozen by the horror of it, convinced it must be some hoax or some ridiculous drug overdose, limited to a few of the poor in a free clinic. They'd not wanted to recognize it as a true epidemic, hadn't taken measures to keep it from spreading through the whole city. By the time quarantine protocols had finally been enabled, it'd been too late. Interference now, be it from the same government or another, stuck in Seth's throat.

The scientist who'd spoken out, a man in his early thirties, glared at Seth and Danny from a distance he probably thought was safe. "We've got plenty of guns and ammunition to defend ourselves if it comes down to it. Don't treat us like kids on a school trip. We don't need you."

"Others have come in with bigger guns. They're all

dead." Seth dropped the fact like a stone. No need to raise his voice for dramatic effect.

The American jutted out his chin. "Your parliament wants us to find out why you haven't gotten this under control. Our government needs to be sure it doesn't reach our shores. We've got their joint backing on this, plus the eyes of the United Nations on us. No one wants this to spread to the main continents. If you stop us from conducting our studies here, they might as well nuke the place!"

Danny held back a sigh. Now the man had gone and done it.

"You have your precious *government backing*." Seth bit out the words. "I've no say in that, then. Bring whatever your bloody papers say are approved. But remember, the British soldiers here don't come past the quarantine lines. Their primary orders are to ensure no zombies or potentially infected get out. You can enter London and bring your blasted equipment with you, but you'll not have the protection of my pack. We will not protect you from your own stupidity. Think hard on that."

"Please, be reasonable." The lead scientist lifted shaking hands.

The other man made a rude noise.

Seth lifted his lip in a snarl. "We have been more than reasonable. We've made our conditions clear. It's a different world in there, ladies and gentlemen. You don't go in following our rules; you go in at your own risk."

Seth turned on his heel and walked away. Danny watched the group of scientists gather together in a babbling huddle, caught the slight shakes of heads from the soldiers at the quarantine border.

This wasn't going to be the end. He'd have to keep an eye out for those damned cages.

SETH BARELY WAITED until they got out of human hearing range. "And what was that all about?"

Danny raised his eyebrows, kept his mouth shut and continued walking toward the center of London. Even at the ground-eating pace they could manage, they'd barely make it back to pack headquarters in time for evening patrol.

Seth growled, his temper still riding him hard. "Don't you pretend you don't know what I'm talking about. I'm in the middle of being the bad guy and there you go flirting about with the lass. You knew I had to tell her what she didn't want to hear. Why draw it out longer?"

Danny dropped his head in apology. "I'm sorry about that. No sense in it, I know. Dunno what came over me. Something about her."

He'd wanted to be around her longer, maybe convince her and her group to take the safer route and stay under pack protection. "She's one of those bright spots, you know? I thought I'd gone numb to all the trophy hunters, these groups of scientists. Seeing them go in every few weeks. But her. I don't fancy having to face her as a zombie some day and give her mercy."

And it'd been happening lately. They'd been fighting the zombies long enough. The walking dead weren't just the nameless tourists and citizens of London who'd been there during the original outbreak. Now, more and more of the faces he saw were familiar, recent acquaintances ... could-have-been friends.

Seth let out a huff. "I'd stop it all if I could. But the

tourists coming in are the only economy London has right now. The people living here need the income and supplies the tourists and trophy hunters bring. Otherwise, we're not self-sustaining and those living here haven't got what they need to make their own way."

"I've sent the government my test results, the data I gathered on the incubation period." A werewolf with a degree in biology? Even the soldiers at the border hadn't bothered to hide their surprise when he'd first approached them with his reports. Danny snarled in frustration. "But they won't set up a holding area for observation. Won't relocate the people that *do* want to leave. Not unless they can prove they can make a living someplace else. Only, how do they know where they'll be allowed to go?"

The people who'd had the means to leave London had gone at the first outbreak. Those with family, friends or business connections elsewhere to give them a place to rebuild their lives. Those who were left were the poor souls with no place to go and no way of fending for themselves even if they did leave. It was heartbreaking.

There was a moment of silence. Then Seth bumped Danny shoulder to shoulder. "Not all of the people living here are lost, Danny."

"I s'pose not." He looked around at the buildings lining the street. Most were empty. But a few had occupants, businesses still open, modified to cater to the trophy hunters and thrill seekers. Bed and breakfasts, supply stores, even pubs and souvenir shops. As long as the werewolves worked with the human police to keep the more populated areas safe, life moved on. And miracle of all miracles, the humans appreciated the werewolves. In his two centuries of living, Danny had never thought he'd experience that. A child peeked out from a curtained upper window and waved at him before disappearing with a giggle.

"Lost, boys?" The tart question floated to them on a breeze as Maisie came around the street corner. "Does this mean we're off to go hunting pirates? I could use a little adventure."

She gave Danny a warm smile, but her gaze heated in a completely different way as she turned her attention to Seth. The pack leader folded her into his arms, giving his mate a hug tight enough to lift her off her feet, careful to set her down with enough time for her to get her feet under her. She was his match, born human and new to being a werewolf.

"Thought you were working at the clinic today." Seth's voice had taken a gentler tone, one he only used with Maisie. A few of the wolves had mistaken it for weakness in the beginning, though they soon learned different. When Seth hadn't bothered to hide the tenderness he showed his mate, several had challenged him. Danny'd had to patch most of them up because Seth had torn them apart so badly they couldn't heal fast enough to keep from bleeding out.

"I helped with a few of the hunting dogs." There was a flippant breeziness to Maisie's statement and her pause had both males waiting for the qualifier. "But then a hunter's wife came in with her bird."

Ah, well then. Couldn't be helped.

Seth reached out to caress her cheek and she leaned her face into his palm. Danny looked away quickly, before he saw the tears he knew must be coming.

Maisie's Change had saved her life. But it'd changed it too. Prey animals couldn't ignore the predatory aspect of her nature anymore, not as a werewolf. The smallest and most delicate went into shock under her gentle touch. The others simply cowered in abject terror. So, when people brought their birds, rabbits, hamsters and guinea pigs to the clinic, Maisie could no longer treat them. She had to focus her efforts on the dogs and cats, the domesticated predators. And even those, more often than not, reacted to her in fear.

Very few, if any, natural animals could take on a werewolf.

"Fat lot of good I am." Maisie huffed out a mirthless laugh.

Danny reached for something to turn her mood. "People still keep those little puffs of feathers?"

"Yeah. Apparently, they do." Maisie drew in air through her nose and let it out slowly through her mouth. "This one was one of those sweet trainable ones that talks to its owners. It froze in its mum's hands when I walked in. Couldn't get it to respond at all. So, I decided it was a good time to take myself out for a breather."

"It'll be fine, sure enough." Seth rumbled his reassurance. "Brian will see things to rights and send the woman on her way so you can get back to your little dogs and kitties. Especially the one who tries to steal my pillow."

That coaxed a smile out of Maisie. The tiny kitten Seth had found and given her had retained his general disregard for his own safety and grown into the pack mascot. A werewolf pack, with a pet cat.

"Besides, it's good you've joined me." Seth slanted a glance in Danny's direction. It was the only warning Danny had. "I was about to ask Danny about the very pretty human he was sniffing about this afternoon."

Bastard tossed him right up onto the proverbial altar as a sacrifice to the gods of distraction. Bloody hell.

"A lady?" Maisie definitely perked up. Aw, now that she

had the scent, she'd not leave off until she'd got the whole of it from the both of them.

"A science-type." Seth didn't bother to hide his amusement. "Not too far from your age, I'd guess."

Maisie had only been a werewolf for a few seasons. Danny was centuries older and Seth ... he was *old*.

"So, you liked her, hmm?" Maisie had paused and planted the ends of her crutches wide. She wasn't planning to budge until she'd gotten what she wanted to know.

Only one answer came immediately to mind. "I don't want to see her dead."

"She did get feisty, didn't she?" Seth was just aiding and abetting.

Danny fought the smile tugging at the corners of his mouth, but he lost. "She did, at that."

Maisie only stared at him harder.

Seth wasn't done, though. "Aye, well, you could've knocked me over with a feather to see Danny with his nose to the ground, one ear cocked to catch every word she said."

"Get on with you." Danny scowled. "I did nothing of the sort. You make me sound like a hound on a scent trail."

And he wasn't *anyone's* hound.

"You took notice of her." Seth said the words slowly, chewing on them. "I've not seen you interested in a woman in at least a year, maybe more."

Now both the alpha and his mate were studying him. If he'd been in wolf form, their thoughtful regard would've had the fur along his ruff standing on end.

"We've had a bit of an apocalypse to be dealing with." Danny tossed up his hands in frustration.

"There's never been a more important time to take notice." Seth jerked his chin toward the trees lining Bayswater Road. "Outsiders like to think we keep the zombies in check, keep them concentrated in the parks and gardens. And we do keep the streets safer, no mistake there. But we've lost half a dozen wolves to the blighters in the last year. A wolf gets too cocky, lets himself get outnumbered, and we die as surely as anything else. It's just harder to kill us."

Danny kept walking, unsettled and not certain where his alpha was going with his line of thought. But he kept his strides short, because Maisie was with them and he'd not cause her the discomfort of trying to keep up, no matter how unhinged he was.

"We're long-lived but we do die eventually." Seth might have been talking to either Maisie or him. "The zombies proved they can eat even the immortal. Sorcha's Seelie lords weren't happy to learn that particular bit of news when she reported back to them. It's a good stroke of luck they agreed to allow her to work with us."

Danny was betting the Seelie lords were more than happy to direct Sorcha's half-berserker blood madness toward the killing of zombies as opposed to watching her go slowly insane in the fae realms Under Hill. He'd helped care for her after she'd cleared literally an entire battlefield of zombies deep in the levels of Notting Hill Gate station. Her mixed heritage was hard on her, every bit as hard as being dual-natured could be for shape-shifters.

Maisie made a thoughtful humming noise, drawing his attention. "Speaking of Sorcha, and Kayden, you make sure you make good use of the time to live while you're busy surviving, Danny. Take notice of the things that interest you, even if you don't properly know why."

Brown eyes flashed in his memory, framed by wisps of dark brown hair. His gut tightened in anxious worry he hadn't realized he'd been experiencing until now. "They don't have a chance without us, not this close to nightfall. Wouldn't put money on them seeing tomorrow. Best we can hope is not to be running into what used to be them again."

The sky was already lighting up gold, the magic hour before sunset. One of the few sunny days they'd had through the winter. It would be brief though. Darkness fell fast in the gardens.

"You're not on the rotation for patrols tonight." Seth was studying the trees, specifically facing away from Danny as they walked. "I'll not be looking for you on your free night.

Danny didn't say a word, only stared incredulously at the back of Seth's head. It was Maisie who craned her neck to see past Seth's shoulder and catch Danny's eye. She raised an eyebrow at him.

"I'll not go back on my decision." Seth continued, "There will be no escort for the group. And mind you, I'd have assigned several wolves to try to keep those sheep safely herded. We've seen enough daft acts of heroism gone wrong."

No. Not for the group. Danny had learned he couldn't save them all. It'd been a hard lesson, a long time ago. But he could check on the woman, make certain she at least made it through the night.

Maisie shook her head and turned her focus back to the street in front of them. "Don't wait for her to shoot you, Danny."

2

—————

"They're dead! They're all dead!" Flecks of spittle flew from his mouth as he screamed. "Ron, Karen, George, all of them. Why couldn't they run fast enough? Th-there was no way to save Professor Reyes. The zombies, there were so many. And where did Jason go? Oh my G—"

Deanna finally caught up with Tom, grabbed two handfuls of his shirt and shook him, hard. His head rocked with the force of it and his babbling ceased.

"Shut up." The warning came out as a low hiss. "The noise. They'll be attracted by the noise. We've got to be quiet."

"We're safe down here." Tom's gaze darted left and right in the darkness. But he quieted. "They stay in the parks, right? We just have to cross under the main roadway and come up outside the park."

Deanna hoped he was right. They should have paid closer attention to the briefing they'd been given, but they'd been so sure they were prepared to defend themselves and their research site. Even the added warnings from the soldiers about what it was like to face a real, hungry zombie hadn't sunk in for any of them.

She loosened her hold on his shirt. It was almost too dark to see. Only a very few lights remained intact in the pedestrian subway and those flickered, leaving ghosted afterimages in her vision. They'd reached a junction point and she peered at the signage in the murky gloom.

"This way. Follow me. The other hall leads to a parking garage. You know, what the Brits call a car park?" Tom murmured, having calmed. "I was here for a conference once, before the epidemic."

They took a few steps and Tom reached back to take hold of her hand, giving it a reassuring squeeze.

"A bunch of us went out bar hopping, stumbled down through here to get to the hotel. Back then, if you didn't go under like this, you were dodging multiple lanes of cars with no cross walk." He chuckled quietly. "If we all found our way back to the hotel drunk off our asses, you and I can get through and come out away from the hell-forsaken park. It's only a few more yards."

Deanna stared at Tom. What little of his face she could see gleamed with sweat and his skin was ghostly pale under smears of dirt. His hand was clammy holding hers. He'd gone off the deep end. Had to. How did anyone go from all out panic to telling stories about blitzed business trips?

A scraping noise pierced her with renewed fear. She tightened her grip on his hand.

"It's fine …" He'd started confident but trailed off in a whisper.

Another scrape, too faint to place the direction. Was it in front of them or behind? The tunnel made it impossible to pinpoint. Deanna drew a ragged breath and almost choked on the stench of decomposition.

Oh please no ...

A form detached from the shadows, towering over both her and Tom. She opened her mouth and a scream tried to claw its way out.

"Shh." The thing was talking. Its voice was low, strangely distorted. But it was talking and they weren't dead. Yet. "Crouch down here, against the wall."

Deanna's knees buckled. The command brooked no argument. She didn't even think to disobey. The rational part of her mind ran in tight little circles as he moved into the light. Six, seven feet tall? Muscular and covered in fur. His face ... mostly wolf but strangely, the eyes, they were human.

"W-werewolf!" The word left Tom in a rush of breath and he fell back on his behind. He began to babble nonsense, getting louder and more shrill. He scrambled crab-style for a moment and then turned, got his hands and feet under him.

"No! Not that way, ya daft ..." The werewolf snarled. Then he turned and fixed his baleful glare on her. *"Stay."*

Nope. Not going anywhere. Did she say it out loud? Were these things people said when they were about to die?

Tom began screaming. The werewolf darted after him. In the darkness of the corridor, all she could see were shapes, too many to be just Tom and the monster. More snarls, and the sounds of something hitting the walls with bone-crunching impact. A head tumbled past her feet and her own scream finally broke free.

The face wasn't Tom's. Not Tom.

Skin hung off the skull in shreds and the eyes were clouded over with a sickly milky grey. Black gunk oozed from the base. Whoever it had been, they had been dead a long time. It was one of the animated corpses.

There were zombies in the dark and Tom had gone right to them.

A strange pressure was building in her chest and a detached part of her mind realized she was holding her breath. She gasped in air.

A thick miasma of rot and bowels had filled the tunnel. The sounds of struggle reached her as she became aware of her surroundings again. She clasped her hands over her ears, trying not to recognize Tom's pained cries in the midst of the ripping and tearing. Wet, black drops splattered across her lap. Blood.

Funny, of all the horror surrounding her, this was the least disturbing. Blood, she'd seen plenty of. She focused on it. Thought about it. Then she pressed her hands over her mouth and squeezed her eyes shut.

The zombie infection was a virus, spread by bodily fluids. She wouldn't allow any fluid to transfer through her eyes, mouth, anything.

"Deanna."

Her eyes flew open and she stared around wildly. Tom was crawling toward her. No, dragging himself toward her on his belly. His forearms were bleeding. Whole chunks had been ripped from his flesh. In one or two spots near his elbows, white showed through. His bone? No. More likely his tendons.

All those thoughts flashed through her mind as she struggled to deal with what was happening logically, as *she* tried to cope.

Tom was reaching for her. "Deanna. The vaccine. We can fix this. We can ..."

She shook her head. "It's preventative only. It can't cure you. It can't."

"You *have* to." Tom's face twisted into an awful, angry

grimace. "Bitch. You are going to save me. All you have to do is *want to* bad enough. I'll bite you myself and make you save us both."

Deanna shrank away from him. He'd been a genial colleague, but not anymore. Now, he was a man trying to save himself ... even if it meant killing her. She didn't want to end here. She had to defend herself.

Harm none.

Even now, she couldn't strike out at him, couldn't kick him away. He dragged himself closer, reached for her again. She fumbled inside her shirt for the tiny leather pouch she always kept with her, prepared for emergencies. Yanking it free of her clothing, she squeezed her eyes shut and focused. Years of discipline cleared away the fear, the panic, and for one brief moment, she had the peace she needed.

Stay away.

No words were necessary, only the clarity of her intent. The ward activated. Tom tried to reach for her and came up against an invisible barrier. His eyes widened as he searched wildly for a way past, but she was surrounded by a protection of her own making. Tom cried out in rage and anguish and balled up a hand, beating at the magical ward.

"You can save me. I know you can save me!" His words turned to harsh sobs. "I don't want to become one of those. Please, no."

Deanna trembled, struggling to hold on to the ward and the power behind it. "Stay away, Tom. Don't come any closer."

"Don't leave me like this." His pleading ripped at her heart.

A shadow loomed behind him, moving too quickly and too silent to be one of the walking dead. The werewolf had returned.

"No one can save you." The words held no cruelty. In fact, the hard fist around Deanna's lung eased a fraction at the compassion in the rough voice. "There's no cure, but you don't have to become one of them."

Tom turned his upper body, his legs not quite working. He craned his neck to face the werewolf. "You mean you'll kill me."

"Yes."

Tom swallowed audibly. "I don't want to die."

"None of them wanted to either." So calm, full of under-standing. "I can make it quick for you. Stop the pain."

Who was this?

"D-don't kill me." Tom turned to face her, despair turning to anger as his eyes narrowed. "You could have saved me. I'll never …"

She hadn't seen the werewolf move. Suddenly he was between Tom and her, and his strong arms gathered her to him. For a moment, she breathed in spicy musk, and then the air left her in a huff as he tossed her over his shoulder. The ground dropped away and they began moving at a dizzying speed.

Her ward. He'd come right through her ward.

"No! I'm sorry!" Tom's scream echoed off the walls. "Don't leave me!"

"Tom. Six."

"What?" Danny scanned the city street for other dangers. Contrary to cretin hunter beliefs, the zombies did leave the parks and were more likely to do so at night when they were more active. When she didn't say anything more, he turned back to where he'd placed her on the steps of an abandoned building. Then he did a double-take.

She stared straight ahead, kept her gaze fixed on a point somewhere beyond his shoulder. He followed her line of sight and saw nothing, heard only the normal sounds of the night. But he wasn't hearing something important from her.

"Breathe." He kept it just shy of an order, tried to gentle his tone. "Breathe for me. That's it. Then you can talk."

Her shoulders relaxed a fraction and her chest rose nice and slowly. The frantic hammering he could hear in her chest eased back to a steadier pace. Good.

A single tear caught the moonlight as it fell down her cheek.

Full moon tonight— plenty of light to hunt by. Her team must have thought it the perfect night to begin their studies. When Danny had come across their tracks, he'd followed the trail from one body covered in feeding zombies to the next. He hadn't stopped or even slowed, not when the zombies would have turned on him and not when he still had the chance to save the living. It'd been Tom's shouting that had led him to Deanna and their fresh trail. Couldn't have saved the stupid male. Only her. And Danny would spare no regrets about it either.

He brushed the tear from her skin and resisted the urge to lift it to his mouth to taste. He must be going mad. "What were you trying to say?"

"Tom." She blew out air in a slow, controlled stream. Tried again. "He was the sixth. The entire team is dead, half a dozen gone. There's only me. Otherwise, I'd ask you to help me go back to save them."

Brave woman.

Every sentence had to have taken effort. She wrapped her arms around her upper body, as if she could hold herself together. It'd be a bad time to tell her he wouldn't have gone back. Even if they'd been alive when he'd rescued her, her colleagues would have been dead by now. As stirred up as the zombies were, returning to that part of the park now would be a suicide mission.

Still in phase-form his hands had claws, so he carefully grasped either side of her head, tilted her face up until she couldn't help but meet his gaze. The fear had receded and only the residual ghosts of the trauma she'd suffered remained. And she wasn't afraid of him. He'd have seen it in her eyes, smelled it in her scent.

He could waste time being glad about it later.

More importantly, her eyes weren't dilated and she wasn't showing any alarming signs of physical harm. She'd suffered a bad scare, yes, but she had the chance to recover from the events of this night.

"You haven't lost any blood as far as I can see or smell. You're not likely to fall into shock." Nor was she likely to turn into a zombie herself. A huge relief, that. When he'd finished killing the last of the zombies in the tunnel, he'd turned to see her colleague reaching for her. Thought he'd been too late. "Still, I'm going to take you someplace where I can care for you better. You might have other, less obvious injuries."

She opened her mouth but no words came out. Finally, she nodded. Mute. Faint tremors began to take over her body, increasing until she was shaking hard enough for her teeth to chatter. Reaction was setting in. He needed to get her to Brian's clinic quickly, where she could be cleaned up, warmed and made to feel safe. Get some food into her.

It was important. The need to take care of her gripped him hard and he didn't want to waste time sorting out the why of it, only get it done.

He didn't toss her back over his shoulder. This time, he gathered her up in his arms, cradled her against his chest. "You're safe now. I've got you."

Her body was stiff against his. "Who are you?"

"My name is Danny. You saw me earlier today." Bollocks. He shouldn't remind her, not when his own alpha had denied them escort.

"Not the man I talked to, not the man who warned us. You don't sound like him." She placed a hand on his chest and leaned away from his as much as she could with him holding her, studying his face. "You were the Asian man, standing to one side."

Why was he relieved she could tell the difference while he was in phase-form? Or maybe he was just glad she wasn't blaming him and Seth for the deaths of her team. He definitely wasn't preening over the way she seemed to remember what he looked like in human form. Not at all.

"My ethnic background is East Asian, yeah." He'd been in London for decades now, a part of the pack. Hadn't thought of where he'd come from in a while. No particular reason. There'd been a lot to do lately, what with the apocalypse and all.

The pressure of her hand against his chest lessened and she seemed to settle against him. She wasn't looking at him anymore, her face turned down. "Thank you for saving me, Danny."

Warmth filled him.

"You're welcome." Aw, and didn't he just sound like an ass? "Let me get you someplace safer."

Her head bobbed once and then she leaned against his shoulder. "Deanna ... my name ..."

She trailed off and he stopped in his tracks. Carefully, he listened. Her breathing had slowed, steadied to the rhythm of someone asleep. Her heartbeat was there too, a touch accelerated, but that was to be expected with as much adrenaline running through her system as she must have. He'd get her hooked up to an ECG at Brian's clinic to monitor for tachycardia. Poor lass had probably just succumbed to exhaustion. Well, he wasn't going to have her safe and warm anytime soon if he didn't start moving again.

Deanna. He'd known already, but she'd introduced herself to Seth and not to him directly. Somehow, it mattered she'd given him her name herself. It'd been a close thing tonight. And not yet over. Now he'd found her, his alpha might boot her clear out of the city.

As he walked, he was careful not to jostle her too much. He split his attention between watching for danger and studying her, or what he could see of her, gathered against him as she was.

He shook his head. What were the chances this woman and her scientific team would break the biggest taboos the alpha of the London pack had?

Ah well, he'd pick that worry up later. She was safe. For the first time since he and Seth had left the group earlier, the wildness inside Danny settled.

Whoever this woman was, whatever else she was besides human, she mattered to him and now he had her.

"WHAT HAVE YOU GOT THERE, DANNY?" Brian's question might have been light, but the human motioned him toward one of the bigger examination rooms usually used for werewolves as opposed to the normal rooms closer to the front.

"A survivor." Danny was loath to put her down, but

neither he nor Brian could examine her properly if he was still holding her.

"Usually it's Maisie who brings in the strays." Brian stepped over, but stopped when Danny growled. "Easy there. You want me to assist or just leave you to it?"

Danny struggled to get his temper under control. What was wrong with him? He'd never gotten this unhinged, not even when it'd been his pack members on the table. "Sorry, Brian. You're a friend to the pack. No doubts there."

Brian held his hands up, a faint smile playing over his lips. "No worries. I met Seth under similar circumstances. I recognize the signs. You think she'll need fluids? I'll just nip out to get an IV and solution while you examine her for further injuries. All right, then?"

Tension eased across his shoulders and he nodded. "Thanks."

And what was he going on about with talk of signs?

"Oh, and Danny ..." Brian paused in the doorway, waiting until he tore his eyes away from the woman. "You might want to shift back to human form to conduct the examination. Just a thought."

Bollocks. He didn't have to sound so damned entertained though. When'd been the last time Danny had forgotten what form he was in when working with a patient? Still, the man had a point. Deanna was a human with an even more delicate bone structure than many. Even though Danny had excellent control in phase-form, he'd be better able to see if she had any broken bones or sprained joints if he handled her with his human hands.

Familiar pain seared through Danny's limbs as bones and muscle, teeth and claws reformed. Shifting to human form took him a minute or two. Longer than Seth, but faster than any other wolf in the London pack. Seth was older and the alpha, so there was no surprise there. But Danny had the best control over his various forms and the volatile nature all shape-shifters had. Some of it might have come from his being the pack medic. Danny had always believed the fundamental nature of any man remained, human or shape-shifter. He'd always been a healer at heart.

His trousers had remained intact throughout the shift from human to phase-form and back to human again. Good thing too. He wasn't inclined to go back out to the front desk to find a spare pair of sweats; the woman needed looking over.

He ran his hands over her limbs gently, paying special attention to her wrists and ankles, her knees. It was only luck that none of the black, rotted blood liberally splattered over her clothes wasn't anywhere near the breaks in her skin. Still, he'd best clean her up and get her a change of clothes.

"How's she looking?" Brian waited for Danny to acknowledge him before stepping back inside the room, IV and saline bag in hand.

"No breaks or sprains as far as I can tell. Minor abrasions only." Danny went to the small sink at the other end of the room and retrieved a few clean cloths and antiseptic wipes. "Chance of infection is low. The blighters attacking her and her team were all the slow, shuffling things. None of the faster, more dangerous ones."

"We've seen fewer and fewer of those since Sorcha and Kayden rooted out the cause and took care of it. Sorcha has been lending us a hand tracking down any of the remaining fae charms used as lures, as well. She said it's not within her talent to make the repelling charms but she'd see if any of the lesser fae returning to the city might have the capability. Never thought I'd live to meet a real fae, half-blood or otherwise. But it's damned glad I am she came along and helped us." Brian brought a small metal tray laden with supplies over to Danny. "Good thing too. Rate of infection from one of their bites was exponentially faster."

"I don't smell rot or gangrene in any of her scrapes." Danny began to wipe down her hands, careful to remove any zombie blood without smearing it. "I'll be sure once we get these soiled clothes off her and there're fewer scents to distract me."

A pause. "Deanna might not appreciate you stripping her down while she's unconscious."

Danny froze. Ally to the pack or not, Brian might become a rival fairly quickly. "You do know her, then."

It'd been Brian who'd asked for the pack's help with this specific scientific team. Danny had figured Brian had known the lead scientist, but hadn't anticipated Brian would know his woman.

"In passing." The growl rumbling in Danny's chest receded. Brian lifted a chin toward the prone woman. "She's why I asked you and Seth to meet them at the quarantine border to offer escort. I've corresponded with her online regarding her research. Not many scientists bother to keep an updated profile picture available, but I recognised her from hers."

Struggling with the odd twisting in his gut, Danny couldn't decide whether to be defensive or relieved the acquaintance was so minor.

Brian chuckled. "I've been around you werewolves enough to know when to keep my distance though. My connection to her is purely academic."

"Good." Danny didn't mind Brian's amusement over the sudden possessive streak, so long as he wasn't a rival. As males went, Brian was a safe one to have around Deanna.

Human and medically trained. Besides, Brian's quick thinking had saved Maisie once upon a time.

Finished with cleaning Deanna's hands, Danny wet a fresh cloth with warm water and wrung it out before turning to clean her face. Beautiful, even liberally splattered and tear-streaked. High cheek bones and a graceful jawline, plump lips. Hell, even her nose was perfect. Symmetrical and pert. More dark strands had escaped her ponytail and he gently brushed them to the side as he wiped away the evidence of what she'd been through, wishing he could do the same for her memories. Encounter like that, losing her friends and colleagues, wouldn't be easy to think on anytime soon.

Long lashes fluttered open and her dark brown eyes darted right and left before her gaze locked onto his. Every fiber of his being responded. His muscles tensed, his pulse quickened, and he was suddenly very glad he had trousers on.

She blinked once. Twice. "Danny."

3

Deanna struggled to swallow against the dryness of her throat.

"Thirsty?" The voice, like the face, was familiar. It conveyed safety in a way she didn't know how to explain. "We can forgo the IV if you think you can sip water for a bit, then we'll get you a proper cup of tea."

It took her a few long moments to make sense of what he was saying. Then the virtual gears in her mind started to turn and she nodded. Yes, a drink would be fantastic. Maybe something stronger than water or tea.

The man, Danny, looked over his shoulder and nodded once, then returned his attention to her. His hair was dark, a perfect ink black. He wore it short and neatly trimmed around the sides but longer on top. And that top was a mess. Models probably paid big bucks to manage the sort of effortlessly mussed, yet hot, look he had going right now. But it was his eyes that caught her attention. Exotic, in a way. Slightly slanted, with just a hint of softness over the eyelid. Hard to pin down why, but those eyes drew her into every expression. His mouth too. So why was it the eyes?

An image flashed across her memory. Fur. A muzzle with gleaming white fangs. And those eyes...sable pools of darkness.

W-werewolf! Tom's voice echoed inside her head.

"Why don't we try having you sit up, slowly." Danny slipped an arm under her shoulders and she clutched the other hand he held out to steady her as he moved her to a sitting position. "Feeling dizzy?"

Yes. But she took a few deep breaths and carefully shook her head. "No."

"Right, then. I'll stay close, just in case." Give her another few minutes to come back to herself and she'd let him know just how bad he was at pretending to believe her.

More memories tumbled through her mind now. How he'd stood out, a wolf amongst the soldiers and other men at the quarantine border, even hanging back the way he'd been. And later, in the tunnel, a huge shadow amongst the others. The monsters. She'd thought he was one too initially, only he hadn't killed her. He'd brought her here instead. Wherever here was.

You could have saved me.

Oh, Tom. Everyone. Gone. And she hadn't tried for Tom. Couldn't.

"Here's water. I put it in a cup with a straw. Makes it easier to sip." Another man came in, pale-skinned with sandy-brown hair. "Sure we don't want to get a line into your vein and hook up an IV, just to help things along?"

She shook her head again. Still not a good idea. She waited for the world to stop spinning.

"Nah. Thanks, Brian." Danny reached out to take the drink without releasing her. She was oddly relieved he'd backed her up.

"Thank you, though." She wrapped both her hands

around the water and sipped. It slid down her throat, wonderfully cool. Her stomach didn't cramp or otherwise rebel, so she took another taste. Brian, Brian? The name, the city ... "We've corresponded, via email."

The other man laughed and took off his glasses, cleaning them with a handkerchief from his shirt pocket. "Yes. I'd wondered if your team would reach out to me before you went into the park."

They should have. Oh, they should have done a lot of things, like paid real attention to the alpha's warnings. "Tom and the others wanted to find a site and get set up right away. Wanted to take advantage of the first night to capture specimens. We'd all figured we could touch base with you in the morning when the zombie activity had gone dormant."

Huge mistake. Even armed, they'd never stood a chance. There'd been so many, coming in twos and threes then all at the same time.

Brian's gaze held sad sympathy. "I'm very sorry for your losses."

Emptiness. She couldn't even be angry, not at the wolves or soldiers or anyone. Her logical mind was too practical and the replay of all they'd done to spite themselves kept her from laying blame on anyone else.

"We brought it on ourselves." Tears welled up, burning her eyes. How could they have all been gone, just like that? But they were.

Danny's arm tightened around her, comforting.

"Well." Brian cleared his throat in the awkward silence. "Why don't I go rouse the boys and send them to fetch some soup? They'll be up for an errand and could do with a bit of a run. You'll be needing some supper too, Danny?"

At first, Danny's eyebrows drew together in a scowl and she thought he'd decline. But then his expression cleared and he sighed. "Protein would be good. A burger or whatever is easy for the lot of them to nip out of the pub at this hour would be fine. There's a wolf on watch along their way."

Brian smiled at them both and left the room, closing the door behind him.

After a moment, she asked, "Where am I?"

Let me get you someplace safer.

She remembered those words, his voice. He'd brought her someplace he considered safe. Gratitude filled her. He could have easily left her out on the street once he'd gotten her away from the zombies.

"At a clinic." He stepped away finally, and her shoulders were cold without the reassuring press of his arm. "Think you can stay right there while I get you a change of clothes?"

"I can manage." The edge she heard in her own words did wonders for her confidence. She was feeling more herself, even if her brain hadn't quite caught up yet.

He lifted one corner of his mouth in a lopsided smile. "Just don't fall off until I can get back to catch you."

Her cheeks heated as he left the room. He'd carried her all the way here. Far? She had no idea. How long had she been out? And what the hell nonsense had she said?

She dropped her head and pressed her palm into her forehead.

"Here now, I was serious about the not-falling-off thing." Danny let loose a few choice curses as he rushed back into the room, a wad of fabric in his hand.

That was fast. Must not have been a long way away.

"I'm fine." And would rather fall off the damned stretcher than admit how embarrassed she was.

He paid her no mind and instead dropped his bundle onto the hospital bed next to her. He lifted her chin so he could peer into her eyes. Then he pulled an electronic thermometer from a nearby drawer and clamped the sensor around her index finger. "Once we get you changed into those, I'd like to take an ECG just to make sure all's right with your heart."

"We?" She cleared her throat. Tried again. "Excuse me, why do *we* need to get *me* changed? I am perfectly capable—"

"Let's get you standing for now and take things easy, why don't we?"

She ground her teeth. Savior or not, there was a limit to the amount of patronizing she was going to take. "Why don't you take a step outside the door? I'll take my time about getting dressed and then we can talk about the ECG."

"I'm staying and you're going to let me help you." His words pushed at her, distinct and demanding.

Dominance. She wondered if he even realized he was asserting it. Hopefully not. Oh, it had come in handy in the situation in the tunnel, but they weren't there anymore. And she wasn't some pup to roll over and give in on nothing but his say so.

"No." She lifted her gaze to his and mustered all the willpower she had to keep from looking away. Moving slowly and deliberately, she swung her feet over the side and slid off the edge, reaching way down until she had solid footing. Why was the bed so freaking huge? Oh. Considering her rescuer, yeah, they treated werewolves here. Big ones. "I can stand. I can get dressed on my own."

Those sable eyes darkened further, if it was even possible. He started to say something, stopped, and the muscles in one cheek twitched. "Compromise. If you want to dress on your own, fine, but I'll not be leaving the room."

"Wha—"

He held up a hand and she thought the corner of his mouth lifted. A little. Maybe. "I'll stand over here and keep my eyes on the wall. You'll have your privacy." He tilted his head to one side. "Outside is too far for me to get back to you if you do have a problem. This way I can stay close enough to help, but you still get to do things on your own and maintain your ... virtue."

She narrowed her eyes. He was teasing her now. But it was better than the patronizing from earlier. "Agreed."

He gave her a full smile then and her heart skipped. When he faced the wall, he presented her with a defined, muscular back. She gulped and this time her whole face warmed. Not that she hadn't seen a man in various stages of undress before, but none of her lovers had been quite as physically fit. Then again, none of them had been shape-shifters either.

As she began to undress, she wrinkled her nose. She'd been too distracted to notice, but the fabric stank of decomposition and was stained with random fluids she'd rather not think about while it was next to her skin. She'd save the clothes though, to analyze later. They were the freshest samples she had access to.

Her hands shook as she stepped out of her pants. How would she collect them? And what would she store them in?

She really didn't want to go back to their camp site to try to get the rest of their equipment. Definitely not alone. Not even in daylight. Would she find the bodies of her colleagues in the area? Or would they be walking dead in the coming nights?

"Alright, then?" Danny remained studying the wall, but his words were tinged with concern.

"Fine." Her response had been too terse. Leaving her underwear on, she fumbled with the simple sweatpants and huge sweatshirt. Hell, she probably could have gone with only the shirt and been covered to her knees. "You can look now."

He was at her side so fast, she hadn't seen him move. He was simply there. All she could focus on was how very near he was, and how incredibly defined his torso and abs were. A rich, earthy musk filled her nose and she wanted to breathe deeper, nuzzle his skin and get more of his scent. The man needed to get a shirt on and she needed to come to her senses.

He lifted a hand and she watched as he reached for her. But all he did was move a strand of hair off her cheek, his fingertip brushing a hot line across her skin. "Let's get some more water into you and hope Brian comes back with some hot tea."

"Tea? We was told to get soup!" a tenor voice called through the closed door.

Danny chuckled. "Would you mind sitting again, before the puppy pack tumbles in?"

Sit? Yeah. Good idea.

He helped her back up onto the stretcher. She assumed because there weren't any chairs in the room. Before he left her, he gave her ponytail a playful tug. Gah, her hair. She pulled the elastic free and quickly finger combed it back it into some semblance of order before tying it up again.

"Soup!" Once Danny opened the door, a gangly boy darted in holding up a brown paper bag. The boy's bronze skin was the deepest tan she'd ever seen. And his pitch-black hair stood up in a shock of spikes as if he'd been hooked up to a Van der Graaf generator.

"Thanks, Ollie." Danny plucked the bag from the boy's hand.

"Oi, I heard Danny brought somebody back." Another

voice piped up from the doorway. Not one head popped into view but four, stacked one on top of the other as the boys all craned to get a look. They must have been piled on each other's backs just outside the door.

"A lady-friend," Ollie confirmed.

"Hi there." Deanna gave them all a wave. A chorus of greetings returned to her and she couldn't help but smile.

Danny let out a huff. "Deanna, these boys are Ollie, Dan, Dan, Dan and Dougie."

She wouldn't laugh. Nope. Not at all. "So, there's four Dans, right here?"

"He's Danny." The one boy with the mop of unruly brown hair indicated the adult werewolf with a thumb. "These are Peas, Goggles and Doc, so as no one gets confused."

"Why ..."

"Don't ask." Danny gave her a pained grimace and a minute shake of his head. "You really don't want to think about it until after you've had your soup."

All righty, then.

"I know, and I don't want to think about it at all." A big man stepped up behind the boys, taller than Danny and maybe a little more muscular. Still lean though, with dark hair and pale skin. He moved forward, making them scatter into the room as he filled the doorway. She remembered him, the London pack's alpha. He nodded to Danny and then turned his attention to her. "Deanna, is it? It's good to see you safe. I'm sorry for your losses."

He sounded sincere, despite the clipped delivery. She was guessing he wasn't a man prone to using his words more often than necessary. "Thank you."

"What were ye doin' out in the gardens, anyway?" the one known as Peas piped up. "Seems a bit daft."

"I'm a scientist." 'Course, she also wasn't going to argue with the kid's assessment either. All in hindsight, of course.

"Ye studying the zombies then? There's some've tried it before." Doc jerked his chin toward Danny and puffed out his young chest with pride. "Only person t'get good samples is our Danny. He and Seth went out and got them."

Deanna nodded. "I studied some of them before coming here. My ... my team and I were trying to isolate the nature of the virus that causes the infection. We were hoping to test a vaccine we'd developed."

"Ye mean a shot, like with a needle?" Ollie shuddered. "Don't hold with needles and things."

Seth simply stood in the doorway, letting the boys do his interrogation for him. Deanna hadn't missed the amused look on his face as he took it all in. She didn't mind, really, but a part of her wanted him to know she was onto him. Irrational, but there it was. Still, it was easier to answer the boys, less of a strain.

"So, how's a virus make a person a zombie? Like catchin' yer death o' cold?" Goggles snorted.

Dougie pushed a lock of hair out of his eyes. "I read in this novel, yeah, that a virus could be used as a carrier. Like it could be used to spread DNA into cells through the whole body, cause mutation. Turned the human heroine into a panther shape-shifter."

Doc shrugged. "Kayden's already a big cat. Bet his blood carries that kind of virus. And the werewolves would 'ave the same kind of thing, only a little different."

"Oi, that book was science fiction *romance*. Why'd you even read it?" Goggles snorted. "They'll not be turning the zombies into big cats. Fat lot of good the idea will do anyone."

"That's not the point." Dougie gave Goggles a shove. The other boy balled his hand into a fist.

"Actually—" Deanna pitched her voice loud enough to cut off the impending scuffle "—you're quite right, Dougie. We can use a virus as a vector to carry the genetic material we want to introduce into host cells so they begin producing certain proteins to defend themselves from other viruses. It's exactly what I'm trying to do."

"Dead things can't catch a virus," Seth cut in. "Shooting zombies up with a vaccine won't cure them."

"No." She drew the word out to give herself time to think. "Not under natural circumstances."

"What kind would you describe, then?" Seth crossed his arms. All the boys grew quiet.

There was a tension in the air, a silence stretching taut. Waiting. Children could be sensitive to those sorts of things, especially those who'd had it rough. She watched the boys, using their body language to gauge the sudden weight of the situation.

They didn't move away from him, which would have made her suspect bad things about Seth and his temper. Werewolves were rumored to be violent creatures, full of uncontrollable rage. But she hadn't seen that in Danny earlier. Rage yes. And violence. But not uncontrolled.

No. The boys just didn't want to distract Seth. Wise of them, probably. When he was waiting like that, it didn't seem like he'd be too happy with what he might hear next. And controlled or not, pissing off a werewolf couldn't ever be a good idea. Too bad she wasn't as smart as the boys.

"Zombies aren't normal in any case. There's a supernatural component animating them."

"True. But then, shape-shifters aren't what anyone would call normal either." Seth scratched his chin. "Actually, there's so many supernaturals in this city, I'm beginning to think *normal* doesn't mean precisely what it used to mean."

At least three of the Dans in the rooms snickered, including adult Danny.

"Maybe supernatural would be the wrong term to use." Deanna shook her head. "Shape-shifters have an affinity with the natural world. Zombies are drastically different. Whatever animates them is a twisting of nature, the kind of manipulation only a witch—"

"Witchcraft isn't the answer." Seth bit out the words. Suddenly, he wasn't just filling the doorway. His angry presence filled the entire room.

Every one of the boys paled. Their eyes grew wide.

"But ..."

Seth lifted a lip and snarled.

Danny was suddenly by her side, not standing between her and his alpha but definitely interceding. "Alpha's decision is pack law. There's to be no witchcraft in London."

Deanna couldn't stop herself. She let her jaw hang open, incredulous. "How can you arbitrarily deny any help that might put an end to this epidemic?"

Seth rolled his shoulders. "You mean well, and because you do, I'll explain. But listen, human, really listen. 'Tis not an academic debate. Witchcraft was attempted early in the epidemic; 'twas a botch job." He sliced his hand through the air in a downward motion. "All it did was turn back on the user, the way it always will, and innocent people died. It's not reliable and it is not a viable solution. Any witchcraft within city limits will mean expulsion or elimination. No exceptions."

The alpha decisively ended the discussion by leaving.

"That's it? Easy as that?" Deanna couldn't help sputtering.

Danny remained silent, staring after his alpha. Every muscle in his body was tense. Glancing down, she wondered if his fingernails were cutting into his palms. He was squeezing his fists so tight.

Deanna's frustration bubbled up. Over? Oh, hell no. She was on her feet and out to the hallway before anyone stopped her. "Hold up."

Seth kept going.

She needed to think, quickly. Playing hardball wasn't any good when you had nothing the other person wanted. He was the one in charge, and thus far all he'd asked for was respect ... which he hadn't been given. She tried a different tact before he got completely down the hallway.

"Please."

He paused. When he faced her, one eyebrow was askance and he did not look entirely open to discussion. But it was better than nothing.

"Okay, no debate. I get that. But the research wasn't my only reason for coming here. It wasn't even the main reason why *I* needed to get here." She tried to convey how important this was to her. 'Course, she'd compartmentalized it, tucked it away under the professionalism of her work. Needed to in order to make herself invaluable to her research team. But the protocol didn't mean anything to this man and she needed to convince him to let her stay. And all she had was a few simple words. "I need to find someone."

Those eyes, they weren't cruel. Hard, yes, surrounded by fine lines of worry and the wear of tough decisions. But they saw what mattered. She met his gaze directly and poured everything she could into the connection.

"I need to find what's left of my family."

Seth sighed but his stance remained rigid, back straight, chin up. "You can stop to make an inquiry with the constable's office on your way out of the city. The human police have records of what survivors—"

"She's not a survivor." Deanna breathed in through her nose and tried to relax her throat as it threatened to constrict around her words. He'd have no use for her tears. She needed to give him something more practical, actionable. "I would know if my sister was alive. Trust me. She's not."

"I'm not sure what there would be to do then." His tone had gentled. There was sympathy there.

"I know the chances of finding her body are next to impossible. I'm not looking for her. I'm looking for something she left me. It's somewhere here and if I can just find it ..." A true part of herself, her thoughts, her dreams, her secrets. "She left it for me so I would know what happened to her. And that's all I need. How she died. Why she died. I came all the way across the ocean to find those answers. Please."

A warm weight settled on her shoulder. She glanced down to see Danny's hand.

"I'll keep an eye on her, Seth. See to it she doesn't get herself into more trouble."

Seth's expression softened, the hard line of his lips easing into a slight frown. "Fine then. You can stay until you find your answers. Then, well, we will talk again."

Hope flared inside her chest. "Thank you."

Danny hustled her back into the examination room.

"That was quick. I thought it'd take more convincing." She was happy to resume her spot on the stretcher since her knees seemed to have gotten wobbly again. The charisma the alpha had was heady stuff, and he was more intimidating than any man she'd ever encountered.

"Seth is decisive. He's very good at assessing situations

and doing what needs to be done." Danny pushed the cup of water back into her hands. "Drink."

"Oi, you're no common lady." Doc ran his fingers through curly hair. "Most'd piss their trousers when Seth stared at them like that."

"You don't, though." She shouldn't have shot back at the boy. It was immature, and the kid had meant it as a compliment.

"It wasn't us he was angry at, was it?" Doc shrugged, unruffled. "We all got experience to know when he's got an issue with us. You're new, and all."

Couldn't refute the logic there. They all knew each other better than she knew any of them. Danny, the boys, Seth. She was the outsider.

"One o' these days, Seth is gonna scare some poor git to death." Dougie pushed away from where he'd been leaning against the sink.

"Don't be daft. Seth, he's scary and all, but he can't kill someone jus' by scarin' 'em ..." Goggles trailed off, chuckling uncertainly.

Deanna tipped her head to one side, considering. "People can die of fright. Don't doubt it for a second. The adrenaline rushing through them is more than their body can handle and their heart just ... stops."

"This used to be Maisie's flat." Danny waved Deanna through the doorway.

The room was neat, sparsely furnished and didn't have a hint of personality anywhere. The walls had been freshly painted. Even the windows looked new, pristine as they were and set into the weathered window frames. "What happened here?"

"Let's just say the rooms on this floor were badly in need of renovation." Danny leaned in the doorway. "Once Maisie moved in with Seth, the pack decided extra quarters above the clinic could be right handy. A good thing too. Turned out to be the best place for the boys to stay."

But what could have happened to trigger a complete renovation? And the boys, where had they come from? Where were their families?

History. Stories behind all of this. And it was obvious she wasn't considered close enough to learn those stories. It shouldn't bother her. She'd come for two specific reasons, and then she'd be returning to the States.

"You seem to be chewing on a few things." Danny sounded curious.

She wandered toward the window, and touched the cool glass. "With the chaos out there, I guess I hadn't thought there'd be families here, making lives for themselves. That's what you all are, in your own way, a large family unit."

He straightened, crossed his arms. "And what was it you were expecting instead?"

"Maybe a more militant atmosphere? I'd thought there'd be more police or soldiers in the streets." She caught her lower lip in her teeth as she considered, struggling to pull her thoughts away from the garbled mess they were in and back into something useful. "I knew the trophy hunters came through, but I thought their hunting was more structured. Maybe passes or tags issued for them, and places for them to check in before going into a park as big as Kensington Gardens. Our team was surprised when there was nothing, no checkpoints or manned posts anywhere. The military had briefed us on the hot zones and provided some basic information on what could kill zombies. They acted as if they'd provided all the information necessary. But they've no real presence inside the city to gather additional intelligence."

"Seth warned you." No censure, no accusation or gloating. "The military doesn't come any farther than the quarantine and the local police work with the pack. In the night, it's safer for even the police to stay indoors and let us take over. But it's a big city, and we can only patrol. We can't be everywhere at once. When your group decided to go against our rules, you went without our protection. Seth tried to be clear what that would mean."

His words were offered as gentle facts. And still, they hurt ... because he was right. They'd all been so confident, arrogant even, in their assurance they'd know far more than any part-beast. They were all the best academia had to offer. Their prejudice hadn't occurred to them consciously, but it had colored everything the alpha had said, and they'd paid the price.

"I'm sorry." It came suddenly, but she meant it. "For what we said earlier today and for the disrespect."

"Ah now, don't go apologizing for words you didn't say." Danny dropped his arms and took a step toward her.

"But I was there and we were all trying to get our way. We didn't stop and truly consider what Seth had to say." And she had a lot to think on regarding what his alpha had most recently said to her as well. Sleep wasn't high on her list of things to do anyway, not with the memories she had lurking at the edge of her mind.

"Well, I imagine you'll have the opportunity to tell Seth yourself, if it still eats at you later. But there's no need to apologize to me."

She nodded. Fine. "But I do owe you my life. 'Thank you' doesn't seem to cover it."

Danny ran his hand through his thick hair. Embarrassed? "Don't think on it too much. Life is a debt not easily repaid and I'd not ask it of you. I'm glad you're safe."

She studied him. Why had he been out there, in the night? He still hadn't put a shirt on and she wasn't inclined to mention it. All those wonderful muscles bunching and sliding under his pale skin. She wondered what it'd be like to run her hands over …

"Well, then." He slapped his hands against his thighs. She almost jumped at the sound. Not almost, she did. "I'll leave you to get some rest."

She was an adult. It wasn't as if she was alone. The boys

were each in shouting distance. Brian was only a floor farther away.

Besides, she had the power to protect herself, if she needed it.

They're dead. They're all dead.

She could keep the physical monsters at bay, but she'd no defense against the nightmares she was sure were waiting for her.

"Wait." It slipped out and she didn't want to take it back.

Danny froze, more than halfway out the door.

She thought he might leave anyway, but he stalked back toward her. He didn't stop until he stood so close the heat of him warmed the chill of her skin. How could he be so near and not touching?

And she wanted him to touch her. She'd only just met him, yet he was the only person who'd ever given her a sense of safety. Ever. Not just tonight.

When he spoke, his voice was deeper, gravelly. "I should be honest with you. I'd very much like to stay and occupy your mind with things having much more to do with living than the things you've seen today." His hand came up slowly, giving her plenty of time to step away. She didn't. He brushed his fingers across her temple and reached past her head, tugging at her ponytail. "But you might not be quite yourself yet, after the scare you had. It was no small encounter out there. It isn't in my mind to be taking advantage of you."

Her cheeks began burning. Pheromones. Of course he could smell her attraction to him. He was probably more attuned to body language than most people were, too.

"Just now, though, your scent changed from very, very interested in me to frightened. I don't want to leave you afraid and alone." Warmth. Concern. His words washed over her, soothing away the momentary spike of panic. "Do you want me to stay?"

A moment passed, maybe two. He was waiting for her answer. No impatience, no prompt or any attempt to hurry her into making a decision.

"Yes." She opened her eyes and studied him, wondering what he'd do next. She wasn't sure what she was hoping for, but her chest squeezed in a good way with the anticipation. "Please."

He pinned her with a searching gaze, his brown eyes inscrutable. She waited, held in his regard as surely as if he'd had her head locked in both his hands. "Then I'll stay."

Her heart skipped and she bit her lip to hold back her smile of relief. He'd think her desperate or silly or ... she had no idea but her thoughts were all sorts of jumbled.

He chuckled and stepped back, opening up the space between them again and releasing the tension. "Well, then, let's get you tucked in, little witch."

Wait, what?

Nerves jangled and her stomach clenched. "I—"

He shook his head. "Only a witch—or someone with experience of them—would mention witchcraft as a potential solution for this plague. And considering what I saw earlier tonight, we'll not pretend."

"But Seth—"

"Is Seth." He jerked his head in the direction of the hallway. "And you mind what he has to say on the matter. But me ... you can be who you are with me, at least."

Her insides settled as she absorbed his statement. She wasn't sure she liked being referred to as "little" though. But she wasn't going to take it to the obvious big, bad, fairy-tale reference either. He wasn't a fairy anything.

"I meant what I said earlier." He'd had no problem

reading her confusion, apparently. "I've every intention of revisiting this once I'm sure I'm not taking advantage, so remember where we were, right there."

She blinked. He had a point. And it wasn't as if she could fault his chivalry. Still, when was the last time she'd ended up frustrated this way? He gave her a lopsided grin and moved to sit on the floor beside the bed, his back against the wall. Reaching up, he patted the bed.

Fine. She seated herself on the edge, legs crossed and facing him. She would *not* sulk, even though she had the irrational desire to do exactly that.

She did have questions for him though. "How did you know I was a witch? You knew, before the discussion downstairs with your alpha. You weren't surprised at all."

The boys had all gone round-eyed at the mention of witchcraft. She wondered if England, maybe all the European countries, had a deeper wariness of witches. Witch families were much older here.

"The man with you, he was going to bite you." Danny's voice was low, but there was a simmering undertone, a hint of restrained rage. "He threatened you to get you to save him, and still you wouldn't strike out."

She hadn't realized Danny had seen so much. She'd thought him occupied by the zombies.

"It was too late." Sadness washed over her and guilt clung to her, heavy. "He was reaching for the impossible."

"He was reaching for you." Warm hands gripped her upper arms, squeezed with only enough pressure to keep her in the here and now. He was on one knee at the side of the bed, facing her. "And I heard what he said. Taking down the remaining zombies took too long. I couldn't get to you in time. Your friend—"

"Colleague." Distancing herself might not help, but it

wasn't anything less than the truth. The entire team had been on good working terms but none of them had been close.

Witches didn't let too many get close, if they were wise. A sacrifice had more power when the victim held sentimental value and too many witches had died trying to save their friends or loved ones, even their familiars. Black witches excelled at double sacrifices, first the loved one and then the target witch.

"Your colleague, then. He couldn't touch you. There was nothing there to stop him and yet he couldn't. I've never seen such a strong ward at that close a range. You had no time to put it up."

His words brought it all back ... the look of hate etched into Tom's face.

So he'd seen witchcraft. It hadn't always been banned, maybe. Or he'd witnessed it elsewhere.

"It might not have been me he was after, so much as what I had on me." She reached into her shirt, pulled out the carry case, holding it in her open palm for him to see. "I had one of the auto-injectors with the latest version of the vaccine we've been developing. It's to be injected as a preventative measure in the living, though. It can't bring back the dead. Didn't make sense for anyone else but me to carry it. I'm the only one who can administer it. But he wasn't thinking clearly."

"None of the others had the power. He threatened to infect you to force you to save you both." Danny's lip curled up in dislike.

"Yes." She gave him the truth in a whisper. Seth had hated the idea of witchcraft so much, she wasn't sure where Danny's tolerance would end. "Witchcraft is required to activate the vaccine during injection."

"Are you that powerful a witch, then?" His voice had dropped to a deep rumble. The anger was still there, underlying, but she didn't think ... hoped it wasn't directed at her.

"No. Yes." She bit her lip. "Maybe."

"Which is it?" He arched an eyebrow at her. "There's only a few ways I know of for a witch to be powerful, and the variable one involves killing innocents to steal their power from time to time."

Anger rushed through her, searing away her hesitation. "I wouldn't. Not ever. My sister and I lived our childhoods in fear, wondering if some coven was going to find us and use us for sacrifice. Do you know how much power could be had from a bond as tight as ours? More so because we are ... we were identical twins?"

His expression gentled, a minute relaxation of the lines around his eyes and mouth, the set of his jaw. "Well, then?"

"With her, I was always more powerful. When our combined intent was aligned. Not just multiplied by a factor of two, but amplified by each other." And the pain of not ever experiencing that gestalt again never left her. "*We* were that powerful. And individually, we had more latent talent than most of the remaining witch families, but our magic was ... quirky."

"How so?" The anger had receded, though his volume remained low. She wasn't fooled. He could still be dangerous. She and her sister had learned early in their childhood to be wary of quiet predators. The loudest bark held no bite.

"Oi, the worst harm you'll suffer at my hands is a firm escort back to the quarantine border." What had he read in her face? His voice softened further. "I can give you my word on it. I'll not harm you, Deanna."

She bit her lip, then nodded to let him know she believed him. And she did. Somehow.

"Helen's magic worked better on the macro world. She could affect animals, people. Her talent made her the best Finder in the country. She could cast a spell to track a person by a simple object they'd held for just a few minutes. Helen was that good." And now, she couldn't be found. Irony there. "Mine has more influence in the micro world. Cells, bacteria, microorganisms. My magic seeks them out, influences them, changes them."

"And so the vaccine ..." Comprehension tinged his words.

Not just a medic, no. He had a fundamental understanding of living things from the building blocks of life upward. Her own intuition told her so. He might not be conscious of it, but she was.

She gazed up at him then. "Without the whisper of my magic, a person could pump themselves full of it and it wouldn't save them. My magic tells the carrier virus what to do, the DNA what to seek out."

And she could have administered it to Tom. Could have taken the chance that the vaccine would move through his system faster than the zombie virus. They didn't have any data on the exact progression of the infection. She could have ...

Danny squeezed her arms again, giving her a slight shake. "Hey, stay with me. You go too far, think too hard on it, and you'll get trapped in all the could haves and would haves. Give yourself a rest and get some distance before you try to look back on it all."

She reached for scattered bits of thoughts, tried to address his earlier observation. "No, he couldn't touch me. The ward. I'd prepared it as a last line of defense against a zombie. Only good for my personal space. Couldn't protect more than one person. The ward didn't have enough power for that."

"That's more than most witches could manage nowadays." Danny eased away from her, giving her room to clear her head.

Latching on to his knowledge, she focused on the tangential topic.

"The old families are scattered and the bloodlines are mostly broken. Talent pops up unexpectedly now, like a random mutation in a gene pool. It'll take generations to breed strong family lines again." She paused. "I thought the European families had gone into hiding, or what was left of them. They broke contact with the witches in the US, especially when the American covens started taking anyone with talent, ignoring family trees. I'm not sure when you encountered witchcraft here, but it was either a long time ago or a rogue witch."

Like her. A witch without a coven.

He chuckled, rich and warm enough to send shivers of a completely different nature down her spine. "Scientists in this age don't believe enough in magic to tie it to any genetic origin."

"Doesn't mean it isn't."

"Ah. But magic has this way of being unpredictable. Sometimes it has a will of its own."

She nodded. "Where have you seen witchcraft?"

"You'll not find it in this city. Not anymore." The corners of his mouth turned downward. "And for good reason. Seth's lover was a witch, though she didn't belong to any coven. A rogue, you call it? Learned on her own. Back then, we were stretched too thin, trying to get the initial outbreak under control. She wanted to help, wanted so badly to show Seth she could contribute, protect the pack. She tried to cast a spell to send the zombies to a specific location, where they could be controlled and put down. It backfired on her, best we can tell. A large number of zombies were drawn to her instead. She thought she had the power to keep herself safe, but she didn't. And good wolves died trying to protect her too. If Seth'd been there, he'd have died himself. As it is, he's not forgiven himself ... or her."

Oh no. "I'm sorry."

Danny lifted one shoulder and let it drop. "It wasn't you. But you need to respect Seth's word as law on the subject. There will be no witchcraft until the zombie threat is neutralized."

"But you, you don't have the same hard line." Might not be safe to fish for it, but she had a hunch. And she'd never ignored those.

His mouth twisted. "Magic isn't much different from weaponry. It's not in and of itself an evil. What Seth is afraid of is ever seeing someone die again because they relied on magic. Same could be said of a weapon. The minute a warrior relies too much on the quality or strength of their weapon and not enough on their given presence of mind, they are lost."

Very true. Too many people looked to magic as the one-stop shop solution to all their troubles. Too often, it only complicated things.

She searched for safer topics and couldn't think of any. Maybe a different direction on the current one would be better. "But you've encountered witches in your life, before this epidemic?"

He made a rude noise. "I've traveled several continents and encountered more practitioners of magic than I'd have liked to. The ones who truly are harmless never did anything to attract anyone's notice. Those doing harm to themselves or others, whether by accident or design, those are the ones I remember."

Anyone would. The desire to protest, to explain to him the witch's promise. She'd long since given up the argument out of practicality. Those who didn't know generally weren't open to being educated. And too often, the purity of the promise had been tainted in any case.

"Some of us still follow the old ways, the traditional promise."

"*Primum non nocere*. Do no harm." Danny raised one eyebrow. "And it almost got you killed. Tells me a lot about you, the way you hold to your beliefs even in the face of a sickness worse than death. And so I'll ask you now to promise. If I am to help you find out more about your sister, you won't practice witchcraft here."

No one knew where the oath originated or how. Only that it began among healers. And Danny must be old to be a traditional healer. Why else would a werewolf, of all beings, state the very core of medical ethics, the precursor to the Hippocratic Oath? And witches had been healers too, once upon a time. Some of them still were ... or hoped to be.

She bit her lip. He'd said so himself. He wouldn't have gotten to her in time.

He reached out then, placing his hand over the auto-injector case for a moment before lifting higher. His fingertips tracing her collarbone until they hooked on the cord holding the leather pouch around her neck, lifting it free of her shirt. "Only these, and only to save your life. Nothing more."

On an intellectual level, she was certain she could find the clues she needed to learn what had happened to her sister. She could search in daylight, avoid the walking dead where her group of scientists had attracted them. But her gut told her she needed this man. Not only because he'd rescued her, but because their meeting had changed the course of their lives and such things weren't always coincidence. He'd met her and he'd saved her.

And would again and again, if need be. Another hunch. A scary one, if she thought on it too hard. She'd never been as good at foretelling as her sister had been. Never had faith in her own predictions. She'd always believed she could change her fate ... if she wanted to.

"I promise."

He nodded in acceptance and withdrew his hand, letting the leather pouch drop back against her sternum. His touch had been featherlight but it lingered, tingled. "You won't need to use it, though."

"No?" She licked her bottom lip as she pushed naughty thoughts to the back of her mind. Not thinking straight. Must remember.

"I'll be protecting you now."

His kiss caught her by surprise. She gasped as the heat of his lips pressed against her own. His tongue swept in, gently tasting, and she answered back in kind. His hands slid over her forearms and glided up to grip her shoulders as he deepened their kiss, sent her drowning. She grasped his wrists, anchoring herself and trying to make sure he didn't let her go. This. She needed this.

He let them both up for air and he let loose a quiet growl. "I meant what I said earlier, but you tempt me beyond reason."

She tightened her hold on him. "Don't leave."

He leaned forward, pressed a kiss against her forehead. "I won't. But you need rest tonight and in the morning we'll talk more on what we'll actually be doing. Let's both work on the thinking part of our brains, shall we?"

Rational thought was highly overrated.

He stood then, and slipped around her on the bed until his back was braced against the wall and his legs bracketed her on either side. Gathering her in his arms, he settled her against his chest.

"Tell me about this sister you're so determined to track down."

"Helen." Sadness washed through her, breaking past the dam she had built to compartmentalize her emotions, to function.

"How did you know where to find her?" Danny's arms tightened around her and she leaned her head against his chest.

"She was here before the zombie outbreak happened, on a trip to do some soul-searching. We'd had a fairly strict childhood. She'd been keeping in touch with an email a day, and sometimes funny postcards she found from the tourist attractions. The last one she sent me was this building in the shape of an upside-down purple cow." She laughed despite the painful memories.

"It was a bit of a circus and comedy festival. Brilliant, really, back when it was still running." He began rubbing her arm up and down in long, soothing strokes.

"In her last email, she said she was going to find her fate." Deanna chewed on the inside of her cheek. "I didn't know what she meant by that, but she said she'd left something for me in 'the place she always wanted to show me.'"

"You've never visited London before this?" His chin rested on the back of her head, tucked as she was against him.

"No. I always wanted to though, and always talked about exploring Hyde Park. It'd always been a place of natural magic nestled in the midst of an old, old city in my mind."

Still was. But the magic was twisted now, tainted. And the horror there ... she gritted her teeth, summoned back the old reasons she'd be interested in the location. "Just walking the paths in there and letting the feel of the place soak into my bones was something I dreamed of."

And now she'd remember running down those paths terrified for her life.

"What kept you?" He'd made the question light, but there was something else there.

And then the guilt crashed over her. "I was finishing my thesis on cellular permissiveness to prion infectivity."

"Prions. Like mad cow disease or transmissible spongiform encephalopathy?"

"Yes to both, though I focused on TSE. I'd wanted to pursue science in conjunction with my witchcraft, whereas Helen poured everything she was into her Craft. My studies took longer."

Danny tensed under her at the mention of witchcraft, but he'd asked to know more about her sister. "Our Craft tied us together, made our bond as twins much more tangible ... It's how I know she died."

A moment of silence. "I wondered why you didn't ask Seth to search and see if there'd been a chance she survived. You already knew."

"Yes." She had to force the word out past the grief closing her throat. "And it wasn't a bite. It wasn't any damage to her body. I'd have the scar somewhere on mine. I'd have felt it, lived it with her. Happiness and hope, frustration and pain, we shared them across our bond."

And other, intimate things. Deanna blushed. Her sister had enjoyed life, including many lovers. It'd been a part of her more adventurous nature.

"What I got from her instead was fear, and a slow aching

pain in every limb. I dreamed of my arms and legs being too heavy to lift and my vision clouding over." She sat up so she could look him in the eye. "Our bond was strongest when we were asleep. I drugged myself to stay asleep longer in the last days, trying to let her know she wasn't alone and that I was coming. But then the quarantine went up and I couldn't book any kind of travel to the UK at all, much less London."

He met her gaze and held it. The strength beneath those dark eyes rose up and buoyed her. "If you manifest the physical damage your twin suffered, it's a wonder you aren't a zombie yourself."

She'd thought the same.

"I needed to know what the zombies were. Prions were theorized as a possible causation, so I got myself a position on the research team. They could hardly refuse me, considering my contribution to the efficacy of the vaccine." Even though the team had known she was a witch, she hadn't ever explained her true interest in the research to anyone, not even to Professor Reyes. Telling Danny was more than giving him the information he needed to know to help her, it was opening a flood gate, finally allowing everything to flow out of her. It wasn't just the worry for her sister or the desire to find out what had become of her. It was the desperate need, her need, to discover what had caused the prolonged suffering and to understand it, so that Helen could finally rest. "And now I'm here, and I have to go and find what she left behind for me."

"Where is this place in Hyde Park, the one she always wanted to show you?" Suspicion tinged his question. He already had an idea.

No use dragging it out. Besides, she had a hunch that honesty, and nothing but, would be a necessity to earning

Danny's help and trust. "The huntress statue, in the rose garden."

"You two didn't make this easy, did you." He pulled her close again, firmly tucking her head under his chin. "Do you think you can go back so soon? That's very near where I found you."

"We set up camp nearby." She swallowed hard. Could only get the confirmation out in a whisper.

His arms tightened around her. "I can't take you back there if you'll go barmy on me." A pause. "I won't take you back if it will hurt you."

"You won't be able to retrieve it without me." She definitely didn't want to go back there. But the need to know overrode the terror of the night.

"Then we go." Simple. No doubt of success. How was he so confident?

5

———

"Are you sure you want to do this?" Danny studied the line of trees edging Rotten Row. It used to be a broad expanse of dirt for horseback riders. Now, the name had taken on a whole new meaning.

Staring at the line of trees and the park beyond, Deanna nodded. "Sure I am. You getting cold feet?"

Her bravado fell a wee bit flat, given her almost imperceptible trembling. Her face was pale and her heart rate accelerated, but she'd also set her jaw and her breathing was steady. Not a full twenty-four hours since her close call and she was facing the terror with the kind of courage people wrote books about.

"If a zombie approaches, let me dispatch it. Keep quiet. Noise will only attract more." He frowned as she kept nodding. "Oi, I need a verbal from you. Let me know you're understanding."

She shot him a sharp glance. "Yes."

He grinned. Good. She had a better chance of keeping it together if she was a touch riled up.

"This isn't the way our team came in." She jerked her

chin to the right, in the direction of Queen Elizabeth Gate. "We didn't see any at all as we entered from the corner gate."

He wondered, briefly, if all humans thought in terms of entrances and gates, roads and paved footpaths. Made sense, he supposed. They'd built them. But he preferred game trails and lesser-used paths.

"Perhaps not. There are a lot of wide-open spaces there. But this is closer to the rose garden you said your sister described." And this route gave him the best chance of getting her in and out in one piece.

"We didn't realize the zombies were active during the day." Her comment had been muttered under her breath, an observation.

Most likely she'd meant it for herself and not for him, but he responded anyway. "They are, but they're slower. Sluggish. And tend to stay to the shadier tree areas. You can walk a good way into the park sometimes without seeing one. It's why I made us wait until the noon hour. This time of day, you can outrun a corpse easily if there's only the one. Don't be daft and run right into the path of others. Keep your eyes open and stay near me."

"But not too near." She'd not sounded irritated, the way someone else might. She was taking his instructions seriously. A good thing. Otherwise, he'd not risk taking her in at all, not after he'd put so much effort into getting her out the previous night.

"Give me room to fight, but be aware of your surroundings while I'm engaged. Stay in the clear, downwind if you can."

"Zombies hunt by smell too?" There might be a faint tremor to her voice. She still held steady in every other way.

"Not as well as shape-shifters." In this, he could be reassuring. "They do seem attracted first by noise and excited by the scent of blood and fresh meat. If they see you, they'll come to investigate, but their vision is poor. Worse the older they get and the brighter the daylight."

"So, stay silent and don't bleed. Got it."

He grinned, and his wolf aspect stirred with the anticipation of a dangerous run. He made the shift to his phase-form. Bones lengthened, tendons stretched and realigned. Muscles grew and bulked. He embraced the burning pain of it and let it stoke the readiness inside him. Alone, he could have crossed the length of Hyde Park into Kensington Gardens and come out the other side in either form. He was fast enough, stronger than half a dozen of the blighters at a time. Here, now, he had someone to protect. He was better equipped in his phase-form.

When he finished, he looked down at Deanna. She returned his gaze, and there was no disgust or rejection there. Only faith and trust. Another thing he had to give the little witch, she had no trouble accepting the supernatural. Tourists came in to see zombies, but weren't prepared for how real the blighters were, or how real the werewolves were either.

"Right, then. In we go." He led her across the street and onto an easy pathway through the widely spaced trees. There were zombies scattered throughout, but all of them were a distance away. Not one turned toward him and Deanna.

He moved on to the dirt of Rotten Row. She kept up with him, slightly behind and to one side. Harder to stay downwind in the open, and virtually impossible to remain unseen. One or two of the undead changed their shambling course and began heading toward them. Danny crossed the road hurriedly. No sense in waiting for more to notice them.

He'd take care of the ones on their trail when they caught up.

He motioned for Deanna to duck under the rail lining the road and then he stepped over it. At his height, it was easy enough, but the rail would slow the blighters down.

Across the asphalt path was the rose garden.

He studied the archways, looking for more of the things in the shade of the trellises. One or two, far down and not paying attention yet. Leading Deanna past those, they stepped into what had become an overgrown maze.

"They're waking up." But Deanna wasn't staring at any approaching corpse. Instead, she was reaching out to lightly touch a thorned rose bush.

The roses had begun sprouting despite the lingering cold. They'd run riot in the nearly two years since the city had been overcome. No longer were they contained in neat beds. Thorned canes reached out across the pathways and upward, as if the roses were creating a fortress of their own.

"Careful." He eyed the plants with suspicion. Sorcha had let the pack know lesser fae might begin taking back parts of the gardens. Perhaps the overgrowth was to protect more than the roses. Something about the feel of this place, the quiet and the way the roses were growing to form a sanctuary made him wonder if one had taken up residence. He'd have to talk to Seth about changing the patrols to ensure this area had what additional protection the pack could provide. Both because of their alliance with Sorcha and because they didn't want zombies tasting any more fae blood.

"Can you feel it?" Her question came in a hushed whisper. "A guardian is here."

"You can sense the fae?" And that had his interest.

"Mmm. Maybe? Not with any certainty. Not here. But

there was one back at the clinic, wasn't there? Call it a hunch supported by logic. Who else would have warmed the towels this morning?" She stepped carefully through the brambles, headed toward the center of the garden. "I wondered why the boys were allowed to stay on their own in the flats above the clinic. At first, I thought it was Brian seeing to breakfast and cleaning up. Wish I'd had a bit of milk and honey to leave for the fae."

"We'll pick some up on the way back for you from one of the supply stores." Danny hadn't wanted to reveal the brownie at the clinic. But he was oddly pleased she'd figured it out for herself and wanted to pay the little fae respect. "He must have liked you."

And might have passed the word on to the fae in the gardens to watch out for her. They were uncanny, the fae. Unpredictable. Still, he'd take help where he could get it.

She turned then and gave him a smile. Here they were, in the middle of the worst place to be in the city, and his breath was catching at the beauty of her happiness over a simple thing.

He opened his mouth, then snapped it shut. He wanted to ask her more about what she could sense. Wanted to know more about what she could do.

But witchcraft was forbidden.

If he asked her, she might have to admit to him she was using it, maybe not even consciously, but instinctually. Likely would be happy to. He was walking a fine line in helping her as it was. If witchcraft was any part of what she was doing, purposefully or not, he didn't want to know. Couldn't know. Because then he'd have to stop helping her.

What he didn't witness he didn't have to acknowledge, and something strained inside his chest to let it happen.

"The huntress statue, here it is." Deanna had caught

sight of her goal and ducked under a few grey-green rose canes.

He moved forward, careful not to trample but not allowing the roses to slow him down either. No zombies in the area yet. "Don't wander too far away from me."

"Sorry." She gave him the distracted apology as she studied the fountain, no longer running with water. Diana, Greek Goddess of the Hunt, stood at the pinnacle on a short plinth in the center of a shallow stone bowl, supported by sculpted figures. "It's here."

The fur on the back of his neck and shoulders rose and he turned to catch the scent of decay on the breeze. "Do what you need to do. Stay next to the fountain."

"Understood."

She'd remembered to give him the verbal, distracted as she was. Good girl. From the edge of his peripheral vision, he saw her step over the low retaining wall of what would have been the pool for the fountain's water. He had to turn away, as not one, but two zombies thrashed their way through the roses.

The roses had slowed the walking dead considerably, no doubt about it. The corpses were torn at the arms and legs from ripping through the thorns. The little anonymous fae had done well.

Danny met the first zombie in a frontal attack, reaching out to grab it by the head and crush its skull as it futilely grasped at his arm. The second one came at him from the side, too slow and clumsy. Putrid flesh hung from the side of its face, exposing the white bone of its cheek and jaw. He swept his left arm out, catching it across the chest and sending it off its feet to land a few meters away. He leaped up and landed directly on its chest, its rib cage collapsing instantly under his weight. He finished the kill, crushing its skull. Had to be thorough with the blighters. Take out the legs or even all of its appendages and it'd still strain toward living flesh until the brain was rendered completely inoperable. For werewolves, that generally meant crushing the skulls, though Maisie had become a handy shot with her .38 Super and 9mm handguns. He'd have borrowed a gun for Deanna, but she hadn't had any training in how to handle one.

He had no desire to end up shot by accident, regardless of how Maisie and Seth met.

"I found it." Deanna's call was quiet, just above a whisper.

He turned to find her standing atop the inner wall of the pool surrounding the fountain. She had a leather-bound book folded in her arms, held tight against her chest. He'd not seen it earlier and he'd no plans to ask her where on the fountain it had been hidden or how. Stone was a natural substance, like wood, and witchcraft could manipulate either of those if the witch had an affinity for it.

"Let's go, then." He waited where he stood for her to join him, listening for the sounds of more of the walking dead coming through the roses. Instead ...

"Do you hear that?" Deanna touched his left arm, above the gore-soaked fur.

"Something banging on metal." He'd heard it earlier, but it had gotten louder. Apparently loud enough for human hearing. "There isn't a lot of metal in this area, just a gate or two, the trellises and the railing over there."

"But this is coming from the direction of our camp. The cage." Her fingers dug into his fur. "Jason was fumbling with the cage when the zombies got past our perimeter."

"You even set up a perimeter?" He regretted the question as soon as the words slipped past his blasted muzzle.

Her hand dropped away from his arm and she moved in the direction of the sound. "Scientists, not soldiers, but we did have a plan. It just wasn't good enough."

"I can come back and investigate after I get you safely out of the park." He tried to reason with her.

"We're here now. And what if someone did survive?"

Not bloody likely. But there was too much hope in her voice and he hadn't seen the size of the cages they'd brought in with them. If they'd been meant to hold a zombie, a man might have locked himself inside to keep the hungry dead away. If he'd survived this long, he could hold a few more hours, but the tension in Deanna's posture told him she'd make him carry her all the way out if they didn't look first.

"If we check, you stay with me." He growled, putting power behind his words. Her back straightened as he spoke and her lips pressed into a thin line. "If, at any moment, I think the danger is too much, I will toss you over my shoulder and leave no matter what we find."

"Agreed. Please, let's go."

DEANNA FOLLOWED Danny as he led her out of the rose garden and back to the main paths. Things looked more familiar. Her group had come in one of the main gates and followed the bigger paved walkways. With all of their equipment packed into wheeled baggage, it'd made the most sense. They'd set up camp as the sun went down, Ron picking off the one or two zombies wandering by. Too easy, really, and for a bunch of brilliant academics, they'd been—

Danny thrust out an arm, holding her back.

She stayed frozen in place as he dispatched another zombie. Clinical detachment was tough to hold on to but he'd killed it quickly and with admirable efficiency. He must've had a lot of practice. It wasn't easy to watch him crush a skull, or see the grey and black matter ooze out. She'd seen pictures and examined the tissue samples, but the reality of the organism as a whole was a thing of horror. More so because it wasn't just any organism, it'd been human.

The entire time, her werewolf protector fought silently. She'd kept a lookout for more approaching zombies. And he motioned to her to follow when it was safe to move forward. Not far.

Minute tremors rushed through her arms first, then her legs. Her hand grew numb and she clenched her sister's diary to keep from dropping it from nerveless fingers.

"All right, then, Deanna?" He'd stopped, watching her. "Take it slow. Don't think too hard, but realize what this is."

Of course. A panic attack. Different from the shock she'd been suffering when he'd first rescued her. She was immobilized, gripped by fear, not only staggered by a close brush with a fate worse than simply dying but terrified of the prolonged existence afterward.

"I'm taking you back." He moved toward her and she stumbled back a step.

No. She reached for something, anything, and found control she didn't know she'd had until she'd needed to look for it.

"Wait. I can get through this. We're almost within line of sight." She fought hard to get the words out, measured and controlled. "Just ... look. Make sure."

You can save me. I know you can save me!

If she could save someone else, maybe Tom's voice would stop haunting her. Otherwise, she was going to need to try a different approach to therapy.

Yes. Wry, clever. That was who she was. Even-keeled and able to compartmentalize even the most distracting emotions in order to get the work done. Her ability to focus gave her power, both in witchcraft and in her research. She'd had the fright of her lifetime, yes, but she'd harness it —use it to drive herself forward—not allow it to hold her back.

The panic attack receded and she steadied. She stared into Danny's gaze, stormy with a mix of emotions that might be equal parts anger and what she hoped was concern or sympathy. "I've got this. Now let's check and get the hell out of here."

Please let there be someone to save.

Danny said nothing, but he lifted his upper lip and snarled at her. The man could be scary as hell. But she held her ground. If she didn't, he'd overrule her and take her back to safety. It was imperative to show him her determination. And it worked; he turned back toward the camp. "For you. And only because you won't be able to let it go until you see."

A different kind of tightness entered her chest, stabilized her heart beat. Even if he didn't call her on it, he was going against his pack, against his better judgment. How many decisions was he making for her sake?

She'd better make it worth it.

No bodies. She'd been afraid they'd be littered around the camp and leading away. Seeing none was worse. It meant awful things and she truly didn't want to face one of her former teammates. But then she saw the cage ... and what was in it.

"Oh, Jason." Her whisper wasn't for Danny or for anyone alive.

Jason had been handsome. His blond hair had been

worn short, neatly trimmed. Ladies seemed to like the sexy five o'clock shadow he had going, especially one of the female soldiers at the quarantine blockade. He'd had tentative plans to hook up with her on her upcoming leave day, outside the city. Professor Reyes was softening to the idea of letting Jason head back to see the woman. Hell, Deanna had helped him wear the professor down, working out a rotating schedule so they all could have some leave time through the course of their planned study.

Now, his brilliant blue eyes were clouded over with grayish-white film. His tanned skin had turned pallid and the only marks on him were bite marks at his wrists. He was missing a finger. The zombies hadn't been able to eat much of him, but they'd managed to infect him.

"He died overnight. The ground all around the cage is churned up. He was irresistible. Had to have drawn them from all over the park. They could reach in, probably got hold of his hands and pulled them into range. Bit him before he could yank his arms back inside." Danny approached the cage, his voice tinged with ... guilt? "Probably died of heart failure, surrounded the way he was. I didn't see him last night. Must've happened after I came through. If I'd seen him trapped like this, I'd have done something."

Jason, or the zombie who used to be him, moved to the edge of the cage and reached for the werewolf.

"Done what?" She edged closer.

"Saved him, if he'd had a chance." Danny leaned closer, studying Jason's outstretched arm. Bone showed white where chunks of skin and muscle had been torn away. "But more likely, he'd already been bitten. I'd have given him mercy. I should now."

He hadn't killed Tom. But then, Tom had asked him not to.

"Don't kill him." She couldn't watch Danny dispatch Jason the same way as the others.

"He's already dead." A fact, given to her in a gentle tone.

"There aren't a lot of coincidences in this world." How could she make Danny understand the hunch nagging at her? "He's here. He's not a zombie we captured and he's right at the beginning of the change, isolated and hasn't fed on anything. I can take samples now and study the change over time. I don't have to come back if you don't want me to. You could take the samples for the rest of the time points."

They'd worked so hard on the protocol, she couldn't let the study go. Not when exactly what they'd needed was right here.

"I agreed to help you find out what happened to your sister."

"This is a part of what happened to her." She tried to convey how sure she was—her conviction, her absolute certainty—that this was connected. She had to convince him. "This. My sister. What's happened to your city. They are *all* tied together and we need to know. The others, they're reacting. The world changes and they move to adapt. They're not asking how or why. But you and me, we need to know, if only to warn them if something worse is coming."

A low growl emitted from Danny's throat. His sable eyes lightened to an odd gold as he clenched and unclenched clawed hands. Violence emanated from every aspect of his posture and she had to lock her knees to remain standing. He wouldn't hurt her. She knew it with the same certainty she had for what she was asking him to do.

This was the right thing.

He charged her. She closed her eyes. Didn't reach for her leather pouch, didn't activate her ward.

A groan, followed by a sickening crunch sounded just over her shoulder. Danny's arm was around her, his hand pressing her face into the fur of his chest. Her heart hammered in time with his. She hadn't been watching for other zombies. Hadn't heard it come up behind her.

"You have collection vials with you?" He never stopped growling, his words barely comprehensible as he spoke.

"Yes." She couldn't lean back to look up into his face. He kept her pressed against him.

"Don't look. Where are they?"

The zombie. It must have been one of her colleagues. Who? Ron? George? Karen? Maybe even Tom or Professor Reyes. It didn't matter. They were all dead but she was about to make sure Jason's death, at least, hadn't been for nothing.

"I have a set in my messenger bag. It should still be in the big crate near the cage." Where else was she going to keep them, in the pockets of her jeans? Jeans nowadays didn't have enough give in the pockets to carry a wallet, much less any of her supplies.

"We'll do this thing. And if you get thrown out of London, it'll be my arse tossed out with you. Probably worse." He cursed. "But it *is* the right thing."

Relief flowed through her, alongside some other emotion she couldn't define. She didn't think. Only wrapped her arms around his waist and held on tight.

6

———————

"When we go back to the clinic, don't talk about the study. Don't ask about the samples." Danny strode up the steps of the helical walkway, shifting back to human form as he did and barely remembering to keep a pace Deanna could manage. It was both difficult and painful, but helped clear his worried mind. It didn't sit well with him, doing this thing. It bordered too close on disobeying Seth.

"I won't." Her words came a little breathless so he stopped and peered out through the huge glass panes to look out over the River Thames.

"Don't even whisper. We hear things humans think we can't all the time. And you never know when one of the boys will be underfoot." He shook his head. "And never lie to us. Shape-shifters can smell a lie, read it in your body language."

"I figured." She stood near him, looking out over the view.

He waited, listening to her breathing and her heart rate. "The boys too. They spent their youngest years doing anything they could to survive. They've not lost their street smarts now they've become wards of the pack. They can tell the difference between a lie and the truth."

"Most children can, once they learn to put a name to each of them." Deanna's voice took an edge. "They usually haven't the guile to lie well themselves, but they recognize the difference."

Ah well, the boys had the guile to manage it too.

Suddenly, she huffed out a laugh. "This is City Hall, isn't it? There's a certain irony to you telling me not to lie in a government building."

The corners of his mouth turned up before he could hold back the smile. Easier to smile when he was in human form. In phase-form he looked like he was snarling. Fair scared full-grown men into pissing their pants. "Well, Seth hates politics and government, so he'd never come here. There're not many patrols as there's few people living in this area. The government officials were first out when those who could evacuate the city, did."

"And did you bring me here just to warn me not to talk or are you going to show me something too?"

He ran his fingers through his hair. Oi, she made him awkward like one of the boys. "You haven't had a chance to see much of the city yet."

And he wanted her to see the beautiful parts of it, those that were left, before she dove into her sister's memoirs. In all she'd been through, he wanted to give her something, some good memories to chase away the horror of it all. He turned and continued up the staircase as it spiraled all the way up to the top of the building. Almost all of the great panes of glass were still intact, though many of the smaller ones were broken by shotgun blasts and possibly angry citizens. Even though he had to stop once to give her a bit of a rest, she was in good shape for a human. Ten stories was a fair bit of a climb.

Once they reached what was once referred to as "London's Living Room," he reached back and took her hand in his. The viewing deck offered a panoramic view of the River Thames and the city up and down its banks.

"Wow." She squeezed his hand as she took in the scenery. "From here, you can hardly tell the city is mostly deserted."

True enough and exactly why he'd brought her. "The population of London proper is a fraction of what it was, but people still make their lives throughout the city. Coming up here, looking out over all of this, gives me a bit of perspective. This is still our home and we're working to take it back."

"There are places so far away from all of this, they pretend it isn't happening." She swallowed hard. "It's too easy to see a streaming newscast and think of it like a movie with special effects. The United States didn't have an "incident," as they call it. Too many people over there just shake their heads and figure maybe it's some sort of hoax or a sort of amusement park."

The people on the European continent, they took it more seriously. Likely because there had been a few strays who made it out before the infection killed them. So far, all of those had been neutralized before they could cause a pandemic, but it was enough to scare the countries involved and the werewolf packs that'd made the other parts of Europe their territories. It'd been Kayden and Sorcha who'd tracked down the blighters to eliminate them but the werewolf packs were ready, in case the time came.

He laughed, but there was no mirth in it. "At least half of our hunters are Americans. None of them listen to the briefings and every one of them wanders about amazed at the change to the city. As if what they saw on the TV couldn't have been real."

"Rubbernecking." She made a rude noise. "That's what I call it. Looking all around and exclaiming about how real it all is. We did it too."

He gave her hand a light tug, careful not to pull her arm out of her shoulder socket. Even in human form, his strength was more than a normal man. When she was closer, he held her against his side and kissed her temple. "It's hard for anyone to truly understand the full impact of a thing like this without seeing it, smelling it, experiencing the reality."

Though some who did went mad.

But not her. No. Here she was, in his arms. Her brilliant mind completely intact despite her close call. She smelled so good. The skin of her hand was silken soft.

"You and your pack have made this livable for the people here. Without you, the entire city would have been destroyed."

"Not going to lie to you, there are days when we look to the skies and expect a missile to come in and end us all."

He watched her hesitate, and then look up at the sky.

"We're all hoping we'll have a bit of warning."

After a moment, she scowled at him. "You've got to be kidding."

He laughed, and this time it lightened the heaviness inside him. "Mostly, yeah."

She balled up a fist and gave him a thump on the chest. He grinned at her. She did get a bit spunky, didn't she? Not too bad a hit for a woman her size either. With some train- ing, she'd be a fighter.

"The hunting attraction is genius." She gave him a wry

smile. "I don't think any government is going to wipe this place off the map as long as there are people willing to pay the fees to get in and hunt the latest 'dangerous game' and come back with the stories of a lifetime."

"Too many don't go home."

"Enough do to prove it can be done. There will always be thrill seekers out there, sure they won't be one of the ones who end up dead."

He clicked his tongue. "Humans have always been a bit mad that way, haring off to dive into some daring deed. It's as if they think they're immortal."

She shrugged. "Some people might think so. Others might be looking for a way to go. Who knows why any of us do what we do?"

"True enough." He rested his chin on the top of her head, content for the moment.

"You know why I'm here." Her voice came softly and curiosity lent a vulnerability to her tone. "But why are you, Danny? Where did you come from? Have you always been here, in London?"

"Ah no, I've not always been here. I'd wandered several continents before my footsteps brought me to this city." Though there were definitely days it felt like he'd been here forever, fighting without an end in sight. "I was born in East Asia two centuries ago, give or take a decade. I wasn't much different from Ollie and the boys. One city street is much like another when you live on it. Though every culture, every region, gives their streets a bit of a different stench. Especially when it's warm all season round."

"Centuries."

Her awed whisper brought a smile to his lips. "Were-wolves live a good amount of time. I'm not even sure how long. I can only tell you Seth is much older than me."

"Yeah? Well, time has definitely made him cranky."

He laughed. "Seth's got good reason. Leading the pack through this crisis hasn't been easy. In point of fact, I'd not thought to see a smile on his face ever again before he met Maisie. She's mellowed him out a bit."

An ache grew stronger in his chest. Wasn't that what he'd been thinking more often lately? He was happy for his alpha, make no mistake. And he was quite fond of Maisie. There was no jealousy for either of them, but maybe if he wanted to be honest with himself he'd been envious of what they had. Oh, and not anything so definite as envy. Only this dull ... ache.

"You are so loyal to him. Is it because you're part of his pack?" She leaned away from him and craned her head to look up. "Do you have no choice about it?"

He'd not take it the way others might have. He touched the tip of her nose with his fingertip and chuckled when she wrinkled her nose like a pup. "My choice *was* this pack. Wandering as I did for several decades after my Change, I was well and truly tired of being a lone wolf. Wolves and humans are both social by nature, for the most part. I needed the support and structure of those who understood me."

He understood—better than anyone else in the pack—Maisie's struggle with the part of herself that used to be a healer.

"With the pack, I have a place and people to care for. I have a leader I've always believed in." Recent doubts aside. He'd not voice those, not even to Deanna. "Seth's a good man. He'll come around once he fights his way clear enough to have a good look and take stock of the changing situation. Without him, there would be no semblance of a livelihood in this city."

"I'll have to take your word for it, since I haven't been here to see it." Her tone was doubtful but he'd let it go.

At least she kept her mind open, despite her judgment. The more he was learning about her, even as she asked him for information about himself, the more he wanted to keep her by his side. She might think she'd be leaving London after her family quest was over, but he thought he'd be able to convince her to stay on.

Or else, he'd follow her.

The realization stopped him cold. Had Seth felt this way when he'd met Maisie? So soon? If Danny thought back on it, Seth had made his choice day one.

She was staring at him and he wondered what expressions had crossed his face. He raised his eyebrows and gave her his best dazzling grin. "Besides, we're making a serious difference here. We have a cause to channel our violence and aggression for the good of the people around us. It's a very positive thing for werewolves. We have a hard time in peaceful places because there's a wild part of us needs letting loose once in a while. Here, we're valued. We might be monsters, but we're good ones at least."

"You're not a monster." There it was again, her absolute conviction.

He caught her mouth with his, drinking in her sweetness. She melted into his kiss, letting him pull her body against him. He ran his hands over her lithe form, over the curve of her bum. When he gave a little squeeze, she squeaked and nipped at his bottom lip in retribution. He liked it. Quite a lot.

"See? I rest my case." She was breathless, her cheeks flushed.

He pressed a quick kiss on the bridge of her nose. "Monsters don't steal your breath away? I can think of a few legends, find references if you like."

Her fist landed on the outside of his arm this time. "Big, bad, scary things don't make me all hot and bothered, thank you very much. And don't you try and say you haven't noticed."

Oh, he'd more than noticed. Her scent was cinnamon and spice, heated like hot mulled apple cider. Her sweet mouth tasted like heaven but he wanted to venture to far more secret places.

"I have." He let his desire darken his voice and watched her pupils dilate in response.

Her lips parted as she licked her bottom lip. "You wouldn't be taking advantage of me now."

"No. But I want to give you proper time and attention." He pressed his mouth to hers again and couldn't resist letting his tongue dance with hers for a few moments. Damn, but he could stand here for hours enjoying her kisses like this. Then again, he wanted to rip away every shred of clothing between them and bury himself inside her. He forced himself to straighten and step away. "Here is not the most romantic place in the city."

She swallowed hard, her brows drawn together in frustration, but she didn't argue. Instead, she turned back to the railing. "You have a point. There's a lot of broken glass on the floor."

Practical woman. He'd bet she didn't fancy making love on sandy beaches either. He'd have to take her on a holiday someday and see. "So that's the Tower Bridge and across the way is the Tower of London, right?" She pointed out over the water. "Historic, but definitely not romantic."

"Unless you like the tragic sort of romances."

She tucked a few stray strands of hair behind her ear.

"Are tragic stories really romances? I thought they were supposed to have happy endings."

"For this discussion, I ought to take you a bit west to the Globe Theatre." He wasn't sure if he wanted to hide her away in a comfortable bedroom or take her sightseeing. Seemed they might be able to do a bit of both. The Globe Theatre might be a bit rundown but there wasn't a mess of glass all over the floors.

"How far is it?" She might be thinking along the same lines.

"A good walk." He paused, glancing at the sky. "We're a fair hike from the clinic too, so we can't stay out much longer. I'm due back at the pack's headquarters to join the patrols."

"Duty calls?" Wistful, but not trying to convince him otherwise. "I should confess, I wouldn't be totally paying attention if you did take me sightseeing. I've got reading to do."

A part of him relaxed. She'd already asked a lot of him today. It helped that she'd not argued with his loyalties at every turn, but only when it truly was a necessity. It firmed his own growing conviction that she was right about the need for the research on the zombie infection, both to uncover the cause and, potentially, a cure.

"Let's get you safely back so I can go out on patrol with a clear head."

7

Deanna sat bolt upright in bed.

"Easy now. It's only me." Danny's voice whispered through the darkness. Faint light from the window reflected off golden eyes as if they were a pair of small mirrors.

"I didn't think you'd be coming back tonight." But she was very glad to see him. She'd been tossing and turning, chased by humans and zombies alike in her dreams.

'Course, she didn't remember falling asleep, hadn't intended to. Helen's diary lay in the tangled blanket next to her. She must have faded out while she'd been reading.

Those eyes disappeared and reappeared. He must've blinked. "I didn't mean to wake you. Only wanted to check in and see if you were settled."

"Are you going to come closer?" Maybe stay? More and more, she wanted his company. Only realized how much when he'd gone out on patrol. "I don't suppose you've got your own bed to get back to."

"Ah, about that, I do have my own room at pack headquarters. But my bed is very cold." Despite the teasing, he sounded so tired her heart ached.

She placed her sister's diary under the pillow and patted the blankets beside her. The guest bed wasn't huge, but the two of them could fit if he was in human form.

He came to her side, but not with the fluid motion she'd come to associate with him. No. Even as he sat at the head of the bed, bracing his back to the wall like he had the night before, every movement was stiff.

"You're hurt!" She scrambled out from under the comforters.

"Shhh, don't wake the boys." He rubbed his ears. "Actually, don't rouse the entire clinic. I don't recall you being quite so loud."

"When you pulled me from the tunnel, I was trying to be quiet." She sat back on her heels and reached out with tentative hands. He was bare from the waist up again, but her questing fingertips found bandages. "Don't you ever wear a shirt?"

"Most of the time, actually, but I find I go unseasonably warm whenever I think of you." His voice sent shivers through her. Suddenly, strong arms came around her and pulled her close. "I'm not hurt badly, so don't worry yourself over it. I just had to get a few stray bullet fragments out and I'll heal up quick as you like."

"Who shot you?" She'd have sat up again, but his hand cupped her neck and pressed her into the curve of his shoulder.

He nuzzled her hair and drew in a slow breath. "You smell very tempting. All spicy and appealing when your temper is up."

She bit her lip. "And you might be out of your head from blood loss."

"Not likely." He chuckled. "This will heal, trust me. It's a shape-shifter gift I rather enjoy, especially when tourists come in fancying themselves big game hunters just because they've got themselves very big guns."

"Humans shot you?" She didn't know what to say.

"Ah well, they'd gotten themselves in a pinch. Our patrol found them on the edge of the park, which would normally be fine, but they'd attracted too many zombies with the daft idea of pouring chicken's blood all about." A growl began in his chest. She laid her hand over his sternum and wondered at the vibration under her palm. His hand pressed warm over hers. "In the confusion, they started shooting at anything, even each other. It was a near thing trying to get them all out of there with minimal injuries."

"This is what you call minimal?" She ran her hands down his torso to the sizeable pad and bandaging at his waist.

"'Course. A werewolf takes a shot and it isn't quite so final as when a human takes the same."

He had a point there. Still, the skin around the bandage was warm, almost fevered. "Any chance of infection? The area around the wound—"

"Is knitting and generating quite a lot of heat in the meantime. No danger of infection." He kissed her forehead, as if in apology for cutting her off.

She wasn't sure what this thing was growing between them. He chased away the nightmares though, and her heart skipped at the oddest moments when he spoke. Earlier, she'd been imagining the cadence of his voice and the soothing touch of his hands as a way of calming her fears as she'd been reading through her sister's diary. It had worked too well, apparently, and she'd fallen asleep without meaning to.

"You're tired." She pitched it as a suggestion, not so much a question.

"Yeah." Fatigue dragged the word out. "Was too full of energy to settle earlier, but now I've found a nice soft spot here, the night might be catching up with me."

There was a sadness underlying his light banter though. "What's wrong? Talk to me."

"We were spread thin tonight, the patrols." His hand began running up and down her forearm, pressing her shirt sleeve up as his fingertips found her skin. His touch sent tingles up and down her arm. "A few zombies broke past the quarantine perimeter and the military needed us to supplement their soldiers."

"You caught them all?" Like any epidemic, it only took one to carry and spread the infection.

"We did." A pause. "We also have a pair specially assigned to hunting down the strays, the ones that find ways through sewer systems or lost underground tunnels out into the countryside. So far, Sorcha and Kayden have been enough to track them and take them down before things spread enough for the governments to notice."

The ramifications of it staggered her. She hadn't known the quarantine had been compromised. And so far? This had happened more than once? "But you've made reports, haven't you? Let them know?"

"We'd prefer not to push them into a rash decision, like dropping a bomb on all our heads." He sighed. "There are still many, many innocent people living here who couldn't get out. We'd like to give them a life of some sort, if we possibly can."

And the pack had done wonders. She'd seen it from a distance earlier in the day. But the boys had shown her more after Danny had left on patrol. They'd gone to the pub around the corner and listened to people laugh and socialize a bit before it got too dark. It'd provided a lively backdrop as she read through her sister's diary, kept her from sinking into grief as she read. No one stayed out very late, but with the werewolves on patrol, they didn't hide in their homes anymore. At least not where the streets were kept reliably clear.

"I'm tired of killing, I suppose." Danny spoke suddenly, as if he hadn't intended to give his thoughts to her.

She hesitated. "Is it because you're a healer?"

A beat, maybe two. "Aye, it's true, a bit more than a medic. I shouldn't be surprised you noticed. I'm always at odds, trying to balance the two sides of me. The predator. The healer. As pack medic, I can do both and help my pack."

"But?" It lingered in the air, his restlessness.

"What we do here is a good thing, but neither side of me is satisfied." His chest rumbled and his arm around her tightened a fraction. "It's no challenge, no real hunt to kill zombies. The only true danger is if they outnumber you. Every night on patrol, you see this epidemic and it's like the flu you can't get rid of. It'll only spring up somewhere else."

"And you can't heal it, can't cure it. Plus, there's the constant worry. It only needs one carrier, one host, and it could spread again." She brought up her own line of thought from moments before. "Next time, it might not be as well contained as it has been here."

He hugged her close. "And this is why."

He didn't say more. They wouldn't speak of it in the clinic. He'd warned her.

"Yes. This is why." She couldn't think of anything else, only that she was glad he'd agreed to help her. Happy he was here, right now. So, she tilted her head up and stretched toward him.

He met her halfway, his mouth brushing against hers.

Hungry, she rose up to her knees, leaning over him with her palms flat against his chest. He opened his mouth, tangling his tongue with hers as his hands slid up to her waist and caught the end of her shirt.

"It's a good thing we found your travel bag this afternoon," he murmured against her lips.

"Mmm?" Words ... why were they using words right now?

"It means you have extra clothes."

Fabric tore, falling to shreds around her. She gasped, incredibly turned on by being suddenly exposed to him.

"Pretty. Very pretty." He sat forward, holding her steady with a hand on either side of her hips, and she wondered how she ever thought he'd have sat back passively as she'd initiated this between them. He pressed a kiss low on her abdomen, and then another one just above her navel. The next kiss was higher but he opened his mouth to suck. She let her eyes flutter shut as he nuzzled the underside of her breasts through her bra. "Blue lace suits you. I like lace."

"Then don't rip this one." She tried for teasing, but the words came out in a breathless whisper. "The others aren't as delicate."

Actually, the others were plain and boring. This set, her sister had bought for her.

One day, you're going to want to actually seduce a man.

Thank goodness her sister had really good taste in lingerie.

Danny licked the curve of her breast above the lace of her bra. Then he gently caught the edge of the fabric in his teeth and tugged it down. Her already taut nipple popped free and he grinned like a child discovering a delightful toy. She began to tell him so, but his mouth closed over her nipple and he sucked. Hard.

She clutched at his shoulders, arching against him, pleasure shooting through her. And he eased the suction, then let go. She blinked her eyes open, but he began to lick and tease at her nipple. The alternating sensations drove her mindless with desire, spiking even higher as he brought one hand up to pull down the other cup of her bra and play with her other nipple between thumb and forefinger. Every flick of his tongue, every tug of his fingers, sent need scorching over every part of her.

"Touch me, please touch me."

He paused. "Where?"

"Everywhere!" It didn't matter that he was already touching her, doing things to her. She only knew she needed to feel him and she couldn't find the words.

His hands curved around her ribs as he rose up on his knees before her and he captured her mouth in a ravaging kiss, all tongue and teeth, with an appetite to match hers. Before she could wrap her arms around his neck, his hands pressed into her sides, turning her. A sound of protest left her throat, but he hushed her. "Trust me."

She let him turn her to face the wall, and placed her hands where he indicated to brace herself. And then his hands began to roam. Across her shoulders and along her arms, back to her torso and over the curve of her back.

"Do you have another pair of shorts to sleep in?" His voice was dark and edgy, the question whispered into her ear.

"I don't care." No more barriers. All she wanted was skin to skin.

He grazed the shell of her ear with his teeth. She shuddered in pleasure. "Good."

There might have been the whisper of something sharp against her skin, but she was so sensitized, she wasn't sure. Her shorts were in shreds around her knees and she was bared to his touch. He spread his hands on the backs of her thighs, cupping below her bottom. When he squeezed, her thoughts scattered. If he tried asking her another question, she wouldn't be able to answer. Not with anything that made sense.

He pulled her hips back, adjusting her stance and encouraging her to arch for him. One hand caressed her, his hot touch gliding over her side and under to her belly, then up to grasp one of her breasts. He used his other hand to tease the inside of her thighs, his fingers exploring until he stroked one finger along her crease. She moaned.

"Shh. Easy. The boys are down the hall."

Easy for him to say. She was wet, embarrassingly so, but before she could blush or feel more than the moment's discomfiture, his finger slid inside her. Every muscle clenched in response and she gasped for breath as he slowly pumped his finger in and out, teasing her opening. His other hand kneaded and massaged her breast. It was so good, and it could be more. She rocked her hips back against him and he made an inarticulate sound of frustration. His hands left her for a moment and she collapsed forward against the wall at the shock of it. But then he was back, the hard length of his erection pressed against her buttocks.

"You're still tight, but I can't wait anymore." His words were strangled, almost the way he sounded in his phase-form, but the hands roaming over her again were human and his hips pressed against her were hot skin, not fur. "Please, Deanna. May I?"

"Y-yes." The request undid things inside her, made this more than sex.

When he started to push into her, another groan escaped her throat and she bit her lip to try to keep quiet. Slow and incredibly good, he filled her and she stretched to accommodate him until he was balls deep.

Oh yes.

He pulled her to him until the length of her back was pressed against his torso. His hands roamed over her, sliding up from her thighs and over her belly to caress her breasts. And as he did, he pumped inside her. She leaned her head back to the curve of his shoulder, only capable of tiny gasps with every thrust as sensation washed over her entire body.

"Everywhere." His whisper in her ear was more erotic than anything she'd heard in her life. "You wanted me to touch you everywhere."

She whimpered.

His hands settled at her waist and he began thrusting harder. She leaned forward again, bracing herself against the wall as he pulled almost completely out and then slid back into her in strong, firm strokes. Her inner muscles tightened as she approached the edge of her ability to process the sensations, the edge of her sanity. His fingers dug into her hips and he picked up his pace. He was so hard, thick, touching her deep inside and setting pleasure points firing with every stroke. She wanted to cry out, needed to, but ...

"Danny." It was a gasp.

He slammed into her and her world blew apart in waves of pleasure. His own muffled cry joined hers a second later as he held himself shuddering through his own orgasm within her.

8

———————

I t's an incredible high, flirting with Death walking. Oh, he might not have known I'd recognized him. But how could I not? I just didn't expect him to be so incredibly hot. No surprise any person—be they straight or switch-hitting—would do anything but offer up their life's blood if he asked for it. The feel of his lips against my neck, the way he whispers cold air across my skin, the way his grip on me leaves me no escape. He could kill me without a moment's notice and it's a heady thought, because he didn't. He's had centuries to perfect the hunt, to hone every seductive skill in seduction, learn every technique for inflicting pleasure or pain at a whim. Probably both.

He could make dying instantaneous ... or last a lifetime.

Just think what it would be like to spend not one, but a hundred lifetimes learning from him. Read every book ever written. Have the time to master every spell.

Any other man I've ever met is like a mayfly compared to him.

I'd let him kill me, if it meant waking up next to him for the rest of the nights in forever.

Deanna wanted to shake Helen, make her think, bring her to her senses. You couldn't die and expect to live. Even love couldn't bring back the dead. She ran through the dark, chasing after her twin.

Only something was coming after her too. Shuffling, stumbling steps echoing against the walls of the tunnel. A wordless groan forced through vocal chords too rotted to make proper sounds. The awful smell of decomposition clogged her nostrils.

She ran harder, hoping to catch up with her sister and reach the end of the pedestrian subway. She had to get Helen to someplace safe. Only the closer she got, the worse the smell. It choked her, made her gag. And somewhere out there, something shot past at inhuman speed. Something dangerous. And it wasn't hungry for rotting flesh. It was after hot blood.

"Wake up." Danny's voice broke through the choking darkness. "It's only a dream, wake up for me."

Deanna clutched at the hand cupping her cheek as she sucked in air. Her heart slammed at the walls of her chest.

"Easy. I'm here." He leaned over her in the small guest bed, propped up on one elbow and still holding her cheek. He bent his head and kissed each of her temples, lingering as his tongue flicked against her skin, tasting the tracks of tears.

It should have freaked her out, but it gave her a strange sort of comfort instead.

"Bad dream." He wasn't asking. What else could it be?

"It's been a rough couple of days." More like a year and more.

"You did come shockingly to dying the other night."

He was lucky his British accent made even that hard truth sound wonderful.

"Black tunnels, hungry zombies, yeah. I was remembering some of what I read from my sister's diary and it got all jumbled up with what happened to my teammates." There'd been the faces of the colleagues who'd died when she hadn't, floating in the recesses of the passageway.

"Oi, if it's guilt you're feeling, stop. Right now." Danny pressed his lips to hers and then drew back to stare into her eyes. "The dead will not begrudge you happiness for living. They will not. Don't let the terror of it keep you from making the most of every day."

Like he did? And yet, since she'd first met him, he was rarely without a grin on his face. Usually the sort of lopsided, mischievous one she wanted to kiss. But every evening he went on patrol and faced the monsters to keep other people safe.

"You must think I'm the worst kind of coward."

He lifted her chin, waited until she looked at him. Then he shook his head. "People who ignore fear are the worst kind of cowards. You face fear, deny it power over you in your waking moments, only give in to it with sleep. I have the very greatest respect for the strength you show in doing so. Never doubt it, not even for a moment."

"Thank you." What else could she say? His words gave her warmth and made her awkward at the same time. What could anyone say to that?

"I forgot to ask you, by the way, if you'd had a chance to read through your sister's diary. Obviously, you had." He rolled back to lay flat and pulled her with him until she was sprawled half across him.

"Oof." Her jaw ached from being clenched and her limbs tingled from lack of blood circulation. She must have been strung tighter than a violin string while she'd been caught dreaming.

"Is that a new way to say yes? Or maybe that was a no?" He raised an eyebrow.

She thumped her fist into his chest. "No. But the answer to your original question is yes."

And what she'd read had been terrifying.

"There were insights to be had, I'm sure. I won't ask you to share the private thoughts, but did you find a clue to help our search?" His sudden formality made her blink. "That's obviously a private collection of your sister's thoughts, not a professional set of notes."

Oh, he had it right, and she had no idea what he'd think of it. Hell, she didn't know what to think of it.

"You said you'd look out for me. But this— I'm not sure this is something you'll want to be a part of."

He didn't respond immediately. Which was a good thing, right? He was listening, not jumping to hasty promises. Decisions like that, made in a rush, usually meant a whole lot of regret on both sides.

"Either way, there's someone I need to find." A man she really didn't want to meet. Or wouldn't, if he hadn't had anything to do with Helen. "He's probably the last ... person ... to have seen Helen alive."

"A friend?"

"More like a lover."

"Would he still be in the city?" Danny tucked her hair behind her ear.

She hesitated, but best to get this one out in the open as soon as possible. "I'd think so. I don't know much about vampires, but they seem to hang out in the same general territory over long periods of time. I doubt something like the zombie apocalypse would make them evacuate right away. I figured they'd wait it out and take advantage of the chaos for a while."

"A vampire, you say." His words were flat, clipped.

Her stomach dropped. Shouldn't be disappointed. He had more than enough to deal with when it came to the zombies. Dealing with another kind of undead?

It was a long minute of silence. She started to curl inward on herself, but his arms pressed her close against his side. "You're right about chaos and supernaturals in general. Easier for us to move about in the confusion of natural disasters and acts of war than under the eye of bored people during times of peace. But most of the others stay in the shadows. It's only us werewolves that come out into the public eye. Still ..." He let out a low whistle. "Your sister liked to live dangerously."

That was an understatement.

"He's not what killed her." Of that, Deanna was certain. "A vampire kill would have been abrupt, immediate. But what I experienced through her was drawn out and slow, over days. And through it all, she ..."

How to describe to someone else the ability to experience the love her twin had?

"... had hope. She thought it would turn out all right." Lame. Deanna couldn't find words for it and really didn't want to use the word "*love*" at the moment.

After a long pause, Danny sighed. "At least we've got the whole of a day to confront this vampire. Come on, then."

"You're coming with me?"

He chuckled. "Seems to me you're going to try to find this vampire no matter what."

"Yeah." No doubt there. She didn't want to, but she'd never even thought about giving up on it.

"Well, then. We should wash, dress and break our fast before we head out."

"Don't you need to know where we're going?" She'd racked her brain trying to make sense of the descriptions her sister had written down, but they'd all been vague impressions of architecture or cute dogs in windows nearby. No practical street signs or landmarks.

"Doesn't matter." Danny's voice had flattened, grim and defensive. "If we want to see any vampire in the city, we see the master vampire first."

"THIS ... was not what I was expecting." Deanna took in the elegant furnishings of the sitting room. "Hotels are still in business in the middle of all this?"

Danny shrugged. "Makes sense, really. Trophy hunters and tourists, some of them are very high maintenance. They're here to sightsee as if this were some amusement park. They don't take in the reality of it all. It's all a great lark of some sort to them. The next big adventure. And for vampires, that selective blindness is ideal. Neighbors begin to notice comings and goings. A hotel like this, full of travelers staying for a weekend or a week at most? All of them focused on going about their own business. It's perfect. Trusted servants run the hotel and the brood has rooms throughout."

Considering the sun high in the sky, he'd have thought the lobby would be empty but a human dressed in a suit came out from behind the desk and had inquired as to whether they'd like a room. While the werewolves had worked on controlling the walking dead, the vampires had found a way to take advantage of the tourism. Practical, that, even if it leaned more toward opportunistic than humanitarian. But then, vampires tended to step away from the messy emotional complication of humanity more so than werewolves. Humans were counted among the prey.

Seth had been the one to communicate with the vampires when the city was first being evacuated. Neither camp had the resources to oust the other and still handle the outbreak of walking dead, though territory had always been an issue between them. Same as in nature when normal animals had overlapping hunting grounds. The exchange had been pretty limited as a result, tending to run along the lines of, "Stay out of our way and we will stay out of yours." Not a peep heard from the vampires since.

Not optimal. But there were some realities regarding the nature of what they all were that had to be overlooked. The werewolves had the zombies to deal with and the vampires had their existence to sustain. In a way, the epidemic had given both supernaturals an enemy to face instead of each other.

The human servant had been smart though, recognizing Danny for what he was. When he'd requested to see the Master, they'd been shown directly to this top-floor suite.

"Did people go missing from the hotel before the zombies started appearing?" Deanna extended a booted toe to the ashes in the fireplace, stirring them and revealing nothing. Her mouth twisted and he wondered if she realized how cute she was when she looked perplexed.

"One of the first things any of us learns as a supernatural predator— don't hunt where you sleep." Perhaps not the best time to draw a comparison, but his woman would need to grow comfortable with his way of life. He could adjust for hers to a certain extent, but there were some realities he couldn't ignore. Someday, they'd have the zombie infestation under control. And then life would offer more choices to the both of them. If she decided to stay with him.

And the certainty was growing inside him. He didn't just want to, he *had* to win her over. She'd become integral to the future he wanted to build. He was grinning when a different human servant entered and began setting a side table with refreshments. This one was female and didn't look up or even acknowledge their presence.

The smell of old death teased Danny's nose, faint and dry like the ashes in the fireplace. Deanna didn't notice when the vampires entered the room on silent feet, so Danny stepped closer to keep himself between the undead and her. Three of them, two lesser and one very old vampire. How he could tell had very little to do with the five senses and everything to do with the vampires. Little cues, and an overall gut awareness of what the other predators in the room were capable of doing.

"It is unusual for one of the werewolf pack to seek me out, even in times such as these. Interesting. Plus, I see a familiar face on a person I do not know." The master vampire of London must have been Turned in his late thir-ties, possibly early forties. Hard lines, square jaw. He was the sort ladies would find attractive, the kind who wore a suit well. He exuded confidence and sophistication.

He also stood perfectly motionless, in a way only the very-long-dead can manage. No heartbeat, no rise and fall of the chest, no flow of blood in his veins or even the minute tensing and relaxing of stabilizer muscles throughout his torso to keep him upright. He was a statue, alive yet without the constant motion of living things. Only the older vampires did that. The younger ones, their bodies remem-bered what it was to be alive. They breathed because they remembered what it was like to need to breathe in order to exist.

This master vampire, he'd long since made his peace with being dead. He could stand there for the rest of time if he had a mind to do it, and never move even a millimeter.

But inertia wasn't a safe assumption for a being such as him. In order to be the Master, he had to be both very old and very powerful. The sense of danger weighted the air, pushing at Danny to shift to phase-form to better face the threat. But he wouldn't, not unless he had to. Doing so would be considered an unforgivable act of aggression. And Deanna needed him to be as cooperative as possible.

"I am Danny, medic of the London pack." He'd bet the Master already knew, but best to go about proper introductions. Vampires had a bit of a thing for protocol. If Seth ever thought he could trust the vampires, they'd be right perfect to handle the political bollocks with the human governments. "This human is under my protection. Her name is Deanna."

The vampire inclined his head. He never blinked. Eerie, that. "You may call me Kenneth."

Informal. Danny let his shoulders relax a touch. Good sign.

"We're looking for someone, or to be more precise, trying to find out how she died." Deanna's voice held only the barest hint of a tremor. His plucky scientist, incredibly brave. Human as she was, she was sensitive. She had to be aware of the danger, like a rabbit in a den of predators.

It was a survival instinct for potential prey, like the tiny pets trembling in Maisie's hands. Even if Maisie meant them no harm, they recognized her for the predator she was.

The vampire, though, his intentions weren't as clear.

"Many have died in this city over the centuries." Flat.

Uncaring. Kenneth might as well have been an automated voice recording.

She persisted. "She would have died a year ago."

"A night, a year, a decade. These are short timeframes, difficult for the long-lived to remember all they encounter clearly. Isn't that so, wolf?"

"I've seen my share of centuries. And yes, the ways humans measure time are brief, their days blend together in a blur. But—" Danny narrowed his eyes "—if I remember a face, I tend to remember a bit more about the person."

One of the lesser vampires snarled and lunged at Danny. He sidestepped and grabbed it by the forehead before it could get inside his guard. Its fangs jutted out as it hissed at him, reaching up toward his face. Bringing his other hand up in an uppercut before it could do him damage, he slammed his open hand into its chest. Its sternum collapsed and he reached through the bone fragments. Closing his fist around its heart, he yanked. Just like that and it was over. Had to be. Vampires were too deadly to allow a prolonged fight.

The dishes rattled as the human servant's hands shook.

"You may go." The master vampire didn't turn his head, but the human servant bolted. "Tell my second and third I do not require their presence. I am to be undisturbed."

There may have been another servant listening or the fleeing girl might have absorbed the message. The master vampire didn't look to be concerned. Of course, his expression had literally not changed since he'd entered the room with his escorts. Obviously, the second and third were more of a challenge.

After a pause, Kenneth motioned for the other vampire to leave as well.

"You owe me a life."

Caution might have been the better approach, but Danny was a wolf and hesitation on his part could have been perceived as a weakness neither he nor Deanna could afford. He had to come at it from a position of strength. "You owe the werewolves a dozen or more. We protect our territory but we do not extend it to foolish humans who do not follow our rules. Your agreement with us was that you'd only feed on those who sought you out. I think you've been stretching the interpretation of the agreement when it comes to tourists, people easily marked as lost to the zombies. What will you do when there are no more humans to feed on in London? Where will you go?"

Deanna sucked in a sharp breath.

He didn't dare look at her, nor worry about what she might think of the wolves leaving humans to the mercy of other predators, the vampires. But one monster didn't deny the nature of another. Their agreement meant only the consenting were prey. It was the best compromise the werewolf pack could make and live with it. Danny would try to explain to her later, if she would let him.

The twitch in the vampire's face was minuscule, but Danny saw it despite his worry about Deanna. He followed a hunch. "Can you even leave?"

Suddenly, the vampire was across the room and facing Deanna. Danny whirled with a growl, but the vampire had her by the throat.

"Ah, ah. Delicate. Fragile." Kenneth stared at Danny with ice-blue eyes, flat and without mercy. "Too easily crushed if you were to threaten me now."

"Let her go." Red edged his vision and logic wouldn't hold for long while Deanna was in danger.

"Werewolves have many advantages over vampires in terms of natural weaponry and defensive form. As we grow older we learn ways to even the odds. Speed, for instance." Kenneth's voice remained void of emotion. "You must blink and we can move in your moment of blindness."

Danny growled. He could kill the vampire, but not before the arrogant prick killed Deanna. She was clutching at the vampire's hand, trying to pull his fingers from her throat. She might as well have been prying at marble.

"Your concern is valid, but unnecessary. I will give you the information you seek."

Falling silent, Danny waited. Both to hear what the vampire had to say and to find an opening to get Deanna out of his grip. Patience came hardest in situations like these, and the gamble to take no action could result in the unbearable.

"Helen was your sister, I am assuming." Though the question was directed to Deanna, Kenneth did not turn his head from Danny.

"Y-yes." Deanna had relaxed in his hold, ready to move when the chance arose. Danny hoped it was that and not a calming thrall of some sort. Most vampires required a taste of the victim's blood to exert that power over will, but Kenneth was old enough to have heightened abilities. Especially if he was fast enough to move in the blink of an eye.

"I wasn't aware she had a twin."

"You knew her."

"Yes."

"She wrote about you."

"She did." No surprise and he didn't phrase it as a question.

Deanna was doing a fine job of keeping her wits, but the scent of her fear was rising in the room. It cut at Danny, made his wolf aspect wild with the need to remove the thing scaring her so badly. But not while it had her by the throat.

"What happened? You didn't kill her. I know you didn't."

"No." A change of inflection. Sadness? Regret? Hard to believe. "She encountered me on the city streets. I had already had a successful hunt. I needed no further sustenance. It amused me to accompany her to a pub and listen to her speak of finding herself. Instead, she'd found me. She was refreshing."

Danny could relate. There were times when every person around a man blurred into every other cretin he'd ever known. Easier to let them all fade into anonymity than hurt for every cherished friend lost to a shorter lifespan. Still, when one personality burned brighter than the rest, grey days of existence took on a splash of color.

Deanna coughed, struggled to speak more. The vampire eased the pressure of his fingers a bit. "You popped up again and again. You searched her out. She said it would've been creepy, but she was so happy to see you."

"Yes."

"And she figured out what you were."

"Regrettably." Kenneth released her neck, but had her chin between forefinger and thumb. Deanna pulled to get free, but couldn't get loose. "I thought her face—your face—singularly beautiful. Ironic that there were two of you."

"What happened to her?" Deanna asked the question again. This time, unshed tears were in her voice.

"She asked me to Turn her. She wanted to spend the rest of eternity with me."

A shocked silence hung in the air. Apparently, Deanna hadn't ever entertained the idea of living forever.

"That's crazy. And you didn't love her back, did you?" The question came as barely a whisper, still crystal clear to Danny's hearing and the vampire's too.

"We do not Turn wielders of witchcraft." Kenneth didn't

blink. Danny couldn't help staring, waiting for him to, but he didn't. "It is not possible to Turn other supernaturals, shape-shifters or fae. The danger in Turning those humans with the natural talent for magic lies in the unpredictable outcomes. It is because of me your sister looked for a different way to see eternity. When I refused, she applied her creativity to the issue."

Deanna's brows drew together. "I don't understand."

That made two of them. More importantly, her skin along her jaw was growing red from the pressure of the hold the vampire had on her chin. Danny couldn't watch her hurt much longer without doing something rash.

"She searched for a spell to Turn herself into a vampire."

"It doesn't exist!" Disbelief cracked her voice, or it could have been fear.

Danny's inner wolf slammed against his control.

"Whether it does or not, I simply give you the information you requested. She tried to create one. She explained, after it was too late, that she'd fused science with witchcraft. It was supposed to have mimicked the vampirism virus and changed the cellular structure of red blood cells."

"She didn't have the expertise to do that, even if it could be done." Deanna was crying, and every tear ripped at Danny. He needed to get her out of the vampire's grip *now*.

"Witchcraft, like other magics, has its own will at times. Instead of recreating a virus that already existed, it created a different one."

Deanna's eyes widened. "No, no, no. It affected prions instead of platelets. Neurodegenerative instead. Oh no."

There aren't a lot of coincidences in this world. Her words echoed in Danny's mind. They were twins with a supernatural bond. Even if Helen hadn't the expertise to guide her spell, the magic had to have followed the template of knowledge from somewhere. It'd recognized through their bond that Deanna had the talent for the micro world and the education to understand the consequences. Helen's talent wouldn't have had the same expertise to guide her intent.

"Yes. Your sister tried to become the vampiric undead and became the first zombie in London instead."

"No, no, no."

The root cause. Patient zero.

"Before she died, she set a ward on the city." Kenneth finally turned his head to look at Deanna. "It is exceptionally strong, unexpectedly so. My brood has not been able to leave, until now."

A ward could survive the death of the caster. Danny had witnessed it in the past. But blood called to power and even if the caster was dead, blood could be used to break the ward. Only Helen's would have been mutated when she died. It wouldn't have broken the ward, leaving the vampires trapped.

Danny went cold.

Deanna's blood would give them the power to break the ward.

Danny lunged. The old vampire moved faster, released Deanna and dodged toward her instead of away. As Danny tried to twist in the air to face him, the vampire backfisted him. Lights exploded inside Danny's head and again as he crashed into the fireplace.

Deanna!

He struggled but the dark closed in around him, yanked him into unconsciousness.

9

D eanna woke as a sharp pain burned along the inside of her right arm. Her eyes flew open and she struggled against the hands holding her, panic shooting cold through her veins. Heavy manacles weighted her wrists.

"L-let go!"

"In due time." Kenneth stepped into her line of sight, or rather, he was just there suddenly. Bastard was too fast to actually see moving.

"What did you do to Danny?" No, no, no. Danny couldn't be dead. But she'd seen him smash into the fireplace.

"On his way, I'd imagine." Not a twitch, nor sign of concern. "But he will not be in time."

This vampire was like the ball-jointed dolls she'd seen. Lifelike, but not. And freaking creepy. His words sank in and relief washed through her, pushing the pain to the back of her mind. Danny was alive.

"I have your blood now, Helen's blood. I can break the ward at any time. But the werewolf owes me a life." Her heart froze. "And your sister's face should not be worn by any other."

The human servants holding her had her by the arms and legs. They lifted her and she yanked, twisted, kicked and fought, but she couldn't get free.

"A singular beauty, her face. I will not see my Helen again. Not even the ghost of her in her sister's eyes. She would want you to join her."

His Helen. He *had* loved her back. Or at least some version of love, whatever a vampire was capable of.

She didn't have time to respond as the servants lifted her over a metal railing and dropped her into a pit sunken in stone. It wasn't a far drop. She was able to land and roll off some of the momentum. Jagged remains of an old, old wall lay scattered across the bottom. From the looks of the sky, the pit was exposed to sunlight when there was any. But as she squinted into the shadows, she realized most of the day must have passed before she'd woken and they'd tossed her in here.

Wait. *Join her.*

There was movement in the shadows. A figure emerged, clothes mostly intact for having been worn for so long without care.

"H-Helen." Tears welled up. Her sister was almost unrecognizable after more than a year. Her body had rotted but was surprisingly whole. Helen had all her limbs, for the most part. The hand that reached toward her was missing the tips of each finger, as if Helen had worn the flesh and very bone of her most distal digits away scratching at something ... like the wall of this pit. "You kept her."

"I'd vowed to care for her all her days even though I refused to Turn her. Stubborn woman. She did this instead." Kenneth stood looking down on them. "She has remained well-preserved with regular feeding. Though she does not always finish. The resultant zombies are removed so they do not inadvertently damage her. And yet, the true spark of her personality is gone."

Deanna hoped so. Staring in horror at her sister's corpse, she was glad she hadn't faced Helen closer to death when the zombie before her would have looked more like her twin.

All the dreams made sense. And Deanna might have always known and not wanted to face it. Her sister had turned into a zombie. Worse. Her sister had *created* the zombie virus.

"You didn't isolate her right away." Keep him talking while she thought. Her sister, no, the zombie was shuffling. It hadn't yet done more than reach a hand out to her and it was still several yards away. She had space to run, a little.

"No. She stumbled into a health clinic, infected others before I realized the nature of her ailment. By then, I chose to isolate only her and let the city resolve the issue. After all, I'd given my word to look after her alone. The rest weren't of my concern." A pause. "It has taken some time, but it is stabilizing."

"You call what's out there stabilizing?" Really?

"Deanna!" Her name echoed across the ground in a roar. Danny. As it faded, a howl and then another rose up in the distance.

"Ah, your wolf has awakened and made his way from the hotel. And he has called in his pack. Excellent." Kenneth motioned and the human servants left the pit railing. "We will be having a discussion as you are reacquainted with your twin. It is time the wolves came to a new agreement with my brood."

Deanna stared up at the place where he'd stood. Too

high. The wall was too high to climb, especially with her wrists and ankles manacled.

A low groan drew her attention. The zombie was sniffing the air. Deanna stared down at the gash on the inside of her forearm. It wasn't deep, but it was bleeding freely. She didn't have much time before the blood loss would make her dizzy. And now that the zombie had scented her, it'd come after her more actively. The pit gave her room, but she couldn't avoid it for long.

"Don't do it, Helen." She shouldn't think of it as Helen. Her ward, her magic, was guided by clear intent. If she believed the zombie was her sister, even for a moment, her power would waver and she would be vulnerable because she'd never shut her sister out of anything in her life, ever. But looking at the face before her, she couldn't ignore who it had been. The ward wouldn't protect her. Fumbling in her shirt, she pulled the auto-injector from her bra. It hadn't been tested yet, not on a human. She stared at the walking corpse and horror crept up in her throat. Oh god, she was looking at exactly what she would become. Exactly.

"Oh, Helen, what did you do?" she whispered the words despite the tightening in her throat. Sorrow. Fear. Horror.

The sounds of snarling and growling came to her. It couldn't be happening too far away. But Danny would have his hands full with the vampire and his brood. She couldn't rely on him to save her this time. She needed to stay alive and find a way to kill her sister ... permanently.

First, the vaccine.

It wouldn't do her any good if the zombie bit her before she could take it.

Her hands shook as she flipped open the cap to the carrier tube and let the injector slide free. Looking up, she sucked in a breath and hissed it out. The zombie had started moving toward her, along the edge where there was less debris. Hampered by the shackles, Deanna retreated along the curve of the wall. If she could get the thing to circle with her, she could come around to the side of the pit where the wall was intact. She might be able to climb up and jump for one of the railings.

Another groan and the thing shuffled closer.

Deanna swallowed hard and pulled off the safety release on one end. She had to hope the vaccine didn't have any serious side effects. Nothing that would slow her down and let her own sister eat her.

No. Focus. She didn't dare close her eyes. She'd always been the twin with the better concentration. She could do this. A clear mind, a definitive intent. That was what the magic needed to act. Otherwise, it had a will of its own.

The zombies. No.

She summoned her magic and gave it her will to be done.

Protect. Do not become.

Stay human.

She gripped the auto-injector in her fist and slammed it into the side of her thigh, watching as the zombie approached in those precious seconds.

One.

The pinch of the needle piercing through her jeans and into her flesh barely registered, not with her right arm burning and throbbing.

Two.

She stepped back, trying to keep the zombie in her peripheral vision as she looked where she was stepping.

Three.

She couldn't fall, couldn't risk dislodging the needle until it had delivered the full dosage.

Four.

"Deanna!" Danny was coming. He was. The vampires hadn't killed him.

Five. Six. Seven.

Around and around they go.

The inane thought made her huff out a laugh. If anyone had been there to call her crazy, she'd have told them to go to hell. She was playing tag with her dead sister, trying to not become a zombie, for fuck's sake.

Eight. Nine.

"Seems like the vaccine makes me curse like a trucker." One of the odder side effects she'd ever noted about a drug. Then again, maybe mice had their own little curses when they squeaked.

Ten.

She pulled the auto-injector out of her thigh and rubbed the injection site hurriedly but didn't drop it. The needle might be small but it was the closest thing to a weapon she had.

Gotta knock the zombie down or something. She glanced around for a decent-sized stone, something she could throw. If she didn't lay it out somehow, it'd be on her before she could try climbing up the shorter wall. It'd definitely manage to sink its teeth into her.

Vaccine or not, she didn't want to test the efficacy if she didn't have to.

Why were all the damned rocks too damned small or too damned big to throw?

DANNY SHOOK WITH RELIEF, and no small amount of exhaustion, when he reached the pit. Changing to phase-form had healed his head injury but taken longer than he'd wanted.

"I've found you."

Deanna looked up and then stumbled backward, retreating from the shambling blighter in there with her. Only seemed to be one. Easily taken care of.

"Don't want to state the obvious here, but I need to get out." She kept her gaze on the zombie, good woman, and had something clutched in her grip. Puny weapon, that, but if it was what she had available he wasn't going to fault her.

Motion swept into his peripheral vision. Seth and the rest of the wolves had Kenneth's brood well in hand. Negotiations were reopened and not going the way the vampire intended, especially not the way Danny had left him. Still, the Master must have left a lesser vampire or two behind, but why? To guard Deanna?

"Any time would be good," she called up. Rocks in hand, she'd begun lobbing them at the zombie as it made its way slowly toward her. She had plenty of room to dodge.

In any case, he needed to take care of these before he could get her safely out. "Bit of a complication up here."

He kept his tone deliberately light. Keep her calm. No need to worry her.

"And these aren't a complication?" She held out her hands and shook them, making the shackles rattle. "These need to come off, now!"

Anger burned through Danny's chest and his lip lifted in a snarl. It wouldn't help her. He tucked it away, channeled it and prepared to slam through the obstacles standing between him and Deanna. He called down to her instead, "If they were fuzzy, would ye be in such a rush to take them off?"

"Danny!"

"In a moment, I've a bit of rage and destruction to carry out. Hang on."

He was done with patience. If he'd acted sooner, she'd not have been taken in the first place. He charged the first vampire, catching it midair as it leapt to one side. Slamming it down to the ground, he snarled as the second landed on his back.

He stepped on the first one's neck and reached back to tear the second off him and throw it into the wall. It hit with a screech and scrambled on the ground. While it was disoriented, he reached down and ripped the first vampire's head off.

Deanna cursed and then cried out in pain.

Red hazed his vision and he met the remaining vampire head on. Its claws tore at him and its fangs bit deep into his forearms but he didn't let it inside his guard. Instead he lifted it clear off its feet and pinned it up against the wall. Freeing his right hand, he landed a solid blow to its head, crushing its skull. He let it fall to the ground, then bent and yanked off its head to be sure. No wood around to stake either of them but beheading worked just as well.

He turned then and leapt directly into the pit. Deanna must have gotten her shackles caught on a cropping of rock hidden in the deepening shadows.

He let out a rumbling growl and yanked the zombie off her, throwing it into the air. It impacted the pit wall with a sickening crunch.

Too late, too late. Again. He'd not been fast enough.

"You're here."

"I'm sorry, love." He ran his hands over her first, assessing her injuries. The gash on her right arm needed stitching. He ripped up her shirt and quickly made it into a makeshift field dressing. The bite ... he couldn't do anything about the bite.

"They'd have ... killed us both ... if you hadn't taken them out first." Her words came in between faint gasps.

Nothing for it. He gathered her into his arms. "I'm so very sorry. I didn't protect you. Hang on, love. Hang on."

He'd do what was necessary. And he'd rip his own heart out after.

"Danny, the vaccine. I had to use it. I'm sorry."

Hope flared. To hell with the witchcraft, so long as it saved her he'd take it up with Seth later. "How will we know it worked?"

She drew a shuddering breath, then another. "As long as I don't die. Should be in the clear. Figure, I need to ..."

She looked up and beyond him, to the night sky.

"Dawn. If I don't survive to dawn, you're going to have to take care of me." She fisted the fabric of his sleeve tight. "Promise me, Danny. Don't let me turn into her."

He looked over to the other zombie. Saw.

"I promise." And this time he'd see it done properly. "I won't fail you again."

Her lips curved in the sweetest smile. "Never failed me, Danny. Not once. You're always here to spot me when I take a fall. I can get back up on my own ... You'll see."

Her eyes fluttered closed.

10

———

"Well, is the little witch awake?"

The voice wasn't Danny's. Deanna sat straight up in the ... bed?

"Now you've gone and done it, Seth." Danny's voice. It had become everything to her, right from the very beginning. She relaxed and looked around. The walls were old stone, once painted white perhaps, but faded over the passage of centuries. Ghosts of red lines and green vines were all that remained of what must have once been intricate wall designs. The furnishings were sturdy but old, medieval-looking. It was all very familiar and though she wasn't a history buff, she recognized the layout from somewhere ... pictures maybe? Had to be someplace famous. And then it came to her. She was in a bedroom of the Medieval Palace at the Tower of London.

"Oi, I didn't intend to scare her. Jumpy, she is. Does she do that a lot?" Seth stood in the doorway again.

Recently, yes.

"Do you ever actually come inside?" Should she offer him a cup of tea?

The perpetually serious expression cracked as he grinned. "Good to see you feeling better, witch."

She swallowed hard as the blood drained out of her head. "I ..."

"Easy now, don't go having vapors when you've only just come back to us." Seth's voice was gruff, gentle even. "Danny here explained after we found you both. And he gave me what for."

Huh?

"It's what I do." Danny sat on the bed beside her and wrapped his arms around her shoulders.

"I'm sorry." She put a hand up to ward off the steaming mug Danny offered her. Seth needed to understand. "It was my decision to use witchcraft inside the city. Danny had me promise I wouldn't."

"Except to save yourself." His growl rumbled next to her ear and his arm tightened around her.

There was a moment of silence. Then Seth sighed. "I'll not lie. I was well and truly ready to throw the both of you out, right on the retreating tails of those vampires. I couldn't believe he'd go against me, not even for love. But it's been Danny telling me I've been rushing forward with blinders on all this time. Too focused, I was, on the problem at hand and not what caused it or how to prevent it getting worse. And hearing how the virus was created, seeing what Kenneth had done, keeping your sister the way he did. Hard to hide from the truth of it much longer." He snorted. "Especially with Danny clutching you in his arms refusing to let me kill you."

She was really glad not to be dead.

"I wouldn't have, mind you. Banishment was all I intended, but Danny was under duress. He'd been assuming the worst."

"It was me." She could barely manage a whisper for the guilt weighing on her chest, making it hard to breathe. "He didn't disobey any of the pack rules, wasn't disloyal. It was me."

"Nah, girl, that's what I'm trying to tell you." Seth stepped into the room but it was Danny who growled low. Seth held up his hands and stepped back.

"My loyalty never wavered," Danny told her quietly. "True loyalty is telling your alpha when he's wrong, trusting he'll eventually listen. I'd always figured my alpha would understand someday, find the answer. I've become too patient, too ready to let things play out. It was you who showed me what I could lose if I didn't take action."

"Let's not get too impulsive, okay? Can you wait a few days to take any further action?" Watching him growl at his own alpha unsettled her. It couldn't be something Seth would allow for long. She craned her neck to gaze up at him. "I need to recover from this latest round."

"You do." Seth spoke up. "And you'll be having more here, once we've got you set up to manage it."

"I don't understand." And maybe she hadn't woken up yet. Maybe this was a fever dream. What did zombies think once they'd died and reanimated?

"Your vaccine works and you're the only one who can administer it." Seth leaned against the door frame. "I've decided to make the grounds here around the Tower of London a clinic for vaccinations. Preventative, as I understand it. Then if people are involved in an attack, they can be brought here for quarantine of sorts so they have a chance to survive. We can't keep bringing strays to Brian's little animal hospital. Danny, here, can provide support. And the boys can run errands, though I'll not have them exposed to possible infection. Perhaps we'll be able to attract a few more willing doctors from outside, or paramedics, medical professionals who work well in dangerous circumstances. Once people test clean for a safe amount of time, say a week or two, they can go back home."

The room started to spin. He was offering to let her continue her work? To establish a real clinic for inoculations and post-attack treatment?

She shook her head, trying to clear it and take in what he was saying.

"Is that a no?"

"No! I mean … no, it's a yes."

"Well, and that was clear as mud."

Danny chuckled and kissed her forehead. "She'll stay. She's got an issue with yes and no, but the gist of it is she'll stay."

"What he said." She let him tuck her against his side and sighed, exhausted.

Seth looked from one of them to the other. "I was not this bad with Maisie."

"Yes, you were," Danny shot back.

"There's only your opinion on that." Seth waved off. "Rest up for now, witch friend, and we'll take care of details once you've recovered. There's also one of those blighters in a cage you'll need to see to. I'll not have you going in there to take samples from the thing over and over without a proper idea of how long you plan to be going on about it. As soon as you have the data you need, you'll let Danny put it out of its misery. Understood?"

"Thank you."

His expression gentled and his smile reached his eyes, gave him a mischievous sparkle. "Don't thank me yet. Maisie's insisted you learn to use guns properly once you're up and walking about again."

With that cryptic remark, he left.

"YOU DON'T HAVE to stay if you don't want to." Danny's voice was quiet as he offered her the mug again.

"What happened to Kenneth, the vampires?" Would they come after her again?

Another growl from Danny. "They've gone. They broke the ward with your blood and Seth made it clear they weren't welcome back. Kenneth wanted to keep his hold on the hotels his people owned, be able to return to London. We had to fight it out, but when the dust settled, it was clear we're the dominant predators in the city. He and his are gone for good."

Relief flowed through her. But ... "They were there all this time."

Danny nodded. "They were here before the pack. But we grew to power while they stayed hidden and he underestimated us. It would've happened eventually. The zombie epidemic only delayed the inevitable by distracting both sides. And before he left, I took payment for what he did to you out of his hide."

There was probably more. Had to be. But she wasn't as worried so long as they weren't after her anymore.

"Are you going to take this or shall I hold it until it gets cold?" The gentle teasing note to his words tugged at her.

She took it carefully in both hands and wrapped her hands around it, savoring the warmth. It was nice to be alive. "Do you want me to stay?"

His arm squeezed gently around her shoulders. "Yes. And there's a life we can make here, with your research and the new clinic, if you'll agree to it. Would save a lot of people. But you have choices. We'll not keep you here against your will. We could find another witch to make the vaccine work—should find more than one to share the burden regardless. If you decide not to stay, I'll hope you let me go along wherever you do decide to travel."

Her heart skipped. He wanted to be with her. Really? "For how long?"

"Well, my forever is likely to be a lot longer than yours. I'll not lie to you about that." They both sat in silence for a moment. "To be clear, I want to spend the rest of your days with you, or as many as you'll have me for."

And she loved that about him too, the way he didn't hold back the truth. She shouldn't hold back either. "Are you sure you want me? I mean, I'm not strong. I'm not a werewolf and I'm not a fae. I'm only human and I'm a witch."

The hatred Seth had for witchcraft might be broken, but it was an old wound recently lanced. It'd linger for a while longer, color her interactions with him and strain Danny's relation with the pack.

"Stop thinking so hard, you. It'll sort itself out given the chance. You're perfect, so long as you hold off on turning me into a newt."

"Wha—"

He pressed his finger to her lips. "Never mind that. Only know you are strong, so very much so. And you are the woman I want to be with, if you'll have me and for as long as you'll have me."

She didn't have any words. Instead, she wrapped her arms around him and peppered kisses over his face.

He laughed. "Oi, we'll need to work on your aim … my mouth's right here."

And he captured her mouth with his, sending them both drowning in a deep kiss.

HUNTING KAT EXCERPT

from Book One of
THE TRITON EXPERIMENT

CHAPTER 1

"Give me back my bra, you little tube rat, or I'll rip out your spine and steal your soul."

Scampering for the open door, he assumed he'd be fast, too fast for anyone to catch. And he would have been—if Kaitlyn had been human.

Lightning quick, she pounced, nabbing him by the scruff and bringing him to eye level. She bared her teeth in a silent snarl.

"You found him!"

The scrawny ferret squeaked, probably relieved at the sweet sound of salvation, as Skuld breezed in from the corridor.

The ship's engineer whisked him out of Kaitlyn's hand and her bra fluttered free. The tiny marauder had dropped his loot. Catching the lingerie, she looked it over carefully. If those sharp teeth had done any damage to the lace...

"Sorry, Katy." Skuld tucked her pet into the front of her rumpled ship suit, raising the zipper until only his furry face peeked out from her cleavage. "I was, um, working with one of the station engineers and Chester slipped out of his cage when we bumped into it."

Uh-huh. Skuld practically glowed, with her cheeks flushed and hair tousled. She always wore her ship suit loose, the sleeves rolled up at the elbows, but the baggy legs had been hastily tucked into magnet-soled boots. Mingled with her usual scent of lavender soap and engine oil was a man's musk.

Considering the ferret's cage had been built of solid plasteel and doubled as Skuld's desk, they had to have bumped it hard. For the cage door to have opened, they'd been going at one heck of an angle. And Kaitlyn stopped considering any further because she *really* didn't want to know.

"He's lucky he didn't damage anything," she growled, letting the sound rumble from deep in her chest in a way no human could.

The perpetrator trembled in his bosom of safety.

"Aw, c'mon Katy. Chester wouldn't do anything intentionally. He thinks your stuff is neat." Skuld fluffed her soft golden brown waves. "Besides, why have fantastic lingerie when you never show it to anyone?"

Kaitlyn turned away, stowing the garment in the appropriate cubby. "I like the way it feels to wear it."

"You'd like the way it feels to let a lover take it off too." Skuld took up the familiar argument. "Slide the straps down your shoulders, unhook the back and let the cups fall away. Or maybe they could play with it on for a while, bite at you through the lace. You've got a great rack."

"Skuld!" For the love of klepto weasels and big ship's engines, the woman needed to shut her mouth.

"You need to get boinked, Katy. Tumbled, screwed, whatever you want to call it." She tugged an oil-stained rag from a hidden pocket and slapped it against Kaitlyn's thigh. And damn but she made it sound easy, but then Skuld had always been comfortable with her sexual desires. Desires she satisfied every time they docked at a decent space station. "Okay, fine, when you first came aboard you had some issues to work through. And it took a while to ease into working with the guys."

"I had my reasons." The kind that gave her nightmares—waking and sleeping. Evils she could never forget because they were burned into her genetic code.

"It's been three years." Each word dropped like a stone. In her own way, Skuld had no mercy. "You can work with our people now and merc teams from other ships. You don't even flinch when strangers come aboard anymore." Skuld paused. When she spoke again, her voice turned gentle. "You've come a long way. You can hold your own and you deserve more than mission after mission, scouting and doing those impossible search and rescues." The rag slapped against her thigh again. "Now go out and get some."

"What makes you think I want some...whatever?" Kaitlyn folded her arms.

Raising her eyebrows, Skuld marched past Kaitlyn to the cubby and yanked out the black bra, turning to wave it under her nose. "No one owns an entire collection like this unless they're thinking about sex or at least want to feel sexy." She swept her arm out to indicate the small medical bay and alcove serving as Kaitlyn's personal quarters. "You're effectively solitary unless someone is bleeding, burned, or full of holes. The rest of us get some interaction, get off ship and socialize. It's not healthy for you to be alone, and regardless of what you want the rest of the crew to believe, *I* know you don't want to be." Skuld raised an eyebrow. "C'mon, give up the specs. What revs you up?"

"No—"

"Ah." Skuld cut her off, staring her straight in the eyes, heedless of how it engaged the predator in her. Probably because of it. "This is me, Katy."

Kaitlyn set her jaw and took a deep breath, reaching for patience or forbearance or whatever it would take to not rip her pretty brunette shipmate to shreds. Only Skuld could harass her with immunity, the only person to constantly prick her temper and walk away unscathed.

"Okay, okay, I think about sex." There, an admission.

"With who?"

No one alive and kicking. Nobody since Katzer. "Haven't met a guy who interests me that way yet."

"I kinda thought you might be omnisexual since you react to just about everyone with the same level of intensity. But you are into guys?" Skuld asked.

"Yes."

"Well, what kind of guy?" Skuld folded her arms across her breasts, making Chester squeak again. "You don't even notice the science guys, so academic types must not be your thing."

"It's more about the lack of balance between intellectual and physical." Kaitlyn figured emotional development was a factor too, but she wasn't in a position to criticize anyone in that regard. "I could bench press any one of them. Pass."

"It's not like anyone would know to look at you." Skuld wrinkled her nose. "You scare more people off with your 'come near me and I'll rip your face off' attitude than your size."

"Didn't keep *you* away. From day one you've popped

right into my medical bay and stomped all over my personal space." Kaitlyn nodded to indicate the current situation.

"Well, I did pause for a picosec or two." Her brows drew together at the memory. "You stepped on board the first day, looking all dark and broody with all your long, black hair and those deep brown eyes staring right through every one of us."

"Uh-huh."

Back then, Kaitlyn struggled to control her cat instincts, still new to the changes. Walking on board Dev's ship for the first time, without bolting or attacking his crew, took every ounce of control she'd had left.

"Then those others came aboard loading cargo and got nasty. When you dropped that spacer on the deck for grabbing my hair, I figured you were badass." Skuld gave her a melting smile. "But badass with a protective edge. Call it instinct."

"More like lack of survival skills."

Seeing the spacer hurt Skuld flipped a switch inside, gave Kaitlyn an outlet and a path of action. It still amazed Kaitlyn how little Skuld knew in the way of self-defense, but her position as engineer rarely placed her in combat or even off ship during missions.

Skuld shrugged. "We're talking about you here. Start simple, Katy. I know this is a stretch of verbal skills for you. What kind of man do you sweat for?"

"Fine." The image of Katzer's lopsided grin and rakish expression floated across her memory. No. He was gone. "I like a guy who looks good in uniform."

"Now we're talking. What kind of uniform?"

Kaitlyn shook her head. "It's not about the kind of uniform, it's about what it takes to wear it and make it something real. There's a difference between a person who looks good because they've got a uniform on and a soldier who makes the uniform look good."

And the thought of that kind of soldier made her blood heat.

Skuld looked ready to pull out a comp tablet and take notes. "It's pretty obvious you're not even going to notice a guy unless he's smart enough and strong enough to take you."

"I can respect a man who can hold his own."

"You don't need to say against you, it's a given." Skuld grinned. "The other merc teams we coordinate with come and go. There's always at least one tough guy in the bunch, trying to make a conquest out of you or prove he's the better merc. You always shut him down. And then once he's beat, it's like he's ceased to exist on your radar."

Because he no longer represented a threat. "So?"

"You get along with every permanent member of this team because we've each got a talent you respect."

Truth. "And this applies to a guy for me how?"

"If it takes respect for you to live with us on ship, it'd take at least that for you to let a man into your bed. He's got to earn it." She paused, pursing her lips as if considering. "And no alpha asshole, either. You're moody enough for the both of you."

"Alpha asshole?" They turned to see Dev leaning in the doorway.

Kaitlyn had fallen silent at the sound of his approach. She absolutely refused to admit participation in the conversation to her captain.

"Kaitlyn gave up her specs on men."

Of course, Skuld would spill every detail anyway.

"And this unique condition enters into this how?" A grin hovered around Dev's lips, just waiting to make an appearance. He stood there dying to laugh right in her face.

"Can you imagine an overbearing, domineering jerk of a guy in combination with Katy? So not good for her. He'd have to be assertive and straightforward, but not an alpha-hole." Skuld rolled her eyes. "Has there ever been a guy who could make her smile?"

"Yes," he said it slowly, watching her. "At least one."

Too much history hung in the air between them. He'd been there, held her, as she stood at the comm the final time Katzer's voice crackled across the link.

Smile, Kitten.

Katzer had even made her smile through her tears before he'd gone offline in a soundless explosion in space.

First kiss, first love, first loss. There hadn't been anyone to call her Kitten since.

"Is it time, Kat?" Dev's voice brought her back to the present, using the personal nickname he'd given her as she grew into her place as one of his crew. He'd bled for her back then, earned the right to use it. "You ready to go looking for a smile?"

The deceptively light question had a world of compre-hension behind it. He'd seen what she'd survived, knew how she'd been broken.

She lifted her lip in a snarl. "I'd sooner take a hole to the head."

"Well now, maybe you don't need a smile so much as a tad less aggression toward those of us of the male persua-sion." Her captain held up his hands in a harmless gesture. He knew how to handle her, how not to antagonize the predator.

She dropped the snarl but lifted her chin in a sharp motion. "You getting too tired to handle it?"

Dev didn't move, but suddenly he filled the whole doorway. "I can handle you just fine, Kat. We both know it." She might be faster, stronger, but he was more experienced. He'd taken her when she'd lost control, contained her before she hurt innocents. If she ever went feral, he'd be the one to help her back to human, again.

Satisfied, she subsided.

He relaxed into the door frame once more. "A little work on your social skills wouldn't be out of place."

Kaitlyn watched him, wary. She didn't just owe him. He'd also proven over time he had a lot to teach her, and his light comment clued her in to a pending attempt to add to the knowledge base. *Shit.*

Dev pushed away from the doorway, stepping into the room and presenting a data stick the size of her pinky finger. "I've got a messenger run for you. It's for a person on Dysnomia station who likes his privacy. Easy hand off, just be sweet and don't maim the nice man."

"You talk as if it's a given I'll want to." It might be, but she didn't like Dev making assumptions.

Dev only grinned. "Now, Kat, you got a true talent for violence anyone can appreciate—from a distance. In fact, you make it into the sort of thing they set to music on occasion." He would bring up the time she'd fought at his back in the middle of a formal ball. There'd been music, all right. A touch of steel threaded through his voice. "As your captain, I'm looking to expand your skill set into the negotiation and diplomacy areas. I know it's outside your comfort zone, but I do like to give you a challenge every now and again."

Also true. And okay, maybe she'd been more antagonistic towards men than necessary. It couldn't hurt to do a single messenger run and try not to scare the bejeebers out of the contact guy.

"Fine," she sighed, taking the data stick. "I'll play sweet and nice."

"Why not check into one of the station hotels and spend a night or two off ship?" Skuld took fire with her own suggestion, following words with action by grabbing one of Kaitlyn's duffels from under her sleep pallet and tossing lingerie into it.

"Oh no." Kaitlyn slapped the cubby closed before Skuld trotted out the whole collection for Dev to see. "I can do the messenger run and be right back aboard ship within a couple of hours max. That'll do me just fine."

"You do have a mighty backlog of R and R time you need to be taking, Kat." Dev peered over Skuld's shoulder to see into the duffel bag. "Those runs you take on the jungle planets after missions don't count as either rest or relaxation."

"Running through jungles and woods *is* relaxing." Absolute truth. Sometimes the wildness took hold and the only outlet Kaitlyn had was to shift to her panther form, burning off the energy in the kind of motion humans couldn't achieve.

Her beast rose up at the thought of shifting. Her paws driving into soft soil, muscles gathering, surging—

"You have relief for the furry you." Dev conceded her point with a nod. He waited, watching, as she swallowed and got her composure back. "But you need to unwind for the human aspect. You need to be thinking about taking some real time away."

Whatever. She and her animal aspect preferred to run, hunt. "I'll think about taking some after the next mission, maybe visit one of those resorts or something for quiet time." Kaitlyn shrugged.

She hadn't fooled Dev, but he let it go. "Messenger run goes at fourteen hundred hours station time." Turning to leave, he tossed a parting comment over his shoulder. "In the meantime, I'm going to try to scrub the images of lacy bits out of my memory like a good captain."

THE TRITON EXPERIMENT SERIES is targeted for re-release in fall of 2022.

ABOUT THE AUTHOR

Piper J. Drake is a bestselling author of romantic suspense, paranormal romance, science fiction, and fantasy.

Gamer. Foodie. Wanderer. Usually not lost.

Piper aspires to give her readers stories with a taste of the hard challenges in life, a breath of laughter, a broad range of strengths and weaknesses, the sweet taste of kisses, and the heat of excitement across multiple genres.

You can read more about her work on her website by using the QR code or going to: piperjdrake.com